Johanna Lindsey

"HAS A SURE TOUCH WHERE
HISTORICAL ROMANCE IS CONCERNED."
Newport News Daily Press

LOVE ME FOREVER

"ENCHANTING ROMANCE . . .
THIS STORY HAS EVERYTHING
FOR EVERYONE: PASSION,
WONDERFUL CHARACTERS, SPICY DIALOGUE
AND A COMPELLING PLOT."
Affaire de Coeur

"GIDDY ENTERTAINMENT . . .
BESTSELLING WRITER LINDSEY HAS NOT
ABANDONED HER WINNING FORMULA."
Publishers Weekly

"THIS ENJOYABLE, ENTERTAINING READ
WILL SURELY ATTRACT THE INTEREST
OF OLD AND NEW FANS."
Booklist

"EXCELLENT . . . LIVELY AND AMUSING . . .
THE QUEEN OF HISTORICAL NOVELS
HAS ADDED ANOTHER JEWEL
TO HER COLLECTION."
Rendezvous

Johanna Lindsey

Love Me Forever

AVON BOOKS
An Imprint of HarperCollinsPublishers

This is a work of fiction. Names, characters, places, and incidents are products of the author's imagination or are used fictitiously and are not to be construed as real. Any resemblance to actual events, locales, organizations, or persons, living or dead, is entirely coincidental.

AVON BOOKS
An Imprint of HarperCollins*Publishers*
10 East 53rd Street
New York, New York 10022-5299

First Avon Books printing: December 1996

Avon Trademark Reg. U.S. Pat. Off. and in Other Countries, Marca Registrada, Hecho en U.S.A.
HarperCollins® is a trademark of HarperCollins Publishers Inc.

Printed in the U.S.A.

20 19

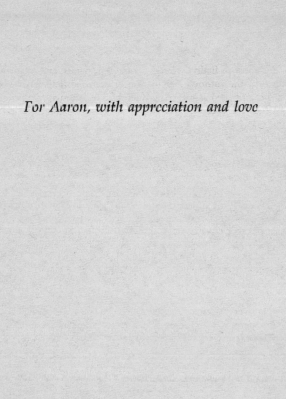

For Aaron, with appreciation and love

LOVE ME
FOREVER

1

"Lachlan, are ye still alive, mon?"

It was doubtful. It wasn't even desirable at the moment. Though the pain of his wound was more annoying than hurtful, as Lachlan MacGregor lay there losing his lifeblood to the sod, he realized it was his pride that had taken the killing blow. That the Laird of Clan MacGregor had been reduced to joining the ranks of common reavers was bad enough. That he'd been stupid enough to get wounded in the process . . .

"Lachlan?" The persistent inquiry came again from his clansman.

"Faith, if I'm no' dead, I should be, so dinna be thinking of carting my body home for burying, Ranald. You'll be leaving it here tae rot as it deserves."

A chuckle came from his other side. "Didna I tell ye no' tae worry, Ranald?" Gilleonan MacGregor said. "It'll take more'n a wee lead ball from a Sassenach pistol tae hurt this great hulk of a body."

Lachlan responded with a snort. Ranald, who'd been prodding him for signs of life, sighed now. "Aye, and I knew that," Ranald said with an odd mixture of boast and relief. " 'Twas worryin' about gettin' him back on his horse that I was doin'. If he canna manage it hisself, then he *will* be rottin' here, 'cause we surely canna lift him, even wi' the both o' us tryin'."

"Och, now, I dinna see a problem in that. I remember lightin' a fire near his big feet once when he was a young'un. Amazin' how a mon as big as the MacGregor will move real quicklike when—"

Lachlan growled low, remembering that time well enough himself. Gilleonan chuckled again. Ranald clicked his tongue and said in all seriousness, "I wouldna be tryin' that, cousin. A fire would alert those Sassenach tae where we are, if they be foolish enough tae still be lookin' for us."

"True, and a fire wouldna be necessary if our laird had waited till we got ourselves home tae be fallin' off his blasted horse. But seein's how he didna wait, and here he lies, have ye got any other ideas?"

"I have one," Lachlan said testily. "I break both your necks, then we'll all three be rotting here."

The two kinsmen knew Lachlan was sensitive about his size, all six foot seven inches of it. Their deliberate goading was their way of trying to get him mad enough to get up on his own—but hopefully not mad enough to kill them.

It was not clear just how mad he was at the moment, all things considered, and so Ranald said, "If it's all the same tae ye, Lachlan, I'd as soon no' rot so near the Sassenach border. Up in the Highlands, now, I wouldna mind so much, but down here in the Lowlands, nay, I dinna like yer idea a'tall."

"Then both of you shut up and let me rest a few moments, and I might oblige you by getting back on my horse under my own steam. Or what's left of it."

He got total silence to that suggestion. They were allowing him the rest he'd requested, he supposed. The trouble was, he didn't think he'd have any steam left for any effort on his part, rest or no rest. He was growing weaker by the moment, could actually feel his strength draining away with his blood. Blasted wound. If he hadn't felt the sting of the bullet going in, he couldn't say for sure that it was somewhere in the general area of his chest. His torso had gone numb long before he'd toppled from his horse, and the hard landing had added other aches to his body. Another problem with his size. When he fell, he fell *hard*.

"I'll wager his mind was a'driftin' again, and that's what got him shot," Gilleonan started in again when Lachlan still hadn't moved an inch after several minutes. "That's all he's been doin' for more'n a year now, moonin' over that bonny redhead the Sassenach stole from him."

Lachlan knew very well that his kinsman was trying to provoke him to anger again, just so he'd get off his duff and stop worrying them. And damned if it didn't work, because Gilleonan's remark was all too true.

When he'd been shot, he had been distracted in thinking about the bonny Megan with her flaming red hair and big midnight blue eyes, a more lovely lass he'd never come across. But he thought about her every time they raided near the

English border, because that was where he'd met her—and lost her. 'Course, he thought about her too much at other times too, but that was his problem and best left to him, not discussed in general, no matter what the purpose.

"I stole her from the Englishmon," Lachlan mumbled. "He merely retrieved her. There is a difference."

"Retrieved her and beat the tar out o' ye—"

That reminder deserved a good clout, and Lachlan's punch, even lacking strength, still knocked Gilleonan out of his crouch. Gilleonan grunted in surprise as he landed on his backside, even though he'd been expecting and hoping for just such a reaction from his laird.

Ranald, on the other hand, laughed. "Verra good, Lachlan. Now if ye'll just put that same energy into gettin' yer big self onto yer wee horse, we'll get ye home so Nessa can see tae that wound."

Lachlan groaned. Gilleonan, having that same thought, snapped at Ranald, "Are ye daft, mon? I'd be runnin' in the opposite direction if I had Nessa fussin' o'er me tae look forward tae. She bullies ye tae wellness, she does—after she cries all over ye first. Och, 'tis a sickenin' sight, tae be sure."

Ranald lifted his brow. "Ye think she'd bully the laird?"

"I know she would," Lachlan mumbled. *And fitting punishment*, he added to himself, for his own stupidity.

With that thought, he rolled over and forced himself to his hands and knees. His vision blurred, not that he could see much to begin with, as dark as it was. A good time for reaving, a moonless night. But reaving and mooning sure as hell didn't mix, and he was going to have to do something about separating them—if he survived this fiasco.

"Point me toward the wee beastie," he told his friends.

They did more than that, they tried to help him up. In the end they were more trouble than help, and he shrugged them both off with a growl. But somehow, he got back in the saddle. And somehow, his two kinsmen managed to get him home, though he had very little memory of that long, grueling ride and the stops on the way that saw his wound tended to before Nessa got her hands on it.

She did get her hands on it though, and on him, and it was a frustrating three weeks before he was able to insist that she leave him be and have her pay attention to that command. The problem with Nessa was she fancied herself in love with Lachlan and took it for granted that they'd be married someday, though he'd never given her the least encouragement. But the fact that he'd never seriously courted anyone else was all the encouragement she seemed to need. Yet when had he had time to do any courting? He'd had the responsibility of the entire clan dropped on him at such a young age.

Nessa lived in his household, as did a great many others of his clan. She'd been underfoot for as long as he could remember, his playmate when they were younger, a nuisance when he started becoming interested in girls, because he didn't put her in that category, tomboy that she was. She was five years younger than his twenty-six, had a devil of a temper, and had pretty much taken over his household when his father died and his stepmother absconded with every tangible bit of the MacGregor wealth aside from the land, forcing him into the unwanted life of a reaver.

He had told the bonny Megan that reaving ran in his family, but it wasn't true. It had been more than two hundred years since his family had actively taken to the roads late of a night, and even back then it had been more to bedevil other clans than to fill the coffers. The MacGregor wealth had come down through the years from royal gifts, a few shrewd endeavors, and one lucky gambler, but there had been a sizeable amount to pay for repairs to the old castle and for the innumerable weddings that cropped up yearly, and to make sure no one ever went without whatever was needful.

The few crops they sowed were seasonal, the small sheep and cattle herds they had couldn't feed the entire household on a regular basis, any more than they ever had. And the one investment that had continued to supply them with ready cash each year had gone sour. Yet they still would have fared well if it weren't for Lady Winnifred.

It put Lachlan in a foul mood whenever he thought of what his stepmother had cost the clan. She hadn't raised him, though she had been at Castle Kregora for a goodly number of his growing years. He hadn't disliked her during the twelve years of her marriage to his father. She had simply been there, part of the landscape, with an occasional smile, but rarely more than that, since she was simply too flighty to be bothered with children, was always concerned only with herself and, of course, his father.

Never would anyone have guessed that she

was a thief, but that she was. Not one week after her husband's death, she up and disappeared, and Lachlan's inheritance went with her. They searched for her for more than a year, but no trace was ever found. It was as if the theft and flight had been well planned, right down to the last detail. But that would speak even worse for her character, and enough had been said to paint a black picture as it was.

Now, three years later, Castle Kregora was falling to ruin, because Lachlan couldn't steal enough from the few Englishmen he robbed down by the border to repair the old edifice. Yet he refused to steal more, as he was afraid someone else might actually be harmed financially by what he took, even if they *were* only Sassenach. He was living with that burden himself, could just barely manage to feed those he was responsible for. As it was, marriages were being postponed, and some clan members who had lived all their lives in the castle or on MacGregor land were moving out of the Highlands altogether.

It had been ingrained in him what his responsibilities were, but an abrupt loss of wealth had never been taken into consideration. At twenty-three he had been unprepared for the burden. At twenty-six, he found the situation much worse and still had no feasible way to rectify it that wouldn't leave more of a sour taste in his mouth than the reaving did. He was already in debt to the few wealthy distant relatives that he had. And everything of value that the castle had possessed had long since been sold.

It was a sorry state of affairs, which was why, while Lachlan was still recuperating from his wound, he called for a discussion on the subject with his two closest cohorts in crime, Gilleonan and Ranald.

Gilleonan was a second cousin and a few years older than Lachlan. Ranald was a third cousin and a year younger. Neither lived in the castle. Both had houses nearby, though they were more often than not found at Lachlan's side, as they were now, sharing a dinner with him on this blustery cold November eve.

Lachlan waited until the meager fare was finished before he made his proclamation, "It isna working."

Since his friends had had prior warning of what was to be discussed, they didn't ask for clarification. "'Twas workin' well enough afore ye got yerself shot," Ranald pointed out.

"My wound has nothing tae do with the obvious. Look around you, Ranald," Lachlan said, and then reiterated, "It *isna* working."

It wasn't necessary to look to see the lighter patches on the wainscotting where paintings had once hung, the china cupboard empty now, fine crystal and silver goblets no longer gracing the table. Of course, it had been so long since these things had gone absent, perhaps his friends had forgotten how the dining room had looked when Lachlan's father was still alive.

"Ye're sayin' there'll be no more reavin'?" Gilleonan asked.

"I'm asking, what's the point? Only once did we bring home a purse fat enough tae make a difference for a short time. We're making that long ride six or seven times a month, and having barely anything tae show for it."

"Aye, I'm no' tae fond o' that ride anymore

meself, especially this time o' the year," Gilleonan agreed. "But our trouble is, we ne'er took the thing serious. It's been no more'n a lark."

Lachlan had to agree with that. Until he'd been shot this last time, they'd had more fun than not, but that was hardly the issue.

"Embrace it in earnest, Gill, and we'd be no better'n thieves," Lachlan said.

Gilleonan raised a brow. "And we're no' that now?"

Ranald snorted. "I dinna consider stealin' from a Sassenach thievin'."

Lachlan had to smile. No, that had been the fun part. The Scots and the English might get along fine now in most dealings, but they'd always be enemies at heart. At least the Highland Scots as well as the border Scots, who'd been preying on the English for too many years to count, saw it that way. On the border, tempers and feuds could still run high, animosity too ingrained and carried over from generations gone by.

"Reavin' was suggested when things didna look so dire," Lachlan pointed out. "But we've reached dire, and something else mun be considered now, afore we lose Kregora as well."

"Have ye something in mind, then?" Gilleonan asked.

Lachlan sighed. "Nay, but as always, I'm open tae suggestions."

His kinsmen settled back in their chairs, Gilleonan swirling the cheap wine in the tin cup he was holding, Ranald plopping a leg over the arm of his chair. Lachlan braced his hands behind his head, prepared to shoot down any suggestions that weren't to his liking.

"I've heard they're findin' gold o'er in that California place," Ranald remarked. "Great nuggets of it just lying around on the ground for the takin'."

Lachlan raised his brow, but before he could reply, Gilleonan said, "Aye, I've heard the same, but the MacGregor here canna venture so far from the hearthstone. Mayhap we could send a few of the clan tae see what's what. Arnald's got the itch tae do some travelin', and his brother would likely agree tae go wi' him. But we canna depend on rumors, nor wait so long as that tae do something ourselves. 'Twould be months afore we even heard from anyone we sent that far."

Lachlan couldn't have said it better, so he didn't add to that other than to nod, though he regretted the fact that he *couldn't* travel so far afield. But Gilleonan was correct. The head of the clan had to be accessible.

"Agreed," Ranald added. "We can put it tae Arnald tae see if he cares tae go gold huntin', but in the meantime . . . I thought o' a solution a while back, but figured Lachlan was tae young then."

"What?"

"A wife—er, that is, a *rich* wife."

Lachlan rolled his eyes, not taking *that* suggestion seriously. But Gilleonan sat forward to say excitedly, "Aye, that's it, Ranald. And time enough the MacGregor gave us an heir tae coddle."

"And where would I be findin' a rich wife around here?" Lachlan demanded, not liking this solution at all.

"Around here, ye wouldna find one that isna spoken for already. But south . . ."

Lachlan cut in, "The Lowlands dinna have an abundance of heiresses either."

"Nay, but England does, and England is but a few days ride away, no' across a blasted big ocean."

Lachlan groaned inwardly that they weren't dropping the idea as quickly as he'd like it dropped. "A Sassenach wife?" he snorted.

"Yer Great-uncle Angus didna see a problem wi' that," Ranald was quick to remind him.

"Uncle Angus, God rest him, was in love," Lachlan replied. "Exceptions can be allowed for circumstances such as that."

"Och, now, isna that what ye would o' done, had the bonny Megan taken a likin' tae ye?" Gilleonan pointed out. "As I recall, she was as English as they come."

Lachlan actually blushed, because that was perfectly true. He'd asked Megan to wed him within minutes of meeting her, had ridden off with her to give her more time to reconsider when she refused him out of hand. And he might have swayed her to his proposal if her fiancé hadn't given chase to retrieve her from him so quickly. But she was a true exception. He wasn't likely to find another lass as bonny as she was.

Faith, they were talking about a *wife* here, a female he'd be stuck with for the rest of his days. Granted, a laird was expected to make *some* sacrifices for the benefit of his kin, if sacrifices were needed, but this one seemed a bit too much in his opinion. Especially since he'd always imagined that he'd be marrying someone to *his* liking, not just to the clan's liking.

He said as much in a very clear grumble. "You'd expect me to wed just any ol' heiress?"

"Nay, no' a'tall," Gilleonan assured him. "Ye're thinkin' o' Scottish lasses and how few rich ones there be. Set your mind tae thinkin' English and the abundance they have. Wi' so many tae choose from, why couldna ye find yerself one tae love?"

That word *love* made Lachlan think of Megan again. Had she married her Sassenach fiancé? Not all elopers to Gretna Green, as she'd been, actually tied the knot. Some came to their senses in time. But a year had come and gone. If she hadn't married that one she came to Scotland to marry, she'd likely married another by now. Then again, what if she hadn't? What if she were still available? That alone was worth going to England to find out.

But still, he had to point out, "You're overlooking the fact that I'm no' a prime catch."

Ranald snorted at that. "Ye're as bonny a lad as they come. There be more lassies moonin' o'er ye than ye ken."

It was true Lachlan was fair to look upon. His hair was darkest auburn, with only mere hints of red appearing in certain light. His eyes were pale green and more often than not, filled with laughter. And his features were put together rather uniquely—at least they'd caused many a lass a heartfelt sigh.

"I think he was referrin' to his great size, Ranald," Gilleonan added hesitantly. "'Tis a bit frightenin' tae a wee lassie."

The extremely tall, brawny size of his body that he'd inherited from his father was and always would be a sore subject with Lachlan. "'Twas the fact that I havena a penny tae my name that I was referring tae," he growled.

Both his friends snorted at that, with Gilleonan expressing both their thoughts in a thoroughly indignant tone, "Ye're Laird of Clan MacGregor, mon. That's all ye need be tae be a prime catch for any lass."

Lachlan sighed at that point. He had turned to reaving at the advice of his kinsmen and had gotten nowhere fast. He wasn't going to jump into marriage just because it sounded like a good idea—to them. Yet it was worth considering and even putting some effort into seeing if it were possible, because he was bone tired of worrying about it all.

"Verra well, but I'm no' going to England wi'out some aid tae get this thing done right and done quickly, if it can be done a'tall. I'll write tae my aunt there and see if she'd be willing tae assist and recommend. But as long as I'll be having tae put up wi' being surrounded by the Sassenach on every front, you two can blasted well come along tae suffer wi' me. And that's the MacGregor telling you that."

In other words, it was an order they couldn't refuse.

2

"You will leave within the week, m'girl," Cecil Richards, the present Earl of Amburough, said to his only child in a tone that would brook no argument. "Their Graces are expecting you at Sherring Cross, and will put you forth in a grand style. Mark my words, you won't have any trouble a'tall finding a husband in that top-lofty crowd."

Kimberly Richards stared blankly up at her father, who had come into the parlor where she was sewing to make his startling announcement. Cecil was in his mid-fifties, a bit portly, quite florid cheeked, with nondescript brown hair and grey eyes. Kimberly had inherited nothing from him in looks or temperament, a fact for which she was grateful.

She shouldn't have been surprised by his announcement, even though she had only ended her period of mourning a mere few days before. For one full year she had veiled herself in sorrow, her grief over her mother's death genuine. She had shunned all entertainments, and her social congress had been restricted to going to church on Sundays. She had also lost her lifelong fiancé because of her year of mourning, for he had been unable, or unwilling, to wait a mere six months more for them to wed.

Yet she had known something like this would be forthcoming, since she had been aware for some time now that her father wanted her out of his house. He certainly made no secret of it, nor of his desire to wed the Widow Marston, who had moved to their small town in Northumberland several years before. She was well aware the widow refused to share a household with another woman.

So the sooner Kimberly was married and gone, the sooner Cecil could remarry. He certainly hadn't mourned for a year over the loss of his wife, Kimberly's mother. Her death had merely been an inconvenience for him.

Kimberly continued to give her father no visible reaction to his announcement, said merely in reference to his mention of the Duke and Duchess of Wrothston, "How did you manage to enlist their aid?"

"A favor owed, and a big one," he replied in a grumble. "I never imagined I would call it in on something so trivial as this, but there you have it."

She raised a brow to that. Trivial was obviously a matter of opinion, and *this* trivial was damned important to him. But she didn't point that out. This wasn't something that she cared to argue with him about, not when she was just as eager to be gone from the only home she had ever known. Unfortunately, it was no longer a home now that her mother was gone from it, but instead a dreary, dismal place that she simply bided time in.

"And don't be taking months to decide," Cecil added sternly. "The duke has been fully apprised of my wishes on the matter, and you know them as well. Don't waste your time on a man you know I won't approve of."

Or he'd disown her. The threat was implicit in his tone. And she'd heard it enough times to recognize it. He even came near to disowning her six months ago, when she'd refused to put aside her mourning for her mother. Though at that time Cecil had backed down. But she could in fact marry without his permission. At twenty-one she was certainly old enough now to do so. And being disowned by Cecil Richards, the present Earl of Amburough, was no great disaster in her opinion, especially since she knew it wouldn't harm her financially. Her mother had seen to that, to her father's utter and recent fury. However, it would be a social disaster, a scandal, as it were, and she would as soon avoid that.

The marriage mart. Kimberly shuddered at the very thought. She wasn't supposed to have ended up on it. She'd had a fiancé since the day she was born, Maurice Dorrien, the son of her father's good friend, Thomas. They'd been only three years apart in age. She'd always gotten along fine with him during their visits at either of their respective homes. They'd never been close friends, yet they came from the same backgrounds, and that had seemed enough.

But they had never managed to set a date. When she'd reached the age to marry, he'd reached the age to go off on his grand tour, and even her father was adamant that he couldn't miss such an important rounding off to his education merely to get married. So she'd been content to wait the year, which was the typical time allotted for such things. The trouble was, Maurice hadn't just taken one year, he'd taken two, because he'd been having such a jolly good time in his travels.

Did anyone ask if she'd mind waiting still another year for him? Of course not. She'd merely been informed that Maurice was extending his trip and the wedding would have to wait.

She was twenty by the time Maurice returned from abroad. The wedding plans were finally made, invitations sent out—and then her mother died and she'd gone into mourning. She'd loved her mother dearly, and she wasn't about to cut short the traditional year of mourning just because her wedding date had already been postponed for two years, and the mourning period would extend that to three. She had waited on Maurice. Fair was fair. He should have had no problem waiting on her, when she'd just lost the only family member she'd ever been close to.

That wasn't the case, however. As it happened, Maurice had incurred considerable debts due to the extension of his tour and the gambling he'd done on it. He was in desperate need of the settlement money and property that would come to him upon their marriage.

She'd never been thrilled with the idea of Maurice for her husband, had merely accepted it as a foregone conclusion, but at least she'd always been sure that he wasn't after her wealth—until six months ago. When his financial situation came out in the open, he'd quickly ended their long

engagement when she refused to wed him immediately. She'd actually been shocked at the
time, it was so unexpected.

And her father had been furious, with her, not
with Maurice. With Maurice, he'd merely blustered and mumbled a bit, but what could he really say? Maurice was his own man now that his
father Thomas was deceased. He needn't honor
an engagement made by parents that he'd had no
say in, not in this day and age anyway. To give
him his due, he had been willing to still wed Kimberly, just not willing to wait another six months
for her mourning period to finish.

When she'd been foolish enough to point out
that Maurice apparently only wanted her money,
Cecil hadn't been even a little bit sympathetic;
he'd said merely, "So? 'Tis the way of things.
D'you think I loved your mother? The only
woman I *ever* loved died because of those bloody
Scots up north, curse and sunder 'em all. Your
mother was a second choice for me because she
came from money, but we did well together."

Did they? Kimberly would always remember
her mother as being miserable, cringing whenever Cecil raised his voice. She was a gentle, almost timid woman, and they didn't suit at all.
She'd needed a kind, understanding husband, not
a blustering border lord. But more to the point,
she'd needed a husband who loved her, which
she hadn't found in Cecil Richards.

But though in tolerance they were much alike,
Kimberly was not timid like her mother. She
could endure much before she actually lost her
temper. And there was no point in losing her
temper over the present situation. She had to find
a husband, and soon. And she was agreeable to

that because she wanted out of her father's house and his control just as much as he wanted her gone. But after her experience with Maurice, she had to wonder how she could ever know for certain if a man would choose her for wife because he really wanted her for wife, or just because he wanted what money and property came with her.

That was something that had never concerned her before. Not that it was the least bit pertinent, as her father would be the first to point out. It was merely important to her in a purely selfish way. She'd just prefer to have a husband who actually cared for her.

When she'd been stuck with the prospect of Maurice for a husband, it hadn't mattered—she'd been resigned to her fate. She had never even considered that she could have something better. But she was no longer stuck with Maurice. And she saw no reason why she couldn't have a man she could be happy with, as opposed to merely "doing well together."

Finding that man wasn't going to be a simple matter, though. She wasn't exactly a raving beauty, capable of making men fall in love with her. Her mother might have always claimed she had a fairy smile capable of casting joy, but that was just something mothers told daughters. Kimberly had never seen anything special about her smile, though it was rather hard to work up a genuine smile when one was staring in a mirror at rather plain features.

She had nothing much to recommend her other than some standard accomplishments, a passing fair voice for song, a little skill at the piano, a neat stitch when it came to sewing, and the ability to run a large household smoothly. That she was a genius at numbers, accounts, and choosing highly profitable investments was something she'd only recently discovered, and not something that a husband would appreciate or utilize, finances being considered a man's domain.

As for appearance, she was slim of build, actually a bit on the skinny side due to her height. Her hair was fashionable enough with its dark blond curls, though light blond would have been more desirable. Her features weren't remarkable by any means, though she did have a somewhat square jaw that hinted at the stubbornness she rarely showed, but was quite capable of. She did have really nicely shaped eyes of a pure, dark green that people remarked upon occasionally. But then most people she knew were rather nice and they needed *something* nice to say to her to *be* nice.

She set her sewing aside and stood up now to look down on her father. Her height of five feet, eight inches, inherited from her mother's branch of the family, gave her the advantage over him by an inch. It was a thing that thoroughly irritated her father and had since the day she'd attained her full height; it was a small weapon that gave her a bit of pleasure simply because it *did* irritate him. Otherwise, her ungainly height was an embarrassment, because it made her stand out in a crowd of average women.

"I have no intention of wasting time, Father, but don't expect immediate results, because I also have no intention of accepting the first man recommended by Their Graces. You won't be the one forced to live with the gentleman for the rest of your days, I will, and if I can't feel a certain compatibility with him, *my* approval won't be forthcoming."

He'd gone red in the face before she'd quite finished, but she'd expected no less. He really hated it whenever she put her druthers forth and stood by them.

"You will *not* drag your feet to spite me—"

Kimberly cut him off, asking, "Why ever would you think that? Hasn't it become apparent to you that I don't like living here? Or, like everything else about me, have you simply not noticed?"

He had no answer for her, but then what could he say? He did tend to ignore her unless he needed something specific from her. Nor did he have the grace to even be embarrassed by her comment.

He merely mumbled a bit before he reiterated, "Just see that you *don't* drag your feet," and then stalked out of the parlor.

Kimberly sat down again with a sigh, but she didn't reach for her sewing. Nervousness came, now that she could really think about what she was facing. She'd be traveling alone, when she never had before. She'd be dealing with a continuous stream of strangers, when she'd lived all her life among people who were familiar to her. And she had to choose a husband, one that both she and her father could agree on. That was the most difficult part, because she couldn't imagine very many offers coming her way. One or two possibly, and that certainly wasn't much to choose from, for someone that she was going to have to spend the rest of her life with.

3

Megan St. James, the new Duchess of Wrothston for all of one year, glanced up over the letter she had just finished reading. When her husband handed her the letter, he'd remarked that he hoped she enjoyed matchmaking. His comment now made sense and she was none too happy about it.

She raised a brow at Devlin, her foot suddenly tapping to indicate her annoyance, if the raised brow didn't quite make her point, and demanded, "And how did it come about that I end up with the responsibility of finding this girl a husband, when *you* are the one who owes the favor to her father? This letter is addressed to you, is it not?"

"Indeed," Devlin replied. "But matters of matrimony and matchmaking are a female's domain."

"Who says so?"

"I do."

He smiled as he said that, because he knew it

would irritate her even more. And she gave him the reaction he was expecting, an unladylike snort.

"You know very well that Duchy is better able to see to something like this," she informed him. "She knows everyone who is anyone, so she'd know exactly who is in the market for a wife, and who isn't. I, on the other hand, am still muddling through just trying to remember the names of this earl and that viscount, and to keep abreast of the current scandals. I haven't even begun on the histories of all these lords and ladies you expect me to become better acquainted with."

"By the by, love, you are doing superbly in that respect." A compliment was just what she needed at that point, but then he knew that, which was why he threw it in. "And it's true, Duchy might be more knowledgeable in this area, but my grandmother isn't up to the entertaining and socializing that will be required to see this thing done right. By all means, enlist her aid and Aunt Margaret's too. They'll be glad to give it. But the favor was asked of me, sweetheart, and so it falls to you, as my wife, to deal with it."

He was right, of course. He was a duke. He shouldn't be required to involve himself in something so trivial. On the other hand, she was a duchess, and in her opinion, the same held true for her. Perhaps there was a way out of this.

With that thought, Megan asked, "Is it absolutely necessary that you do this favor?"

"Absolutely," he assured her. "The favor I owe is a serious one. This is nothing compared to what could have been asked of me, and quite a relief that this matter can be disposed of so simply."

She felt like snorting again, but restrained herself this time. Simple for him, certainly. He'd already delegated the responsibility, washed his hands of it. That's what he thought. If she was required to do a lot of entertaining above and beyond the normal required of her to get this girl matched to some worthy fellow, she'd see to it that Devlin would attend said entertainments.

Then again, she suddenly recalled that they were soon to have a guest aside from Lady Kimberly. Maybe it wouldn't take long at all to find the lady a husband . . .

"Your Aunt Margaret mentioned something about her nephew-by-marriage coming for a visit—"

"That's fine, fine—"

"It means we're going to have a house full of guests again."

"When have we ever not had a house full?" Devlin replied dryly.

She chuckled. With more than a hundred servants under their roof, a house full was a bit of an understatement. Yet he was referring to guests, and he was quite right. So many people had occasion to do business with Devlin, and since Sherring Cross was quite a ways from London, when Devlin was in residence, they came to him and all tended to stay over, some for weeks at a time, before heading back to the city.

"What I meant to suggest, before you attempted to ignore it," she said with an admonishing look for his "fine, fine," "is Margaret's nephew is husband material, I believe. We could well avoid inviting the entire ton here, if he and Lady Kimberly take to each other—as long as we're going to have him in residence for a while anyway."

"Excellent." He smiled. "I trust you can see to it that they *do* 'take to each other'?"

"I suppose I can put some effort into that. Much easier than planning several balls and dozens of smaller affairs—all of which you would have to attend."

He looked aghast at the very thought. "I believe I shall take up residence in London for the duration."

She gave him a thoughtful look. "Now that you mention it, it would be easier to plan these things for London. Less likelihood of *everyone* staying over."

He quickly changed his mind. "On second thought, I'll remain here in the country."

She smiled innocently. "As you wish. If you want to put up with thirty or forty people at our breakfast table each morning—"

The look he gave her now was quite sour. "You're determined to involve me in this, aren't you?"

"Absolutely."

Devlin sighed. "I believe I'll have a talk with Aunt Margaret about this nephew she acquired through her marriage. If he's suitable, and I can't see how he would be otherwise, I'll put my own effort into matching him with the earl's daughter." He gave Megan a brief hug. "An excellent idea you had there, sweetheart. Let's get this thing accomplished with all due speed, shall we?"

She hugged him back, not so briefly. "And then maybe we can have a vacation ourselves for a little privacy, just you, me, and the baby? After all, we haven't had any real time to ourselves since Justin was born. It's been months now, and people are still showing up to get a look at your heir. Perhaps we could hie off to that cottage of yours near Bath?"

He chuckled. "That cottage is twenty rooms, with a full staff. Hardly conducive to privacy, sweetheart."

She frowned, having pictured something much smaller. Scratching that idea, she suggested an alternative. "Actually, Sherring Cross is large enough that we could probably move to one of the unused wings and no one would ever know the three of us were there."

He glanced down at her to determine if she were joking. Since her expression gave him no clue, he said, "Was that a complaint about the size of my home?"

"Not a'tall. Tiffany is the one who calls Sherring Cross a mausoleum, not I."

Tiffany was Megan's childhood friend, and, in fact, they'd both been children the first time they saw Sherring Cross. Tiffany really did consider it a mausoleum, but then, they'd been truly amazed at the size of the ducal estate.

"I've always considered it the perfect size myself," Megan added, "even if I do get lost occasionally."

"You do not," he protested.

"Only once or twice."

"Megan—"

"All right, only once, and not for long." She grinned.

She adored teasing her husband, she really did. It worked well to get him out of the stuffy, pompous manner that had been his usual demeanor—

before he met her—which he sometimes fell back into from habit. She much preferred the hot-tempered, argumentative stableboy she thought she was marrying when they'd eloped to Gretna Green. Quite a surprise to find out that she'd married the very duke—sight unseen—that she'd set her cap for last year.

"You know," Devlin said now, in response to her teasing, "I haven't explored the back wings of Sherring Cross in some time. They were quite private, as I recall. You're absolutely sure they still are?"

The look in his turquoise eyes told her exactly in what direction his thoughts had gone. A tiny thrill shot through her, as it usually did whenever he looked at her with heat in his eyes. A tryst, in the middle of the day, in an unused portion of the house, sounded quite enjoyable.

"Why don't we go and find out?" she suggested, her voice a bit huskier than it had been.

"My thought exactly."

4

It was the grandest edifice Kimberly had ever set eyes on. She'd been to Victoria's palace to be presented to the queen the last time she had gone to London with her mother, so she was familiar with grand edifices of the royal kind. But this, Sherring Cross, the ducal estate of Ambrose Devlin St. James, outshone any palace in sheer size, stretching out over acre after acre of beautifully manicured lawns. It was intimidating to say the least, and she was already nervous enough.

The more she had thought about her reason for being here, the less she liked it. Imagine, asking someone of such consequence as the Duke of Wrothston to assist in finding her a husband. Her father's gall knew no bounds. And His Grace, the duke, couldn't be any more pleased about doing this favor than she was to reap the benefits.

Nor had it been a pleasant journey getting here. It wasn't enough that she was bone-weary from three straight days of traveling, but during that time, the carriage also lost a wheel and she had to stand around for hours while that was fixed. Then the weather turned even colder than normal for this time of year, and the little coal-burner she had in the carriage wasn't enough to take the chill off.

Then she had a bad experience at one of the inns she stayed at, where a group of rowdy Scots in the room next to hers kept her up half the night. She had nothing against Scots herself. It was her father who denounced them all because he blamed them for the death of the woman he loved. A death that in her opinion, and the opinion of the courts, had been accidental.

Even having been reared with his sentiments—he'd never kept his undying love for another woman from his wife; it was something he brought up quite frequently, in fact—she wasn't affected by his prejudices, likely because she felt no true closeness toward her father. Actually, she had on occasion felt that that other woman was lucky she had escaped a life with the earl, even through death. But those occasions were rare, and usually when she really detested something her father had done.

But she did have something against blatant public disturbances of the kind those Scotsmen had created that night at the inn. Three complaints to the manager and those men still didn't quiet down. But at least her father hadn't been there to cause a scene. As much as he hated Scots, it would have turned into an embarrassing situation, rather than just an annoying one.

It was bad enough that she had herself snapped at one of those Scots when she ran into him in the hall the next morning. The poor fellow had barely had his eyes open yet, but they were agog by the time she flounced off, after having vented her spleen on him. It wasn't until hours later, back on the road, that she regretted her rash words. She so rarely lost her temper. Being tired, and therefore irritable, was no excuse.

And her new maid was no help. Mary took to traveling even worse than Kimberly did. Her constant complaints at every little bump, delay, or drop in the weather would have tried a saint. But at least *she* had been able to get some rest each night in the rooms she shared with Kimberly. The girl slept sounder than the dead.

And if all that wasn't enough, Kimberly had caught a cold. Her nose was likely as red as a cherry from all the sneezing she'd been doing. Her body ached from the jarring ride. Her head felt like it was splitting apart. And protocol insisted she put her best foot forward to make a good impression on Their Graces? That was a laugh. They'd take one look at her and wonder what they'd gotten themselves into.

Yet there was no help for it. She'd arrived at Sherring Cross. Footmen in fancy livery were already stepping forward to assist her out of her carriage. And the massive front doors were swung wide. There was really nothing to do but step through them.

Under the circumstances, she had hoped, prayed even, that she would be shown to a room and could be presented to Their Graces after she'd had sufficient time to recover. No such luck. The Duchess of Wrothston herself was standing in the large entryway to greet her.

Meeting for the first time, they were both, to a degree, dumbstruck, Kimberly because she'd had no idea that St. James's new duchess was so petite or so incredibly beautiful. But she should have guessed. She'd met the duke some ten years ago when he was but twenty, and even though a young girl would take little note of such things, she remembered him as being extremely handsome. So it stood to reason that his wife would be lovely. But this lovely?

Megan St. James defined beauty, albeit, a bit vividly. Her bright copper-red hair wasn't a bit fashionable, yet it suited her perfectly. Her midnight blue eyes were warm, friendly. Her figure, after her first child, couldn't have been altered much, it was so slim and ideally curved.

Beside her, Kimberly felt like a gangly dowd. Granted, there had never been much call to dress in high-fashion in her small town in Northumberland. And she had only just put away her mourning wardrobe, which meant what clothes she had left were several years old and didn't take into account the weight she'd lost. Not that that was noticeable in the bulky winter wool coat she was traveling in; at least, it hadn't been until one of the footmen requested her coat, and wouldn't go away until she shrugged out of it and handed it over.

As for Megan, now that her initial surprise was over, she was thinking that a new gown, cinched in properly, a new hairstyle that wasn't so plain, and a little less color in the nose would do wonders for Lady Kimberly. She wasn't going to be the season's new reigning beauty, and that was too bad, but it couldn't be helped. Not every young miss joining the marriage mart each year could be.

Things could be worse, Megan decided. At least the lady wasn't downright ugly. Kimberly

Richards was just, well ... average-looking came to mind. And she did have nice eyes of a pure dark green, really beautiful the more one looked into them. It just might take a little longer than they had imagined to get her married.

Kimberly, to make her first impression more memorable, sneezed quite loudly at that point. And worse, she discovered she had left her lace handkerchief in the carriage. She was about to panic as she felt her nose starting to run, when Megan's dimples suddenly showed up in a smile so stunning, Kimberly didn't even think to wonder about it.

"A cold?" Megan said, her tone on the hopeful side. "That expla—ah *is* a shame. But expected, with the dreadful weather we've been having."

Kimberly did wonder about that smile now, and the tone accompanying it, which belied any sympathy implied in her hostess's words. In fact she stiffened, somewhat offended. Then she decided that before she said something she would undoubtedly regret, she ought to give herself a few moments to consider that she just might be so exhausted from her trip that she was imagining things.

To that end, she said, "I'll be right back, Your Grace. I seem to have left something in my carriage."

Without further explanation and giving the duchess no opportunity to stop her, she turned to open the door that had been closed behind her. The carriage would still be there, since Mary was overseeing the unloading of their baggage. And that was all that Kimberly expected to find when she opened the door. That wasn't the case, however.

Standing there, about to knock with a very large fist that was drawn back just before it reached her forehead, since she'd taken the place of the door, was a very fascinating man. He was tall, as in very tall, as in approaching seven feet tall. And if that wasn't enough to hold Kimberly momentarily spellbound, he was also extremely handsome.

He had dark auburn hair, clubbed back to keep the rowdy wind from playing havoc with it. A brief ray of sunshine, come and gone in a flash, showed mere hints of red in those thick locks. There had been laughter in his light green eyes that didn't last long as she continued to stare. And he wasn't just tall, but brawny huge, with legs like tree stumps, and a barrel-wide chest, all tightly wrought in muscle rather than excess flesh.

"Instead of gawking, lass, why dinna you step aside tae let me in?"

His voice was deep, rumbling, and surprisingly lyrical in its lightly accented Scottish brogue, but at the moment, the tone was quite curt. He was a man who didn't like being gawked at apparently. But how could anyone help doing so? Kimberly had never seen anyone that tall, let alone that handsome—well, with the possible exception of the Duke of Wrothston—and she doubted anyone else had either.

She was so flustered she didn't speak or move, and when she felt the tickle on her upper lip that suggested her nose wasn't going to wait for that handkerchief she'd been after, she automatically lifted her arm to wipe her sleeve across the area. It was a no-no of the worst kind, a mistake a child would make, not a grown woman, and she didn't even realize she'd done it until she heard him snort.

Her embarrassment was made a hundred times worse by that sound. And it was followed by his hands attaching to her waist and physically setting her out of his way.

But her hot cheeks, now as bright as her nose, went entirely unnoticed, due to the Duchess of Wrothston and the newcomer finally seeing each other, now that his path was cleared. Kimberly, still gawking at him, immediately noted his delight at seeing the duchess. Pleasure and joy fairly oozed out of him, his smile brilliant, the laughter back in his light green eyes. She expected him to dance a jig at any moment.

Megan St. James, on the other hand, was not. "Good God, the Scots reaver!" she said with a hand drawn up to her chest. "You haven't come to rob us, have you?"

His smile turned abruptly sensual, and it had the oddest effect on Kimberly, sort of like a mild punch in the gut, just enough to make her lose her breath, but not enough to hurt. And it wasn't even directed at her.

"If you'll be letting me steal your heart, darlin', aye, that I have," he replied, then, "Faith—the bonniest lass in all of England living under the same roof wi' my Aunt Margaret? I canna be that lucky."

Megan was shaking her head in denial after hearing that. "*You're* Margaret's nephew? Impossible. We can't be that unlucky. The relatives Margaret gained through her marriage are MacGregors, not Mac"—she paused to try and remember the name he had told her so long ago—"Duell, wasn't it? Yes, Lachlan MacDuell, you said you were."

"Och, now, you dinna expect a reaver tae hand o'er his real name, d'you, when he's in the process of reaving?" He asked that with an unremitting grin. "Nay, I'm a MacGregor, *the* MacGregor, actually, present laird of my clan—and the Lachlan was correct. 'Tis pleased I am that you remember."

That was still blatantly obvious. He couldn't stop grinning. Also obvious now was Megan's displeasure at this unexpected turn of events.

"This won't do a'tall, MacGregor," she warned him. "Devlin will never permit you to stay in his home. He didn't like you one little bit, if you'll recall."

"Devlin Jefferys? What's he got to do with Sherring Cross?"

"Perhaps the fact that he owns it?" she said a bit dryly, before she explained. "And Devlin isn't a Jefferys. Like you, he also had a fondness back then for using names that weren't his own."

The man suddenly looked appalled. "Wait a moment, you dinna mean tae say your blasted Englishmon is my aunt's grandnephew, Ambrose St. James?"

"Shush, he really hates that first name of his, and yes, he most certainly is."

Now he groaned. "Och, please, darlin', say you didna marry the mon."

"I most certainly did," Megan huffed.

His groan turned into a growl, which abruptly ended with another smile and a shrug. "No matter. I've surmounted worse obstacles, that I have."

Megan's eyes narrowed on him. "If that means

what I think it means, you can forget it this instant. I *am* married, and *very* happily so," she stressed. "Furthermore, I can almost guarantee you won't be staying at Sherring Cross as you'd planned. And besides, I could have sworn Margaret said you were in the market for a wife."

The look he gave Megan said clearly that he'd found the only wife he could ever want. It caused the duchess to blush. Kimberly, seeing that look, was annoyed for some reason, although it was no business of hers. She tried clearing her throat as a reminder that there was a witness to this very personal conversation that she definitely wanted to end, but she still went unnoticed.

"Whether I stay here or near here, I'll be pursuing my heart's desire. I'd be a fool not tae."

"You'd be a fool if you do," Megan replied, then added with a sigh, "Dense, that's what you are," and a shake of her head, as if she simply couldn't understand it. "Just as dense as you were a year ago, when I told you I was spoken for, but you refused to listen."

"Determined," he corrected with still another grin. "And what's one wee husband matter when two hearts were meant for each other?"

At that, Megan rolled her eyes. Kimberly, getting more annoyed by the moment, cleared her throat again, much louder. This time Megan heard her and glanced her way, though her look was totally confused for a moment, as if she couldn't for the life of her remember who Kimberly was or what she was doing there.

And then it must have dawned on her, because she gasped. "Oh, my dear Lady Kimberly! Please forgive me for my distraction. You must be exhausted from your journey, and here I've kept you standing there while dealing with this incorrigible Scot—" She paused to give Lachlan a reproving glare, which placed the entire blame where it belonged, at least in her opinion. Then to Kimberly again, she made a sincere apology: "I'm so sorry. Come along and I'll show you to the room that has been chosen for you, and we'll see to that cold you've caught as well. As it happens, I know that Duchy, Devlin's grandmother, has some wonderful remedies—"

Lachlan interrupted at that point, as Megan started to lead a relieved Kimberly away. "Ah, darlin', don't be leaving me yet. 'Tis been way tae long since I've basked in your glorious sunshine."

Megan snorted beneath her breath, loud enough for only Kimberly to hear. She continued to lead Kimberly away for a moment, but must have thought better of it.

She paused to swing around, frowning sternly, and hissed at Lachlan, "I have a guest to see to who *is* welcome here, whereas you are not. Have one of the servants fetch Margaret for you, and see that you inform her of your previous involvement with Devlin. She'll tell you herself that you have to change your plans, I have no doubt, for that dear lady couldn't have been aware of your nefarious activities. She never would have knowingly invited a thief into our home."

"Reaver, darlin'," he corrected with a pained expression. "Kindly make the distinction."

Megan sighed in exasperation before she replied, "There is no distinction, MacGregor, not when it was Englishmen you were robbing. You Scots might see it so, but we English certainly don't."

"Ah, but 'tis a moot point, since my reaving

days are behind me now," he assured her. "I canna undo what was done wi' good reason afore now, yet you'll give me credit for turning o'er a new leaf."

"Will I? Not likely. And we've discussed it long enough. Good day."

Kimberly was witness to his chagrined look just before she was led off, then the determined look that followed. He apparently was a man who refused to accept defeat easily, yet in the case of acquiring Megan St. James's affections he was bound for failure. All of England knew that the Duke and Duchess of Wrothston were madly in love with each other. That news had come to the far reaches of Northumberland, but apparently it wasn't common knowledge in Scotland.

A Highlander. Too bad. Kimberly had felt somewhat attracted to Lachlan MacGregor—well, that was putting it too mildly. She'd been very attracted. There was no point in denying it. But it was a moot point for two very good reasons. His affections were already taken, albeit by a married woman. And he was Scottish. And even if the first reason could be overcome, the second one was insurmountable. Her father would never approve of a Scotsman for her husband. He would flat out disown her first, and bedamned to the scandal that would cause.

A Scotsman. That was really, really too bad.

5

"You poor, dear boy," Margaret MacGregor said in sympathy after Lachlan had finished explaining to her, in full honesty, the circumstances that had led him here looking for a wife. "And Winnifred? Who could have guessed she'd do something like that. She seemed like such a nice gel."

Lachlan had to smile. Winnifred was close to fifty, not exactly a girl. But Margaret, being in her seventies, tended to call anyone sixty or below a girl or a boy. She was a dear, sweet lady, a little on the plump side, and always cheerful, at least whenever Lachlan had ever been in her company. But he had to agree with her on that point. No one could have guessed that Winnifred was capable of such a dastardly deed.

As Margaret refilled Lachlan's teacup—they were alone in the mammoth parlor at Sherring Cross—she admonished, "Why did you never come to me for monetary assistance? Your Great-uncle Angus left me quite well in the pocket, God love him, though he knew it was unnecessary. I have more money than I'll ever find things to spend it on."

Lachlan was embarrassed enough by the subject, but it would be even worse if he tried to explain his reasons. Borrowing from blood kin was one thing and perfectly acceptable. But Margaret wasn't that. She had married into his family instead, and her husband was no longer living, or Lachlan wouldn't even be here. He'd have gone to his Uncle Angus for assistance long ago.

So he said simply, "I mun do this on my own, Aunt Margaret," and hoped she'd leave it go at that.

She did, though she made a tsking sound to indicate she didn't agree. "Very well. And you do seem to be on the right track now. A wife with plump pockets is just the thing to put an end to your difficulties. Why, it's done all the time, don't you know."

He nodded his agreement, even though he wished he didn't have to take advantage of this method himself. "But there's another thing I need tae be telling you, Aunt Margaret, that I didna ken would be a problem until I arrived here. I've met your nephew Ambrose under less than ideal circumstances. He was using a different name at the time, which is why I was unaware that I'd met him—until today."

"A different name?" She frowned. "Would that be when he was in Scotland last year?"

"Aye, exactly then. I'm afraid I stopped him to—ah, relieve him of a few of his coins, but instead, I relieved him of his fiancé."

Margaret's faded turquoise eyes widened briefly, then crinkled as she began to chuckle.

"Good God, that was *you*? My sister and I had heard a bit of that story from Megan—Devlin, of course, would never have repeated such a story, even though his rescue was quite heroic. But Duchy and I had a great good laugh over it, I must say."

He was relieved that she found it amusing. He didn't, and he knew damn well Devlin wouldn't either.

"The thing is," he pointed out, "Megan seems tae think he'll no' let me stay on here."

"Oh, bosh, of course he will," she scoffed, only to amend seconds later, "At least, he will after he is apprised of your situation, and I'll see to that. Don't you worry, dear boy. We'll have you married in no time a'tall."

Lachlan smiled his acceptance of that, though he couldn't help blushing over the thought of Devlin learning of his dire straits. What rotten luck, that the bonny Megan had married his aunt's relative. Then again, if she hadn't, he likely would never have found her again.

That he had found her changed his plans somewhat, well, completely, actually. He wasn't going to be looking for a wife now, at least, not until he'd given it his best effort to win Megan away from her duke. If he could accomplish that, then he'd just have to find some other way to rectify the family fortune, though faith, he still couldn't think of another way to do that just yet.

Megan—he'd actually found her, and she was as beautiful as he remembered, more so, if that was possible. And just as feisty, he thought fondly. The irony was uncanny, though, that his quest for a wife should lead him to her. Aye, she was meant for him, not for the Englishman. He just had to convince her of that, and he meant to do that very thing.

"My sister and I have come up with quite a few possible heiresses for you to consider, m'boy," Margaret was continuing, unaware of his decision. "In fact, we're lucky enough to have one of them arriving here anytime now for a protracted stay. In search of a husband herself, don't you know. A rich earl's daughter, she is. You can't do much better there. Her dowry's rumored to be immense, and includes several prime properties."

Lachlan nodded, because he couldn't very well tell her that his plans had changed, that he was no longer interested in any heiresses. He'd be banished from Sherring Cross if he did. Also, he still needed her help so that he *could* stay here, because he certainly couldn't see himself appealing to Megan's husband to let him stay so he could seduce his wife. That really wouldn't go over well at all.

So he said, "She sounds ideal, Aunt Margaret. You'll have tae be introducing me tae her when she does arrive—that is, if I'm no' on my way back tae the Highlands afore then, which seems more likely the case now," he ended with a sigh.

She leaned over to pat his hand. "Don't you worry about that now. Our Dev would never be so churlish as to give you the boot just for some little misunderstanding that occurred ages ago. In fact, I will go and speak with him now, just to put your mind at ease. So do make yourself at home, Lachlan, m'boy, you'll be staying."

6

"He's not staying, and that's final!"

It wasn't the first time Devlin had said that in the last few hours, but no one seemed to be paying any attention to him—at least on that subject.

Megan had been the first to find him and inform him who his aunt's Scottish relative was, and she had left him to mull over what rotten luck that turned out to be. Then Margaret had shown up in his study to drop some ridiculous tale of woe in his lap, explaining that the Highlander had actually been robbed of his inheritance, and so had turned to reaving merely as a means to keep kith and kin together.

A stepmother absconding with the family jewels, as it were, and completely disappearing? Not bloody likely. More likely it was a tale the Scot had come up with because he knew it would stir the sympathies of their mutual aunt, and other such gullible ladies. But now even Megan was changing her tune, when she had at first seemed highly indignant that Lachlan MacGregor was under her roof.

They were in the parlor where the household usually gathered before dinner. His grandmother and her sister, Margaret, had their heads together on the sofa, speaking so softly their voices wouldn't carry to Devlin and Megan, who stood by the fireplace. Lord Wright, who had come up from London to purchase one of Sherring Cross's prize thoroughbreds and so was staying the night, was speaking with Lady Kimberly about the weather, of all mundane topics. Too bad he was in his fifties and already married, because he showed a marked interest in the lady.

At least the subject under discussion had the decency to not make an appearance. This was fortunate, because Devlin couldn't be sure of his own reaction if he came face to face with that scoundrel again. He was still in the house somewhere due only to common courtesy, allowing him to get a fresh start in the morning for his journey back to the Highlands, or wherever he now chose to go.

That Devlin had had to restate his decision was due to Megan now suggesting they let the Highlander stay on. She had yet to say why she had changed her mind, but he was sure she would get to her reasons in her own sweet time, since she never let him wonder for long about her motives—at least, not overly long.

As for his statement, she merely said, "You're not really angry over some silly thing that happened more than a year ago, are you?"

Devlin raised a brow at her. "Silly thing? The man got down on his knees and proposed marriage to you upon meeting you, and when you refused him out-of-hand as any sane woman would have, he abducted you."

"Yes, but you got me back *and* soundly thrashed him for it," she reminded him. "Or had you forgotten that you've already had your revenge?"

Anyone who didn't know Devlin very well wouldn't have recognized that slight turning of his lips as a sign of smug satisfaction. The pleasant memory that prompted it didn't last long, however.

"That hardly pertains to what he does for a living," he said. "Good God, he's a bloody thief. Why do you ladies keep overlooking that simple fact? And because of that, he could be my aunt's stepson, rather than just her nephew, and he would still not be welcome in my house."

Heads were turning their way, and Megan whispered to him, "Not so loud, if you please. And might I point out that you haven't even noticed Lady Kimberly, she's so—unnoticeable—which means we're going to have a devil of a time finding her a husband, and here you are kicking out one of the possibilities. Have you forgotten already that we were going to try and match those two?"

Now he realized why she'd changed her mind, but it made no difference at all in his opinion. " 'Were' is the operative word, Megan. His past activities do *not* make him a suitable match for an earl's daughter."

"Oh, give over, Dev," she cut him off impatiently. "He's a Scottish lord, and head of his clan to boot. That makes him highly suitable for an earl's daughter, and well you know it. And his objectionable past activities can be overlooked, due to the circumstances that prompted them. You heard what your aunt said. The poor man was desperate. Yet he's put that behind him. And he's here to find a rich wife so it will *stay* behind him. With the dowry that comes with Lady Kimberly, he'd hardly have reason to continue his reaving ways, now would he?"

He snorted. "Unless he enjoyed them, which would be a very good reason for him to continue haunting the border for victims, wife or not. And you can't deny he did seem to enjoy robbing us, Megan."

"Seemed to, maybe, but we don't know that for certain. And the very fact that he's here looking for a rich wife is proof, as I see it, that he doesn't want to continue in that vein. I don't see why we can't give him the chance to show that he's sincere. Even your grandmother is willing to do that."

"If he's sincere, I'll eat my—"

"Don't make promises you might regret," she cut in with a grin. "And admit it, you just don't like the chap. *That* is your main objection."

"That is only a small part of it," he insisted. "And enough has been said about that blackguard. He is *not* staying, and that's final!"

7

So the Scotsman really was a thief. MacGregor had said it himself, called himself a reaver, but Kimberly hadn't taken that seriously, since the conversation she'd been forced to overhear between him and the duchess in the entryway had seemed more like simple banter than fact. But now the duke had confirmed it.

MacGregor was an actual thief, *and*, he had once tried to rob Their Graces. And that wasn't even the worst. He was not just a thief, but an abductor of women. Amazing. Though even more amazing was that a magistrate hadn't been summoned posthaste to deal with the fellow. But Kimberly assumed that was because he was somehow related to the duke's aunt.

The only reason she had gone down to dinner tonight, feeling as miserable as she did, was on the off chance that she might see the Scot again. Silly of her. And he hadn't even made an appearance. She would have been much better served to have gone to bed early, particularly since now that she was trying to get some sleep, whoever was in the next room to hers was making that impossible.

There was banging going on, creaking, an occasional burst of laughter, and voices just loud enough to be bothersome, but not loud enough to distinguish any words. She was reminded of the sleepless night at that inn, though those walls had been thinner, allowing her to distinguish the Scot's brogue in the occasional words she'd heard. This racket was just as bad, however, and if it persisted much longer, she was going to be forced to do something, though she wasn't sure what.

Pounding on the walls, she supposed, would cause her the least effort. As tired as she was, she had absolutely no desire to go seek out the housekeeper, if that lady happened to still be up, just to be moved to another room, which would require even more time. Not for the first time, she wished she weren't such a light sleeper, or she might have at least had a chance of getting to sleep even with that racket going on.

The proper thing to do would be to suffer in silence, but Kimberly simply didn't feel like suffering any more than she already was. So fifteen minutes later, when the noise hadn't even lessened a little, she finally pounded on the wall behind her bed.

In response she was treated to immediate silence. She had made her point, obviously. She sighed, fluffed her pillow, and lay back down— only to be startled half out of her bed with a much louder pounding on the wall coming back at her.

Well, that did it. So much for doing it the easy

way. She'd get herself moved to an empty wing—there had to be one in a home this large—but first she'd give those inconsiderates in the next room a piece of her mind. If the same thing hadn't happened to her so recently, she would never have considered a confrontation. But she was furious now, she had gone through this just two nights ago, and because of that, she had no thought at the moment for doing what was proper or lady-like.

She yanked on her robe, nearly cut off her breathing in belting it too tight, slammed her door back against the wall when she opened it, and a few seconds later was banging her fist on the next door down from hers with all the strength she could muster. That it opened immediately wasn't all that surprising. With that loud crashing in of her own door, she'd given ample warning. What did surprise her was that Lachlan MacGregor stood there.

But Kimberly wasn't dumbstruck by him this time, though she found him no less fascinating. She was simply too furious for that to matter.

She glared up at him and demanded, "Have you no sense, man, to not realize how late it is and that you might be disturbing others with the noise you've been making?"

To that he merely raised a curious brow and said, "So the little wren has a voice after all?"

She blushed at being reminded of her earlier gawking. But that didn't cut through her anger, especially when another voice drew her eyes to a man lounging in a chair farther in the room, the very man she'd upbraided a few mornings ago for keeping her up half the night.

"Aye, I can vouch for that," the fellow said

with a drunken nod. "A voice? More like a banshee wail she's got. 'Tis her who screamed me ear off at that inn a couple days ago, and for nae good reason."

"Och, well, I'm no' surprised they stuck me in the servants' wing," Lachlan replied, supposedly to his friend, though his eyes remained on Kimberly. "But I'll be settling down in my own good time. 'Tis sorry I am that you're being disturbed, lass, but"—he shrugged—"you can blame your employers for that, inasmuch as this is where they put me."

He might have mistaken her for a servant when he lifted her out of his way earlier in the entry hall, but unless he was deaf, he must have heard the duchess use her title when she'd apologized to Kimberly. Megan had also mentioned that she was a guest here. So his inference now that this was the servants' wing simply because she was in it, she saw as purely an insult, a deliberate one.

Odious man. His manners left much to be desired, but then, she'd already known that, given the way he had completely ignored her earlier. But Kimberly wasn't going to knuckle under just because he chose to be odious.

"It's obviously your habit to make disturbances no matter where you are. But this is not the servants' wing, MacGregor, which you know very well. I am visiting Sherring Cross just as you are. Furthermore, I am sick. I am exhausted. I desperately need some sleep, but I can't get any with you doing your best to wake the entire household."

"I'm thinking that wouldna be possible wi' a household this large, lass, though I'll allow the idea does have some merit just now, in the mood I find myself in."

He said the last with a somewhat evil grin that brought her brows further together. Obviously, he had no intention of doing the decent thing.

That just added exasperation to her fury, enough to cause her to snap, "And I'm thinking you don't have a brain to think with. Are you Scots truly this inconsiderate? Or are you simply so self-centered that you don't care who you upset or disturb with your rudeness?"

She'd managed to make him angry. His sudden black expression left her little doubt of that. And he took a step toward her, making her gasp and step back. Yet he took another step, then another, then another, causing a smidgen of fear to rise in her chest, and the wish that she'd sought out the housekeeper after all, instead of taking her complaint to its source.

"So you're thinking I'm rude, are you?" he said in a low, menacing tone. "You havena seen rude, lass, at least no' from me, but that can be arranged if you dinna cease haranguing me wi' your blathering."

By the time he finished, he'd backed her right back into her own room. And he seemed somewhat satisfied that he'd done so, since he merely ended with a curt nod, grabbed the handle of her door, and closed it, loudly, behind him.

Kimberly was left standing there wide-eyed and trembling. He'd frightened her, no doubt about it. But only because she'd had no idea what he might do. And she'd let him get away with it. How smug that Scot must be feeling at the moment.

Laughter came again from the room next door.

Color flooded Kimberly's cheeks, since she was certain that laughter was at her expense. The wren had been frightened back to her nest. She wanted to march back over there and give them a further piece of her mind, she really did—yet her heartbeat hadn't returned to normal yet. And she couldn't be sure that ill-mannered Highlander wouldn't manage to frighten her again.

But it absolutely infuriated her that she couldn't deal with the situation as it deserved. And that was because the Scot was an unknown quantity, when she was too accustomed to dealing with known quantities. She was plain and simply too intimidated at the moment to confront him again.

With a low sound of disgust, mainly for herself and her lack of courage, she locked her door, discarded her robe, and crawled back into the large four-poster. A very comfortable bed, but she gave up the idea of getting any sleep in it, at least for tonight. It was still too noisy and she was still too angry.

Yet she decided not to seek out a new room in some other part of the mansion. She'd wait until it quieted down next door, then *she'd* start making some noise. If she couldn't get satisfaction in an acceptable way, at least she could pay that wretched man back in kind. And thankfully, he'd be on his way tomorrow. She'd overheard Ambrose St. James clearly in that regard. The Scot wasn't staying.

8

"Did ye frighten the poor lass tae death then, Lachlan?" Gilleonan asked as soon as Lachlan returned to his room. "I dinna hear her screamin' for help, so she mun be shocked into silence or dead o' fright."

Lachlan gave his cousin a dark look. "And why would she be screaming for help? I didna lay a blasted hand on her."

"Och now, maybe ye should have, a soft hand that is. Ye've always been able tae cajole and seduce much better'n ye frighten, and wi' less complaints. At least when ye set yer mind tae it ye do."

"Wi' lassies familiar tae me, aye, that may be true. But those who dinna ken what a nice lad I am tend tae run if I look at them wrong."

Ranald, sprawled in a comfortable reading chair, hooted with laughter over that contention. "Nice, he says? They can call the laird of the MacGregors many things, but nice?" More laughter followed.

At the darker scowl that produced, Gilleonan said, "Dinna mind him, Lachlan. He's had one ale tae many, I'm thinkin', but wi' reason."

The censure in Gilleonan's tone did not go unnoticed and Lachlan found it vastly irritating. Ranald had been hitting the ale ever since he'd learned who their hostess had turned out to be. Neither of his cousins was one bit happy that he'd found his Megan again. And Ranald was too far gone in drink to even notice that the subject had subtly changed back to where it was before they were interrupted by that uppity termagant next door.

In fact, Ranald went on to say, "When that one gets her courage back, she'll be raisin' hell again, I dinna doubt. Burned me ears off but good at that inn when ye and Gill were still abed, and me barely awake tae even ken what she was after complainin' about. If she werena so blasted loud about it, I might've enjoyed meself just lookin' at her, for she's got a right fine figure on her, that she does."

Lachlan rolled his eyes. Gilleonan, standing with a pint of his own ale by the slow-burning fireplace, was now softly chuckling.

Ranald was partial to fine figures. A woman could be ugly as sin, but if she was shaped exactly the way he liked them, then he'd be panting after her right quick. And Lachlan had to allow, even he'd taken note of those shapely curves that had been cinched in so tightly.

Actually, he'd noted a few other things as well that he'd overlooked earlier when she'd been wearing her drab, loose gown. She had quite hefty breasts that hadn't been apparent before. And she was tall. For a man who usually topped

a woman's head by more than a foot, it was rare
to find one with a bit of height on her, so he
didn't feel like a blasted giant next to her. And
spectacular green eyes, she had, all sparkly with
her ire, as well as a complexion as silky smooth
as fresh cream. Also noted was her splendid
golden hair, loose and flowing to her waist,
which gave her a somewhat wanton look that
was quite sensual.

Unusual woman, she was. She'd seemed so un-
assuming at first glance, the shy little wren easily
awed, easily ignored. Yet she had some hidden
plumage apparently. And she certainly had no
qualms about brandishing a scolding tongue on
a stranger, which took a degree of courage on her
part—or a complete lack of good sense.

Aye, Ranald would definitely find her of interest. Lachlan might have himself, if he weren't already smitten with his sweet Megan. But he was,
and Megan was the one he meant to have and to
hold for the rest of his days. There was just the
wee problem of her already having a husband.
And his cousins seemed to think he wasn't aware
of that fact.

When Lachlan had confided earlier who the
Duchess of Wrothston was and that he was going
to win the lady for himself, Gilleonan had asked
quite plainly, "Are ye daft, mon, tae be thinkin'
o' stealin' a duke's lady? Or perhaps ye're forgettin' she's already spoke for?"

It wasn't something Lachlan could forget, but
he didn't give it as much importance as his cousins seemed to think it deserved. He'd simply replied to that, "She made a mistake in her choice.
I mean tae convince her of that. Divorce is no'
unheard of."

"For the gentle folk, 'tis ruination," Gilleonan had pointed out. "And ye'd be askin' her tae give up a dukedom. I canna see any woman doin' that."

"Och, well, a true test of love—"

Gilleonan had snorted. "A true test o' idiocy, I'm thinkin'. And besides, Lachlan, ye're forgettin' ye're here tae find ye a moneyed miss with deep pockets. What if she has none tae speak of?"

"A duke marryin' a poor lass?" Lachlan had likewise snorted at that possibility. " 'Tis more like she comes from a line of dukes herself, or marquises. Dukes dinna marry verra far beneath them."

" 'Tis more like dukes would marry anyone they please, and a mon as rich as this one wouldna care if the lass were poor. He'd no' be needin' aught from a wife but herself and the bairns she'll give him. And this one he'd be wantin' regardless, just as ye do, because she's such a bonny lass. But ye, on the other hand, are needin' the money. Or have ye also forgotten that wee fact?"

Their disagreement had been interrupted at that point by the loud pounding on the door and the annoying complaints that had followed from the curvacious wench next door. If Lachlan hadn't already been exasperated with his cousins for not seeing his point of view, he might have given in to the lass's demands. On the other hand, she'd jumped right in with an insult, a look meant to fry him on the spot, and a belligerent tone guaranteed to raise a man's dander, so he still might have taken offense, no matter the mood he'd been in to begin with.

He was still in that mood, which prompted the

remark now, "If your voice didna get louder and louder wi' each pint of ale you down, Ranald, we wouldna get angry visitors in the wee hours complaining about it."

"Och, aye, 'tis all me . . . fault then . . . I suppose?" Ranald slurred. "Ye werena shoutin' . . . right back at me . . . I suppose?"

"Only tae be heard over your own racket."

"If ye havena noticed," Gilleonan interjected calmly, "ye're both shoutin' again."

They both glared at Gilleonan for pointing that out, but then Lachlan ran a hand through his hair in exasperation, grumbling, "Faith, now I'll *have* tae be apologizing tae the wench come the morn, and as like receive another set-down for the effort."

"As if ye wouldna have done so anyway," Gilleonan chided, reminding Lachlan, "When ye let yer temper guide ye, ye always regret it after and correct any bad feelin's that get left behind."

"No' always," Lachlan replied. "Just when I ken I'm in the wrong. And in this case, having that lass attack first, instead of requesting, cancelled any wrong I might have felt. That we're still disturbing her rest puts me right back in the wrong." Gilleonan and Ranald both got a glare at that point, to tell them where Lachlan placed the blame. "Faith, why canna you two just be happy for me, that I've found the lass of my heart?"

"Because the difficulties ye face tae obtain her, Lachlan, are more than any mon can surmount lightly. 'Tis more reasonable tae assume ye're going tae fail and be crushed."

"You've no faith in me then, is that it?"

Gilleonan had the grace to blush. " 'Tis no' a matter o' faith, just the facts before us. Would she have wed the mon if she didna want him?"

"A duke?" Lachlan snorted.

"Och, well, there's that, yet this duke has more'n his title and position tae recommend him. Ye forget that we've all had a good look at the mon, Lachlan, and 'tis certain sure he's been turnin' the lassies' heads wi' the same ease as ye do, and for just as many years. 'Tis verra likely she's in love wi' him. So ye're expectin' her tae forsake her love and her exulted position, tae run off wi' an impoverished laird instead? If ye were usin' yer head instead o' yer—er, heart—it'd be as plain tae ye as it be tae Ranald and meself that that isna going tae happen."

"There be other things I can offer her that her stuffy Englishmon never will."

"Such as?"

"Such as joy and laughter."

Gilleonan rolled his eyes. "Not every lass appreciates those things. And ye dinna even ken if she'll suit yer purpose for being here."

"As tae that, I'd find another way tae obtain the silvers afore I'd give up my Megan."

"We had no luck coming up wi' any other way, Lachlan, or has that, tae, slipped yer mind?"

It was the sarcasm that earned Gilleonan another glower. "I *will* win her, Gill," Lachlan asserted, "and I'll have the bonniest lass in the kingdom tae call my own when I do. So leave me be on this."

Gilleonan shook his head. "I canna do that. I'd no' be doing me duty if I didna point out tae ye the folly o' this decision ye've made. And furthermore, a bonny-lookin' lass doesna always make an agreeable wife, Lachlan. Aye, this one be bonnier than most, as I recollect. No one can

deny that. But she be worse'n Nessa in her blath-
erin', as I also recollect. Yet there'll be other lassies out there who'll be just as fine tae look upon,
but no' so irritatin' on the ears. But ye willna even
search them out."

"Because it would be a waste of my time tae
do so, now that I've found Megan again. And the
circumstances under which we met her, Gill, is
no' an indication of the woman's true temperament. She was understandably upset at that time,
wi' my carrying her off as I did. That doesna
mean she has a high temper all the time."

"Or it means just that."

Lachlan narrowed his eyes on his cousin.
"Then we'd be well suited in that, I'm thinking,"
he said in a dark tone. "And ye'll be givin' it a
rest now, Gill, afore I do something I'll have tae
apologize tae you for as well, come the morn."

Gilleonan smiled innocently, "Och, now, 'tis
time I found me bed. And I'll see tae our cousin
here for ye." To that he hefted the now snoring
Ranald over his shoulder and headed for the
door. But there he turned to add one parting shot.
"I've every faith ye'll come tae yer senses in the
morn, Lachlan me lad. 'Tis a fine quality ye have,
yer ability tae avoid mistakes afore ye make
them."

Lachlan snorted as the door closed on his cousins. The mistake would be if he didn't pursue Megan, and that would be a mistake he'd never
outlive the regret of.

9

When Lachlan strolled boldly into the breakfast room the next morning, a room quite larger than most formal dining rooms, though much smaller than the formal dining hall at Sherring Cross, it was with the assurance of a welcomed guest. Devlin, at the head of the table, mumbled beneath his breath as he eyed the man with a degree of vexation and resignation, because the fact was, the Highlander *was* welcome now—at least by the ladies in his family

Megan had convinced Devlin to her way of thinking, of course. He didn't know how she managed it, but she did. And obviously, she'd wasted no time in informing the Scot of that change this morning. But Devlin wasn't going to pretend to be happy about it, and the cold look he gave MacGregor left little doubt of his true feelings.

Lachlan didn't miss that look or misinterpret it. He assumed it was his Aunt Margaret who had changed St. James's mind. He would never have guessed that only Megan had that ability, and he would have been appalled if he knew her reason for wanting him to stick around. The same reason had prompted her to have the servants remove half the chairs at the long table, so that when Lachlan arrived, the only seat available was next to Lady Kimberly.

Kimberly and Lachlan noticed the shortage of chairs at about the same time. She blushed profusely at what she considered rotten luck. If she had been the one who had just come in to find the only chair empty would force her to sit next to the Scot, she would have made an excuse not to stay, no matter how hungry she might be.

But it would be too rude of her to make an excuse to leave now, too obvious that her exodus was a result of the Scot's arrival, no matter how good an excuse she could have mustered. Not that she wouldn't have hesitated to do so if only she and the Scot had been present. But Their Graces were both there, as well as the rest of their family, and she wasn't about to embarrass them just because she found one of their other guests so odious.

Lachlan could have spared them both, but he gave no thought to doing so, not with Megan in the room. Instead, he flashed their hostess a brilliant smile, kissed his aunt on her cheek as he passed her, then plopped down in the only empty chair. There was an uncomfortable moment when Margaret, unaware that they'd already had bad feelings and words between them, introduced them to each other.

Kimberly survived that, but as soon as protocol allowed, she proceeded to ignore the man next to her and started up a discourse with the nice Lord

Wright, whom she'd met the night before and who now sat across from her. That didn't last long, however, since some remark by the duchess drew Lord Wright's attention to her.

Before Kimberly could follow that conversation enough to join it, she sensed MacGregor leaning toward her just before he whispered, "I owe you an apology, for disturbing your sleep last night."

She was surprised, surprised enough to glance toward him. Considering that he'd frightened her back to her room and threatened further rudeness of that kind, an apology had been unexpected. And considering that she had paid him back in kind—at least she hoped she had and that he wasn't such a sound sleeper that she'd stayed up the rest of the night for nothing—his apology was unwanted too.

He sounded sincere, yet she had to wonder about that, as badly as he and his friends had behaved. And he seemed to be waiting for a like apology from her. Not bloody likely, she thought to herself.

To him, all she said as she looked back at her plate was, "Yes, you do," in an equally hushed tone.

She didn't have to glance at him again to know she'd caused his cheeks to flush with color. Whether in anger or embarrassment, though, was undetermined, nor did she particularly care. His apology, after the fact, did not erase the sleepless night she'd suffered through. And she sincerely hoped that he was just as exhausted as she was this morning, though to look at him, that couldn't be determined either.

"I had my kinsmen on my back, lass," he said by way of explanation, "due tae a decision I've

made that they dinna like. What was your excuse?''

It was Kimberly's turn to flush with heat again.
Of course, he was referring to the noise she'd
made as soon as his side of the wall had quieted
down. And she had no excuse for making that
noise, other than pure retaliation. Yet she still
wouldn't apologize.

He and his kinsmen *could* have taken their arguments elsewhere, after they had become aware
that they were disturbing her peace. But no, they
hadn't done that, they'd continued to keep her
awake . . . and she did *not* have to justify her own
behavior. She was the one who was still sick and
could barely keep her eyes open to finish the meal
set before her, while he had come in seemingly
in great good spirits and in perfect health.

"Trying to justify your behavior last night does
you no credit, MacGregor. I have had very little
sleep in the last three days, two of those days due
to your own lack of consideration for others.''

"Och now, so that's your excuse, is it?''

"I am *not* apologizing to you," she hissed, "I
am merely pointing out that your behavior was
even worse than you supposed it to be.''

"Had you asked nicely for some peace, darlin',
you might have got some, but that wasna the
case, now was it?'' he drawled rather smugly.

She gasped. He actually dared to place the
blame for his behavior on her shoulders. But that
was no better than one could expect of a . . . Kimberly nipped that thought in the bud as she realized what she was doing, letting her father's
prejudice affect her own thinking. She knew better. And besides, she needed no prejudice whatsoever to dislike this particular Scot. He managed

to instill that emotion in her all on his own.

His comment didn't deserve a reply. To continue in this vein was letting him bring her down to his level of rudeness. Yet she still couldn't resist saying, "Is it necessary to remind you that had the disturbance you were making last night been of a tolerable level, it wouldn't have been necessary to speak to you a'tall. And you may address me as Lady Kimberly. I am *not* your 'darlin'.'"

"And 'tis glad I am of that," he retorted.

She had an urge to stand up and slap him soundly. But she recalled where she was and with whom, and made an effort to keep the heat out of her cheeks instead.

"So we are agreed, MacGregor," she gritted out, then added in a mild mimic of his lyrical brogue, "And 'tis glad I am that I will not have to suffer your company again after this meal is over."

That got her a chuckle and a cheeky grin. "You're leaving Sherring Cross then, are you?"

"No, you are."

He shook his head. "I hate tae disappoint you, lass, surely I do, but I'm no' leaving."

She frowned at him. "You're lying. I distinctly heard His Grace—"

"His Grace has had himself a change of heart," he cut in and was frowning himself now. "And 'afore I take offense at being called a liar, I'll be having an apology from you."

"No, you won't. I'll allow that changed circumstances do not make you a liar in regards to this, but considering your profession, MacGregor, I have little doubt that lying comes as naturally to you as stealing. And since you will, unfortunately, be staying on here, I will be sure to put my belongings under lock and key."

She could not have insulted him worse if she'd tried to. But in fact, she hadn't been trying to. She was simply so flustered and chagrined to be having this conversation with him at all that she was answering him without giving her responses full consideration.

But he was insulted, gravely. It was one thing to be called a liar when he was lying, but something else again to be called a liar when he wasn't.

"The only thing I'd be stealing from you, lass, is that vicious tongue of yours. You'd be wise tae put that under lock and key as well."

She gasped for the second time, then in a tone as stiff as dried leather, said, "This habit you have of threatening women speaks for itself. You might have gotten away with intimidating me last night, but you may be sure that you won't manage it quite so easily again. So might I suggest that you refrain from speaking to me at all, and I will in turn be glad to spare you my 'vicious tongue.' "

" 'Tis what I deserve for trying tae apologize tae a shrew," he mumbled to himself.

She heard him, of course. He meant for her to hear him. But the silence—finally—that his remark produced had him feeling somewhat ashamed. Trading insults with a lady was unique for him. Not that he minded so much, not with *this* lady in any case. But—it was his habit to charm and tease, not to provoke hostility, and he wasn't even sure why he was doing it.

This morning, in her frill-less, serviceable brown morning dress that hung loosely on her frame, her hair in an unbecoming, plain style that merely emphasized the redness of her nose, Lady Kimberly was infinitely ignorable, and yet— Lachlan couldn't seem to ignore her. She rubbed him wrong, she truly did. Every word out of her mouth pricked at his ire and had him hot to retaliate in kind.

She had managed to disturb his sleep a number of times throughout the night. This morning he had awakened as tired as he was when he'd finally gotten to sleep. That hadn't annoyed him, had amused him actually, that an Englishwoman could be that vindictive. He'd merely accepted that as his due and came down to breakfast hopeful, after a servant had delivered the message that he would be welcome at Sherring Cross indefinitely. Yet he'd been tired, and even the sight of his beautiful Megan hadn't perked him up as it should have. But damned if he wasn't wide awake now, after exchanging barbs with the spiky lady next to him.

Refrain from speaking to her at all? The devil he would. The MacGregor wouldn't back down from a challenge like that. But he'd won this round. So he could desist for the moment.

Guts she had aplenty, although she was bolstered by the presence of others, he didn't doubt. She'd likely sing a different tune if they'd been alone, one not so grating on the ears. Then again, maybe not. But he'd find out. He wasn't leaving, had all the time he needed now to win his heart's desire. And in the meantime, he had little doubt that he and Lady Kimberly would cross swords again.

10

Kimberly spent a good portion of the day sleeping. It wasn't very sociable, it being only her second day at Sherring Cross, but she'd had no choice. And even the duchess agreed she should do so when Kimberly had nodded off just as Megan was beginning to discuss the "plan" that would see her on her way to matrimony.

Megan had herded both Lucinda, Devlin's grandmother, and Kimberly to her sitting room directly after that—how should she put it?—torturous breakfast. The "plan," as Megan called it, was a strategy that they could all agree on, in other words, how to expose Kimberly to the widest assortment of bachelors at the soonest opportunity to assure her a wide range of possibles that she could then have ample time to consider.

It was mentioned that a number of social events were already scheduled in the coming weeks at Sherring Cross. And a slew of invitations to entertainments elsewhere also needed to be sorted through and decided on, including several imminent balls.

Kimberly had fallen asleep just as Lucinda, or Duchy, as her family fondly called her, mentioned that one of those balls was in London and a mere four days hence. Kimberly had been about to confess that there was no way she could prepare for an event of that formal magnitude in that short of time, having not a single ball gown to her name, when her eyes had closed for the umpteenth time and stayed closed.

The next thing she knew, Megan was shaking her awake, laughing softly, and telling her to go to bed.

It was, of course, the height of bad manners to fall asleep on one's hostess, and Kimberly was truly embarrassed. She made her excuses, blamed her cold and the journey. And she wasn't sure why she didn't put the blame where it belonged, on the guest in the room next to hers, but she didn't.

Now, as she dressed for dinner, she also wondered why she hadn't requested another room today. Having that Scot sleeping nearby was going to disturb her peace of mind, she knew it was. Knowing that she might run into him in the halls, coming to and from her room. Knowing that she was bound to hear him, whether he decided to have a little more consideration for the sort of noise he made or not. She had decisions to make that were going to affect the rest of her life. She didn't need distractions.

Yet she'd said nothing to her hostess, and now that she thought about it, she still probably wouldn't ask to be moved. The simple truth was, that even as exhausted as she'd been, and mis-

erable with her cold, she'd never in her life been
so stimulated. Excitement, fear, thrill, fury, whatever she wanted to call it, MacGregor made her
feel it. And she ought to decide whether it was a
good or bad thing, before she put an end to it.

The dowager duchess had sent a God-awful
tasting concoction along with Mary, to treat Kim
berly's cold, and by the time she was dressed and
ready to leave her room, she was actually feeling
somewhat better. At least her nose was no longer
threatening to run away at the first sneeze. In fact,
she'd stopped sneezing, enough so she was able
to camouflage some of the lingering redness, or
as the case was, rawness, with a little powder.
The achiness was also gone from her limbs, adding a little perkiness to her step.

Actually, she was quite pleased with her appearance, all things considered. The lavender
dress that she'd had Mary press for her had a
draped and sashed waist that allowed her to tie
away the looseness in that area. But she really
was going to have to do something about her current wardrobe, and decided to ask the duchess if
she had a personal seamstress at Sherring Cross,
or at least one located close by that she could visit
tomorrow. Parties and balls in London? Not until
she was properly girded for them.

She'd heard not a sound from the room next
door all afternoon, though she doubted anything
could have roused her from the deep sleep she'd
fallen into. But she'd heard nothing this evening
either. Perhaps *he'd* requested a new room elsewhere, now that he was being allowed to stay on,
to spare them both any more disturbances. She
still couldn't understand why the duke had
changed his mind about letting the Scot stay; he'd

sounded so adamant the night before.

This evening there were several new guests that Kimberly was introduced to when she joined the nightly gathering in the parlor. Lady Hester Cowles and her daughter, Cynthia, were visiting the dowager duchess, and had agreed to stay for the coming week. Cynthia was a lovely young chatterbox of about sixteen years, which made her old enough to socialize with the adults on certain occasions, but not quite used to that privilege yet.

Tiffany Whately was also present, introduced as Megan's "dearest friend." She had come with her husband, the Honorable Tyler Whately, for the weekend, and pretty much monopolized the duchess, as the two friends had much to catch up on. Kimberly had wanted to get back to discussing that "plan" she'd fallen asleep on this morning, but it looked like it would have to wait a bit more.

However, she was able to find out that a Mrs. Canterby, an excellent seamstress, according to Margaret MacGregor, was retained full-time by the ladies of the house, and they kept her so busy that it was necessary as well as convenient for her to permanently reside at Sherring Cross. And Megan had already arranged for her to meet with Kimberly first thing in the morning.

That did put Kimberly's mind to rest on the matter of a new wardrobe. And hopefully the ball that had been mentioned only a few days hence wouldn't be on the agenda. She had hoped to gradually work her way into the social whirl, until she was comfortable meeting a great many strangers, not start out immediately with extravagant events. However, from the little that she had heard about the "plan" this morning, the duchess apparently had other ideas.

As it grew near the dinner hour, and Lachlan MacGregor had yet to make an appearance, Kimberly began to hope that she wouldn't have to endure his company again. She wasn't to be that lucky.

She was sitting next to Cynthia Cowles, listening to the girl complain about the lack of color variety in her wardrobe—young girls were still trotted out in the inevitable pastels that had been favored for the last century and Megan's rich green gown had prompted an envious sigh—when the Highlander sauntered into the room, looking exceptionally handsome in a dark burgundy dinner jacket that nearly matched his hair color when the light reflected in it just so. And his thick, unclubbed hair floated about his shoulders, highly unfashionable. Yet when had Highlanders ever conformed to fashion, and on him, well, the style seemed just right. A bit of lace at the neck and cuffs of his white silk shirt added to the dashing effect he presented.

Cynthia's mouth dropped open. Kimberly had nearly the same reaction, though she managed to keep her mouth closed. No doubt about it, he still attracted her on every level, causing her senses to become vibrantly alive and expectant.

But he didn't notice her or anyone else for that matter. He came in wearing his charm-the-ladies smile, but there was only one lady he was interested in charming and he moved straight to her.

That lady was the duchess, of course, and since Megan was on the other side of the room, it was impossible to hear what words were exchanged between them. But it became comical, watching them, as Megan realized he was going to reach for her hand and tried to prevent it. She swiftly moved her hand out of his reach, but had to do it again and again since Lachlan refused to give up, was actually chasing her hand with his until he finally caught it to bring to his lips for a lingering kiss, or at least, he meant for it to be lingering. But Megan immediately snatched her hand back, giving him a frown for his efforts.

Everyone, of course, was watching them. Lucinda chuckled. Devlin scowled. Kimberly shook her head.

Into the silence that followed, Cynthia found her voice, saying in an awed tone, "He's a veritable giant, isn't he?"

Kimberly had thought so at first too, but having stood next to him since, she'd been forced to change her mind. "I don't think so," she replied.

Cynthia should have been mortified, having made a thoughtless remark like that, and in a voice that would carry. Her mother certainly was. But the girl seemed quite unaware of her faux pas.

As for Kimberly's reply, Cynthia simply looked at her as if she were daft. So she stood up to demonstrate why she might not consider him a giant. Cynthia's eyes followed her up and up and finally her expression mirrored some mild self-disgust, as if to say, now why didn't I notice that before?

"Well, no wonder you wouldn't think so. You're a giant too," the girl said.

Poor Lady Cowles was beet red by that point, but the comment struck Kimberly funny for some reason, and she laughed out loud. It had been so

long since she had done so that it felt strange—
yet good. But when she wound down, ending in
a smile, she happened to catch Lachlan giving her
an odd look. She had *not* meant to draw his notice
to her, and having it now, she found herself flustered again. But fortunately, dinner was announced at that moment and the exodus began
toward the dining hall.

Megan had made an effort to again limit the
chairs at the dining table, but without actually
assigning seats and being obvious about her strategy, it didn't work this time. In fact Kimberly and
Lachlan were the first seated and as it happened,
at opposite ends of the long table.

Megan was a bit put out. But having witnessed
Lady Kimberly's smile in the parlor, she was still
so pleased that she realized the seating arrangements didn't matter that much.

That smile, genuine as it was, had completely
transformed the lady, surprising Megan at first,
then delighting her. Amazing what a couple of
dimples could do for one's appearance, not to
mention disposition. And although Kimberly still
couldn't be called beautiful in the classic sense,
when she smiled, there was a warm, sensual ap-
peal to her features that made her quite lovely
indeed. And Megan was thrilled that Lachlan
MacGregor had also taken note.

Along that same line of thought, another idea
occurred to Megan. She tested her theory at dinner, putting her best effort forth to be amusing
and to keep those around her smiling, if not
laughing. And it worked. Kimberly relaxed and
seemed to thoroughly enjoy herself, and each
time she laughed, Lachlan seemed to turn her
way.

Of course, it was too bad of him that he was also sending seductive smiles and looks Megan's way.

Megan sighed, realizing she was going to have to have another talk with him about his continued interest in her—before Devlin took note of it. The only way she'd been able to get around her husband's stubborn refusal to allow the Highlander to stay was to stress the possibility of matching him with the Earl of Amburough's daughter. If he happened to notice where MacGregor's interest lay, albeit temporarily—Megan would see to that—there wouldn't be any talking around him again. The Scot would be given the boot immediately, if Devlin didn't take him to task with his fists again instead.

That was, unfortunately, an ongoing possibility, considering Devlin's antipathy toward the Highlander. But sitting near each other tonight, with only Duchy between them, they seemed to be doing an admirable job of ignoring each other. Too admirable, possibly.

Though it might become apparent to those around them how *completely* they were ignoring each other and cause speculation and gossip, they didn't have that to worry about quite yet, not until they started socializing outside of Sherring Cross. But then, plans had been made for doing just that within the next few days.

Duchy had managed to convince Megan that putting all her eggs in one basket wasn't a brilliant idea. As much as she liked and had settled on the notion of helping Kimberly and Lachlan on the path to discovering true love, and as convenient as it was, having both of them in residence to hurry that along, it might simply not be meant to be. So in all fairness, they each needed to be exposed to a nice range of eligibles. And the Wigginses' ball in London, only a few days away, was just the thing to get that out of the way.

11

Kimberly was feeling pleasantly tired as she slowly made her way down the many hallways back to her room. She still hadn't caught up on her sleep yet, but hopefully she would make up for that tonight. And her cold, miraculously, seemed to be gone completely, thanks to Lucinda's wonderful, foul-tasting concoction.

All in all, she'd actually enjoyed herself this evening. She'd been looking at all these upcoming social gatherings with something more like dread than anticipation. But Megan St. James had been such a charming and amusing hostess tonight that Kimberly had actually forgotten her reason for being at Sherring Cross.

Amazingly, she'd also been so distracted by her hostess that she'd managed to forget, for brief periods anyway, the presence of the man who so fascinated her. It had helped that he sat at the far end of the table from her, far enough that she couldn't even hear his voice in whatever conversations he joined in.

It was only when she had the strangest feeling of having MacGregor's eyes on her that she recalled him at all. Not that she looked even once to confirm if he was staring at her or not. And it was more likely just her imagination giving her that feeling, because he'd have no reason to pay attention to her when the lovely Megan was present.

Kimberly knew exactly where his interest lay. After all, she had overheard everything he'd said to the duchess when he arrived. And not for a moment did she think that their banter had been the kind of harmless flirtation that men and women engaged in. He'd been serious. He meant to pursue a married woman. And that married woman had been obviously annoyed and exasperated with him because of it, not in the least bit receptive to the idea. But that wouldn't stop him. His behavior tonight proved that.

Kimberly heard the footsteps behind her just as she turned into the hallway where her room was located. The sound caused her heart to skip. It could be a servant, though she doubted it, with such a heavy tread. It was more likely the Highlander, and yet she had left the gathering early, to avoid just such a possibility.

After dinner they had moved from the dining hall to the music room, where Cynthia had entertained them with her skill on the harpsichord. Because it was such a small gathering, by St. James standards, the men had brought their brandies along rather than remain behind to finish them, and those who wished to smoke did so in the back of the room.

When Kimberly left, MacGregor had still been swirling a good portion of brandy in his glass, as well as being deep in conversation with Lady Hester, so by all counts, he should *not* be coming up the hall behind her. And she knew for a fact that he kept late hours. But her senses were telling her otherwise, were leaping with alarm or excitement—she really wished she could distinguish the two.

Wisely, Kimberly chose not to have another confrontation with him, if it was him, however brief or even if it were no more than a nod in passing. She was positive she'd never get to sleep tonight if she did. So she hurried her step, was actually running the last few, only to realize as she turned the latch on her door that she'd locked it.

Now, why had she done a foolish thing like that? He hadn't been serious about stealing anything from her, he wouldn't dare. For her peace of mind, she really only needed to lock the door when she was behind it, not when she wasn't. Yet it was locked tight, those footsteps were growing louder, and when she finally located the hidden pocket tucked under the folds of her skirt and yanked the key out, she was so anxious she dropped the damn thing. Worse, after snatching it up again, she couldn't find the keyhole.

And then a large hand spread wide against the door, level with her face, and a Scots brogue was breathing down her neck. "So you dinna think I'm a giant?"

After her haste and anxiety, it was strange to have a calmness come over her now, but that's what happened. Possibly she'd had one too many glasses of the sweet wine with the meal tonight, or possibly it was no more than resignation. But she was definitely calm now, and when she turned around to face him, she wasn't *too* disconcerted to find him practically looming over her, he was so close.

So he'd heard her remark to Cynthia? Amazing that she wasn't embarrassed by that.

Kimberly raised her eyes to meet his, not too far a distance, really it wasn't, and answered in a somewhat dry tone, "Hardly."

That response seemed to amuse him, though he pointed out, "You did enough gawking at me the first time you saw me, as I recall."

"Possibly because you're an exceptionally handsome man?" she said.

Putting it in the form of a question had him blushing, though that was likely to have happened either way. He also dropped his arm and stepped back slightly, so that he didn't seem quite so threatening.

"Then perhaps I'm owing you an apology for my abruptness yesterday when I arrived."

She could have been gracious, accepted his apology, and let it go at that, which would undoubtedly have hurried him along to his own room, and gotten her into hers without any further ado. She didn't do that.

Instead she said, "You're making a habit of owing me apologies, aren't you?"

It was a provoking question. She realized that as soon as she spoke. Yet she didn't try to retract her comment or lessen the subtle challenge it issued.

His reaction, however, was to laugh and say, "D'you think so, darlin'? And here I was thinking what a good lad I've been—all things considered."

Kimberly ignored his attempt to put the blame

for his behavior on her, and said instead, "I've asked you not to call me that."

The smile he offered now was somewhat on the wicked side, or perhaps her imagination was running rampant again. "Asking willna always get what you want from me, unless 'tis what I'm wanting tae hear."

She should have known she couldn't have a conversation with this man without getting annoyed with him. "And what would that be?"

"From you, maybe—please?"

She quirked a brow. "Humble myself because you haven't sense enough to see that I am not nor will I ever be your darling? I think not."

It was another challenge. His hand came back to the door behind her head, bracing him against it. That definitely crowded her and forced her to tilt her head back even farther if she wanted to keep eye contact. Perhaps she should reconsider about his being a giant . . .

"Never deny what's possible, and anything's possible, given fate's intervention, as well as the quirks of nature and one's own determination."

"Then would it be *possible* for you to take yourself off and let me retire in peace?"

He chuckled. "Aye, 'tis possible, but here is an instance when determination's going tae delay it."

"What do you mean?"

He smiled a bit too sensually, which should have given her some warning of what he was going to say, but it didn't. "Just that I havena kissed you yet, darlin', when I'm feeling this powerful urge right now tae do so."

"Don't even—!"

That was as far as she got in her protest, because he bent his head and he *was* kissing her. For an unexpected happening, this one could have won a prize. Never would Kimberly have thought that something like this was possible, yet Lachlan MacGregor's lips were moving over hers in a light, hesitant manner, and then suddenly, with no hesitancy at all as his kiss deepened for a full tasting.

Kimberly was thoroughly entranced. She didn't move. She barely breathed. She certainly didn't think. She simply stood there and experienced the wonder of that kiss and all the pleasant sensations that accompanied it. Even when his tongue made a foray into her mouth, her shock that he would do such a thing didn't counter the pleasure of it. There were too many unique feelings coursing through her to be overly disturbed by the unexpected.

When he finally leaned back, she was totally bemused. He could have left right then and she wouldn't have known it. But he didn't leave. He was staring down at her rather intensely, and when her thoughts finally returned in a rush, they bombarded her with contradictions. Utmost was outrage alongside a desire to kiss him again, which *really* didn't mix at all.

Kimberly had certainly never experienced anything even remotely similar to what had just occurred. Maurice had given her a short, awkward kiss when she was sixteen, which had been her first. Then he'd given her a more manly kiss before he left on his grand tour. Neither had affected her in the least, but she certainly couldn't say that about the Scotsman's kiss. And she had no idea why he had decided to show her the difference.

She resolved to find out, asking him frankly, "Why did you do that?"

He suddenly looked as confused as she was. "I dinna ken," he admitted. " 'Tis possible I have overimbibed and should take myself tae bed, afore I make more of an ass of myself than I have."

She was disappointed in his response though she had no business being so. What had she expected to hear, that he had kissed her because he simply couldn't help himself, that it was something he had to do because he wanted to so badly? She nearly snorted at her own thoughts.

To him she said, "Yes, that's a capital idea. And don't bother apologizing yet again in the morning, MacGregor. Too many apologies tend to weaken the sincerity one should expect from such endeavors."

She turned about to make another attempt to open her door. His hand came to her arm, stilling her, and he was once again breathing down her neck, sending a shiver down her spine this time.

"I never apologize for kissing a lass. 'Tis something I'm never sorry for, and that 'twas you I kissed doesna make an exception to that. So dinna be expecting to hear that I'm sorry, because I'm no' the least bit sorry."

With that he walked away, leaving her even more confused than she had been.

12

Three days later, Kimberly couldn't quite believe that she was going to the Wigginses' ball. She could have sworn she wouldn't be ready for it in time, but she was. The St. James party was to include both Their Graces, Lady Hester—Cynthia was still pouting because she wasn't old enough yet to attend—and Lachlan MacGregor, all of whom made the journey to London on the morning of the ball. They would be staying at the duke's townhouse for just short of a week, since a few other London engagements had also been accepted, including yet another ball. And Lucinda and Margaret would be joining them tomorrow, along with Cynthia.

Incredibly, Mrs. Canterby had been able to create a stunning ball gown for Kimberly in only a day and a half, and another one would be delivered later in the week. With the help of an assistant or two, she had also managed to complete two day gowns before they departed that morning, and more would arrive in London daily, she had promised.

With their servants along, as well as the amount of baggage that the duchess traveled with, it took two carriages besides the grand ducal coach to transport them. Even so, the duke elected to ride one of his magnificent thoroughbred horses instead, possibly because he didn't want to be cooped up with the Highlander for the many hours that it took to get to London. Kimberly wished she could have been spared the same, but she wasn't that lucky.

She had managed to avoid Lachlan the last two days, except at meals, which was fortunate. The morning after he kissed her, he arrived for breakfast and sneezed, repeatedly, and she had burst out laughing. It was just deserts, in her opinion, that he had caught her cold because of that kiss. But he'd been scowling at her ever since, apparently having a different opinion entirely. And she really couldn't say why she had found it so funny, but she did. She also assumed that Lucinda had sent him one of her foul-tasting remedies, because he hadn't sneezed much after that one time.

This morning, sitting beside him in the coach, but nowhere near him as the seat was so long, she was still able to ignore him somewhat. Megan and Hester sat on the opposite seat, and Kimberly could just imagine the looks that Lachlan was passing on to the duchess when Lady Hester wasn't paying attention. In fact, Kimberly had no doubt that if Hester weren't along, she would herself be ignored again and the two of them would be discussing, quite openly, his interest in the duchess. She felt certain that he would at least make that attempt.

As it was, Megan maintained a mulish expression that indicated her annoyance with the Scotsman. The only time it left her face was when she had to turn to Hester, who kept up a steady stream of chatter, to make some reply. Kimberly was avoiding those brief conversations herself by admiring the passing scenery, or pretending to.

There was nothing scheduled for the afternoon, and in fact when they arrived in London, Megan suggested they all rest, since the ball would undoubtedly last into the wee hours of the morning. Kimberly was all for that. Trying to ignore Lachlan at such close quarters had been a strain, making the journey very tiring.

But it seemed like in no time at all, they were departing for the ball. Kimberly was actually excited, probably because, she had to admit, she had never looked quite so nice. And that wasn't only due to her splendid gown, which fit her exceptionally well. The silver grey satin was interspersed with powder blue lace that circled the narrow skirt at intervals and bordered the lengthy train in the back. It also draped off her shoulders and edged the deeply scooped neckline, which was the current style. A choker of the satin and lace had been made to accompany it, to which she was able to attach a lovely cameo that had been her mother's.

But it was the coiffure that Megan's maid had created for her that actually made her feel pretty. And to think she had fussed at the girl when she arrived with her scissors and curling irons, and had started snipping away at Kimberly's bangs. She was apparently adept at the current hairstyles, which was why Megan had sent her to Kimberly for the ball.

By the time she was done, many long golden locks littered the floor, but the short fluff of bangs that now framed Kimberly's face and the curls at her temples softened her features considerably. With a bit of powder and rouge added, she hardly recognized herself.

Lachlan didn't recognize her either, not at first glance. When he stepped out of his room just as she was passing by he began a general greeting, assuming the St. Jameses had yet another new guest. She didn't stop, didn't acknowledge even noticing him, continued to sashay down the hall, and his mouth dropped open as it dawned on him who she was.

It wasn't often he was taken so by surprise, yet Lady Kimberly seemed to be making a habit of surprising him. He wanted to grab her back and ask her what the hell she thought she was doing, looking like that. He didn't. And he kept his mouth shut before he sounded as ridiculous as he felt.

She'd also surprised him the other night, when he first saw her smile. She was pretty when those dimples made an appearance, really pretty. And he had to wonder how that smile was going to enhance this changed appearance that gave her a unique sort of beauty. He supposed he'd find out during the course of the evening, but he *wasn't* looking forward to the effect it would have on him.

And what surprised him the most was that the woman was affecting him in the strangest ways.

From the night she'd come pounding on his door in high dudgeon, and he'd reacted out of

proportion to it, he'd been doing his best to ignore her and concentrate on his Megan, yet he
somehow couldn't. She kept flitting through his
mind when she had no business there. And that
kiss they'd shared certainly hadn't helped.

He still couldn't understand why the urge to
kiss her had been so compelling. But he certainly
wished it hadn't happened, because he couldn't
stop thinking about that either.

There was something about that kiss that he'd
found highly stirring, the way she'd clung to him,
the way she'd opened her mouth to his ravish-
ment, the complete yielding of her soft, supple
body against him. And for once he hadn't gotten
a stiff neck, bending to reach her lips. There were
some definite benefits to kissing a tall woman, but
he could have done without finding that out with
this particular woman.

Tonight, he planned to further his campaign
against Megan. He would have the opportunity
to dance with her. She wouldn't refuse him at
such an affair. And once he held her in his arms,
anything was possible. He had high hopes of
breaking through her ridiculous assertion that she
was happy with that stodgy Englishman she'd
married. She was merely putting on a good face
for what was a terrible mistake, and he meant to
prove that to the both of them.

Aye, high hopes, and they did not include
mulling over that shrewish, albeit lovely butterfly
that just broke out of her cocoon.

13

"What the devil? I could've sworn she was dancing with someone else just now."

"Who?"

"Lady Kimberly."

Megan nodded in a distracted manner, as if her attention didn't just perk up. She was dancing with Lachlan only because he wouldn't stop pestering her until she agreed. But that he could notice another woman, at least Kimberly Richards in particular, while he'd been whispering outlandish blandishments and compliments in Megan's ear . . . well, she couldn't have been more pleased.

Not that she hadn't thought he was sincere, or rather, she was sure that *he* thought he was sincere. But for someone who'd heard just about every compliment that could be thought of, she wasn't impressed.

She was impressed, however, by the remarkable change in Kimberly Richards, and apparently, so was Lachlan. And just in case he wasn't aware of it, she decided to emphasize it.

"She *was* dancing with someone else, now that you mention it," she said now. "They're cutting in on her partners. Not very sporting of them, but young men are so impatient, don't you know."

"I dinna know," Lachlan grumbled.

Megan smiled inwardly. He actually sounded a bit jealous. That was certainly more than she could have hoped for at this early date.

"She's very popular, it seems," she continued, watching his expression carefully. "Not flighty, not giggly like the younger girls tend to be, and a very good listener. Men like that in a woman. Oh, and she's very lovely besides, if you haven't noticed."

He grunted. "You are verra beautiful, Megan, but I dinna see them standing in line tae dance wi' you as they are wi' her tonight."

She laughed. "I should hope not. Devlin broke these young bucks of that notion long ago. But as for our Kimberly, I would imagine she'll have a few proposals before we return to Sherring Cross. I should ask her if anyone in particular has caught her fancy yet. Perhaps you would be so good as to take me to her as soon as this dance is over?"

He nodded curtly. And she noticed his compliments had ended. Actually, he barely spared her another glance, and it was all Megan could do to keep from laughing and patting herself on her back.

This matchmaking business was really much simpler than Megan had first thought it was going to be. Either that, or Lachlan and Kimberly were simply destined for each other, no matter what anyone did to aid them in figuring that out for themselves.

Lachlan did lead her straight to Kimberly the moment the music stopped. Dragged her there was nearly the case. And not a moment too soon. Megan knew the young gentleman about to escort Kimberly back onto the dance floor, and she quickly forestalled him, sending him after some refreshments instead. As for Lachlan . . .

"If you'll excuse us now," Megan told him in a no-nonsense tone, "I'm going to take Kimberly out for a quick turn on the balcony—"

"Nay, what would your husband be saying, darlin'," he cut in, "if I didna lend you my protection for such a dangerous undertaking?"

Megan nearly snorted at such nonsense, but she was in fact glad he wanted to stay close. However, she didn't want him to know that, so she shrugged and said, "Suit yourself, but do keep your distance."

She didn't wait for him to agree, but took Kimberly's arm and led her outside, though not too far outside. Windbreaks had been set up along most of the balcony edges to keep the worst of the winter cold at bay. It allowed the guests an area to cool off without it being so cold that they couldn't enjoy it for very long, but you still didn't mistake what season it was.

Megan hadn't actually planned to grill Kimberly about the men she was meeting, but with Lachlan eavesdropping on them, and he was doing just that, it was an opportunity she couldn't pass up.

"Are you enjoying yourself, Kimberly?" she began, her tone merely casual.

"Yes, Your Grace."

"None of that now," Megan admonished gently. "I'd like to think we are becoming friends, you and I, and my friends call me Megan—if not worse."

Kimberly smiled shyly, though her eyes kept drifting to where Lachlan was standing several feet away, pretending not to be paying them any mind.

"So tell me," Megan continued. "Have you met anyone yet that you might be interested in?"

"John Kent."

That answer came too quickly, surprising Megan. "Well, yes, a fine young man he is. Conservative. Comes from excellent—are you quite sure? Don't misunderstand, but he seems a bit stuffy to me."

Kimberly couldn't help herself. She laughed at that description, which she'd noticed for herself. "Ah, but you see, I've lived all my life with a—how shall I put this? Highly emotional parent."

"A bit hot-tempered, your father?"

"Yes, exactly. So for me, stuffy isn't so bad, it's actually refreshing."

"Never say so," Megan said in mock horror. "My Devlin has occasional bouts of stuffiness, nothing like he used to have, mind you, but still every once in a while that old stuffiness comes through and drives me up a wall in no time a'tall. If you want a change from hot tempers, you'll want a quiet sort, or better yet, someone with a nice sense of humor who'll make you laugh a lot."

They both glanced furtively at Lachlan at that point, who was whistling quietly to himself as if he hadn't heard a word they'd said. Kimberly was flustered as usual, having him near. And he was sinfully handsome tonight in his black formal wear, which made it even worse.

She had tried to concentrate on the gentlemen she was meeting, but it was next to impossible with Lachlan MacGregor in the same room. And she was disappointed too. For some reason, she'd actually expected him to ask her to dance—at least once. But he hadn't. He'd been dancing with Megan or not dancing at all.

"There was also Howard Canston," Kimberly mentioned. "I found him quite interesting."

Megan frowned without realizing it. The trouble was, there wasn't a single thing she could think of that was wrong with Canston. He was athletic, yet also active in the House of Lords, where he had taken over his father's seat since old Canston had become ill. The family was wealthy, owning some prime properties right in London. No scandal had ever been associated with their name. And Howard was due to inherit the title of marquis as soon as his father passed on, which rumor had it, wouldn't be much longer.

No, Viscount Canston was one of the prime catches of the season, ideally suited for any young miss, Kimberly included. He was also quite good-looking, if one liked those golden Adonis sorts.

Megan *wished* she could say something disagreeable about the chap, simply because she already had it set in her mind that Lachlan was the man for Kimberly. But she couldn't, and to be fair, she supposed she ought to at least invite Canston to Sherring Cross in the coming weeks. And if she *had* to be fair, she might as well invite Lord Kent too. Actually, if she was going to go that far, she might as well give Margaret the go-ahead to invite some of the young women she had come up with who would be suitable for Lachlan.

Megan sighed to herself. There were times when fairness just went against the grain, it really did.

And this was definitely one of those times. She forced herself to say, albeit a bit tersely, "Howard will make a fine husband. Anyone else?"

It wasn't all that surprising, at that point, that Kimberly mentioned three other names. The girl was here to get married, after all, and apparently, wasn't going to waste any time just enjoying herself.

Megan would really like to know, though, why, with such a prime specimen of manhood on hand from the very beginning, Kimberly didn't seem the least bit interested in Lachlan. And if she was interested and just wasn't letting on, well then, it was certainly a well-kept secret.

But that wasn't something that could be asked at the moment, much as she wanted to. Not with Lachlan barely pretending not to be eavesdropping on their conversation.

It was a moot point, at any rate, as the balcony doors opened again to reveal Devlin standing there, filling the space. He didn't have to look far to find them, and he was there with a purpose. Cupping a hand to his mouth, he imitated a whisper, which in fact had no trouble reaching all three of them.

"Megan, love, I need you to rescue me from Henrietta Marks, who is determined to espouse her husband's political views to me, which all and sundry know I don't agree with one little bit.

Be quick, she's right on my coattails."

He sounded huffy and expectant all in the same breath, and the expectancy won out. He didn't give Megan a chance to answer either way, nor make the appropriate excuses to her companions. He stepped forward, gave Kimberly a generous smile, gave Lachlan no glance at all, and abruptly whisked Megan back into the ballroom.

And the first thing Megan noticed was no dragon breathing down his back, which she immediately pointed out. "I don't see Henrietta anywhere."

"No, you wouldn't," he replied as he patted her hand, grinned at her, then gathered her in his arms to finish the current dance in progress. "The Markses never come to these fancy affairs."

She was surprised for all of five seconds, then she was smiling up at him. "That was brilliant timing, if I do say so myself, allowing me to leave Kimberly and Lachlan alone out there."

"Yes, I know," he said rather smugly.

She raised a brow at him. "You mean you saw us go out to the balcony?"

"My dear, I am always aware of where you are and what you're doing."

To that she made a face. "I don't know whether I should be extremely pleased about that, or wonder whether or not you trust me."

"Since I trust you implicitly, I suppose you will have to settle for being pleased."

She smiled again. "Yes, I suppose I will."

14

Kimberly was still staring at the closed balcony door, still amazed at how quickly she had been left alone—with him—when she heard Lachlan's deliberate cough, meant to draw her attention to him. She decided to ignore him, and turned about instead to overlook the square behind the Wigginses' townhouse. Lights flickered down there, showing plainly a mist in the air, some lonely benches, a large statue of some forgotten war hero at the center . . .

"It does you no good tae ignore me, lass. I am singularly unignorable."

"Oh, I don't know," Kimberly remarked, still without looking his way. "I'm actually very good at ignoring things that don't interest me."

"Ouch," Lachlan said, close enough that she realized he'd come quietly up behind her. "You wound me tae the quick, darlin'."

"I sincerely doubt that's possible, but on the off chance that it is, well, I'm sure you'll survive."

"On the off chance that you're no' lying, I'd

expire here on the spot." He paused before adding with feigned surprise, "Och, now, I'm still here. Fancy that."

She almost laughed. It was very hard not to with the urge so strong. Silliness like that was what she needed in her life—but not from a man whose true interest lay elsewhere, and they both knew where.

"You'll have to excuse me, Mac—"

"Did those stuffy English tell you how beautiful you look tonight, Kimber?"

A warm glow filled her. She had been in the process of moving away from him, but that stopped her. And yes, she had been told already, by several men tonight, that they thought she was beautiful, but it just wasn't the same as hearing Lachlan say it.

His hand came to her arm, as if he still needed to physically detain her, when her feet had no thought of moving at the moment. She liked to think he simply wanted to touch her, albeit innocently.

"Have I embarrassed you?" he asked softly.

She wasn't embarrassed, she was tongue-tied. She really didn't know how to receive compliments gracefully, having had so few in her life, at least from men. So she shook her head briefly and kept her eyes lowered, but that only seemed to encourage him to further intimacy.

"I'm thinking I like this shy side o' you. 'Tis unexpected, but verra nice."

"I'm not—"

"Och, now, dinna get defensive. 'Tis no' a bad thing, a wee bit o' shyness."

She didn't *want* to argue with him tonight, but

she didn't want him to get the wrong impression about her either. "I'm really not—"

"Makes a mon want tae kiss you, and I mun confess, I've that urge again."

Her breath caught in her throat. Her eyes rose up to meet his, and the moment they connected, his lips were pressing against hers. Unlike their previous kiss, this one was much more serious. He gathered her in his arms. He held her extremely close. And his tongue intruded immediately beyond her lips to forage deeply. It was the kind of kiss she should have learned nothing about until she was safely married. It was the kind of kiss designed to provoke passions, and hers were ignited quickly.

Where that kiss might have led Kimberly wasn't to find out, however, since several other of the Wigginses' guests chose that moment to seek some cooling on the balcony. As the doors swung open, Lachlan sprang back, putting a decent distance between them. Unfortunately, the immediate loss of his support left Kimberly swaying unsteadily on her feet, forcing him to lend an arm to her back again. And the easiest way to cover that intimacy was to lead her back inside and straight onto the dance floor.

By the time she was thinking again with any semblance of clarity, it was too late to upbraid him for what he'd done. Not that she had any true desire to do so, when she had enjoyed that kiss so thoroughly. But to say nothing was to let him assume that he could kiss her anytime he liked, which wasn't so. She would get around to saying something, just—later, after the pleasant glow left her and he wasn't still lavishing her with his attention.

And Lachlan was doing that.

He wasn't paying the least bit of attention to where he was leading her in the dance, he was staring at her instead. And there was heat in his light green eyes that continued to warm her. When one of the gentlemen who had previously cut in on her partner tried to do so again, he found Lachlan willing to defy convention with his refusal.

He went so far as to snarl, "Get lost, English. She's taken."

Kimberly was embarrassed and thrilled at once, a difficult combination, and she made no remark at all. She simply enjoyed his hand on her back, his other hand clasping hers gently, and every so often her pulse would leap when he *accidentally* moved too close so that her breasts would brush against his chest.

She had no idea that these were practiced moves on his part, that he was setting her up for seduction, and succeeding very well. He was subtle about it, not even using half of his usual tactics, afraid that anything obvious would have adverse effects rather than benefits. And he couldn't say when or why he'd made the decision to have her, come what may. It hadn't even been a decision. There was no choice involved. He simply had to have her now, his desire was that great.

15

Kimberly returned to the St. James townhouse in a romantic haze that night. And with Lachlan in the same coach, that haze had no time to clear.

Her opinion of him, of course, had undergone some major changes tonight. In fact, she was already wondering how she might avoid the scandal when she married him, and her father disowned her for it. Not *if* she married him. The decision was already made as far as she was concerned.

There was simply no reason to look any further for a husband, when Lachlan MacGregor would suit her so well. The only reason she hadn't entertained the idea before was his apparent interest in Megan St. James. But after tonight, that was obviously at an end. His attention was turned to her instead. And it would be very easy to love him, she had no doubt. Besides, his devil-may-care, nonsensical, charming manner was just what she needed in her life.

She was still smiling to herself, still daydream-

ing of what her future could be like with him,
when she reached her room and slowly readied
herself for bed. Vaguely she was aware that Lachlan had been assigned the room next to hers
again, having passed him in the hall earlier. Quite
a coincidence that, with the St. James townhouse
another really large home. But she didn't wonder
about it. She'd changed her opinion in that too,
now liking the fact that he was so close.

Mary had been told not to wait up, and Kimberly managed to get out of her gown without *too*
much difficulty, and without really noticing how
much stumbling about she was doing.

She would have liked to continue daydreaming
about Lachlan—they were such thrilling fanta-
sies. But due to the amount of champagne she
had consumed at the ball, she was asleep within
moments of crawling into bed. So she was quite
disoriented when she awoke a while later, so disoriented that she still thought she was at the ball,
still standing on that balcony being kissed by
Lachlan.

All the wonderful feelings she had experienced
then came immediately to life again. But they
were enhanced. She was being kissed quite pas-
sionately. And where the balcony had been cool,
there was now so much heat.

It took a while before she realized that Lachlan
was doing more than what one might expect from
a kiss. His hands weren't just holding her, they
were roaming quite freely over her limbs, and en-
countering skin where satin should have been.
That confused her, but she never got around to
questioning it, since his hands continued to roam,
sometimes evoking sensations so pleasant, she
couldn't hold back her delight, the sounds of

which encouraged him to explore further.

But there was something else present that had not been felt before, a vague kind of frustration she couldn't pinpoint, but she knew, somehow, that all the wondrous things he was making her feel just weren't going to be enough, that something even more delightful was missing and she wouldn't be replete without it. And with that feeling a sense of urgency developed, as if her body were telling her, *there is an end to this rainbow, and if you hurry, you just might find it.*

The heat continued to escalate. Her gown seemed to stick to her, and yet . . . it no longer felt like satin. It seemed like she'd grown another layer of skin and it was heavy, weighing her down, hard and unyielding where she was usually soft. But his kiss continued to bedazzle her, allowing her no time to analyze what was happening to her, much less ask questions about it. And besides, she was no doubt imagining things, an unfortunate consequence of consuming too much champagne, which she was not at all used to.

And then she felt the pain, a quite sobering effect, that. And she realized two things with crystal clarity. She wasn't on the Wigginses' balcony, she was in her bed, where she ought to be. But Lachlan MacGregor was lying on top of her, and that wasn't where he ought to be.

Her mind reeled with the implications, which in her innocence, she still didn't fully grasp. She could only think to demand, "What are you doing here?"

He leaned up, but she could barely see him in the dark room, which had only a banked fire giving off no light to speak of. "Och, now, darlin', is that no' obvious? I'm making love tae you."

"The devil you are," she said indignantly and nearly snorted, "Without my permission? I don't think so."

"Aye, 'tis true," Lachlan replied. "And sorry I am for your pain, but—"

"Pain?" she cut in, and then recalled it with a gasp. "Why did you hurt me?"

"It wasna intentional . . . well, it was—sort of, but 'twas unavoidable, and I swear tae you, lass, it willna happen again."

"No, it won't, because you're leaving," and she stressed, "This very second."

"Now why would I be doing that, when 'tis no' what either of us wants?"

"Do not presume to know what I want—"

"Och, but I do know. You've been telling me all night that you want me, darlin', and right now I'm wanting you something powerful as well."

To hear him say that sent a thrill through her, but he was confusing her too. She couldn't recall telling him any such thing, and in fact, she couldn't imagine herself being that bold, whether it were true or not. That it was true, well, at least that she did want him, was beside the point . . . or was it? She was going to marry him anyway, so did it really matter if they did this lovemaking thing now, before the fact? And everything he'd been doing to her had been so very nice, until that pain had intruded.

Recalling that pain again, she said in a small voice, "Why did you hurt me?"

He groaned and immediately started *showering* her with kisses. "Ah, darlin', 'tis no' something I *wanted* tae do. Did your mother never explain tae you about—ah, well—about a virgin's blood having tae be spilled 'afore she can be truly joined wi' a mon?''

She did recall something vaguely about that, but she'd been so young when that conversation had come up that she'd completely forgotten it. And she imagined that Lachlan was blushing profusely, having to mention it. She was doing some blushing herself.

"Are you saying we've been 'truly joined'?"

That he might give those words a different meaning than she would didn't occur to her.

His response was rather simple and to the point. "Can you no' feel it?" he asked in a tone gone husky.

It was hard to feel anything at the moment other than his weight on her, because his body was so still. But then it wasn't and her eyes flared wide as she felt a movement deep within her. No further pain, true, and a pleasant rush that felt like her blood had stopped, but was now racing to catch up to where it should be.

"Did you do that?"

He chuckled at the awe in her tone. "That I did, darlin', and 'tis only the beginning. You're going tae like the rest even better, you've my word on that."

He proceeded to show her what he meant. Better? That hardly described the exquisite sensations accompanying his movements inside her. And he was kissing her again, deeply, so even if she thought to remind him that they shouldn't be doing this now, before they were actually married, she didn't find a chance to.

Not that she wanted to now. Too quickly, she was so immersed in pleasure that all thoughts ceased, leaving only her feelings to govern her responses. And she did respond, innocently at first, yet with an inherent passion that soon took over to match the rhythm he was creating. Fast, slow, she followed him, she kept up with him, so much feeling consuming her—and then too much. She cried out in surprise. It was so unexpected, the pinnacle he took her to, such a glorious burst of sensation and then the incredible aftermath, floating back down in a bubble of pulsing pleasure, the lethargy that followed, the complete sense of repletion.

How could she thank him for that? Was one supposed to thank the gentleman for introducing you to such sinful delight? She'd figure it out in the morning, she was sure. Just now she sighed happily, wrapped her arms around her gentleman's neck, and promptly fell asleep.

16

Mary came into Kimberly's room as she did each morning, to begin her chores. Kimberly roused gradually to the soft sounds the maid was making as she started a new fire. Familiar sounds. Nothing out of the ordinary. Nothing to remind her that her life was irrevocably changed.

When she roused enough to lean up on an elbow and get her eyes open, she did so too quickly. A pain streaked through her temples. She immediately brought her hand up to cover her eyes from what seemed like the brightest, most glaring sunlight she'd ever experienced. The ball. She'd gone to the Wigginses' ball and consumed too much champagne. So this was the result of the sins of overimbibing? A throbbing headache, an aversion to light, and a sense of dread?

Dread? What could she possibly have done to elicit that feeling?—kissing on the balcony, dancing repeatedly with the same man, those potent, sensual looks Lachlan kept sending her way. Lachlan . . .

It took one memory to trigger another, but they piled up swiftly now, and in the order she had received them. When she reached the final ones that had been acquired in this very room, her hand dropped back to the bed and she groaned inwardly. Impossible. She couldn't have done that, allowed it to happen. The rest might be real memories, but that last, no, that had to be a dream. And yet, when had she ever dreamed anything that real—or that nice?

And then she spied her nightgown lying on the foot of the bed and with some trepidation, she glanced down to find that it wasn't a second gown that she had taken out and then decided not to wear in favor of another one. She was actually naked beneath the bedding that was at the moment clinging to her breasts. The chill on her bare shoulders should have pointed that out sooner, but she supposed her headache was keeping her from noticing such minor things as that.

But hot color spread up her cheeks now, then just as quickly drained away, leaving her quite pale. Coincidence, that the one night out of her life that she hadn't donned a nightgown to sleep in was the one night she dreamed she'd been made love to? She was afraid it wasn't, afraid too that she was now utterly ruined . . . and now she knew why that feeling of dread had been lurking.

At least Lachlan wasn't still there in the bed with her. She couldn't imagine her embarrassment if he was, when it was Mary's habit to enter her room in the morning without knocking first, so that she could start the fire and have the room warmed by the time Kimberly awoke. But then, what difference would it have made?

One big difference, actually. Mary loved to gossip, and being only recently employed, held no real loyalty to Kimberly that might keep her mouth shut. But though she'd been spared that embarrassment, she was still ruined. Young women of good breeding just didn't do such things as she'd done and . . .

She groaned again and buried her head under the covers, hoping Mary would simply leave her alone to her misery. She couldn't understand how she could have veered so far off the straight and narrow path, she who'd never done anything untoward in her life. The only somewhat suspect thing she'd ever done was to defy her father and refuse to end her period of mourning, and rightly so, since it would have been merely to accommodate her fiancé's gambling debts. That bounder. If Maurice hadn't been unreasonable she wouldn't be in this predicament and . . . and . . .

She was working herself into a fine panic, and all because she was forgetting one little fact. She sighed as she remembered it now, that she had concluded last night that Lachlan MacGregor would suit her quite well for a husband. That she hadn't been exactly clearheaded when she'd come to that decision was—well, that hardly mattered now.

She had decided to marry him, and now she couldn't change her mind even if she wanted to. They'd made love. That was to be done only with one's husband—or in her case, one's soon-to-be husband. And she could find no fault with him in that area. It was something she was very much going to enjoy doing with him on a regular basis—as soon as they were officially wed. She could have *wished* he'd waited until they actually were married to show her how nice that part of wedded life was going to be, but he hadn't, and she would bring him to task for that later, to be sure.

She at least wanted to know *why* he had come into her room to wake her with his kisses, and proceeded from there to seal their fate. He'd mentioned some nonsense about her telling him she wanted him. But that was ridiculous. Of course she'd done no such thing.

Yes, she'd consumed more champagne than was obviously good for her, and because of it, her memory was a bit fuzzy as to even why she'd decided to marry Lachlan in the first place. But she would never have been so bold as to tell him she wanted him, even if it were so, especially when in her innocence, she wouldn't even have *known* it were so—would she?

She recalled sensing that she was missing something when he was making love to her, but she hadn't known what it was, could never have imagined the incredible pleasure it turned out to be. She knew now what wanting him meant, but she hadn't known at the ball, as he had implied.

She heard the door click softly shut and sighed, thankful that Mary had taken the hint that she wasn't ready to get up yet. She would have liked to lose this problem, at least temporarily, by going back to sleep, but she was sure sleep was something she'd never do again.

However, she hadn't wanted to face her maid just yet. She was positive that the girl would take one look at her and somehow *know* what she'd done last night. And she wasn't being fanciful.

Her own guilt would likely tell the whole story at a glance. Yet she couldn't hide in her room all day either, much as she would like to.

She would have to find the duchess and tell her she needn't plan any more social engagements on her account. Hopefully, Megan would be relieved. Kimberly would have been relieved as well, to have the matter decided, if it had been decided some other way. And she would have to speak to Lachlan, just to make sure he knew they were getting married. It was possible, she supposed, though not very likely, that he hadn't realized that yet.

It took two hours for her to bolster herself with courage and decide that her changed status wasn't really visibly apparent. The only thing that had been visible, proof positive in fact, had been the stains on her sheets. But she had immediately disposed of those herself, before Mary had a chance to see them. She prayed the housekeeper wouldn't notice.

She had dressed in one of her new gowns, a light green that seemed to intensify the color in her eyes, making them, as one of her nicer features, more prominent. And without Mary's help, since the girl showed no signs of returning without being summoned, the coiffure she managed was rather loose. But she had to admit, it was becoming that way, at least it was with the new feathery cut to her bangs. In fact, she was quite pleased to find that she appeared almost as pretty as she had looked last night in her formal finery. And it was a relief that she could be pleased about anything this morning.

Lachlan, unfortunately, didn't answer the knock on his door. After she had stood there for nearly a minute reinforcing her courage before rapping her knuckles on it, his absence was deflating. Seeing him for the first time after last night was *not* going to be easy by any means. Never had she been so intimate with another person, and she was afraid his knowledge of her was going to render her tongue-tied and too embarrassed to broach the subject of their marriage.

It had to be done, however. And if he wasn't still sleeping, which was a possibility since it wasn't quite midday yet, and they had returned so late from the ball, then she needed to find him.

Kimberly had to allow that it would be prudent to speak to him before the duchess. After all, she was going to tell Megan that they were getting married, and he really ought to be apprised of that fact first, since he might not take kindly to hearing about it from someone else. Although she assumed he had to expect it, after the kind of intimacy they'd shared. But it was only common courtesy to let him know she was agreeable to the match, just in case he might be thinking otherwise.

Questioning each servant she came across about his whereabouts—oh, they'd each taken full note of him in passing, and probably with their mouths hanging open too—she was led first to the breakfast room, empty now, then the terrace, cold and empty now, then the library, where she stopped in the doorway, having found him.

But he wasn't alone.

The duchess was also there, apparently searching for a book on one of the higher shelves, since she was halfway up a ladder. Lachlan was holding the ladder steady for her, though it seemed a sturdy enough ladder not in need of his help, that help merely putting him closer to the lady.

Kimberly was about to draw their attention to her presence when she heard Lachlan ask Megan in a somewhat frustrated tone, "You dinna believe I could love you? Is that what you're saying?"

Megan didn't even bother to glance down at him to reply, "I believe you are simply enamored with this face of mine, which has forever been a problem for me. Think about it, Lachlan. What you feel, or think you feel, can't be real when you know absolutely nothing about me."

"I ken you have been constant in my thoughts this last year. That is more than passing fancy."

"Perhaps because I was the bird that got away?" Megan suggested.

"I'm no' so grasping that I mun have everything I have a wee desire for." Lachlan's tone had passed mere frustration now, as if he considered himself gravely insulted.

Megan's sigh was loud as she plucked a book off the shelf and climbed down the ladder to face him. "This is all redundant, Lachlan. How many times must I repeat that I love my husband? No man could make me happier than he does. So whatever you feel or think you feel, I would appreciate it if you would henceforth keep it to yourself. You're here to find a wife, and a rich one as I understand it, who will solve the distressed state your stepmother left you in when she absconded with your inheritance. It's high time you set your mind to that, don't you think? And find one who isn't already in love with someone else *and* already happily married."

Kimberly had heard enough, too much actually, and if she was noticed now by either of them, she would likely expire on the spot. So she stepped quickly to the side of the door, putting the wall between her and the occupants of the room. Then she ran for the stairs further down the hall, something she would never ordinarily do since it wasn't the least bit ladylike, but that was an indication of just how upset she was.

But when she reached the upstairs hall, she stopped and leaned back against the wall there as the full magnitude of her predicament caught up with her. Her groan was audible as she closed her eyes and banged her head back against the wall a number of times.

Lachlan MacGregor wasn't going to marry her, he was still in love with Megan St. James. *Why* had she thought that had ended? Just because he'd kissed her, and more than once? Just because he'd made love to her? How naive could she be? One of the oldest professions in the world supported the contention that a man didn't have to be in love with a woman in order to make love to her.

Apparently he'd merely toyed with her, perhaps out of boredom or even the frustration she'd witnessed, because he wasn't making any progress with the woman he really wanted. And from what she'd just overheard, it didn't sound like he ever would make any progress there. Yet where did that leave her? Socially ruined and without a husband—well, not *really* ruined, with no one but her and Lachlan aware of it. Not yet anyway. But there were two things that could happen to change that real quick.

She might not have known much about lovemaking, how to go about it or what to expect from it. But it was nearly universally known that babies were created from that sort of thing. Not always, but sometimes. And she would have to face that *sometimes* and hope it didn't visit her from her one indiscretion.

If she could be that lucky, she would at least have time to face the second thing that could see to her ruination in quick order. If and when she received a proposal of marriage, she would have to own up to what she'd done before she actually accepted. She would have to tell the gentleman that she had—that she was no longer—well, that she wasn't quite as pure as she ought to be.

She wasn't so cowardly that she would keep it secret and hope he wouldn't notice. There had been a major scandal in her town a few years back because a groom had been able to tell, in some mysterious way, that his bride wasn't pure. He'd let the entire town know it and insisted on an annulment because of it. So men were able to somehow know.

But if she owned up to her own disgrace, her gentleman could either be generous and accept her as she was, or be furious and let all and sundry know about it.

She could just imagine her father's reaction if that happened. He would either disown her outright in his fury, which was highly possible. Or he would have to literally buy her a husband, and she wouldn't have much choice in the matter of who if it came to that.

And then that voice she was coming to know so well asked her, "Are you hiding up here, Kimber? Or is it daydreaming you're doing?"

17

Kimberly slowly opened her eyes. That her head was still dropped back against the wall allowed her to see Lachlan's face immediately. He was wearing a tender expression as he looked down at her. That, more than anything else, gave her the strongest urge to slap him soundly.

Of course, she wouldn't do anything of the sort. Slapping wasn't the least bit ladylike and . . .

She moved away from the wall with her arm swinging in the direction of his face. Her palm connected with his cheek sharply, loudly, and it was wonderfully satisfying to see the imprint it left behind. Definitely worth the hot stinging she now felt on her hand.

But she was surprised that she'd done it. Lachlan was, of course, even more surprised. And before he recovered, she almost slapped him again, just because he *was* surprised and hadn't expected it, when his behavior practically demanded it.

But she managed to restrain herself now, and instead said with all the contempt she could muster, "You are despicable beyond redemption. Stay away from me, MacGregor, or I will not be responsible . . ."

She didn't finish. She was about to cry, and as far as her pride was concerned, it wouldn't do at all for him to witness the emotional state he'd brought her to. So she retreated, running down the hall instead. Running again—she didn't even notice this time.

When she reached her room, she dropped back against the door, her hands fisted and pressed hard against it. She didn't want to cry. She wasn't the sort who condoned self-pity. But she had so much emotion welling up in her. At least half of it was anger, however, and she concentrated on that to hold back the tears.

And then she was shoved forward as the door opened behind her. The gall of him!

"This is my room, MacGregor, not yours! How dare you enter here again without permission?"

His expression was thunderous. He'd obviously recovered fully from his initial surprise, and felt himself undeserving of her attack. In fact, his temper was on the border of exploding.

"Again?" he said in a barely contained roar as he slammed the door shut behind him. "Are you implying I wasna invited in previously?"

"You were most certainly not!"

For some reason, he hadn't expected that answer, and it had him frowning, as well as lowering his tone to tell her, "Then you've a short memory, lass, if you dinna recall your behavior last night."

"What has my behavior to do—"

"Everything," he cut in. "You didna refuse my kisses, Kimber, you returned them full measure.

And your eyes fairly devoured me all evening long. D'you think I'm so inexperienced in these matters that I canna recognize an invitation when I receive it?"

She stared at him aghast. "You're saying you came in here last night and made love to me because you *thought* you'd been invited to do so? You didn't hear me say the words, you just assumed?"

"You're denying it?"

"I'm telling you that if I looked at you in a way that could be considered inappropriate, I certainly wasn't aware of it. And if I accepted your kisses, it was because of the silly notion that you were seriously interested in me, more fool me. Furthermore, I had consumed too much champagne, Lachlan. Couldn't you tell that?"

"Nay, you just seemed more agreeable," he said, his frown turning thoughtful now. "And wi' as agreeable as you were, 'tis possible I may have convinced myself you were experienced in these matters."

"Experienced! I *never*—"

"Aye, I ken that now," he cut in curtly, impatiently. "And I dinna take tae well tae champagne either, so I wasna exactly clearheaded myself, at least no' enough tae think this thing through. You were a beautiful woman who gave every indication of wanting my attentions, and I'm no' a man tae turn down a beautiful woman."

The compliment didn't even come close to touching her. She was simply too furious, and at the moment, too filled with disgust.

"Then you're as faithless as a barnyard cock," she said scornfully, "to claim to love one woman, yet be so quick to dally with another."

Hearing that, he had the audacity to grin at her and shrug. "Och, lass, you've a lot tae learn. A man will be faithful when his needs are seen tae on a regular basis. When that isna the case, he'll be randy enough tae take whatever comes his way and be grateful for it."

He'd managed to make her blush with such base talk, yet she couldn't take him to task for it since she'd started it. However, she could point out, "True love should make an exception to that."

He shook his head at her, even sighed, indicating he was really disappointed in her contention. "Now you're spouting romantic drivel, Kimber. The body is an amazing thing, and you'll learn that it has a mind of its own when it comes to certain things—lovemaking one of them. Did you no' discover that for yourself last night? Or perhaps you're needing another demonstration?"

She put out a hand to stop him if he thought to approach her, understanding him clearly. And she refused to admit that there was some truth to what he was saying. She did indeed remember her body's reaction and how her will had succumbed to it.

But it was a moot point. The relevant point was that she hadn't invited her own ruination. He had forced that on her because he had *misinterpreted* her behavior.

But she'd said enough about that. "I've already had a demonstration, for which I'd like to draw and quarter you. If you weren't aware of it, I am here expressly to find a husband. How am I going to do that now after what you've done to me?"

"Is it marriage you're wanting from me then?"

She should have said yes. She should make him

pay for what he'd done. But her pride reared up, and it was the truth she gave him.

"When you're in love with another woman?" she said tightly. "No thank you."

"Och, well, it has been brought tae my recent attention that 'tis possible I dinna ken my own feelings," he said in a tone laced with disgust. "So if you'll have me, lass, I'll be marrying you."

"How self-sacrificing, but unnecessary, since I won't have you. I won't have a man who'll always be pining over another woman. My mother had just such a marriage, so I know exactly how intolerable that can be."

"You're sure?"

"Oh, I'm most definitely positive. And I'll thank you to vacate my room, Lachlan, and don't step foot in it again. And just in case you misconstrue any more looks of mine, let me assure you now, you will never be welcome here again—not that you ever were."

His expression turned mulish as he demanded, "And if I insist?"

She gasped. "On coming in here?"

"On marrying you."

Her eyes rounded. "Why ever would you do that, when you don't *want* to marry me?"

He didn't answer at first, just stared at her, but after a moment more he growled and raked his fingers through his hair in exasperation. "I dinna ken what I'm wanting just now." And then his light green eyes pinned her to the spot and there was a wealth of meaning in them that she couldn't begin to understand, until he added, "But I usually pick up the gauntlet when 'tis tossed down."

"Don't—" she began in a choked whisper, but he cut that short.

"I'll be seeing you later, darlin'."

She was so flustered by what his previous remark implied that the door had closed on him before she managed to shout, "And don't call me that anymore!"

It was another moment before she actually realized that she was alone and leaped for the door to lock it. And locked it would stay from now on when she was behind it. The gall of that Highlander. The brazen impudence to suggest that she had challenged him to change her mind.

She snorted to herself. As if he could.

18

The socializing continued apace, with several more events in London, including a night at the theater. Kimberly was actually able to enjoy that, since it allowed her to step away from her own worries for a while to become immersed in those of the actors.

There was also a ball their last night in London, where she was able to further her acquaintance with Lord Kent and Howard Canston, who both informed her that they had received invitations to Sherring Cross. They both seemed thrilled, it apparently being quite a social coup to claim an acquaintance with the Duke of Wrothston.

There had been several other gentlemen of interest at that ball, one of whom became completely intoxicated and actually proposed to Kimberly on the dance floor. She had not taken him seriously, of course, considering his condition, but she had been quite flattered.

Her first proposal—actually, not her first, though the other two she wasn't counting. Her first betrothal had been arranged when she was a baby. And Lachlan had said he would marry her, not exactly a proposal that, but she supposed it was somewhat the same thing—except there was a world of difference between "would" and "want to," and she hadn't heard any "want to" in his proposal.

As for Lachlan, it was impossible to avoid him altogether, though Kimberly gave it her best effort. Dinners, formal as they were and at a set time, were still the one time of the day she was required to see him. Also, he went to each social gathering that she did, but now she understood why. He also had come to Sherring Cross for the express purpose of finding a spouse, and as far as everyone *else* knew, that was just what he was doing.

It was too bad his pursuit of the duchess had gotten in the way of that, too bad also that Kimberly had known about that from the very beginning. Otherwise, she would definitely have been more agreeable to him, and to hell with her father's antipathy toward Scots. Lachlan would have been well worth facing that problem. And he did seem to have *some* kind of interest in her, or he wouldn't have kissed her on more than one occasion or made love to her.

But unfortunately, she did know where his true affections lay. And even if Lachlan came to his senses and gave up on Megan, even if he tried to find an available and willing wife, which he apparently needed to do for financial reasons, that wife would be his second choice. He'd always be pining over his first choice, and Kimberly could only pity his wife because of that.

Sherring Cross had quite an assortment of

guests by the end of their first week back, not counting the usual crop of daily visitors. John Kent and Howard Canston had both settled in. And included among the newcomers were three young women who, like Kimberly, had entered the marriage mart this season and had been invited for an extended visit by either the duchess or Lachlan's Aunt Margaret.

Kimberly disliked them instantly. They were each younger than she, and prettier in her opinion. And if two of them hadn't brought handsome, unmarried brothers along as their chaperones, Kimberly might have packed up her bags and returned to Northumberland, because she certainly had no chance of drawing a fair share of the gentlemen's attention with those three lovelies around.

Lady Monica Elgar was blond—and a very light blond at that—and blue-eyed. She was also very petite, had a droll sense of humor that kept everyone around her laughing—especially the gentlemen—and she had John Kent's undivided attention from the moment he laid eyes on her.

Lady Edith Winestone, vivacious, auburn-haired, with lovely light grey eyes, was a bit loud, but so pretty no one seemed to notice except Kimberly. The young lady didn't have a shy bone in her body either, and thought nothing of jumping into any conversation with her own differing opinion, though half the time Edith was proved to be wrong. She wasn't all that intelligent, actually, and often made ridiculous remarks, but the gentlemen certainly didn't seem to mind that.

Jane Carlyle, now, personified the ideal lady in every respect. Slim to the point of emaciation, at least in Kimberly's opinion, she was also blond with amber eyes, a truly fashionable beauty. And her decorum was impeccable. She ate correctly, spoke correctly, followed every social etiquette rule to the letter, and was sweet-tempered besides, or so her overbearing mother kept assuring everyone who cared to listen. No one in their right mind would doubt that indomitable lady. Though what gentleman in his right mind would want that lady for a mother-in-law . . .

Besides Hector Carlyle and Christopher Elgar, new to their growing group, there was also a widowed marquis who had come to see the duke on business and had accepted Devlin's suggestion that he take a holiday and stay on to enjoy some of the festivities Megan had arranged for the coming weeks. James Travers was his name, and in his early forties, he was a bit older than Kimberly had been hoping for. Yet no one could deny he was a splendid catch.

Rakishly handsome in appearance with his black hair and blue eyes, James was also disgustingly rich, according to a whispered aside from Lucinda. And although not in the market for a wife, having two young sons from his first marriage, he wasn't avoiding the matrimonial state either. Megan had assured her he just hadn't found the right woman to replace his departed wife yet.

Kimberly came to like James in the days that followed. Her conversations with him were always lively and never lagged, which was nice. Long, shy periods of silence were always embarrassing for both parties, but she never encountered one with him. And once he'd noticed her smile and remarked on it, he made a concerted effort to make her laugh frequently, which he accomplished with ease.

Yet Lachlan was always somewhere near at these gatherings, and she was *always* quite aware of him, no matter who she was speaking to at the time. Avoiding him was one thing, ignoring him completely when he was in the same room was quite another. And there were times . . .

She passed him in the hall once before their return from London, and in one breath he said to her quite formally, "How fetching you look today, Lady Kimberly," and in the very next, "D'you ken that bairns are a possible consequence of what we did?"

That she had started to blush from the compliment only added to the mortified color that spread clear to her roots. And he'd sauntered away before she could even think how to respond. So his intention had been merely to apprise her of that fact if she hadn't been aware of it.

And she'd thought that was a really rotten thing for him to do, adding one more thing to her worries if she *hadn't* already known that little fact. Except that apparently wasn't the reason he'd mentioned it to her. He'd just been giving her warning of his next outrageous remark, delivered again out of context.

They'd been at a dinner with a good thirty other guests, yet somehow he'd managed to get the gentleman on her left to leave the room. She couldn't imagine how he'd accomplished this, yet he had proceeded to take the man's seat, apparently assured the fellow wouldn't be returning. And although Kimberly had done an excellent job of pretending he wasn't there, the conversation

around them had centered so they were all involved in it.

And between one comment and another, Lachlan had leaned toward her to say, "You *will* tell
me if you're going tae have my bairn, Kimber. I
would be extremely angry if you think tae keep
something like that from me."

She'd been delighted to find him and tell him
a week later, "I won't be having any babies,
MacGregor, until I'm properly married."

Incredibly, he hadn't seemed relieved by that
news as she had expected. She certainly was,
since it at least put her back on a normal time
schedule for finding a husband, as well as pre-
cluded her from having to tell her father about
what she'd done. Not that she could procrastinate
for long over her choices, with her father so eager
to have the matter settled. Nor did she want to
impose on the St. Jameses indefinitely.

But the fact that Lachlan hadn't been relieved
confused her. He had given nothing away, really,
of how he felt about her news. And Howard Canston had come upon them before anything further
might be said, and had invited her to go riding,
it being one of their nicer winter days.

Kimberly was pleased that Howard still
showed a marked interest in her, despite the arrival of the "three lovelies." John Kent, however,
she could scratch from her meager list.

As for Lachlan making an effort toward finding
a wife, well, he didn't seem to be making any
effort at all. Edith he barely noticed, though she
did her fair share of batting her eyes at him, and
although he did show some attention toward
Jane, it was cordial at best.

Kimberly wondered, more than once, if he

hadn't been devastated by what she had inadvertently revealed to him at that last ball they'd attended in London, and had been brooding about it ever since. She'd chanced to pass him near the refreshment table, and had noticed that he was staring at Megan and Devlin dancing, and a kernel of resentment had bubbled up in her that he was still mooning over the lady and undoubtedly always would be. If that weren't the case, she might have allowed herself to fall in love with him.

Her resentment had gotten the better of her and prompted her to say to him, "You really think she'd leave her adoring husband and her baby for you?"

He'd swung around to face her and had nearly shouted, "Her what?"

She'd frowned at his incredulous expression. "You didn't know they have a baby son?"

"Nay, how could I know? I've never seen her wi' any bairn."

"Then I'm sorry—at least, that you learned of it from me." And then she'd added gently, because she was regretting more the reason she'd told him, "All of England knew, Lachlan. It was in every paper, and just about all the gentry was talking about it for a while. I thought you knew, that surely your aunt would have mentioned it at sometime or other, but it just didn't make a difference to you."

"No difference that 'tis no' just the tae of them, that they're a blasted family?"

He'd laughed, but it was a hollow sound, and then he'd walked away. And she hadn't seen him again that evening. But she'd been disturbed, because the look he'd given her before he'd disappeared could have implied that she'd insulted the hell out of him with her last remark, or that he found her contemptible for pointing out what he felt was trivial. And she really wished she knew which it was.

19

"I tell you I don't care! I want the Scotsman, Mother. I'm sick and tired of hearing what *you* want!"

Kimberly had just entered the breakfast room when Jane Carlyle had started her screeching. And screeching it was. It was likely she'd been heard as far away as the stables. And everyone in the room, at least fifteen of the current guests, the Scotsman included, was a little bit in shock over this unprecedented outburst from what had previously appeared to be the perfect lady.

There was a cough, then another, then an outright snicker. And into the silence that followed, a Scottish brogue drawled thickly, "I'm thinking the Scot may have something tae say aboot it."

Conversation burst forth now from everyone at the table in an effort to pretend that little outburst hadn't happened. Jane, standing at the sideboard with her mother where a buffet was laid out, glanced back at the table with a look of bewilderment, as if she weren't even aware of what she'd done. Her mother certainly was though. Red-faced, the lady grasped her daughter's arm and marched her out of the room. Kimberly just barely got out of the way before they bowled her over.

The conversation returned to a normal level as soon as they were gone. And Edith, that little nit-wit, said in her usual loud tone, "But I thought she was sweet-tempered. Her mother said so."

Kimberly happened to meet Lachlan's gaze at that moment, and almost burst out laughing when he rolled his eyes. She restrained the laugh, fortunately. She would have been mortified if she hadn't, under the circumstances. But it was impossible to keep from smiling, briefly, and that audacious man winked at her.

Moving on to the buffet now, which had been the standard setup each morning since the house had filled up with so many guests, Kimberly passed Jane's brother at the end of the table and heard him remark to Christopher in a snide aside that shouldn't have been overheard, "I could've told you what a little bitch she is. My father's always said the same about my mum. It's been bloody hell living with the two of them all these years, I don't mind saying."

Monica's brother, to give him credit, appeared embarrassed to have been given that confidence. Kimberly tsked to herself and mentally crossed Hector Carlyle off her list. Telling tales about his own family . . .

Having heard that, however, she actually felt sorry for Jane. A man might not mind at all that his wife was a bit dense, might even prefer it that way, to assure himself that he was more intelligent. But most men didn't want a wife with an uncontrollable temper, which could be socially embarrassing.

It wasn't surprising that Jane's mother, poor woman, packed her daughter off that very afternoon. Jane had ruined her chances with the crop of eligibles at Sherring Cross. It was just too bad that they hadn't taken Hector with them.

There were two activities planned for that afternoon. The duchess was heading an excursion to the nearest pond for some ice-skating for those who enjoyed the outdoors in fair weather or foul. And for those who didn't, there would be charades in the parlor.

Kimberly elected to go ice-skating. It was a difficult decision to make, and made finally because she simply didn't like charades and *did* like ice-skating. But what with Megan chaperoning the excursion, it was guaranteed that Lachlan would also be there.

Finally, she simply determined to enjoy herself despite his presence. Besides, she'd purchased a new winter coat in London, one much more fashionable that conformed nicely to her figure, and she hadn't had much opportunity to show it off. And she was rather good at ice-skating, it being something she and her mother had enjoyed doing together.

And Megan had a large selection of skates in all sizes on hand, as well as providing woodburning stoves to be set up along the bank of the pond for when the cold got to be too much. A number of servants had also come along to roast a continuous supply of chestnuts for treats, and there were mugs of hot chocolate, and warmed spiced brandy for the gentlemen.

Kimberly was rather surprised that Howard Canston didn't come along, as athletic as he was, and surprised yet again that James did, especially when she learned that he'd never worn a pair of skates in his life. But she had a rousing good time trying to teach him, even when she ended up on her backside several times because he couldn't find his balance. She had to admire him though, for he was absolutely determined to get it right. He even elected to continue practicing when she headed in for some hot chocolate and a little heat from one of the woodburners.

Kimberly joined John and Monica, but they returned to the ice after only a few minutes of excited chatter. She'd been out there too long herself without a break though, so the burner was welcome, and she took her hands away from it only long enough to wave to James each time he passed. He didn't much take his eyes off the ice though, so he didn't notice.

Megan was skating between a pair of her older guests, their arms all locked together. Quite a few people had elected to come along for this outing, including several families with young children. And Lachlan . . .

Kimberly had no sooner been handed a mug of chocolate by one of the servants than the fellow was called over to another burner. And the minute she was completely alone, Lachlan came to a perfect stop on the edge of the pond and climbed the low bank to join her.

"Faith, but you looked fair enchanting out there, darlin'," he remarked as he removed his gloves to extend his hands toward the fire.

For some reason his compliment warmed her even more than the fire did and she blushed becomingly. But that seemed to be a regular occurrence when this man was around. And she assumed he was referring to her ice-skating skill, since she was certainly not looking her best after those two falls. Her coiffure had come undone with the second fall, the pins scattering on the ice, and it had been pointless to even try and put her hair back in order.

But she was pleased enough to say, "Thank you, I've been skating since I was a child."

She ought to return the compliment, since he was quite skilled himself. But she refrained. Saying so would be admitting she had covertly watched him, when that was the last thing she wanted him to know.

But he surprised her by correcting her assumption. " 'Twas your hair I was admiring, Kimber. All loose and flowing about you like that, it reminds me . . ."

He didn't finish—deliberately. He didn't have to. And her blush turned scalding. She couldn't believe that he would mention their lovemaking all these weeks later. She, despite her wish to the contrary, thought about it frequently, too damned frequently actuall'. But he should have all but forgotten it by now.

And then, as had been typical of him in each of their last encounters, he said completely out of the blue, "Why are you encouraging him? He's old enough tae be your da."

She didn't pretend to wonder whom he meant. "What has that to do with anything?" she asked him. "And he's far from *old*, Lachlan. James is in the prime of his life, perfectly healthy, physically fit, and women find him very attractive, myself included. Or is it that you don't think two people of widely differing ages can have anything in common? I'd have to disagree there, since James and I have already discovered a wealth of things we share an interest in.''

He mumbled something under his breath before he grouched, ''But can his kisses make you forget yourself, darlin'? Does he fire you with passion the way I do?''

It took every ounce of will she had to keep from blushing yet again and to reply in a thoughtful tone, ''Hmmm, I don't know, he hasn't kissed me yet. Perhaps I should find out. But I would imagine, considering he's had more years to practice that sort of thing, that he'd be quite good at it by now.''

''Then let me refresh your memory, so you can make a better comparison—''

''Don't you dare!'' she hissed. ''Are you mad? We're not alone here.''

He was grinning widely, now that he'd managed to disturb her. ''Och, what a pity. But I suppose I can wait until we are alone.''

She gasped. ''The devil you will—I mean, you can get any notions of kissing me again right out of your head, Lachlan MacGregor. I won't be allowing it, and besides, why ever would you want to?''

''Kiss a beautiful woman?'' He smiled. ''Did I no' warn you how fond I am of doing that?''

It occurred to her then that he was teasing her. She might have realized it sooner if she were used to being teased, but she wasn't. Her reserved nature pretty much kept people from taking that liberty with her. But Lachlan was a bold devil. Just because she didn't seem teasable, that wouldn't stop him. And she wished she could figure out exactly when the teasing had actually started, and how much of what he'd just said he really meant.

For his efforts, though, she gave him a sour look. "Yes, you did warn me, and I'm sure you've been quite busy of late doing just that, with so many beautiful women around. And I wonder now if that isn't why Jane lost her temper this morning with her mother, that she was so set on having you because you'd turned her head with a few kisses."

He snorted. "That little paragon of exactitude? I dinna trust a lass wi' no apparent faults, and rightly so, as 'twas proved that lady has at least one fault in the extreme."

"I have a temper myself," she reminded him, trying to tamp down her relief that he hadn't been interested in Jane at all. "But that didn't stop you from—"

"You've got spirit and courage, darlin'. There's a big difference there, if you dinna see it."

Of course she blushed again. The man was really doling out *too* many compliments her way lately, and she wished she knew why. Was he trying to make amends to her? A few compliments could hardly make up for one's lost virtue, and she had yet to even face the consequences, when she would be forced to tell whomever she married. But then some men tended to be quite illogical in their thinking, so he *might* assume he was clearing his conscience in that fashion.

"Well—Jane wasn't the only beautiful woman around lately," she pointed out. "So I imagine you've still been busy. Lady Edith—"

"Hasn't enough sense tae ken when she's being a twit," he was quick to cut in. "She'd drive a mon tae drink in a matter o' days wi' her witless chatter.''

She almost nodded, since that had been her opinion as well. But she was having to deal with contradictory emotions, annoyance that he was shooting down each point she was making, and delight that two of the women she'd been so sure he would court hadn't interested him at all.

But there wasn't a thing he could say against Monica Elgar. Even Kimberly had been drawn into liking her, she was such a nice person. And she *did* want Lachlan to admit he'd been kissing someone else. She wouldn't like hearing it, but she was sure that knowing it would help her to stop thinking about him so much.

So she said, ''What about Lady Monica?''

He sighed at that point. ''If you didna notice, Kimber, that lady is no' more'n five feet tall, if even that. Every time I'm near the lass, I get the urge tae lift her up on my hip like a wee child.''

In exasperation, she asked, ''Then who have you been kissing?''

''As it happens, darlin', no one.''

She blinked. ''Why not?''

''Perhaps I'm waiting for you tae come tae your senses and have me.''

Her heart skipped a beat. And just as quickly, her temper shot up. Teasing again, and this time she really didn't appreciate his humor. Obviously, he just wasn't going to tell her whom he was amusing himself with now while he continued to pine over the duchess.

She took a sip of her chocolate, then set it down to put her gloves back on. ''Well, if that were true, Lachlan,'' she said with a tight little smile, ''I'd probably suggest you hold your breath while you're waiting.''

For an insult, it surely missed the mark. He laughed.

"When you get angry like that, darlin', d'you ken your eyes flash wi' green fire? 'Tis verra tempting.''

"Tempting?''

He sighed. "You're still an innocent in many ways, I'm thinking. Run now, lass, or I'll be kissing you here, wi' no care for who's watching.''

She hadn't understood what he meant by tempting, because he hadn't said how she was apparently tempting him. For all she knew, he could have meant tempting him to clobber her. But she understood that last well enough. And although running in skates on a snow bank was hazardous, she managed to get back on the ice quickly.

That his chuckle followed her as she hurried away put her in a rotten mood for the rest of the day. Had he only been teasing her again? She wondered about that later, when it was too late to find out.

20

"I'm thinkin' we should've stole his fancy stallion when we had the chance tae," Gilleonan remarked in a grumbling tone as he and Lachlan stopped to watch a pair of young thoroughbred horses being exercised in the training yard attached to the closest stable. " 'Tis no' as if he would've missed it, as many's he's got here and even more breedin' each year. And it would've fetched a fair price."

"No' so loud," Lachlan admonished.

He glanced to Gilleonan's right, where a couple of the other houseguests were leaning against the fence, also admiring the pair of young horses being put through their paces. The other guests weren't actually close enough to have heard Gilleonan, and they certainly weren't paying attention. As far as Lachlan could tell, they were deep in a discussion themselves about the prize thoroughbreds bred and sold here at Sherring Cross.

Still, he moved down along the fence a few more feet, tugging his cousin with him, before he added, "There was no point tae stealing his horse, Gill, when he would've took it back same as he took the lass back. Besides, I dinna steal horses, and well you ken it."

It was the Duke of Wrothston they were discussing, and the horse he'd had with him the day Lachlan and his cousins stopped his coach to rob it, and Lachlan took off with Megan instead of the money they'd been after. Lachlan was beginning to wish he'd stayed home that day.

"Och, well, 'twas just a thought," Gilleonan admitted. "Though all in the same thought, I'm thinkin' ye're no' takin' this wife-findin' business seriously."

Lachlan raised an auburn brow at his friend. "And just where does horse stealing and wife finding have anything a'tall in common?"

"Ye dinna see it?" Gilleonan replied. "Why, in the money they'd both bring, which is the reason we're here, or have ye forgotten that again?"

It was the question, not the answer, that brought a frown to Lachlan's brow. "Tell me something, Gill? Is it that you dinna think I take my responsibility seriously? Or d'you just feel a need tae complain more often wi' us living among the Sassenachs?"

Gilleonan at least looked suitably embarrassed now and even sighed. "It mun be the latter, aye, it really mun be, especially after bein' here well nigh a month now. Has no one caught yer fancy then, now that ye've come tae yer senses and give up on the duchess?"

Lachlan's expression changed to one of vexation and he mumbled, "Aye, one lass has."

"Faith, why did ye no' say so? When will ye be proposin' then?"

"I already did."

"And?"

"She willna have me."

Gilleonan snorted. "That's no' the least bit funny, Lachlan. Any lass would be pleased tae—"

"Except this one."

Gilleonan paused. "Ye're serious?"

"Aye."

"She—ah, had another commitment then?"

"Nay, she just doesna like me."

Gilleonan almost chuckled at Lachlan's look of vexation but managed to restrain himself, just, and shook his head instead. "Och, well, 'tis lucky we are that there be more lassies showin' up here nearly every day, thanks tae yer aunt's efforts. Ye'll find another, Lachlan. 'Tis heartenin', though, truly, that ye *are* gettin' serious aboot it finally, and have put aside yer feelings for the duchess for the sake o' the clan."

Lachlan snorted to himself now. Put aside his feelings? That certainly hadn't been very difficult to do, when all things considered, it should have been extremely hard. And that made him wonder if Megan hadn't been right.

Had he been deluding himself all along about his feelings for her, wanting her only because she was so beautiful, and because she'd escaped from him before he'd had a chance to charm her? Or did the fact that she and the duke had a child, and a son at that, change his mind?

That child did make a world of difference, especially since a duke would never give up his heir, and rightly so. Lachlan could never be so cruel as to take a mother away from her child, no matter his own feelings about the lass. But he gave up trying to figure out what those feelings had been. They simply were no more, as if they had never been.

Odd, though, that he had no trouble figuring out his feelings where the other lass was concerned. Anger was hard to mistake, and that's what he'd been experiencing more and more of late, and in particular, when he saw Kimberly enjoying herself with other men.

It wasn't jealousy—well, it couldn't be. Most times he felt annoyed when she was with James Travers, laughing, dancing, partnered with him in a game of cards, or just in quiet conversation. But Travers was a man in his middle years. Lachlan couldn't possibly be jealous of a man nearly twice his own age. That was ludicrous. And besides, when had he ever been jealous of anything? Never that he could recall, so it obviously wasn't in his nature to be bothered by that silly emotion.

Yet he couldn't deny his anger. It was there, and wouldn't seem to go away, no matter how much he ignored it. The most likely reason for it was that the lass had refused to marry him. His pride must have been sorely pricked by that. First Megan wouldn't take him seriously, then Kimberly, after showing plainly that she wanted him, refused to have him permanently. When had he *ever* had such rotten luck with women? Never. And that had to be why he was having such difficulty in dealing with it.

It was really too bad, though, that he'd put aside his pursuit of Megan after he'd seduced Kimberly, rather than beforehand. If he could have handled that whole matter with her differently, if he hadn't been still foolishly thinking it was Megan he really wanted, he might have been successful. But he'd been thinking that Kimberly was just a temporary diversion. Some diversion.

She was the one he couldn't stop thinking about before or after that one glorious night with her. So it wasn't all that surprising that the moment he'd finally decided to get serious about finding a wife, he'd thought of her. But it was too late. He'd burned his bridges there. She'd made it perfectly clear she wouldn't have him.

Yet when had that ever stopped him from going after something he really wanted? Aye, he still wanted her. Faith, but she felt so right in his arms, the few times he'd managed to get her there. It was a unique experience, that rightness, something he'd never felt before. And he wanted to know it again and again.

21

"See them, sweetheart? See the horsies?" The baby, held up to the window with the view of the stables, merely gurgled. "You'll have one for yourself in a few years," Megan continued. "Well, not one as big as those two, but—"

"And not in a few years either," Devlin cut in, coming up behind his wife and son. "Justin isn't even a year old yet, Megan."

"Shhh, he doesn't know that. And besides, I'm just giving him something to look forward to."

Devlin chuckled. "You're adorable when you get ridiculous. As if he understood a word you said."

"I'll have you know, Devlin St. James, that my son is *very* intelligent," Megan said huffily. "He understands more than you think."

"If you say so, love. Far be it for me to disagree when you get that 'ready for battle' look."

She snorted. He chuckled again, then added, "But it's time for his bath, so give him to nurse now. The poor woman has been searching high and low for you, had to drag me out of my study to help."

"Begging yer pardon, Yer Grace, but—"

Devlin's abrupt throat clearing cut the woman off and she blushed. Megan giggled, knowing exactly what her husband had just attempted, but failed dismally without the woman's cooperation. He seemed to think that if he could make Megan feel contrite about something, that she wouldn't fuss at him about anything for the rest of the day. It rarely worked, yet he kept trying.

"Actually, we did have a devil of a time finding you this morning," he insisted. "Why do you persist in bringing Justin to these unused rooms?"

"For the different views, of course," she replied as she kissed Justin's cheek before handing him over to his nurse. "It's too cold to take him outside this early in the morning, yet I don't want him to miss how pretty the grounds are in the early light—sooooo, I find him different views from different rooms. I hadn't even realized you could see the stables from this one, did you?"

"Certainly," he lied with aplomb.

Devlin might have been in every room in the mansion at one time or other during his life, but it hadn't been to look out the windows. He did so now, however, and ended up frowning at the view below him.

"Quite a few early risers about," he remarked, his tone gone stiff.

Megan, aware of whom he'd seen down by the stable, said, "Now, now, when are you going to stop getting annoyed every time you see that Highlander?"

"When I stop seeing him."

She grinned. "Stubborn."

He shrugged, then put his arm around her shoulder and squeezed it. "By the by, since nothing came of your matchmaking scheme, d'you think you might put some effort into finding a lady who'll suit him, so the bloody chap doesn't end up darkening our door all winter long?"

"I already have. I've asked Margaret to double her invitations, but—"

He sighed loud and long. "When is our home going to return to normal?"

She grinned, since "normal" meant only three or four guests at any given time. "Soon, Dev, but as I was about to say, I haven't given up completely on our original plan."

He shook his head. "You mean *your* original plan. And you call me stubborn."

"But I've noticed him watching her recently."

"And I've noticed how completely she ignores him," he countered.

"I think she only pretends to ignore him."

"Well, a damn fine job of pretending she does, if I do say so. Face it, Megan, the lady isn't interested in that Scot one little bit. And besides, she's all but wed and our obligations at an end."

"What?!"

"Well," he quickly amended, "James has mentioned to me that he is seriously considering matrimony again."

"Oh, I do hope not."

"Megan—"

"Oh, don't misunderstand. I think James Travers is a fine man, and he'd make anyone a fine husband."

"I wish I didn't hear a 'but' in there," Devlin mumbled only just loud enough for his wife to hear.

She narrowed her eyes on him before continuing, "*But* I've gotten to know Kimberly during her stay with us and, well, I think she would be happier with someone else."

"Why, might I ask, when she and James are perfectly compatible?"

"Yes, too compatible, actually, and you know what that can lead to, don't you?" She answered before he had a chance to, and as if he were in agreement. "Exactly, boredom."

He rolled his eyes. "Dare I suggest it might also lead to perfect accord and hence—happiness?"

"No, you may not."

"You are the only stubborn one in this family, brat. You know perfectly well . . . that . . ."

What began in exasperation trailed off as Devlin stared out the window. Megan followed his gaze to see that Kimberly had returned from an early morning ride with several matrons. Her youth and vitality radiated in the company of the older ladies, yet she was also looking quite splendid this morning in a new riding habit of ruby red velvet, cinched in nicely to display her fine figure.

Megan smiled to herself. She'd warned Mrs. Canterby before she got started on the lady's new wardrobe that she wanted all of Kimberly's clothes just a tad on the tight side, to show off her curves to advantage. And Kimberly hadn't suspected a thing except, perhaps, that she might be putting on a little weight.

What had caught Devlin's eye was that Howard Canston was suddenly there, waving away the groom heading for Kimberly so that he could assist the lady in dismounting. It was an old ploy in Megan's opinion. It allowed a gentleman who was interested in a particular lady to put his hands on her, and quite firmly at that. And although most gentlemen would release said lady the very instant her feet touched the ground, some men weren't so meticulously proper.

Howard apparently fell into that latter group, because his hands remained on Kimberly's waist all the while she made some remark to him, and all the time it took him to answer, which was much too long to be considered proper. And that was too bad of him, as Kimberly's riding companions, Abagail and Hilary, were known to be notorious gossips. Then again, perhaps that was his intention, to have his interest in Kimberly become common knowledge.

But that still probably wasn't what had gained Devlin's undivided attention. It was the Scot, who had abruptly ended his own conversation when Kimberly showed up, and had been staring at her intently ever since. He'd gone all stiff when Howard appeared at her side, and his stance had turned to outright aggressiveness when the viscount reached up to assist Kimberly to the ground. But when Howard didn't release her immediately, Lachlan actually started toward them, and there was simply no mistaking his fury.

Devlin must have guessed the same thing Megan did, because he said, "Oh, good Lord, he's not going to . . . he really wouldn't . . ."

There was no point in continuing, because Lachlan did. He no sooner reached the unsuspecting couple than his fist landed in the vicinity of Howard Canston's right eye. The blow also knocked the man off his feet. He lay flat on the ground now, apparently dazed, possibly even knocked out, because he was making no effort to get up.

Beside her, Devlin growled. Megan quickly grabbed the lapel of his morning coat to keep him from running down there in high dudgeon. The coat was pulled halfway down his arm when he pivoted toward the door.

But he did turn back to her. He even lifted a black brow, his subtle way of saying, "Let go or you'll be dragged along with me."

She straightened out his coat and said practically, "Now, Devlin, there's no reason a'tall for you to get involved in that."

"Isn't there?" he gritted out. "Howard Canston is a guest in my home."

"Oh, give over. You've been itching for a reason to give the Highlander the boot, and you think you've found it. But you haven't. That disagreement involves two of your guests, three actually, and is quite personal. Not one of them would appreciate you becoming involved. Besides, that black eye isn't going to hurt the viscount a'tall. The ladies will all ohhhh and ahhhh over him and he'll love it."

"That is hardly the point—"

"Perhaps, but what *is* exactly the point is you have one man behaving improperly and another overcome with jealousy because of it, hardly the stuff to trouble one's host over."

"Ah-ha! Now comes the real reason you want me to stay out of it. You're just delighted because you think MacGregor is jealous."

She grinned up at him. "There's no 'think' about it. That was a glorious display of jealousy and you know it. So why don't we just continue to watch from the sidelines, and if they attempt to *kill* each other, then it would be appropriate for you to become involved."

"And what if the lady attempts to kill one of them?" Devlin asked dryly.

"What?!"

Megan swung back toward the window to see that the parasol that Kimberly had had attached to her wrist instead of a riding crop was now quite bent over Lachlan's head. Completely ruined, of course—the parasol, that is. Lachlan's head would likely survive.

"Oh, now that was really too bad of her," Megan said in disappointment.

"I'm sure he feels the same," Devlin replied smugly, but ended with a chuckle.

"This isn't funny. She should have been impressed and flattered."

"Why, if she doesn't like the chap?"

"Ohhhh! You're just never going to see this my way, are you?"

"Hardly, when it's *my* fist that aches to be planted in *his* face."

"Do continue to restrain that urge, will you?"

After several heated words passed between the couple that was still standing, Lachlan marched off, and Kimberly bent to do some ohhhing and ahhhing over Howard, or so Megan assumed. It was too bad she and Devlin were so far away and behind a closed window. She was dying to know what had just been said down there, but she supposed she'd have to wait until Abagail and Hilary got around to repeating the entire story. Actually, knowing them, that shouldn't take any longer than the first person they ran into.

22

"I think it's sooooo romantic."

"But I thought Lady Kimberly and the marquis were all but engaged."

"Apparently not, or—"

"Well, I heard—"

"Barbaric, if you ask me—"

"Scotsmen usually are—"

"Now I take exception to that, indeed I do. M'father's cousin hails from the Highlands. They play golf, don't you know. Highly civilized, that."

"I meant breaking her parasol over his head. Waste of a good parasol."

"Well, I heard that—"

"Thought that was rather funny, m'self."

"You would, Abagail. You've broken four or five over your Elbert's head, haven't you?"

"Only two, m'dear."

"*Well, I heard that he—!*"

"Good God, Mabel, you don't have to shout. *What* did you hear?"

149

A low voice mumbled, "Well, now I forget."

A chuckle. "Actually, I have it on good authority that she's already turned him down three times."

"Who? The marquis?"

"No, you ninny, the Scot."

"But what about the viscount? A prime catch there, and obviously he's interested."

"Canston? He's always interested, though not in matrimony, if you catch my drift."

"Now, now, Hilary, don't be catty. Just because nothing came of it when the viscount was courting your niece a few months ago—"

"Courted m'daughter last season, but never got around to proposing to her either."

"Taking after his father, if you ask me. Old Canston was a rake in his day—"

"Nonsense, they're just laggards at making up their minds. Runs in the family, don't you know."

That was pretty typical of the conversations Kimberly had been overhearing all day long: at the late breakfast, at the recital she attended afterward, at teatime in the late afternoon, and then again at dinner, she either heard the whispers, or the complete silence when she was noticed, or the unrestrained talk when she wasn't. Tight-lipped, she slipped out of the card room before she was noticed and ended up embarrassing that particular group, even if they deserved embarrassment.

She really deplored being gossiped about. It was so unsavory. But it had been too much to hope that that little drama Lachlan had instigated this morning wouldn't make the rounds at Sherring Cross.

It was too much to hope that it wouldn't travel far afield by tomorrow. In fact, she would be surprised if it didn't reach her father by the end of the week, and even more surprised if he didn't show up soon thereafter in a fine rage. A Scotsman was being linked to her name, after all. He would want to know why.

What wasn't surprising was that each accounting of the incident was wrong in some respect. But then that was quite typical of gossip. After it had made a few rounds, it was barely recognizable.

One retelling had poor Howard thoroughly thrashed by the Highlander. Another had Kimberly breaking off an engagement with Lachlan, which was supposedly what caused him to go berserk when he saw her with Howard. Still another account had it that James Travers was the one who had delivered that punch to the viscount. The marquis hadn't even been present, yet he was being dragged into the tale because of his recent association with her. And then she'd heard that she'd turned down Lachlan's marriage proposal twice, thrice, and one gentleman claimed it was six times—just to give an excuse for his jealous behavior, she supposed.

Jealous behavior? Now nothing could get more absurd than that. Perhaps if Megan had been involved, but her? Her only involvement with him, aside from several arguments, had been that one night they'd shared together when they had both imbibed too much champagne. Ever since, they'd been somewhat on the close side of enemies. His one proposal of marriage, which hadn't even been a true proposal, had come belatedly, and that, undoubtedly, merely to clear his conscience.

Is it marriage you're wanting from me then?

Hardly a heartfelt declaration by any interpretation.

So what did cause him to attack Howard Canston?

Now that Kimberly had had time to think about it—she'd thought about nothing else all day—she suspected there must be a disagreement of some sort between the two men, something recent, or even something long-standing, but just unresolved. Something that had been building toward an explosion since they'd been under the same roof—something that had absolutely nothing to do with her. And she, unfortunately, just happened to be present when they caught up with each other and tempers finally snapped—in this case, Lachlan's.

But at the time, it had happened too quickly. She'd been utterly shocked. She hadn't even seen Lachlan approaching, which might have at least given her warning of what was about to happen. But there'd been no warning, and in her incredulous state, she'd reacted impulsively. And two wrongs certainly didn't add up to a right.

She shouldn't have hit him. She had regretted it instantly. An act of violence like that was as bad as the one that prompted it, even if breaking her flimsy parasol over his head hadn't hurt him one little bit.

And Lachlan certainly hadn't expected an attack. He'd been surprised enough to demand, shout in fact, "What the devil did you hit me for?"

Perhaps if he hadn't yelled at her, she might have apologized—might have. But she was appalled by her own action by then as much as with his, and instead countered in nearly as loud a voice, "What the devil did you hit *him* for? This is England, not your savage Highlands. People actually discuss things here without resorting to violence."

To that little gem of idiotic enlightenment, he'd taken a very long look at the broken parasol she was still gripping, even raised a sardonic brow at her, and her face had exploded with brilliant color. And just in case she hadn't understood his pointed look, he said derisively, "You've a fine way of discussing things, darlin', that you do."

He'd marched off then without another word, and every line of his tall body proclaimed loudly the high state of fury he was still in. And Kimberly hadn't seen him again all day, nor Howard either, for that matter. The viscount had been so dazed from that single punch that it had taken him a good ten minutes to stand. And by then it was obvious that he was now angry too, and who could blame him? Though he tried admirably not to show it, the glint in his deep blue eyes, at least in the one that wasn't starting to swell closed, was quite chilling.

But when asked why Lachlan had attacked him, this from nosy little Abagail, he'd merely said, "Deuced if I know."

That hadn't satisfied anyone's curiosity, certainly not the two gossips. The general assumption was that jealousy had been Lachlan's motive. Well, Kimberly knew better, and if she ever spoke to that infuriating man again, she just might ask him the real reason. However, it was seriously doubtful that she *would* ever speak to him again.

Once again he'd caused her to behave in a manner she found utterly unacceptable, and she was infuriated. She wished she knew what it was about him that could make her so forget herself, that she could repeatedly throw etiquette and good breeding to the wayside when she *knew* what was proper and acceptable.

Actually, she had experienced more exasperation and real anger in the short time she'd known Lachlan MacGregor than she had in the last several years at home with her tyrant father—although, she had to admit, she'd developed a long-standing habit of ignoring her father. She couldn't quite manage that with the handsome Highlander. No, not at all.

23

"Goodness, you gave me a start," Megan said as she entered the conservatory and noticed the sudden movement to her left. "What in the world are you doing in here in the dark?"

Kimberly shrugged, trailing a finger along a prickly leaf on the table of plants next to her. "It's not all that dark in here, I can see the mansion all lit up through the windows."

"Hmmm, you're quite right," Megan allowed, after a quick glance toward the solid bank of glass facing the house. "Haven't been in here before at night myself, which is why I brought this lamp along—that I won't need now."

Kimberly smiled halfheartedly as Megan extinguished the light. She had wanted to be alone. She was in no mood for conversation, but wasn't going to be rude to the duchess, who had been nothing but kind to her.

So even though she'd avoided answering the question herself, she asked the duchess, "What brings you here this time of night?"

Megan's chuckle was somewhat wicked. "I've come for a rose. My Devlin's been gloating about something all day that has annoyed me no end. He needs a reminder of what to expect if he doesn't stop. I thought a nice long-stemmed rose might get the message to him rather quickly, placed on his pillow tonight—without the rose petals, of course."

Kimberly's laugh was spontaneous; she couldn't help herself, and it felt really good to release it, after the horrid day. Trust the duchess to think of something so cleverly subtle. A stem of thorns on her husband's pillow. Yes, he was bound to figure out exactly what that implied— and have a good laugh over it himself.

Kimberly grinned now. "Well, let's hope he notices the thorns before he lays his head down."

"Oh, I'll make sure of that. Now, care to help me find the perfect rose?"

Kimberly nodded, and they moved down the aisle together to a bed of dark red roses in varying stages of bloom. And then nonchalantly, as she bent to sniff one of the flowers, Megan said, "You know, I'm glad you're here, actually. I've been meaning to ask you, but just haven't managed to find you alone recently, if you've considered the Scot?"

"Considered him?"

"For matrimony."

"No."

Kimberly's answer came so quickly, Megan blinked in surprise. "No? But he's such a handsome devil and so charming, why, he'd make a splendid husband. And he's looking for a wife himself, don't you know."

"Yes, he has many good points," *and just as*

many bad ones, Kimberly added to herself. "But he won't do for me."

Megan scoffed at that. "Of course he would— why don't you think so?"

Kimberly could have said, "Because he's in love with you," but that would have unnecessarily embarrassed them both, so she said instead, "I suppose I should have told you that my father would never approve of a Scotsman."

"You're joking?" Megan said, her expression indicating surprise bordering on shock.

"No, regrettably it's true," Kimberly replied reluctantly, wishing this subject had not come up. "He's quite prejudiced against them."

Megan frowned. "I suppose it's because you live so close to the border? All that violent history there, border raids and all that? Actually, now that you've mentioned it, I know several families who feel that way. Even though hostilities of that sort have mostly ceased in this generation, the animosity has still been inherited—"

"Not in this case," Kimberly cut in. "With my father, it's a personal matter that he's, unfortunately, let encompass all Scots."

"Personal?" Megan pounced on that. "Then you don't share his views?"

"No, I have very few views in common with my father, and certainly not his narrow-minded prejudices."

The duchess sighed in relief. "Well, that's nice to know. But it's—ah, absolutely necessary that he approve of the man you marry?"

"If I want to avoid a scandal."

Megan gasped. "You don't mean he would actually disown you?"

"Most definitely, and without a qualm."

The duchess was back to frowning. "That's—rather hardhearted if you ask me."

"Yes, quite. But I did tell you he's something of a tyrant. Quite unbending and set in his ways."

"Well, I am quite put out about this, I must say—for your sake, that is. I just can't imagine—what if you fell madly in love with a Scot? Not MacGregor, of course," Megan quickly added, "but some other Scotsman you might chance to meet, and he adored you as well. For you to never know the kind of happiness that I do—"

"Ah, but that's different."

"It is?"

"Certainly. It's not as if I have any strong desire to please my father, any more than he's ever had any desire a'tall to please me. No, if something like that occurred, I believe I'd face the scandal."

"Wonderful—I mean, well, a scandal of that sort would be unfortunate, but I can't imagine it being ruinous. Why, even the queen would take your side, as fond as she is of her Scottish subjects. Your father would more likely be condemned for his harshness and stubborn prejudice. If anyone would get the cold shoulder, he would. You would be—ah—well . . ."

"Pitied?"

Megan became flustered. "Well—no—"

Kimberly smiled, patting Megan's arm. "It's all right. It's a moot point anyway, since I have no intention of falling in love with any Scotsman."

Megan sighed again. "Quite right. But you know, I really can't comprehend a father like yours. Mine spoiled me terribly. I can't remember him ever denying me anything—well, except when I wanted Devlin dismissed. He did refuse to do that."

"Dismissed? From what?"

Megan chuckled now. "Ah, but that's a *long* story, m'dear, and as late as it is, best left for another time. I should be getting back to the house, before Devlin sends a brigade of servants looking for me." She bent to pluck one of the roses first, then added, "By the by, what *were* you doing roaming about in here?"

Kimberly groaned inwardly. But there was no point in lying. The duchess, after all, couldn't have missed the gossip making the rounds today. No one could have.

However, she still said, somewhat evasively, "I felt the need for a little solitude, but I couldn't manage to find a room in the house that didn't have someone already in it. I should have just retired, I suppose, but I didn't feel like it at the time."

Megan smiled in understanding and hooked her arm though Kimberly's to lead her back down the aisle. "I get that urge myself sometimes, but in your case—you must know that the kind of gossip running rampant today can't hurt you, m'dear. Actually, it's beneficial. Shows the rest of the gentlemen how popular you are."

Kimberly was *not* going to get into a debate, but so much for evading the subject. "I notice the gentlemen involved choose not to face it."

Megan grinned. "Well, I have it on good authority that Lord Lachlan went off to our nearest tavern to get foxed. And Lord Canston spent the day with his solicitor. He was determined to bring the matter to the courts."

"What?!"

"Oh, never fear, there won't be any more food for the gossip mill on this count. Devlin managed to dissuade him from making matters worse, which that would surely have done. He's been— well, pouting isn't a very dignified word for a viscount, but that describes his temper very well—ever since."

Kimberly couldn't quite manage to envision the virile, athletic viscount pouting, she really couldn't. "Is he planning to end his visit then?"

"No," Megan replied, sounding somewhat disappointed. "I'm sure he'll be back into the thick of things tomorrow. We're having that fox hunt in the morning, remember? I know he wouldn't want to miss that."

Kimberly would be missing that herself. She'd never cared much for hunting of any sort, but she thought foxes were rather cute . . .

"Are you coming back to the house?" Megan asked as they reached the entrance to the conservatory.

"Shortly."

Megan nodded, then glanced once more about the room. "You know, I ought to arrange a picnic in here. Yes, now that I think of it, that's a splendid idea."

Kimberly grinned, shaking her head as she watched Megan saunter off, her single, thorny rose in hand. Now that *she* thought of it, it must be hell to play hostess to so many people, especially when you had to continuously think of ways to keep them entertained.

The duchess had been doing admirably in that respect though, and a picnic in here did sound like a nice idea. The air was moist, humid, but quite pleasant with so many floral scents floating

about. If someone was going to have a picnic in
the heart of winter, a warm conservatory was the
place to do it, and the one here at Sherring Cross
was larger than most. Yes, it actually sounded
like fun and . . .

Got foxed, did he? Good, and she sincerely
hoped Lachlan had one of those horrid headaches
in the morning because of it. The wretched man
deserved no less.

24

Some very loud pounding on her wall came first, then, "Kimber, are you awake?"

She was now. Wide awake. And she also couldn't quite believe that Lachlan would make that kind of racket in the dead of night—once again. He'd been so quiet the past few weeks, she'd begun to think he'd been given a different room when they'd returned from London.

God, what time was it? The heavy drapes in her room were drawn closed, giving her no clue. Yet she recalled the difficulty she'd had in getting to sleep. Midnight had come and gone when she last remembered pounding her pillow . . .

"Kimber?"

The sound she made could only be called a growl as she tossed her covers back, shot to her knees to face the wall, and gave it a hard pound herself. "Be quiet in there! Have you lost your mind? Do you have any idea what time—"

"I'm . . . dying."

"What?!" she shrieked.

Her heart had skipped a beat. She got no further answer, even when she pounded again on the wall. Fear coursed through her the like she'd never felt before. She bounded off her bed and ran toward the door with no thought of anything except getting to him. She'd break his door down if she had to—but that wasn't necessary. It opened to her touch, slammed open actually, because she hadn't paused in her race to get there.

She found him where she expected, by the wall where he'd been pounding. He was on his knees there, bent over, his head nearly touching the floor, and so still. Not a movement could she detect in the candlelight that flickered about the room, not a breath, and her own breath was held as she slid to her knees beside him.

"Lachlan?"

She grasped his head, heard his moan, and felt such incredible relief, she would have cried if it wasn't temporary. But it didn't last. He wasn't dead yet, but she still didn't know what was wrong with him, and her panic shot right back up there.

"Where do you hurt? Tell me! Are you bleeding? Have you been shot or—"

"You came?"

"Of course I came. You said you were dying. Now tell me, *how* are you dying?"

"Poison."

"Oh, God, I don't know what to do for that," she cried. "How did it happen? How long ago? I'll send for a doctor immediately—"

"Nay, dinna leave me."

One hand came out from under him, where his arms had been wrapped across his belly. It reached blindly for her, encountered her ankle, and squeezed tight around it. His condition hadn't affected his strength yet. His grip was like steel, making her wince.

"You have to let me go for a minute, Lachlan, just long enough to find someone who can go for a doctor."

"A doctor canna help me, lass."

Her fear made her snap, "Don't say that! You're not going to die, do you hear me? There must be something that can be done for you, and a doctor would know what."

"A bed is all I'm needing, Kimber, and a gentle hand tae see me through the worst of it. D'you think you could find a wee bit of compassion tae help me?"

"I'm *trying* to help you," she began, but then said more gently, "All right, come, I'll help you to your bed first. Sit up for me, so we can get you to your feet."

She tried lifting his shoulders, but without his cooperation, they wouldn't budge at all. There was just no way she was going to be able to move him without some assistance on his part.

And then his torso rose on its own, with his other hand pushing, then bracing against the floor to keep him upright. Facing him now, seeing him completely, she realized he was still fully clothed, had apparently only just come to his room when he'd started pounding for her. He was also a mess, his hair bedraggled, dirt and straw clinging to him as if he'd taken a tumble in a stable but forgot to dust himself off. But what gave her pause was the alcohol fumes, so strong that he could have been doused in the stuff.

She had forgotten that Megan had told her he'd

gone off to get drunk, and she demanded now, "Have you been drinking *all* day?"

"Nay, I slept—I dinna remember where."

"And went right back to drinking some more?"

He smiled lopsidedly. "Och, I had a powerful thirst as I recall."

Kimberly sat back on her heels. He didn't look like a man who was dying. He merely looked sotted, smelled it, and come to think of it, sounded it too.

"How did you get poisoned, Lachlan? And do you know it for a fact, that you are?"

"Poisoned?"

Her eyes narrowed on him. "You said you'd been poisoned, remember?"

"Och, aye, the drink'll do that tae you. I've never felt this rotten—"

"You wretch! You scare me half to death, telling me you were dying, when all you are is foxed?"

She leaped up, furious, but she forgot he still had hold of her ankle. She didn't even manage a full turn toward the door before her balance was lost and she fell backward, landing on her behind. She was able to catch herself on her elbows before she ended up completely prone.

"Now that's an invitation I canna refuse, darlin'," she heard him drawl.

"What?"

She'd been startled by the fall, and his remark made no sense until she took her eyes off of him to glance down at herself. Her nightgown—there'd been no thought for grabbing a robe in her haste—was twisted about her hips and hiked up, one side above her knee, the other halfway up her calf. And her knees, God help her, were bent upright, her feet flat on the floor, and spread wide apart.

She understood his remark now, crude as it was. And worse, he was already starting to crawl toward her, albeit slowly and not too steadily. But apparently, he had every intention of placing his body on top of hers to accept that "invitation" he'd alluded to. Just the thought of him doing so sent a core of heat straight to her vitals, which amazed and appalled her at once.

Her reaction to that, however, aside from a choking sound of embarrassment, was first to snap her knees together, then bring her foot, the one he wasn't still holding, straight up to plant flat against his nearing chest.

"Don't *even* think about it," she warned.

"Nay?"

"Absolutely not."

He sat back on his haunches, swayed once, righted himself, then frowned down at her. "You're a coldhearted woman, Kimber, that you are."

"Where you're concerned, I have to be," she mumbled in reply. She hadn't said this for his benefit, yet he still heard her and actually perked up.

"Really? Now why is that, darlin'? Can it be you're tempted and fighting it?"

That was much too close to the truth for her comfort, and she sat up straight. "Can it be you've lost your mind again? Look at you, reeking of spirits, bedraggled, blurry-eyed. Tempted? By what, pray tell?"

She came just short of snorting. And to her ears she sounded believable, had used just enough scorn to make him wince. The trouble was, Lachlan was too handsome to begin with. A little messy and inebriated wasn't going to make him any less desirable.

"I wish I could say the same about you, lass. You're blurry-eyed yourself, and after that tumble, just as bedraggled, yet I'm wanting—"

"Not another word!" she cut in frantically, afraid she would hear something that might sway her. "And let go of my foot so I can leave. You had no business waking me in the first place, and I've got no business being in here."

He looked down at his hand on her ankle and seemed surprised that it was there. But he did release her with a sigh. "Go on then, back tae your warm bed. I'll abide the night here on this cold floor, since I canna make it tae my own bed."

Her eyes narrowed on him as she rose to her feet. "Was that supposed to make me feel sorry for you?"

"Nay, that would take a wee bit of compassion, which you're proving you dinna have."

"I'll have you know I have just as much compassion as any other woman," she replied stiffly. "Why else would I have come running in here?"

"Aye, you did come. But you can see how miserable I am, yet you'll no' stay tae help me."

"What I see is that you're in a condition that was self-inflicted, and so undeserving of sympathy. What possessed you to drink so much?"

"You dinna want tae be knowing the answer tae that, Kimber, believe me."

She ground her teeth in exasperation. And now, as so many times before, it was on the tip of her tongue to retort that she didn't like hearing him shorten her name to Kimber, any more than she liked his calling her darling. Usually she was too angry to tell him or some other point was more pressing, which was why she hadn't mentioned it sooner. And this time it would really be pointless, since she doubted he'd remember her complaint in the morning.

"Fine. Don't tell me. I only asked to be civil, since I hardly care. Your motivations don't concern me in the—" She stopped when she realized she was protesting far too much, and switched to a blasé tone to finish, "Well, good night, Lachlan. Try not to make any more noise, will you?"

He said nothing as she moved to the door, nothing when she reached it. She wasn't going to look back at him, wasn't going to feel sorry for him. If he still felt wretched, well, it was no more than he deserved.

It wasn't until she was on the other side of the door and closing it that she heard, "I need you."

Kimberly groaned. She dropped her forehead against the door, closing her eyes, fighting the wealth of emotions those three words provoked. But it was no good. There was no way in hell she could ignore that plea. Not from him. Not put that way.

She supposed she could be grateful, though, that it was only aid he was needing from her, because she wasn't sure just now if she could resist those same words if said in that other context. And for her to end up in bed with him again, just because of some small thing he said, God forbid, she couldn't be that much of a fool, could she?

25

Kimberly moved the heavy drapery aside to peer out the window. Incredible. The vague sounds of activity out in the hall and outside the mansion, a cheery whistle, a bang, a bell tinkling, a low-voiced greeting somewhere, all should have given her warning, yet she still found it hard to believe that dawn had arrived—and she was still in Lachlan's room. How many hours had she been there? Too many.

She glanced back at him now, sound asleep in his bed. His apparent unconsciousness was deceiving, of course, as she'd learned to her exasperation. But this was the first time she'd been able to move away from that bed without him drawing her back.

She shook her head with a sigh. She should have stuck to her guns—helping him was undoubtedly a mistake that she would live to regret, yet what else could she have done? At least she'd been brisk and surly about her assistance, so if he remembered anything at all, which was really doubtful, he'd think her help had been given grudgingly.

But help him she did. She'd even relented and removed some of his clothes once she got him into his bed, at least his shoes and coat, to make him more comfortable. And the moment his head had touched the pillow, he'd fallen asleep.

However, that didn't last, as she discovered the first time she tried to leave him. When she'd moved away from the side of the bed, he would groan as if he were dying. And he never even opened his eyes. He just somehow sensed it. And each time it happened she thought he'd settled down enough so that she could get back to bed herself.

It wasn't a mere ploy either, as she first suspected. For all his talk and cajolery earlier, he had been in a really wretched state. And she had attended it all, with cold compresses when his body tried to sweat out the poison, with a gentle hand when it came out quicker into a handy basin. He'd rested easier after that, yet still, when she left his side, he'd make some sound to draw her back.

She could barely keep her eyes open now. She'd had only an hour or so sleep before he'd disturbed her last night, and none afterward. But moaning and groaning from him or not, she was going to be in her bed this morning before Mary arrived to wake her. That gossipy maid of hers was not going to be given the opportunity to speculate on where Kimberly had spent the night.

She moved back across the room to stop by the bed for one last time. Lachlan's sleep did seem to be more peaceful now. And he looked so innocent she had to smile. But even the devil, she supposed, might look innocent in sleep. And there was nothing innocent about the things this man could make her feel. Even now, she had an urge to smooth back that unruly lock of hair that had fallen over his forehead again—just as she'd done a number of times during the night. She got out of there before she gave in to the urge.

It wasn't all that much later that Kimberly was rudely awakened, not by Mary's gentle tones, which had come and been ignored, but once again by pounding on her wall. It brought her sitting up in bed, blinking, trying to get her eyes to open, or at least, to stay open.

It came again though, not the pounding, but a very obvious crash of some sort. Something, or someone, had definitely fallen to the floor. And it was that noise that recalled to her sluggish mind Lachlan's condition and what had passed during the night. The fool man was up and about already, yet his head was probably coming off with the worst headache of the century, and that was why he was stumbling into things and making another God-awful racket.

Her head turned slowly to glare at the wall behind her, but she knew damn well she wouldn't get back to sleep until it was quiet again. However, there was no rush this time as there had been last night. She wasn't even angry. She was too *tired* to be angry. So she took some time to slip on her robe and a pair of slippers, and even spared a glance in the mirror above her vanity— which was a mistake.

She really did look as exhausted as she felt. Her eyes were still drooping, refusing to open fully. Her hair was in wild disarray. It was the wanton

ook that Lachlan had found so appealing, but
Kimberly found it unladylike, and so totally unacceptable.

But a brush and a quick splash of water righted
her appearance to some degree, the best she could
hope for, she supposed, when all she wanted to
do was crawl back into her comfortable bed. But
during the few extra minutes she took, there was
yet another crash next door, and some serious
sounds of complaint, grunts and groans and the
like. She was beginning to think that Lachlan was
just falling out of his bed, albeit more than once—
except, there had been that pounding against her
wall again, and his bed was nowhere near the
wall that separated their rooms.

She sighed, wondering how the devil she had
been drafted to be his nursemaid. But there was
no help for it. No one else would come to his aid
so early in the morning. And where *were* those
two clansmen who had come here with Lachlan?
Sleeping off the same overindulgence in their
own beds? They should be assisting their lord,
not her.

Kimberly left her room before she worked herself into a real disgust. But all thoughts in that
direction ended abruptly, as did her step, when
she discovered Lachlan's door wide open, and the
Duchess of Wrothston standing there, biting her
lips, wringing her hands, and otherwise looking
quite distressed as she gazed into the room.

Moving again, quickly now, Kimberly came to
stand beside Megan, but she had trouble believing what she could now witness in that room for
herself. The Duke of Wrothston was in there and
he was quite simply beating Lachlan senseless.
And Lachlan, that idiot, wouldn't stay down to

put an end to it—*if* that would put an end to it. Kimberly wasn't so sure. The duke was clearly enraged. Yet it was a moot point as long as Lachlan kept getting to his feet each time he was knocked down. And how many times had that happened already?

By the look of him, too many. His nose was bleeding, his cheeks bore the prints of Devlin's fists. A punch to Lachlan's belly produced one of those grunts Kimberly had previously heard through the wall. Another to his jaw sent him back to the floor again, his arm slamming against a side table, which managed to topple with him.

Kimberly winced, imagining how each pain he was receiving was likely being multiplied a thousand times by his headache. He was holding up remarkably well, all things considered, but he certainly wasn't defending himself; he seemed to be too dazed to even know what was happening to him . . . and Kimberly was unable to just stand there and watch as Megan was doing.

She was definitely awake now, wide awake, and she demanded, "What, may I ask, is going on?"

Megan was startled at first, not having noticed Kimberly's quiet arrival. But she glanced her way and tsked before she answered, "You know, I was actually starting to like that Highlander, now that he's stopped pest—ah, well, it's a shame he reverted to form and tried his thieving here. I am really quite disappointed, truly I am."

Kimberly was given pause, nearly blinked, did finally gasp. "Thieving? Are you saying he has stolen something from Sherring Cross?"

Megan nodded. "Not just something, mind you, but one of our finest stallions, as well as two of the breeding mares. It's obvious he had intentions of starting his own breeding farm, to assist in his financial difficulties, I suppose. And so unnecessary, when a wife was all that was needed to put an end to those difficulties of his.''

Kimberly was about to point out that it really was unnecessary. So why would Lachlan take that risk? But she got distracted by another crash. Lachlan had slammed into the wall next to one of the windows. Someone had flooded the room with daylight by opening the drapery, possibly Devlin before he dragged Lachlan out of bed, so he could better see to slam his fists into the Scotsman. But with the drapery open . . . if Lachlan had fallen back just one foot to the left, he could have gone right through that window, or at the very least, severely cut himself by breaking the glass.

Seeing that, Kimberly's temper exploded. ''Stop it this instant!'' she shouted into the room, or to be more accurate, right at the duke. ''Can't you see he's in no condition to receive such treatment? He was so foxed last night, it will be days before he is completely sober.''

When there was no immediate response from the duke, Megan added her worried tones, ''Devlin, she's right, stop it. Haven't you noticed that MacGregor isn't defending himself?'' and turning to Kimberly in a whispered aside, ''How did you know about his condition?''

Kimberly blushed, but recovered quickly and improvised, ''He woke me, a number of times, with his retching, falling down, groaning. I could have sworn he was dying, he sounded so awful— and you did say he'd gone off yesterday to get foxed, so I assumed . . .''

"Yes, quite right and a logical deduction—Devlin, stop it, d'you hear me? You're killing the miserable wretch."

"Did I . . . neglect to mention . . . that was my . . . intention?" the duke huffed between blows.

Megan tsked again, but in another side whisper to Kimberly, she confided, "I believe Devlin wants to know what MacGregor did with the animals. Otherwise, he'll have him carted off to gaol. He could possibly be made to see reason if he gets the horses back. Possibly, mind you. Although with the way he feels about that man . . ."

It wasn't at all likely was what Megan had left unsaid. Not very encouraging.

"Has he bothered to ask where the horses were taken?" Kimberly thought to ask.

"Certainly, but the Scot denied any knowledge of the theft."

"But you had proof, of course?"

"Well, yes—I suppose." Megan frowned. "The young man who discovered the theft, one of the grooms, claims he heard a Scottish brogue just before his head was bashed. And with Lachlan's well-known, as well as admitted, history of reaving, I'm afraid that's all the proof my husband needed."

It did sound bad. And Kimberly certainly had no reason to defend the man, despite the most ridiculous urge she had to do so. However, that wasn't concrete proof by any means. A mere accent? There were other Scots on the property, including some of the servants. If the duke and duchess would think about the theft logically, it was much more likely the thief had sneaked onto the property to do his stealing and was long gone by now.

There was, of course, the fact that Lachlan obviously resented the duke, just because he was married to his true love, and so would probably have no qualms about stealing from him. There was also the straw that had been clinging to his coat, proving he'd been in a stable, though that could have been any stable, and at any time prior to his reaching his room last night.

However, from what little Kimberly knew about him, she was sure he had more honor than to steal from a man who had offered him hospitality, no matter how he felt personally. He might be despicable in some ways, but she would wager that wasn't one of them.

Furthermore, the fact that Lachlan was a known thief did not convict him out of hand, especially since he had no need to take such a risk. Also considering his sottish condition yesterday, considering he hadn't actually been seen taking the horses . . . His condition . . .?

"When was this theft supposed to have occurred?" Kimberly asked.

"About an hour before dawn."

Kimberly swayed in her relief. "But he was wi—"

She stopped abruptly, horrified that she had almost said *with me*. There was no way she could admit that, unless she wanted to destroy her reputation completely. There had to be another way to prove Lachlan's innocence, and now she knew he *was* innocent, without condemning herself.

She coughed to cover her blunder, even sputtered a bit, then finished, "—was in a wretched state, from what I could hear of it. And I'm sure he woke me with his groaning long before dawn. Actually, I'm sure it was closer to midnight the

first time I heard him stumbling about in here.
Are you certain of the time?"

It was the duke who answered. Apparently
Lachlan had been knocked out cold by his last
punch.

"My man said he checked the time before he
left his room in the stable to investigate the noise
that woke him. An hour before dawn, it was. Are
you certain, Lady Kimberly, that it was Mac-
Gregor you heard in here, or could it have just as
likely been one of his lackeys, deliberately making enough noise to wake you so you would assume it was this blackguard?"

Kimberly groaned inwardly. She couldn't answer that truthfully either. But she was angry
again, because Lachlan was lying there on the
floor unconscious, severely beaten, when he was
innocent.

So she said in a condemning tone, "I'm certain
of one thing. I don't see a mark on you, Your
Grace, so I can only assume the Highlander there
did not fight back a'tall. I can only assume that
he didn't defend himself, either because you are
his host, or because you are the Duke of Wrothston, or perhaps because he had consumed more
spirits than any man could tolerate and was still
too foxed to understand what you were accusing
him of. And in that case, which is the more likely
case, he would also have been in no condition to
have committed this crime."

"Or he could have been so foxed he foolishly
thought he could get away with it."

Devlin St. James obviously wasn't going to listen to reason. He'd found Lachlan guilty in his
mind, and that was that.

However, Kimberly wasn't about to concede

now. The alternative was the truth, which could be used as a last resort, but hopefully, that wouldn't be necessary.

"I would say more investigation is called for," she said. "I believe I have raised doubts that can't be easily ignored. At the very least, this matter should be postponed until Lord MacGregor sobers up completely and can answer your accusation with a clear mind."

"Perhaps she's right, Dev," Megan intervened. "He really didn't seem very clearheaded when you woke him."

He glared at them both. He really was in no mood to postpone anything.

But he finally nodded curtly and allowed, albeit in a grumble, "Very well, I will wait to summon the magistrate. However, guards will be posted at his door. He's not going to escape this time, by God, without paying for his actions, I promise you that."

Kimberly sighed with relief. Well, she'd bought Lachlan some time at any rate. Now, hopefully, he would be able to defend himself to everyone's satisfaction, without dragging her into it—that was if he could talk at all when he regained consciousness and sobriety. Those swelling and cracked lips from one of Devlin's meaner punches suggested he might have some difficulty in that regard.

Damn, she was going to have to play nursemaid again.

26

The door opened after one brief knock. Not that Lachlan would have said anything loud enough to be heard, to keep the intruder out, when he didn't want to disturb the lass who had fallen asleep in his arms. But he did swear beneath his breath, and again when he saw it was his cousin Gilleonan who had just barged in.

Lachlan scowled at him as an attempted warning to keep him from saying anything, but his scowl turned into a wince before Gilleonan noticed it—his face was just too battered to accommodate a scowl comfortably. And his cousin was too surprised to pay attention to it anyway. That was if he could get his eyes off of Kimberly to even notice anything else.

"What is *she* doin' in here and—" Gilleonan paused to bend down so he could better see Kimberly's face, tucked away as it was on Lachlan's chest. "Sleepin'? D'ye ken she's sleepin' on ye, mon?"

Lachlan could hardly miss that fact, as he'd

been sitting there holding her for more than an hour, without moving an inch for fear of waking her. They'd been sitting on the edge of the bed, after she'd managed to rouse him with her wet cloths, and she, sitting sideways, had been dabbing at one of the cuts on his lips when between one moment and the next, she'd simply nodded off to sleep.

He'd caught her just before she started to topple over—toward the floor. So she'd swayed against his side instead, dropped one arm into his lap, snuggled her head halfway onto his chest, and, after a small sigh, she hadn't made another sound since.

But Lachlan wasn't going to explain all that to his cousin. "Be quiet," he mouthed.

"What?"

"Shhh!"

Gilleonan blinked, then comprehended, "Oh, aye," he said, reverting to a whisper. "But what *is* she doing in here? And for that matter, what're those two braw Sassenachs doin' outside yer door as if they be guardin' it?"

"Perhaps guarding it?"

Gilleonan snorted at his dry tone, but finally happened to glance at Lachlan, and that prompted a sharply indrawn breath that was quickly followed by, "Faith, who took a mallet tae yer puir face?"

Lachlan winced, this time intentionally. "It looks that bad then, does it?"

"It doesna look good, mon. Did she—"

Lachlan tried again for a scowl. "Dinna be ridiculous." He settled for scoffing. " 'Twas our hot-tempered host—at least, I *think* it was."

"Think? How could ye no' be sure aboot the

worst beatin' ye've ever taken? And believe me, Lachlan, ye've never looked this bad."

Lachlan half hissed, "Because I was no' quite awake when it began, or completely sober yet, for that matter. I was seeing double, triple—"

Gilleonan's eyes widened. "So ye did go off and get foxed? I figured as much, as angry as ye was yesterday mornin'. Punching that puir lord, and for no good reason as I could see. Knew ye'd be regretting that—"

"Let's no' discuss that, if you please. I canna imagine what devil got into me either. But the condition I ended up in somewhere in the wee hours o' the night bears no description that I know of," Lachlan said in self-disgust. "I dinna remember half o' it, if you mun know."

"Dinna remember?"

Gilleonan started to chuckle, but Lachlan managed a scowl finally, despite the pain it caused him, and he sobered quick enough, coughed a bit, then asked, "So why was he beatin' on ye—och, dinna tell me ye finally bedded his duchess and he found out?"

"I did not," Lachlan said indignantly.

"Then why?"

"I've a wee vague memory that he's thinking I stole some o' his bonny horses."

"Ah, did ye then?"

It was a bit hard to whisper and threaten at the same time, but Lachlan managed it with, "I'm going tae be murdering you for that, Gill."

"Och, since when can ye no' ken I be joshin' ye?" Gilleonan demanded.

"I could say the same."

Gilleonan blinked, then softly chuckled. "Oh, aye, I knew that."

That being one of Ranald's favorite phrases, rather than Gilleonan's, Lachlan would have grinned if it wouldn't have hurt to do so. "I'm no' sure about any of it, Gill, but if I've got guards at my door, I'm sure I'll be hearing about it all soon enough."

"And the lass there?"

Lachlan glanced down at the dark golden head tucked carefully under his chin, his expression softening. "Lady Kimberly has been an angel, trying tae patch me up. But I'm thinking I may have disturbed her sleep a wee bit last night, since she couldna stay awake long enough tae finish wi' me."

"She wasna able to tell ye what this was all about, then?" Gilleonan questioned.

"I didna get around tae asking her 'afore she fell asleep on me."

That wasn't true at all. He'd asked her a number of times what she knew of the duke's visit, but each time she'd put him off with a "Be still," or "Shhh," or "How can I tend you if you don't keep your mouth shut?" So he'd stopped asking, figuring he'd get answers soon enough. But she'd fallen asleep instead. And his pleasure in holding her was far greater than his curiosity, so he'd had no thought to waking her for any more questioning.

But Gilleonan didn't need to know any of that. Lachlan suggested, "Since you dinna appear to be under suspicion wi' me—at least no' yet, see what you can find out."

"Aye, I'll fetch Ranald and we'll nose about the stables till we have the whole of it. 'Tis probably no more'n some guest wanderin' off in the dark wi' the wrong horse, and he hasna realized it yet."

"Aye, no doubt."

But Lachlan didn't really think so. St. James wouldn't go berserk over something like that. He'd require something in the way of proof, but for the life of him, Lachlan couldn't imagine what that might be.

Gilleonan had turned back toward the door, but stopped to suggest, "Ye ought tae carry the lass tae her room so ye can get some rest yerself."

"I'm in no condition tae be doing that."

"I could—"

"Nay," Lachlan cut in a bit too quickly. "She's no' bothering me."

Gilleonan raised a brow at that, but when he got no further response, he shrugged and left. Lachlan sighed as the door closed again.

Kimberly might not be bothering him in the sense he had implied, but with her soft body pressed against his side she was definitely bothering him in another sense. And as miserable as he felt, with aches noticeable in just about every part of his body, he found it rather incredible that he could want her right now, and want her badly. Particularly when he couldn't do a damn thing about it at the moment, even if she were awake and agreeable.

He should have let his cousin take her out of there, or at least, he ought to nudge her awake long enough to get her moving back to her own room. But he was loath to let go of her, even to relieve the state she had put him in. What was one more discomfort, after all, when he had so many? And besides, he *liked* having her right where she was.

So he turned his mind to other thoughts, and foremost in those thoughts was the Duke of Wrothston and the beating he'd received at his hands.

The man might have felt justified, for whatever mistaken reason, to administer such a thorough trouncing. That Lachlan hadn't been sober enough to protect himself even a little was a moot point.

Actually, one lucky punch in the beginning that had been intended for his eye, but had slammed into his forehead instead when Lachlan attempted to duck, had pretty much decided the outcome. From then on Lachlan was too dazed to even know he was being pounded on. But he would wager the beating wouldn't have been quite so vicious if St. James didn't feel he had past grudges to settle as well.

He'd have to wait and see what the duke had to say for himself. On the one hand, he felt St. James was justified in getting a few licks in, whether he knew it or not, and not for any past grudge, or this current thing, but because of Megan. It was permissible to love another man's wife as long as you did so from afar, no one else knew about it, and there was no active pursuit involved. But he'd lost his head a wee bit when he'd found the bonny Megan again. He'd tried to lure the man's wife away from him, and at the moment he wasn't feeling too proud about that.

On the other hand, he'd already taken a beating for that past grudge, and wasn't willing to accept another for it. Nor was he willing to take the blame and beating for something he didn't do. Steal some of the primest stock in England that would be so easy to find simply because they were such outstanding specimens? He'd have to be utterly crazy.

But he wasn't going to react, one way or another, until he'd heard all the facts. So all he could do now was wait and see what St. James had to say for himself.

27

"Well, shall we see what the blackguard has to say for himself?" Devlin said.

Beside him, Megan frowned, and not for the first time that day. "I still don't think you've calmed down enough. This could wait until morning, after you've had a chance to sleep on it."

Devlin shook his head emphatically. "You've held me off the entire day, and even managed to get me to sit through a bloody uncomfortable dinner, with Lady Kimberly glowering at me the whole while, though I can't imagine why she should find fault with me."

Megan restrained the urge to snort, just. "Perhaps because she thinks you've been a bit unfair in your dealing with the Highlander thus far? He really wasn't in any condition to face your wrath this morning. Actually, with you as angry as you were, I don't think perfect health would have helped the Scot a'tall, though Kimberly might think otherwise."

That merely produced another glower. "Not another minute will this be delayed."

That said, he gave his wife no further opportunity for protest. He opened the door and marched into the Scot's room. She followed on his heels, as did the three burly servants who'd been brought along to cart MacGregor off to the magistrate after Devlin finished with him. Of course, with as big a man as Lachlan was, it might have taken more than three if he hadn't already suffered a beating.

The room was dark and quite chilly. The fire that had been lit at some time during the day had completely burned out, and the guards at the door had probably scared the maids away. But from what little light filtered in from the hall, MacGregor was located in his bed, and once again was apparently asleep.

Megan tsked. The man's condition supported her contention that this interrogation really should be delayed until morning. But Devlin was already giving orders to the three servants to get the fire going and light the lamps about the room, and in his obvious sour mood, they were quick to obey. So she didn't suggest *again* that this ought to wait. Further aggravating him at this point wouldn't benefit the Highlander. Not that she wanted to benefit him.

Lady Kimberly might have raised a few doubts that morning, but Megan still tended to agree with her husband. She just felt—well, rather sorry for Lachlan, all things considered. And she dreaded having to tell Margaret what he'd done. So far, the matter had been kept under wraps, so to speak, but soon enough it would become common knowledge. And Margaret was going to be terribly upset. Not only that, but she would un-doubtedly hold herself responsible as well, for having invited him here, nephew or not.

"That's enough light," she heard Devlin say now. "Fetch that basin of water over there. I want to be certain he's completely awake—"

"Oh, for heaven's sake," Megan interrupted and marched over to the bed, ordering loudly on the way, "Get up, MacGregor, and go splash some water on your face—before it's done . . . for you . . ."

Her words trailed off and her step halted as she got a good look at the man in the bed, who had opened his eyes and was even attempting to sit up, though with some very obvious difficulty. His cheeks were bruised, the left side of his head was also swollen, his lips were puffy and scabbed, and there was a knotty lump on his forehead that the lock of hair that had fallen there couldn't quite conceal.

The only undamaged area of his face appeared to be his eyes. Devlin had missed them com-pletely. But Lachlan, or someone, had removed his shirt to sleep, and with the covers now dropped to his waist, the damage to his chest and stomach area was also revealed. With that mass of dark bruises, he could count himself very lucky indeed if he didn't have a few cracked ribs.

"If the look of him distresses you, m'dear, you need only leave the room," Devlin said behind her. "There's no reason for you to be here—"

"Not a'tall," Megan cut in, steeling herself to continue briskly, "Are you awake enough to an-swer to the charges you've been accused of, MacGregor?"

"Nay, I'll be partaking of that cold water, if you dinna mind giving me a moment—"

"You haven't...begun yet...have you?" Kimberly huffed from the doorway.

She was completely out of breath. As soon as she realized the duke and duchess had disappeared from the gathering below, she had raced all the way upstairs. She took a deep breath now before continuing, "You were supposed to inform me when you were ready to question him, Your Grace. I believe I told you I wished to be present."

Devlin sighed. "Lady Kimberly, there is absolutely no reason for you to be present—"

"Nonetheless, I must insist. After the treatment I witnessed him receiving this morning, *someone* should be here who is impartial."

"Your defense can hardly be considered impartial," Devlin replied.

Kimberly gasped at that. "I am not defending him. I merely pointed out —"

"Enough!"

It was Lachlan who interrupted, and so loudly, even he winced at his tone. But he'd stood up beside the bed, and looked quite furious, and that fury was directed straight at the Duke of Wrothston.

"Oh, God," said Kimberly.

"You've roused me from my sleep twice now," he continued more moderately in tone, if just as angrily, "beat me senseless, and left me locked in this room wi'out sustenance the whole day long. So I'm thinking you'll be answering my questions, St. James, and you'll be starting wi' what the blasted hell I'm being accused of."

"That has already been—" Devlin began.

"Repeat it, mon," Lachlan interrupted again, a stony glint in his light green eyes. "I wouldna be asking if I had the memory of it, would I now?"

Devlin scowled for a moment, but then nodded, if curtly. "Very well, I have three very valuable missing horses, and a groom who heard your voice in the stable just prior to being rendered unconscious."

"*My* voice?"

"Now just a minute," Kimberly inserted. "The duchess said it was merely a Scots brogue that had been heard, and that hardly—"

"Lady Kimberly, I appreciate your concern for justice," Lachlan said. "But if you please, would you be letting me do the questioning?"

Put so gently, it would be churlish of her to refuse. She nodded, without meeting his eyes. She was, in fact, still mortified over her own behavior that morning. To have fallen asleep on him, literally *on* him . . .

Lachlan noted her pink cheeks and guessed the cause. When she had finally awakened in his arms, she had been so embarrassed that she had fled the room with a few mumbled excuses that he hadn't caught. He had seriously thought about going after her, until he remembered the guards at the door. So he'd gone back to sleep himself, and, apparently, slept the day through.

But he was finally going to have this bizarre incident explained to his satisfaction. He addressed the duke again, asking, "What the lady just said, is that true?"

"That was the young man's accounting when he first recovered this morning and was still somewhat muddled from the blow he received, and that was sufficient evidence for *me*," Devlin

replied. "However, he has since been reques-
tioned thoroughly about it and has put a name to
the voice he heard—yours, MacGregor."

"Och, now, I've ne'er met the mon," Lachlan
said, "but he knows me so well he can recognize
my voice, is that what you're telling me?"

"He doesn't claim to have met you either,
MacGregor, but he knows you by sight. You're
bloody well hard to miss. And he's heard you
speak before."

"Now that's interesting," Lachlan pointed out.
"When I'm no' in the habit of talking tae the
grooms, at least your English ones, since I can
barely understand them and their local dialects."

Kimberly, apparently, was the only one who
found that amusing, considering Lachlan's own
Scots brogue. She had to actually struggle to keep
the serious look that everyone else was wearing.

But Lachlan hadn't finished his remarks. "So
let me see if I have this right, St. James. You're
accusing me of bludgeoning your stableman and
making off with three of your prize stock?"

"Exactly."

"And I suppose I am tae have hid them nearby,
since here I am wi'out them? Or perhaps sent
them on tae the Highlands, where no one would
take note of them on the road, common animals
that they are?"

"Your sarcasm isn't called for," Devlin said.
"There are any number of ways that you could
have planned for their transport, including a covered wagon that would keep them hidden."

"Och, so now this was a well-planned crime,
was it? No' just some spur o' the moment plan
that my drunken mind concocted? Yet I decide

tae go through wi' it, when I'm so drunk I can barely stand on me own feet?"

"Were you really foxed, MacGregor, or only pretending to be?"

"Well now, I believe you've a tavern nearby that can answer that for you, and in some detail, I'm sure. I vaguely recall they kicked me out o' it at one time during the day, or was that night already? I'm no' too clear about that. I had tae sleep off a bit o' the drink 'afore they'd let me back in, which I did in their stable—I think. I'm no' tae sure about that either—except I did get back in, though they werena tae happy tae see me again."

"That will, of course, be checked out, though it hardly matters. You were still overheard in the stable just moments before my groom was attacked."

"And who was I supposed tae have been talking tae, that your groom overheard me? One of my two kinsmen here wi' me? As it happens, neither of my cousins joined me yesterday in my folly, that being my drinking, mind you, not my supposed horse stealing. And knowing my cousins as I do, they each—begging your pardon, ladies—likely had company throughout the night, of the fair kind, which can be easily verified or no' by asking them. But then—when am I supposed tae have committed this crime? In the day, when anyone could have seen me? Or late in the night?"

Devlin snorted. "An hour before dawn, as if you didn't know."

Lachlan's eyes narrowed. "I was in my bed at that particular time."

"So you say. Or perhaps, like your cousins, you weren't alone and can prove it?"

Kimberly's cheeks started to heat up. She imagined Lachlan's eyes on her, though it was probably her guilty conscience that made her think so. All she had to do was speak up at that point and admit that she was with him all those late hours of the night—and ruin her reputation for good.

"Nay, there was no one lying 'aside me that I recall," Lachlan finally stated. Kimberly's cheeks still bloomed with color. He had worded his denial in an entirely truthful manner. She'd been sitting beside him all night, not lying beside him.

But glancing around the room, she saw that no one was noticing her hot cheeks; all eyes were still on Lachlan. The duke now said somewhat triumphantly, "Then as I thought, you can't prove that you were in your bed."

"I dinna have too many memories o' last night, but getting tae my room a wee bit after midnight is one o' them—among a few others. 'Twas no' a pleasant night. I was sick a goodly part o' it."

"So now you're going to say you simply don't *recall* the theft?"

" 'Tis true I drank too much; however, I wouldna do something in that sotted condition that I wouldna do when sober, and I'm telling you, St. James, I wouldna steal your blasted horses."

Devlin all but sneered. "If that's the best you have to say in your defense, MacGregor, then I'm wasting my time here."

"I'm telling you I didna do it, and you'll be giving me a chance tae prove it."

"You mean a chance to escape?"

"Escape tae where, St. James? You know where

tae find me. Or do you think I'd be giving up my home for your horses, ne'er to return tae the Highlands?"

Even Devlin must have realized that wasn't likely, because instead of addressing that point, he demanded, "Then how do you mean to prove it?"

"By finding your horses and the real thief," Lachlan said simply.

"I'll find my horses, and I've already got the thief. You."

"Nay, you dinna. Or are you afraid you'll have tae be apologizing tae me for being wrong?"

There was a long moment of silence before Devlin growled, "Very well, I'll give you a week. And then you'll be eating those words."

Lachlan grinned slowly, or at least, what he thought passed for a grin. "Or you'll be feeling my own fists—my way of accepting your apology."

To that, Devlin merely snorted before he stalked out of the room. Kimberly, still standing in the doorway, quickly moved out of his way. But she didn't realize Megan would leave so abruptly behind him, herding the burly servants with her. She was, in fact, suddenly alone with Lachlan again, and acutely aware of it.

Embarrassed again, she still felt compelled to tell Lachlan, "Thank you."

His brow quirked up. It actually still worked correctly, when most of his other facial features refused to do his exact bidding.

"For what, darlin'?"

"For not asking me to verify that you were telling the truth."

"Would you have?" he asked softly.

She wished he wouldn't use that tone. It made her feel all mushy inside. But as for his question, she couldn't admit that yes, she wouldn't have let them cart him off to the magistrate, if it came to that. He might get the wrong impression, that she cared about him, when she didn't, she really didn't.

So she steeled herself to say, "Of course not. That would be throwing my reputation away, and I have too much sense to do that. Besides, I've already helped you more than you deserve. I even went so far as to tell the duchess that I'd heard you in your room last night, that you woke me a number of times."

She could tell he was disappointed in her answer, but still he asked, "Did she believe you?"

"Yes, certainly—but the duke pointed out that it could have been one of your kinsmen, there to make me *think* it was you."

"Aye, he'd think o' that, so sure he is that I'm guilty," he grumbled.

"Well, I won't admit I spent the night in your room to prove you innocent," she reiterated stonily. "You'll have to find another way."

"That was my intention. I'd no' ask you tae ruin your reputation on my account."

"Then you think you *can* find the horses?" she ventured, then groaned inwardly when she heard the hopeful note in her voice.

But he didn't seem to have noticed. " 'Tis no' a matter of 'can,' darlin', 'tis a matter of 'have to.' "

She nodded in complete agreement. And she was about to leave, when he sat down on the edge of the bed and she saw him wince. She had to bite back her concern. Yes, he was in pain, he had to be, but he was a big man and he could get through it well enough without any more assistance from her.

But he looked so pathetic she reconsidered the uncaring facade. "I'd like to help—that is, if you need help in your search. I don't like it, that you're being blamed for this, when I know you didn't do it."

He chuckled softly. Those last few words of hers had really brightened his mood. Actually, she felt a little lighter in the chest herself for having owned up to what she really felt.

"No more than I, darlin'," he said. "But I have tae allow my past deeds did make me a likely suspect. In that I canna really blame St. James. But he'll be eating his words in the end, or I dinna deserve tae be Laird of Clan MacGregor."

Put that way, she didn't doubt him at all.

28

"Is name is Will Ables," Gilleonan was saying. "And I've a strong feelin' he's no' just confused on the matter, he's lyin' for some reason."

"Why?" Lachlan asked.

It was the next morning. Gilleonan had shown up bright and early at Lachlan's door to report on what he and Ranald had found out yesterday about the missing horses.

St. James might have given Lachlan a week to prove himself, but it was going to take him longer than that just to recover from the beating. So he was going to have to depend on his cousins to do most of the investigating, at least to begin with, and in all haste. The most he could do right now was give them direction.

"He's tae defensive," Gilleonan answered. "And tae insistent that 'twas yer voice he heard. No' just a Scot, mind ye, but ye in particular. Now I'm askin' ye, where would he even ha' heard yer voice 'afore, when he doesna work in the common stable, but in the breedin' ones?"

"I was wondering that myself, when the closest I've gotten tae the fancy stock here was the other morning when we wandered over tae the training yard."

"Aye, the mornin' ye socked that viscount for no good reason. Or is there a reason ye'd care tae be sharin' wi' us less discernin' Scots now?"

Lachlan gave a mental sigh. He knew his cousin was feeling excluded, but he couldn't very well explain what had prompted his attack on Howard Canston, when he didn't understand it himself. To call it jealousy, a logical excuse, was absurd, so he'd as soon not discuss it at all.

In answer, Lachlan said, "Dinna fash yourself about that, Gill. I've already forgotten it myself. Drunk it out o' my system, so tae speak."

That got the expected chuckle he was hoping for. Anything else on the subject could wait until Lachlan figured it out for himself, if he ever did. But for now, he got back to the matter at hand.

"As for this groom, keep your eye on him, wi'out him knowing it, if you can. Take note of who he talks tae, where he goes, what he does when he's no' working. Also, talk tae everyone who works wi' him. Find out if anyone—un-usual—has been around tae see him in the last weeks."

"What is it ye be thinkin'?"

"I'm no' sure, but the possibilities are many. Young Will could be the thief himself. Those who live in the stable would know when no one else would be around tae take note o' what they're up tae."

Gilleonan shook his head slowly, "Nay, he doesna strike me as havin' enough sense, let alone the gumption, tae try somethin' like that on his own. More like one o' a group and followin' orders."

"Aye, there's that," Lachlan agreed. "Or he could simply have been paid tae put the blame on another, tae give the real thieves more time tae cover their tracks. Though why he would pick me I canna guess."

"I can." At Lachlan's raised auburn brow, Gilleonan explained, "I doubt there's many here hasna heard aboot yer reavin' past, at least in the servants' wing. 'Twas discussed openly when ye first showed up, 'atween Their Graces, wi' servants close enough tae hear more'n they should be hearin'. It's made for some lively talk down in the kitchen, or so Ranald claims. And he should know. The lass he's been passin' time wi' is the cook's assistant, so he spends a goodly amount o' time down there."

"Well, that doesna help tae narrow the chase down, does it now?" Lachlan said in disgust.

Gilleonan grinned. "Nay, what it did was make ye the first one tae come tae mind, for such a plot, which is also why the duke looked no further for a culprit. But we'll be figurin' this thing out, dinna worry."

"Aye, I've got every confidence o' that," Lachlan agreed. Though that wasn't exactly true.

Gilleonan nodded, adding, "I had Ranald scourin' the countryside and the nearest villages for likely places the animals could be hidden, and I'm thinkin' tae keep him at that for the time bein'. Considerin' the time o' day that the theft occurred, wi' most folks up and aboot soon after, 'tis doubtful the horses were taken verra far from here, or the thief or thieves would've risked bein' noticed."

"That's true, and why I was also going tae suggest the roads nearby be covered for the next few mornings at that early hour," Lachlan said. " 'Tis likely anyone found traveling them at that time does so every day and can be questioned if they saw anything."

"A good point, and I'll even help Ranald wi' that, since 'tis only an hour or two that we need be concerned wi'. Any later and whoever travels the roads would be at their jobs. And I'll still have all the rest o' the day tae keep watch on Will Ables."

"It should be easier tae find the horses than tae find the thief, though if we get lucky, we can find the one wi' the other. The horses by themselves willna prove anything, but at least we'd have more tae go by, and a place we can be sure the thieves will return tae. There's the possibility, also, that the groom, if he is involved, could lead us tae them."

"Aye, I'll be watchin' for that, you can be sure," Gilleonan assured him.

"Verra well. I'll be paying him a visit myself— as soon as I'm up tae a wee bit o' browbeating. At the moment, I dinna think I'd be inspiring anything but contempt, wi' this face o' mine. 'Tis good for frightening maids in dark corners, but no' much else."

"Actually it's—well—" Gilleonan had meant to be encouraging, but ended up sighing. "Aye, there's no improvement yet."

Lachlan chuckled. "I've eyes and mirrors tae be showing me that—as well as the horrified look o' the maid who brought me breakfast this morning."

Gilleonan winced. "Och, I didna think o' that,

but this will be delayin' yer wooin' for a spell."

"Indeed," Lachlan said.

But actually, he hadn't gotten around to any serious wooing, because of the simple fact that he couldn't get Kimberly out of his mind long enough to decide on which of the ladies currently at Sherring Cross he ought to pursue. In truth, all he could think about was pursuing her.

He'd figured that would be pretty hopeless. She'd made that very clear. But that was before she'd shown up in his room the other night to give him such tender care—and come to his defense the next morning. She might have been brisk about it all, but he was beginning to think her attitude was a ruse. She always tried to be correct and proper—and so often failed.

He smiled to himself. He loved it when she failed, and most times she amused him when she didn't. The lass had a hard time containing her spirit, she really did.

She might have refused to get him out of this predicament the easy way, but then he hadn't expected her to go that far. As it was, in the end she *had* offered to help. So perhaps she'd changed her mind about him. And perhaps he ought to find out for sure, because there was no point in denying it. He wouldn't mind marrying Kimberly Richards.

Who was he kidding? It was becoming more and more obvious to him each day that he *wanted* to marry her.

29

Will Ables was a lanky young man with wiry black hair and large, owl-like blue eyes that gave him a somewhat forlorn look. It tended to make one feel sorry for the chap on first sight, without actually knowing why—at least until you became acquainted with his cocky attitude.

Upon first seeing him, Kimberly thought he appeared so miserable. She had been hesitant to even approach him. She had to actually remind herself that for whatever reason, the man had lied. She knew for a fact that Lachlan hadn't been here, yet this groom swore that he had been.

For two days now she knew something wasn't right in Will Ables's accounting of the incident, and it bothered her. But she couldn't tell anyone about it, or come right out and accuse him without explaining how she knew. But her forced silence went against the grain. And the fact that she couldn't do anything about it was making her angry.

And with three days of the mere "week" that

Lachlan had been allowed gone now, with nothing new coming to light that she'd heard about, she'd decided to speak to the groom herself. If she could find out anything, anything at all, that might suggest he was indeed lying, then that could be used to clear Lachlan. It was worth a try at least.

She also realized there could only be one reason for him to lie, because he was somehow involved himself. And that made her wonder if he'd even been hit on the head, or if that had just been a ruse.

Had someone checked out that injury? Actually seen proof of it? Or in the excitement, had that been overlooked? She intended to find out.

Of course, there was the unlikely possibility that Will Ables was just confused, that he really did think that he'd heard Lachlan. But this was too serious a charge to not be a hundred percent certain.

She had to ask each groom she came across if he were Ables, since she did not know the man. But by a process of elimination, she finally found him sitting on a bale of hay, eating a large meat pie. And he really did look miserable, with those large soulful blue eyes. But it was just an appearance, not really an indication of what was going on in his mind, as she was to find.

"Will Ables?"

He came to his feet immediately and doffed his cap, a bit too quickly for a man recently injured. Surely a sudden movement should have caused him some head pain, but not a wince did he show.

"That be me, mum," he said.

"Please, don't get up," she told him, smiling.

"I've heard of your mishap. Actually, I came to see how you are faring, after such a harrowing experience."

"A what, mum?"

"Your run-in with the horse thieves. That was rather brave of you, if I do say so."

"It weren't nothin'," he replied, blushing at the compliment. "Just part of me job."

"Yes, I suppose. But did the doctor say you would be all right?"

"Didn't need no doctor. Me head's taken worse knocks before."

"But surely a doctor came to examine you?" She'd need the man's name, so she could talk to him as well.

"For a little lump?" he scoffed. "I told 'em it weren't needful."

Kimberly lifted a brow. No doctor, no one to verify that the groom really had been hit over the head. Well, hadn't she suspected that might be the case?

"Was that wise, Mr. Ables? What if you had needed stitches or the like? Here, why don't you let me have a look at your lump, just to make sure—"

He jumped back from her so quickly, he nearly toppled over the bale of hay. And his look, when he found his balance, was a bit accusatory. Clearly she'd taken him by surprise. But he soon recovered, putting on a pretentious smile.

"No need to bother, mum. I told ye it weren't nothin'. No broken skin, no bleedin'. Actually, the lump's all but gone, it is."

Kimberly nodded, though she'd eat her winter bonnet if there had been a lump on his head to begin with. It was really too bad the duke hadn't insisted a doctor examine the man when the injury supposedly occurred. He could have found out then and there that the man was lying, and lying he was. Kimberly was almost positive now.

But too many days had passed to prove it. A lump, if there had been one, could have receded already. Since it offered no proof, she had to think of some other way.

She wondered what he'd say if she just flat out called him a liar. Deny it, of course. She sighed inwardly. That would accomplish nothing.

"It's such a shame, the horses haven't been retrieved yet," Kimberly remarked. "But at least that Scot didn't get away with it, thanks to you. Imagine, stealing from your host? Such utter gall, not to mention bad form. Why, that's as bad as stealing from your employer."

His blush came again, a guilty one this time, she'd warrant. But it was her praise he latched onto.

"I don't know the bloke personal-like," Will said. "But I'd 'eard 'im a time or two. It's 'ard to mistake, that voice of 'is."

"I know what you mean. His brogue is so thick, isn't it? Very easy to recognize."

"Aye, that it is."

He was lying again, agreeing with her, when she was stating untruths herself. Lachlan's brogue was light. It made her so furious, she had to look away from him for a moment, until she could get her anger under control.

But this was something she could at least make use of, she realized. Will Ables *didn't* know Lachlan's voice, he'd probably never heard it before. If he heard three Scots together, including Lachlan, he'd have a devil's time trying to figure which was which.

The duke needed to be apprised of this—no, not Devlin. He didn't like Lachlan, had wanted him gone from the beginning. He was satisfied with his guilt, pleased about it, she didn't doubt, since he could now oust the Highlander with a clear conscience. Short of having the real thief in hand, he would scoff at anything that suggested Lachlan's innocence.

No, she'd tell Megan about what she'd discovered. The duchess might have been exasperated and annoyed with Lachlan, but Kimberly didn't think she personally disliked him. She'd be fair. And the two of them might even be able to arrange a little demonstration to force Will Ables to prove his claim.

Now *that* was an excellent idea. Kimberly was so pleased with it, she was even able to look at the man again without her eyes frying him on the spot.

"Well, I'm glad to know you're feeling up to scratch and able to resume your duties," she told the man in parting. "Of course, you've fewer charges to look after at the moment. But hopefully that will be rectified soon. I'm sure the duke won't rest until he has the animals back where they belong, and that audacious thief behind bars."

"Are you sayin' 'e's still around, the Scot? 'E's not been locked up yet?"

She realized he hadn't been informed about the outcome. Of course, there was no reason to inform a servant about the doings of lords. Considering that, he likely didn't know that Lachlan had been beaten either, and was keeping to his room while he recovered.

He appeared worried, but that wasn't conclusive guilt. Considering Lachlan's huge size, anyone who accused him of anything, true or not, wouldn't feel safe about it until Lachlan was arrested and unable to show up for revenge—or an accounting.

She wondered now if the groom might not disappear if he thought there was a chance Lachlan would come looking for him. That in itself might point toward his own guilt—or not, since fear of retribution from that Highlander could be just as motivating, she supposed.

No, she didn't think that would actually help, so she said, "He claims he's innocent, don't you know, and the duke, being a fair man, has given him time to prove it. But there's not much he can do in that regard, injured as he is."

"Injured?"

"Yes, he was soundly thrashed. No more than he deserved, of course."

The man visibly relaxed, hearing that. Kimberly *hoped* she hadn't made the wrong decision in trying to keep him from disappearing. But he did seem to be the only lead to proving Lachlan's innocence, and they needed him.

Kimberly offered him a parting smile and bid him good-day, eager to get back to the house. But just as she turned to leave, Howard Canston came around a corner and stopped abruptly.

"Lady Kimberly!" he exclaimed. "What are—ah, I've been looking for you. Was told you'd wandered this way. Thought you might like to go for a ride, what with the sun making a rare appearance today."

She didn't. She wanted to go have a talk with the duchess, to discuss what she'd just learned. However, she'd also been meaning to explore the immediate areas around Sherring Cross, on the unlikely chance that she could find the missing horses herself.

The duke undoubtedly had his own people out looking for the animals, but there was a lot of area to cover, including forest and uncultivated meadows. And she would really like to be the one to actually locate them, to make up for her silence.

So she agreed to the ride. It certainly couldn't hurt to further her acquaintance with Howard too. She did still have to get married after all, and he was still on her list of likely candidates.

But Kimberly frowned to herself as they left the breeding stable to walk to the common one down by the house, where she could get a gentle mare for riding. If he had been looking for her, as he claimed, why then had he seemed so surprised when he found her?

30

A small table with several chairs had been brought into Lachlan's room for him to take his meals at, since he wasn't up to venturing downstairs to join the other guests. Gilleonan plopped down in one of the chairs now and lifted the cover off of the meal that had been delivered before he arrived, but hadn't been touched yet.

"They're feedin' ye well, at least," he said, sniffing at the baked salmon and creamed potatoes, the huge slab of fresh baked bread smothered in soft butter.

Lachlan turned away from the window where he'd been staring thoughtfully at his own reflection in the glass. "Did you think they were starving me?"

" 'Twas a possibility."

"Rest easy then, I've got maids showing up throughout the day wi' tarts and cakes and full-course meals. They mun think I'm starving, too. That's my second dinner there, so help yourself."

Gilleonan grinned. "I dinna mind if I do," he

said, and pulled the tray over to himself. But after a few bites, he glanced up at Lachlan to make his report. "That Lady Kimberly showed up tae talk to Ables today. She really despises ye, dinna she?"

Lachlan stiffened. "Why d'you say so?"

"She was after agreein' wi' the mon, sayin's how ye got thrashed and deserved it, callin' ye an audacious thief." Then Gilleonan frowned as he remembered something else. " 'Course she did get him tae state that ye had a thick brogue, when she and I both ken that isna so."

Lachlan looked confused for only a moment. Then he laughed. "I do believe she was there tae help, Gill. Consider this . . . if he thought the lady sympathized wi' him and didna suspect a thing, he might be telling her things he wouldna tell you."

"Hmmm, now ye mention it, I suppose that could've been what she was doin'. Actually, she tried tae have a look at the bump on his head also, but he was havin' none o' that, nearly fell on his arse tae avoid her touchin' him."

"No lump then," Lachlan said.

"I'd suspected as much," Gilleonan agreed, adding, "Then I almost got discovered, hidin' 'round the corner from them, when that viscount showed up lookin' for the lady. I only had seconds to dive out o' sight."

"Lord Canston?"

"Aye, tae take her ridin'."

"Did he?"

Gilleonan shrugged. "I didna follow them tae see. I stayed close tae Ables, though no one else showed up tae see him today."

It was hard to take his mind off of Kimberly

and Canston going off together, but Lachlan finally managed, "What of Ranald? Did he have any luck?"

"Nay, though he did say he thinks the official search has been called off."

"Why?"

"His guess is the horses have been found, but no one's lettin' on aboot it."

"Blast, I was hoping we'd have a place tae set up watch, tae catch the thief when he shows up tae feed the animals or move them . . . wait a minute. If no one's letting on—then the horses havena been returned here. So St. James has set up a watch for himself, has he?"

"Ye think so?"

"Aye, 'tis what I'd do. But he's hoping tae catch you or Ranald, I dinna doubt. And I'm hoping he doesna botch it. But call off Ranald's hunt. I dinna want him walking in on this place by accident in his own search."

"Och, that'd be the worst luck, and no one would believe he was innocent."

"No more'n they did me," Lachlan said bitterly.

"Nay." Gilleonan chuckled, stuffing another bite of tender salmon into his mouth before he added, "I'd say all the lassies around here had more'n a wee bit o' faith in ye, or ye'd no' be eatin' so well."

Kimberly had wanted to ride toward a desolate glade she'd spotted that afternoon, with what appeared to be an old woodcutter's hut in the center of it, seemingly abandoned. It had occurred to her when she saw it that the hut was large enough to fit three horses, and she'd wondered if anyone had investigated it yet.

But as soon as she pointed it out to Howard, he had insisted they turn around, that he had an appointment he had forgotten about and would be late for if they didn't head back immediately. She didn't doubt him. He had certainly appeared agitated. He even whipped his horse unnecessarily for extra speed, at least until they cleared the woods, and the poor animal showed signs that it wasn't the first time he'd been so misused. But when she had suggested he return without her, he wouldn't hear of it.

So she hadn't been in the best of moods when they'd returned to Sherring Cross, and what was worse was she wasn't sure if she could even find her way back to where she'd seen that woodcutter's hut that she still wanted to investigate. Then she'd gotten even more frustrated when she tried to find Megan and couldn't.

Not until dinner was served that night did Megan make an appearance, and alone. The duke wasn't with her, nor would he be joining them that evening, she announced. That was fine with Kimberly, since she was still infuriated with him for convicting Lachlan out of hand.

But she had to wait until the meal was over to find a chance to draw Megan away for a private word. And when they finally slipped into the library together, Megan had some of her own news to impart.

"The horses have been found."

Kimberly blinked. "They have?"

"Yes, in an old hut on the west side of the woods," Megan said.

"Amazing," Kimberly replied, shaking her

head in bemusement at the irony. "I think I came across that place just today. I wanted to go and check it out, but I was with Viscount Canston at the time, and he had some kind of appointment he was late for, so we returned here. But I was going to try and find it again tomorrow."

"No, no, don't do that. Devlin is there now, with a dozen or so men, just waiting for someone to show up. And he's even more furious than he was before, because whoever put the horses there, left them there *together*. Two mares and a stallion, without anything to separate them . . . it's a wonder that old building is still standing."

Kimberly blushed. This was not a subject for a lady's ears.

"I assume, since His Grace is still there, that the thief wasn't. But was there no clue left behind as to who he really is?" Kimberly asked.

"M'dear, I know you think Lachlan is innocent—" Megan began gently.

"I don't just think it, I—"

Kimberly hesitated. Now was the time for the truth, the real truth, that was. And she was reasonably sure that if she told Megan, it wouldn't go any further—well, only a bit further, since the duke would also have to be told. And there is where she balked.

St. James, stuffy duke that he was, would feel obliged to tell her father. A matter of responsibility and such. He would also feel it his duty to ask her if anything untoward had happened during that night she spent with Lachlan. She could honestly say nothing did—that night. But her guilt from that other night might show through and then . . . no, she still couldn't do it, especially after what she had discovered about Will Ables today.

So she began again, saying instead, "Let me ask you something, Megan. Would you say Lachlan's Scots brogue was thick?"

"No, actually, it's very light, sometimes not even noticeable, now you mention it. I have a footman whose brogue is so heavy, I can barely understand him, yet MacGregor's burr is quite lyrical."

Kimberly nodded, continuing confidently now, "I always thought so myself, but did you know that your groom, Will Ables, thinks otherwise?"

"He does?"

"Doesn't that make you wonder?"

"Yes, actually—but how do you know this?"

"I went to see him today," Kimberly admitted. "Did you also know that Mr. Ables refused to have a doctor look at his head injury? It wouldn't have cost him anything, so why would he refuse?"

"It does sound strange, doesn't it," the duchess agreed, frowning.

While the duchess was digesting this, Kimberly said, "Megan, he was lying about Lachlan, I know he was, and it would be so easy to prove."

"How?"

"You mentioned your footman is Scottish, and there are others here, including Lachlan's clansmen. If you gathered them all together with Lachlan, and had them each say something identical, with your groom able to hear them, but unable to see them, he wouldn't be able to say which was Lachlan, and that would prove he was lying."

Megan grinned. "That's rather clever, but what

if he picks one of Lachlan's kin? That would still indicate Lachlan, albeit indirectly."

Kimberly sighed. "You're right. Lachlan's kin shouldn't be used a'tall. I don't suppose you have a few more Scotsmen working for you?"

"One that I know of, yes, and another that can be fetched. He doesn't work for us, but he lives just north of here and I'm sure he'd be willing to participate."

"Wonderful!"

"I'd say we could try this tomorrow, at the latest, the next day. But I should still point out, Kimberly, that if as you say, Ables was lying, then he'll be guessing when asked to pick out Lachlan's voice, and there is still that possibility that he just might guess accurately."

"There is that," Kimberly allowed. "But if I'm right, then he wasn't really injured, it was just a ruse, and that makes him involved in this thing. So I'm hoping the very situation will so fluster him that he might just do something stupid."

"Like confess?"

Kimberly grinned. "That would be nice. You—ah—won't tell your husband about this, will you? At least until after we've tried it?"

Megan chuckled. "I imagine Devlin will be spending the next few days out in the woods, he's so bloody determined to catch the chap red-handed. Don't worry, m'dear, he can find out the good news—or bad, after he returns."

31

After her talk with Megan, Kimberly was finally feeling a bit more optimistic. Their plan was going to work, it had to. The alternative was—unacceptable. And once this was behind them, she could get back to concentrating completely on what she was here for—a husband.

As a matter of fact, James Travers had leaned forward to whisper to her, when he held her chair for her at dinner, that he wanted to have a private word with her sometime tomorrow. She had little doubt that he was going to ask her to marry him. Just the thought should have thrilled her. Instead she had still been engrossed in the meeting she'd had with Ables and how she was going to put her suggestion to Megan.

But now, with that done, she had time to consider James—and she wondered why the thought of marrying him *still* didn't thrill her. They were ideally suited. She knew he could make her happy—well, she was reasonably certain that he could. And her father would be extremely pleased, could find no fault with him whatsoever.

There was still Howard Canston, of course, who had apparently cooled on his former flirtation and had been showing much more interest in her just lately. He was younger than James, even more handsome, was also going to be a marquis when his father passed on, and was certainly just as wealthy as James.

A prime consideration, that last, for her anyway. At least with both James and Howard, she had no fear that they were solely interested in her for the money that would come to them from her father. They wouldn't even know, until after the marriage when she chose to mention it, just how wealthy she really was. When they learned of the inheritance she had from her mother, it would merely be a nice surprise.

Returning to her room that evening after her talk with Megan, she was still wondering what she was going to say to James tomorrow when . . .

"You're keeping late hours, Kimber."

"Good God!" She gasped. "Frighten me to death, why don't you!"

A chuckle came from the dark. "Och, I'd no' be wanting tae do that."

"You could have fooled me," she mumbled as she moved to fetch a twig from the fireplace to light the lamps. "And what, may I ask, are you doing lurking in my room, Lachlan?"

She, at least, had no trouble identifying his voice in the dark. No one could, really, who'd actually heard him speak before. His voice was distinctive.

"Lurking? Nay, merely waiting," he said, explaining, "I didna want tae miss seeing you and have you return tae your room and slip into bed wi'out my hearing it. So I came here to await you."

"Seeing me?" she said just as the first lamp was turned up. She glanced around the room then, until she found him in the comfortable reading chair by her window. "Well, you can see me now, so . . . ?"

"Aye, and a pleasure it is, as usual," he replied, his green eyes moving slowly over her.

The compliment, so unexpected, made her blush. But his eyes, in their slow perusal, ignited a warmth.

Kimberly was suddenly too flustered to continue to upbraid him. And besides, he needed to be informed about the little experiment they had planned with Ables, among other things. In fact, she had intended to stop by his room in the morning to do just that. So it was just as well that he was there. Highly inappropriate, but well, that seemed to always be the case with this man.

So as she headed for the next lamp, she started with, "They found the horses."

"I know."

She raised a brow at his tone. "You don't sound too happy about it."

He shrugged before leaning forward in the chair, his elbows on his knees. "Because I wanted tae find them—and sit on them, till the thief showed himself."

"I believe the duke is doing that."

"But I dinna trust him tae do it right. He'll have tae many men in there, and in the surrounding woods, I dinna doubt. They'll be giving themselves away and our thief will be gone for good."

Put that way, it didn't sound at all encouraging, so she told him her other news. "Well, I've come up with another way to end the thing."

Now he raised a questioning brow. She noticed that his face was looking better, some of the bruises already faded and the lump on his forehead gone. Even his lips had returned to their normal size, though several scabs remained. But with only the one lamp going, and that not very bright for such a large room, he was looking too damn handsome again by half.

When she realized she was still staring at his lips, Kimberly blushed again and blurted out, "The duchess is going to arrange it, for tomorrow or the next day at the latest, an experiment."

She finished quickly with the lamp on her vanity, then moved to toss the twig back in the fireplace. But turning back to face him, she found that the extra light didn't help. He was still so mesmerizing with his dark auburn hair lying against the white shirt he wore, the light catching the seldom seen reddish tints, his light green eyes watching her intently . . .

"What experiment?" he had to prompt.

She actually had to think for a moment, to remember what they were talking about. That produced still another blush that she could only hope he didn't notice.

"I paid Ables a visit today," she said. "And proved, to my satisfaction at least, that he doesn't know your voice a'tall. So we're going to have him listen to you and a few other Scotsmen, and he'll have to point out which is you. He won't be able to do it. He'll have to guess."

Lachlan was silent for a moment, mulling that over, before he pointed out the same thing Megan had earlier: "He could get lucky."

"Yes, and that'd be rotten luck—for us." She

sighed. "If it doesn't work and if . . . well, if the time runs out without the thief being apprehended, I'll own up to where I was that night."

She'd managed to surprise him. He stood up, reached her in seconds, surprising her now, and causing her a great deal of internal alarm with his nearness.

And rightly so, she quickly found, because he grasped her face gently in his hands to ask her, "You'd do that for me, darlin'?"

His gaze was too intense, forcing her to lower her eyes. And his touch, dear Lord . . .

"I'd have to," she confessed in a whisper. "I'd have no choice. I couldn't let you be sent to prison for this, when my being with you at the time proves—"

His kiss cut her off before she got any further. And somehow she'd known it was going to happen. She could have prevented it, moved away—maybe. But now, now it was much too late. Now she had the taste of him again, the roughness of his scabs, the softness of his tongue, the scent of him intoxicating her senses.

His lips moved carefully over hers at first, almost hesitantly, yet there was a firmness now in his hands to keep her captive for the moment, in case she thought to end the kiss. She had no such thoughts, none at all. She knew she ought to, but . . . "ought to" never did seem to work when she was around Lachlan MacGregor.

Her senses were alive again, wildly alive, rippling with exciting anticipation. From the heat on her lips, the fluttering in her belly, the tingling in her breasts, and his body wasn't even touching her yet, just his mouth, just his palms on her cheeks.

She sighed into his mouth, put her hands against his chest, not to push, to touch, and it seemed it was a sign he'd been waiting for, because he then gathered her fully in his arms, fitting her curves to his hollows. His tongue thrust more sensually now, deeply invading her privacy. His hands roamed her back and hips, pressing her closer to his hardness, closer to his heat, then finally lifting her, carrying her, laying her carefully on the bed.

She knew what he was going to do. Somewhere in the deepest recesses of her mind, she knew that what shouldn't have happened before was going to happen again. But she was bedazzled by the pleasure he'd created and continued to lavish on her, the heat of his large body surrounding her now, the gentle caresses of his hands upon each bit of skin he uncovered as he slowly undressed her. She knew . . . and there was no part of her willing to stop him. If anything, she wanted him to hurry.

But he was not going to rush something he'd dreamed of nightly since he'd last held her thusly. He'd ignited a fire and he was going to fan it slowly, and fan it he did.

She trembled when his tongue circled her ear, then delved inside it. She groaned when it soon flicked and teased the hard little nub her nipple had become. But she soared half off the bed when it licked a path down her belly and then . . . God, she couldn't let him do that! But she was powerless in her desire, mindless in her ecstasy, and he was so damned determined to know every facet of her, to bring her every pleasure.

It was a pleasure almost too intense as it took her and swept her along on its pulsing waves.

Even the aftershocks were profound, so much so that when Lachlan entered her, filled her with his warm flesh, and buried himself to her core, she climaxed again within seconds, and minutes later, yet again, when he groaned his own release.

She was asleep before her breathing quieted, and so deeply, she didn't feel him gather her close, or hear his sigh of contentment.

"You're mine now, darlin'. Like it or no', come morning you'll be knowing it."

Kimberly didn't hear that either, which was a good thing, or she might not have slept a wink.

32

Lachlan had meant to stay awake, he really did. Mostly because he'd had every intention of making love to Kimberly again, and again, throughout the long night. She was going to have little doubt, come morning, that they were meant for each other. No more excuses. She'd not be talking her way out of marrying him this time. And he couldn't have been more delighted.

And the irony was, he hadn't come to her room with the idea of seducing her. Not that it wasn't always on his mind, but last night, he'd merely wanted to know why she'd gone to see Will Ables.

And he hadn't even needed to ask. She'd explained it quick enough. What he hadn't counted on hearing was that she was willing to prove his innocence at the expense of her own reputation. She had in fact been willing to do so all along, if it became necessary.

He'd been so moved, in realizing that she really did care about him, must care about him, despite her assertions to the contrary, that he'd been unable to resist claiming her then and there. And she'd let him. If he'd had any doubts left, her passionate, yielding response to his lovemaking put them to rest.

Aye, he'd meant to stay awake, and leave her as he did the other time, before the dawn. He would have returned at a decent hour to settle things between them. But the first indication that that plan had gone awry was the soft humming that woke him, of a cheerful little tune, and the sounds of the fire being stoked.

Any rekindling of the fire in his own room he had to do himself. The maids who attended such things simply wouldn't enter his room until midday, long after there could be no doubt that he'd be up and about.

Yet there was no mistaking that a fire was being tended to across the room, and not by Kimberly, because there was definitely no mistaking her warmth still beside him in the bed. In fact, she was so wrapped to him that the arm about his neck was nigh choking him, and she had a leg flung clear across his hips. Hard to miss either of those limbs, he thought with a mental chuckle.

But this was an unexpected turn that Lachlan certainly hadn't counted on. And he didn't imagine that he could go unnoticed, great hulking body that he'd been cursed with, not unless the maid was near blind. That would be stretching his luck a wee bit too far, when he'd had little enough of it lately for any stretching at all.

But what happened was rather comical, at least he was to think so later.

At the present, though, there was nothing amusing about it, with Kimberly stretching sensually against him, having also been awakened, apparently, by the sounds the maid was making. That wouldn't have been so bad either, faith, was damn pleasant actually, but no sooner did he think so than she was sitting up and screaming her head off. And not a second later, the blasted maid was doing the same thing, screaming loud enough to bring the roof down.

Lachlan sat up himself then, mumbling a few unmentionables about his poor ears. The maid was staring at him boggle-eyed, her sooty hands covering her shocked cheeks. One glare from him and she ran out of there, with Kimberly yelling after her, "Mary! Mary, come back here this instant!" but to no avail. The door was slammed shut and wasn't reopened. Then there was a half growl, half shriek as Kimberly buried her head beneath her pillow.

Lachlan lay back down, his arms crossed casually behind his head, his brows half-lifted, and remarked in an exceedingly dry tone, "It could've been worse, darlin'. She could have stayed."

"Ohhh!" Kimberly exclaimed, coming out from under the pillow to scald him with her eyes. "You have no idea, no conception . . . she's the biggest gossip this side of the Atlantic! Do you know what that means?!"

"It means we'll be getting married."

And then he smiled at her. He couldn't help himself. He wouldn't have sealed her fate quite so dramatically, not for the world, but now that it was done, he couldn't manage to be displeased.

Kimberly, on the other hand, wasn't a bit pleased. She looked like she was about ready to pound her fists against him, or at the very least, her pillow.

"You're a fool, Lachlan, if you think anything is that simple."

Having made that cryptic statement, she flounced off the bed in search of a robe. He had to remind his body that this wasn't the time to pay attention to the fact that she was stomping about naked. After last night, his body wasn't inclined to listen.

Kimberly was furious, more so at herself than the man in her bed. This time there'd been no champagne to blame. She hadn't had a single glass of wine at dinner last night. She had been perfectly sober, perfectly aware of what she'd been doing.

What she'd done was ruin her life. And for what? Pleasure. She'd wanted the pleasure Lachlan could lavish on her, did lavish on her. But this time she was going to pay for it with not just one, but two scandals, and with a husband who loved someone else. And all because she didn't have enough will to ignore Lachlan MacGregor.

She came back to the bed now, knotting the belt on a pink velvet robe that barely covered her breasts. In fact it left a deep V down to her belly, designed as it was to be worn over a nightgown, not without one.

But Kimberly was too upset to notice, too intent on releasing some of her fury. Lachlan, sensualist that he was, couldn't help but notice, despite the emerald green eyes shooting sparks at him.

"Why are you still here?" she demanded, glowering down at him. "Are you waiting for someone to barge in here to verify Mary's shocking tale? You'll no doubt find ten maids out in the hallway waiting to do just that as soon as you leave. Why disappoint them?"

He ignored her sarcasm. "I'm waiting tae hear you say you'll marry me."

"Did I miss something, MacGregor? Were you not just found in my bed as if you belong there? As soon as the duke hears of this, there will be no alternative."

Mentioning his nemesis was not why Lachlan suddenly shot off the bed, showing some annoyance himself now. Shocking Kimberly wasn't his intention either, though he managed to do that just the same.

She blushed profusely. She was still too new to lovemaking to accept easily the sight of him standing there across from her in all his masculine glory.

"There *was* no alternative, Kimber, no matter who hears of this. But I still havena heard you say you'll marry me, and I'm no' leaving until I do."

That snapped her out of her shock. "Yes, I will! And I hope you're satisfied, because you surely won't be after all is said and done. When my father finds out—"

"I'll deal wi' your da, darlin', never fear," he said with complete confidence.

She started to correct the impression that he'd obviously gotten, that it was only an upset parent he had to face, rather than a prejudiced one. But she was too angry at the moment to get into that, and she'd given him warning. If he chose to scoff . . .

"You know, Kimber," he continued as he located his clothes and started to dress, "it occurs tae me that they'll no' believe you if you tell them now that you were wi' me the night the horses were stolen. They'll think you're just trying tae protect me. 'Twould seem we've no choice now but tae find the real thief.''

She was not feeling the least bit agreeable at the moment and so didn't offer a reply. She just wanted him out of there and as quickly as possible, so she could go about the business of bemoaning her fate in private. But her look said, there's no "we" involved here.

To her chagrin, his look said, there is now.

And there were only eight maids lurking about in the hallway when Lachlan finally walked out the door.

33

The summons came about noon, to join the duchess in her formal sitting room. Kimberly groaned. It certainly hadn't taken very long for her shame to reach Megan's ears.

But then Kimberly shouldn't have been all that surprised. Just minutes after he left, Lachlan had pounded on the wall to her room to yell, "You were off by two, darlin'. I only counted eight maids."

She'd thrown a book at the wall, wishing it were his head instead. And she was going to dismiss her maid the minute she dared to show her face. That wouldn't help her predicament, but might teach the girl a thing or two about loyalty, though that was doubtful.

Kimberly arrived at the ducal rooms precisely on time. She was prepared for the most uncomfortable and embarrassing meeting of her life. She'd dressed in somber hues accordingly. She couldn't have been more nervous if she thought her father was inside. Actually, she did expect

Devlin St. James to be on hand, summoned from his vigil in the woods to lend his official displeasure to the proceedings.

As it happened, only Megan's secretary was in the formal sitting room to let her in. The doors to the connecting rooms on either side of it were closed, though the secretary wasted no time in knocking on one now, and a moment later, Megan entered through it.

"Ah, good," the duchess said, smiling at Kimberly. "Will Ables will be escorted here shortly, and I've got four Scotsmen waiting in Devlin's room there." She nodded toward the other connecting door. "I had a bit of luck in that, I'm pleased to say. My neighbor to the north, Mr. Kennedy, had his uncle visiting, and that gentleman has agreed to help us as well—you look surprised, m'dear. Didn't you think I could arrange our little experiment this quickly?"

Kimberly's mouth had dropped open. She forced it closed now. Surprised? She almost laughed. Her relief was incredible. Megan was merely giving her an inquiring look, certainly nothing in the way of condemnation. She obviously hadn't heard yet about Kimberly's disgrace.

Which wasn't to say she wouldn't be having the meeting she had expected later, but for the moment she was reprieved. And yes, surprised. With her current dilemma taking precedence over Lachlan's problem, at least in her self-castigating thoughts, she had completely forgotten about Will Ables and the demonstration.

So she said, "I did think it might require a bit more time."

"No, no, I arranged everything early this morning. The only thing that would have delayed us was if Mr. Kennedy hadn't been at home. And I must admit, I'm rather excited about this. I had my doubts all along about MacGregor, you know, but my husband was so certain and—well, I do like to prove him wrong occasionally." Megan grinned. "Keeps him on his toes. And I do have a good feeling about this, especially with the odds improved now against Mr. Ables being able to guess his way out of it."

Kimberly nodded. That would be the worst luck, if it happened, but Megan was right, the odds were better now with four Scotsmen, rather than just three.

It *had* to work.

Lachlan was undoubtedly right about the thief's not showing up at that hut again. With so many people involved in that vigil, he was bound to know it was a trap and stay away. Yet she was now personally involved, was going to have to marry the man accused of the crime. If he wasn't cleared, well, there was yet another scandal to add to the other two. Two she might weather, but a husband in prison? She might as well pack her bags and move to another country.

It *had* to work.

But she couldn't count on it. Ables could, in fact, get very lucky. And then what? Yes, this did seem to be their last hope, but if it didn't work, then an alternate plan was needed. But what? Damn, she should have thought of something sooner.

Quickly, she put the known pieces all together again while they waited. Had she missed anything? She went over and over again each little thing from the day it happened and beyond, even the fact that the thief had so little care for the horses that he didn't bother to try and separate them. The bashed head that wasn't really bashed, the hour the theft had occurred, the fact that Lachlan was so sick with drink that night and why he was, the obvious lie from Ables, obvious to her and Lachlan . . .

One thing did finally stand out that she hadn't really considered before. The very fact that someone of Ables's social class had accused a lord, albeit a Scottish one. That seemed quite out of place, not something that someone like Ables would do, unless, of course, it was true. But since it wasn't, it seemed more like something someone would tell him to do, someone who would have no qualms about accusing a lord . . . perhaps another lord?

" 'Ere now, what's this all about?"

Two menservants escorted Will Ables into the room. Apparently, they hadn't told him why the duchess had requested his presence. At the moment, he was looking quite leery and nervous, which was a logical reaction possibly, except, if he had nothing to be worried about, wouldn't simple curiosity be more appropriate?

Megan smiled to put him at ease. "Thank you for coming, Mr. Ables. This won't take long a'tall, just a few questions and a brief demonstration, then you can get back to work."

"Questions?"

"About the theft."

His expression turned defensive. "Didn't I answer all there was to answer for 'is Lordship?"

"Yes, I'm sure you did, but my husband was quite upset at the time. After all, no one had ever stolen Sherring Cross horses before. So he may have missed a point or two. For instance, what exactly did you hear Lord MacGregor say that caused you to recognize his voice?"

"Ah, I don't rightly recollect, Your Grace."

"Try, Mr. Ables. Was he talking to someone else, or to himself, or possibly to the horses he was stealing? Was he mumbling or shouting or—"

" 'E were talkin' normal-like, which is why it were easy to recognize 'is voice," Will answered, having found some confidence.

"Very good, and what did he say? Take your time, if necessary, Mr. Ables. We do want to be accurate."

"What's it matter what 'e said? I 'eard a noise. I went to 'ave a look-see. I 'ear the Scot talkin', and the next thing 'appens, I get coshed on the 'ead."

"Yes, very simple, except he might have been talking to an accomplice, might have mentioned a name. Or you might have been confused in what you heard. After all, you were wakened from a sound sleep. It's possible you weren't fully awake when you heard the voice."

"Beggin' your pardon, Your Grace, but I know what I 'eard. It were that Scot MacGregor's voice. There be no mistake in that."

"Then you'd recognize his voice again if you heard it?" Megan asked casually.

"Certainly."

"Very well, just for the sake of clarity, would you tell me which of these voices you're going to hear belongs to Lachlan MacGregor?"

"What voices?" Will frowned.

Megan nodded to one of the servants, who then crossed the room to open the door to the connecting suite. No one was seen beyond that door, just the usual furniture one would find in a very elegant bedroom.

Kimberly spared barely a glance in that room, she was watching Will Ables, whose frown had grown deeper. He still didn't quite understand what was going on or expected of him. But when that first voice spoke from the other room, his eyes rounded and he turned quite pale.

"Was it me ye heard, laddie? If sae, speak up now an' say sae."

"Or was it me ye were hearin' tha' night, mon? Dinna hesitate. I've been accused o' worse, an' there's naething muir I'll be sayin' aboot tha', I'm thinkin'."

"Or mayhap it was myself you heard, laddie? As it happens, I've a fondness for both horses and head bashing."

"Och now, it mun ha' been meself ye heard, wasna it, lad? Aye, I've a verra distinctive voice, I'm tald, verra hard tae be mistakin'."

Kimberly was amazed herself, at the strong difference in each man's voice, either in his tone or the thickness of his brogue. No two of them had sounded a bit alike really, which should have made it quite easy for Will Ables to pick the third voice, which she had recognized as Lachlan's— unless he'd never heard Lachlan's voice before.

And yet he stood there, his owl-like blue eyes about as wide as they could get, apprehension in every line of his face. And he said nothing. His very silence condemned him as far as Kimberly was concerned, because he knew he'd be condemned if he made the wrong choice.

Megan must have realized it also. Her smile was a bit on the triumphant side when she said, "Well, Mr. Ables, which is it then? Which voice did you hear in the stable just before you were attacked?"

He was so panicked at that point that he blundered badly with the question, "MacGregor's one o' them?"

Megan lifted a brow. "You have to ask?"

He lost a bit more color. "No, no, I 'eard 'is voice just now, I did. It's the order, the counting—I 'ave trouble with numbers, ye see. If I could 'ave a look-see at the gentlemen, I could point 'im out—"

"Come now, Mr. Ables, that would defeat the purpose of this little demonstration, now wouldn't it," Megan said sternly. "Aside from the fact that Lord MacGregor is well known due to his lofty height, how else would you have been able to identify him that night unless you had heard *and* seen him before?"

He latched onto that remark swiftly. "Exactly," he blustered. "I did identify 'im, so what's the point of this, eh?"

Megan sighed. "Did I not mention clarity? Or perhaps you haven't realized what a serious charge this is? It would be extremely unfortunate if due to no fault of your own, you were a bit confused in the matter, especially with Lord MacGregor being related to my husband—"

" 'E's *what*?"

"Related to my husband—you weren't aware of that? They share the same aunt through marriage."

Megan must have realized, as Kimberly did, that fact might influence Ables into changing his story. But that *wasn't* what they were after, which is why she quickly added the assurance, "That is no concern of yours, of course, Mr.

Ables. If MacGregor is guilty, he will be dealt with accordingly. I mentioned it only so that you understand why we wish there to be no doubt whatsoever."

"I 'ad no doubt," Will grumbled.

"Of course not, but Lord MacGregor does deny the charge, and with no other witnesses to be called upon, that pits his word against yours, doesn't it? Which is why we are here now, to put any doubts that anyone might have firmly to rest. Simply identify him again, and that will prove him to be a liar as well as a thief."

Silence again, and the man's panic could almost be smelled. He'd tried to talk his way out of cooperating, but had failed. And he hadn't been smart enough to simply grasp the excuse Megan had inadvertently handed him, to admit to uncertainty now. Most men wouldn't bite the hand that feeds them, and condemning a member of your employer's family could definitely be considered biting that hand.

Yet that wasn't the outcome they'd been hoping for. It might have gotten Lachlan off the immediate hook, but it certainly wouldn't have proved his innocence as far as Devlin St. James was concerned. And Kimberly was sure that Lachlan would prefer to be completely exonerated. Especially since he had been beaten for something he didn't do.

Megan sighed once again as the silence continued, then called out, "Very well, gentlemen, Mr. Ables needs to hear your voices again, and give yourselves names this time, if you please. Matthew, Mark, Luke, and John ought to do it, so he doesn't have to deal with—counting."

The Scotsmen complied, with only a slight

thread of impatience in a couple of their tones. And they each claimed one of the names Megan had supplied, and in the same order she'd said them, so Ables didn't have to tax his counting ability by coming up with a "first" or "second." But when the last voice was heard, the groom still hesitated, and hesitated, in an agony of indecision. It was so *obvious* that he had no idea which voice belonged to Lachlan. He couldn't even make up his mind which one to guess at.

Megan finally lost her own patience and said brusquely, "Mr. Ables, this is not a matter for guessing. Either you know or you don't know—"

"Luke," he blurted out with a cringe, as if he expected the ceiling to now fall on his head.

It felt instead as if it had fallen on Kimberly. No! Thrice bedamned luck! And probably because he associated Luke with Lachlan, the closest he could get to a similarity in his mind. Damn Lachlan, why hadn't he picked another name, instead of following in order . . .

"So," Megan said, disappointment clear in her tone. "You do know."

Will Ables didn't relax until then, and now you could almost see the tension slide off his shoulders. He smiled. It was a wonder he wasn't laughing.

"Aye, and didn't I say as much," he bragged.

It was the bragging that infuriated Kimberly the most. She was so furious she took a leaf from Ables's book and managed a wild guess of her own. Looking him right in the eye, she told him firmly, "It doesn't matter. Howard Canston has already confessed everything to me."

"Oh, my," Megan said, as surprised as Kimberly to see Ables lose all his color again, then start turning bright red as anger replaced his horror.

"That bleedin' bastard!" he burst out, half whining, half yelling, and then in his own defense, " 'E offered me five 'undred pounds, more money than I'd see in me lifetime. I couldn't refuse that, now could I?"

"Obviously not," Megan said dryly. "But you had no qualms about sending an innocent man to prison."

"I swear, Your Grace, it weren't to be like that. 'E said 'e just wanted a little revenge, 'cause the bloke there embarrassed him. 'E said after the Scot suffered a little, 'e'd turn the 'orses loose so they could be found, then tell the duke 'e'd overheard a couple Cornishmen in a tavern bragging 'bout stealing 'em, which would clear the Scot."

"And how would that clear you, Mr. Ables, when it was you who named MacGregor as the thief? Sort of makes you still involved, doesn't it?"

There went the man's color again. "That bleedin' bastard!" he was shouting now. " 'E never mentioned that part, and I never thought . . ."

He bolted out of the door before he finished, overcome by his panic. The two menservants went after him immediately. Kimberly sank down in the nearest chair, her relief making her legs weak. The man's wild guess had saved him. Hers, just as wild, had condemned him. Amazing.

And from the doorway to the duke's suite, Lachlan remarked, "I'd say let him go, if I werena still feeling twinges as a result of the false words out o' his mouth. But 'tis Canston I'm wanting."

"I don't blame you a'tall, Lachlan," Megan replied, somewhat abashed. "But I really think you should let my husband deal with this."

"Your husband hasn't dealt well wi' it so far, lass," he reminded her.

Megan blushed. "He's going to feel awful about this, I do assure you."

"Aye, he will," Lachlan agreed, then pinned Kimberly with his light green eyes. "And why did you wait so long tae mention that blasted confession?"

She stiffened, not liking his accusing tone. "Perhaps because there was no confession. I merely guessed about the viscount, the same as Ables guessed about you. But you should have had more sense than to pick the name Luke. You practically asked him to choose you."

He blinked at her. Then he laughed. Then he crossed the room to lift her out of her chair and kiss her.

Behind them, Megan cleared her throat and said, "So . . . I'll put Duchy and Margaret to work on the wedding preparations immediately . . . all things considered."

34

All things considered.

Kimberly's cheeks were still burning as she rushed down the hallway. What a polite way for Megan to say she knew wherein Lachlan had spent last night. But that made it no less embarrassing. And to think the duchess had conducted that whole interview with Ables without letting on at all that she'd already heard the gossip.

"And where d'you think you're running off tae?" a soft burr asked at her back.

Kimberly started in surprise. She hadn't heard Lachlan following her. But she'd reached the stairs and didn't pause.

"Running?" she tossed back over her shoulder. "Hardly. I'm hungry, starving actually. Does that tell you where I'm going?"

"Aye, but it doesna tell me why you're running."

"I am *not*—" she turned to say, but stopped when she found him grinning at her.

Teasing again. The man had the worst timing

for it, he really did. And obviously, he wasn't going to let her go off about her business. He should be just as embarrassed as she. At the least, he should be upset that the love of his life knew he'd spent the night with another woman. But no, he stood there grinning at her.

"Did you want something in particular?" she asked in a tightly constrained tone.

"Aye, I'm wanting tae know how you concluded that Canston set the horse stealing up just tae blame me? No' once did I think o' him."

So that was it. He still had the thieving on his mind, and his relief over being cleared. She'd had no time to relish her own relief, what with Megan's mention of wedding plans setting her mind back to her own problems. But she allowed that he'd had a bit more to lose if the truth hadn't come out about the theft.

So she shrugged. "I'm really not sure what made me come up with his name there at the end. Possibly because I'd finally thought of *everything* that had happened that day, rather than just from the theft on. And I included your punching him that morning."

"One blasted punch and he wants tae see me in prison?" He snorted.

"Well, you see, I knew that he *did* want to press charges against you for it. I also knew that the duke talked him out of it."

"St. James did?" he said in surprise, then derisively, "No' on my account, I'll warrant."

She had to agree with that. "No, he probably did it to avoid a scandal among his guests," she replied pointedly, since she could lay each of the scandals she had been and would be involved in at his door. "However, Megan claimed Howard was—well, she called it 'pouting' after that. But I never gave it another thought until today."

"And that's it? You save me from prison because the duchess claimed he was 'pouting'?"

"Well . . . there were a few other things that when viewed all together, finally added up. Such as yesterday, when I was talking to Will Ables in the breeding stable, Howard showed up. He said he'd been told he would find me there, that he'd been looking for me to invite me riding, but—he seemed surprised, actually, when he first saw me there. It was more like he wasn't expecting to find me there a'tall, and yet the only one else there was the groom."

"So he was there to talk to Ables, but your presence stopped him?"

"Something like that. And then when we did go riding, I couldn't help but notice how ill-used his horse was. Its hide was liberally laced with spur and whip scars."

He lifted a brow at her at that point. "What has that tae do wi' horse stealing?"

"Nothing, except when I was reviewing all the facts, I remembered Megan told me the horses had been left in that hut without any effort made to keep the stallion separate from the mares—"

"Faith, the beastie mun have had him a fine time, I'll warrant."

She glared at him. "I believe the duke was quite furious about the condition the animals were in as a result."

"That mon is always in a fury, Kimber, or havena you noticed that?"

"I wouldn't say always, more like only when you're around. But I digress. The fact that the horses hadn't been cared for properly suddenly reminded me of Howard, who also showed little care for horses. And to top that off, when we came upon that hut yesterday in the woods, and I wanted to examine it, he suddenly recalled an appointment that he was late for, and rushed us back to the mansion.''

Lachlan shook his head, grumbling, '' 'Tis no wonder I gave no thought tae the viscount in this matter. All these things you've mentioned, I wasna aware of.'' And then he grinned. '' 'Tis well for me that you were on my side, rather than his, and were able tae piece it all into a whole picture 'afore my time ran out.''

''It still wasn't enough to point a finger at Howard. It was merely a good guess, and fortunately, Ables was gullible enough to believe that the viscount might have confessed. And I wasn't *on* your side,'' she stressed. ''I just wanted the truth to come out.''

''Well, I'm thanking you, darlin'.'' He took her hand and squeezed it very gently. ''No matter the how or why behind it, you've kept me from the magistrate's clutches—so I can remain in yours.''

She blushed. There was no accountable reason for it, other than he *always* seemed to make her blush. And there was a warmth in his light green eyes now that . . .

''Kimberly, might I have that private word with you now?'' Lord Travers asked from the bottom of the stairs.

James, she mouthed, and remembered . . . Good God, he was going to propose marriage to her— at least, she had assumed that was his intention. And if it was, she'd have to tell him about Lachlan. But it was going to be so unexpected for him, such a blow, especially if he really had intended to ask her to marry him.

She groaned inwardly. Who would have thought she'd end up facing a situation like this, when she had come here doubtful of getting even one proposal?

She turned to face James. She offered him a smile, though it came out very weak.

"Certain—" she began.

"Nay," Lachlan said behind her, cutting her off and placing his hands possessively on her shoulders. "Kimber and I have wedding plans tae discuss just now."

"Whose wedding?" James frowned.

"Ours," Lachlan replied, and Kimberly could almost feel his wide grin. "You're now among the first tae be told, the lady has agreed tae marry me. So I'm thinking anything you have tae say tae her can be said in my presence—if it willna take tae long. We've much tae discuss."

"No—it wasn't important and . . . my felicitations, of course. This is rather . . . unexpected news."

"Och, well, I'd been after asking her for some time now. Wearing her down was no' easy, you ken, but my luck finally changed."

If Lachlan hadn't sounded so *happy* about it, she would have murdered him on the spot. She was still furious. And poor James was utterly shocked. He tried to conceal it, but he simply couldn't. There'd been no call to tell him so abruptly.

She would have eased into the subject, prepared him, but no, she hadn't been given a chance to say a word. And Lachlan had no right to be that high-handed with her—yet. Even when he did have that right, she wasn't going to meekly accept him speaking for her. He even knew her well enough to *know* that by now.

She tried to lighten the blow, saying, "I'm sorry, James," but he had already turned away and was now hurrying off.

"Sorry, are you?"

She swung around, her eyes as stormy a dark green as they could get. "Sorry you shocked him! You didn't have to do that. He could have been told more gently."

"Nay," he disagreed. "These things are best dealt with quickly."

"How would you know?" she demanded, then, "Damn it, the man wanted to marry me himself. He had no idea that you and I—that we—"

"I am aware of that, Kimber." Lachlan's hand suddenly gripped her face. "But you're mine now." He kissed her hard while he held her thusly. "And I'll be making sure anyone else who had designs on you knows it."

She was dazed for a moment, but only a moment. "Do you realize that smacks of jealousy?"

"Do you realize that you're going tae be mine forever?" he countered, his hand now caressing her cheek before he let go of her. "That you'll love me forever? That I'll—"

"Don't say something that we both know isn't sincere, Lachlan," she cut in, sounding disgusted. "We're both being forced into this marriage—"

"Speak for yourself, darlin'," he interrupted right back. "I'm rather pleased that I'll be marrying you myself. Now go feed that noisy belly of yours. Faith, but you're a veritable termagant when you're hungry," he complained, though there was laughter in his tone.

He then turned her about and gave her a soft whack on her behind, to send her on her way. Kimberly didn't move a step, mortified that someone might have witnessed his audacity. No one had, but by the time she finished blushing and looked back, he was gone.

35

"**B**loody hell!"

"Somehow I knew you'd say that," Megan remarked from the doorway where she stood watching her husband pace back and forth in his study.

It was several hours after he'd been told about Will Ables's breakdown and confession. Both men had already been turned over to the magistrate, with Howard protesting his innocence, of course.

In fact, he'd had the gall to ask, "You aren't going to believe a servant's word over mine, are you?"

As if that wasn't exactly what he'd expected to happen when he'd set up Lachlan. And that was exactly what *had* happened.

Through it all, though, Devlin had contained his emotions quite admirably. But in order to do so, he had to revert to the duke of old, the stuffy, unflappable one who never lost his control, when Megan knew he'd wanted to tear into Canston just as he had the Scot, if not more so.

The viscount, after all, had arranged a situation that allowed Devlin to release his fury on the Highlander, something he'd wanted to do but couldn't—without a good reason. And now he was faced with making amends to a man he could barely tolerate, and that stuck in his craw but good.

But now that he was finally alone in his study, or almost alone—he wouldn't count her—he wasn't containing any of those emotions any longer. And Megan knew well enough that he'd be working himself into the dark side of a rage if he weren't distracted very quickly. But that wouldn't do at all, since Lachlan had been sent for and he would be arriving shortly for some of that amends making.

So she cleared her throat to get his attention. "Did you mean it, what you said earlier, that you were finished with this matter, that Canston and Ables could fight it out in the courts themselves?"

He didn't bother to stop, just nodded curtly. "I have the animals back. I don't intend to waste my time further. And besides, Canston has got some powerful relatives. I don't doubt his uncle will endeavor to sweep this under the rug. But his family will know they now have an enemy in me that they'll regret. They won't let him off without *some* punishment because of that."

"And that's enough for you?"

"I made a bloody fool of myself, Megan. I would just as soon not be reminded of it further."

"Well, perhaps this will make that crow you're going to eat taste a little better."

"What will?"

"The news that MacGregor seduced Kimberly."

Devlin stopped his pacing so abruptly, he almost tripped. "He did *what*?"

She nodded now, and quickly clarified, "Seduced our Lady Kimberly, spent the night with her as well, and was found in her bed this morning."

"Bloody hell!"

"Oh, come now, I thought that would make you feel a little less foolish."

"What it means is I'll have to explain to her father how I let it happen!"

"Nonsense," she scoffed. "There wasn't a thing you could have done. Something like that, if it's going to happen, it's going to happen. It can't be prevented."

It could, of course, by simply separating the two lovers, as in kicking that Highlander out of his house as he'd wanted to do to begin with. But he didn't say that. There was no point. His lovely wife would somehow counter whatever he said with some romantic drivel.

So he narrowed his eyes at her and demanded, "I suppose you're delighted?"

"Well . . . I'm not disappointed. It would have been nice if they had gone about getting married in the acceptable fashion, but—I'm no hypocrite, Dev. We—ah, sort of did the same thing, if you'll recall."

A bit of color in his cheeks said she'd made her point. "He's going to marry her then?"

"Of course," she replied. "Seems rather happy about it, if you ask me. She doesn't, poor girl. At the moment, she's quite embarrassed."

"As well she should be."

Megan gasped. "Don't you *even*—" she began to rail at him, until she saw the slight turning of his lips. She finished with, "Wretch. We are the last two people who can cast stones. As for her father—"

"Yes, her father, who's going to be in a fine rage and rightly so." Devlin sighed.

"Ah—I think his rage might not be so fine, but a bit on the ugly side," Megan confessed uneasily.

He raised a brow at her. "How so? What *else* do you know that I haven't been informed about?"

"Just that the earl doesn't like Scotsmen, any and all Scotsmen."

"He's prejudiced?"

She made a disgusted face. "Yes, very. In fact, he hates them so much, he'd probably disown his daughter if she married one."

"Bloody hell!" Devlin exploded again at that little tidbit. "You've known about that and you still tried to get those two together?"

"I only learned about it the night the horses were stolen. I've hardly been matchmaking since that happened," she added indignantly.

"I beg your pardon, then."

"As well you should," she retorted. "And besides, this isn't a case of wanting to get married and having the earl withholding his approval. It's a matter of *have* to get married. The man will just have to see reason about this, and I'm sure you'll help him to that end."

"Me?!"

"Certainly. You don't expect me to do everything, do you?" she asked huffily, then turned on her heel to flounce out.

But she nearly collided with Lachlan, who had come up behind her. Her eyes narrowed on him.

"How long have you been standing there, MacGregor?"

"Just," he replied with a curious look.

"Well, do go in then. But don't keep my husband long. I don't want him late for dinner. I'll be serving a large helping of cro—"

"That's enough, Megan," Devlin growled.

She turned and gave him a tight little smile. "Certainly, dearest."

Lachlan closed the door behind her, remarking, "I wish my Kimber were that agreeable."

"No, you don't, MacGregor, believe me you don't," Devlin mumbled.

That said, they each recalled, at exactly the same moment, *why* they were having this meeting. Lachlan crossed his arms over his chest and smiled. It was a devilish smile, full of anticipation and no small amount of gloating. Devlin leaned back against his desk with a sigh, his own expression mirroring his self-disgust.

"Lord Canston and my stable groom have both been arrested and charged."

Lachlan stiffened. "Before I could get my hands on him? D'you think that's fair, mon, considering—?"

"Considering you started the whole bloody thing when you attacked him that morning?" Devlin interrupted. "Yes, I'd say you didn't need to take him on again, especially when you aren't quite in any condition for it, and he's in the best of health, and a bloody Corinthian at that."

Lachlan started to protest again, but allowed the duke might have the right of it. It wouldn't be all that satisfying if he ended up the loser again because he wasn't completely healed from the last bout.

Devlin continued on a different note, "The horses have been recovered."

"Aye, I was aware o' that yesterday."

"There were enough teeth marks to indicate the stallion enjoyed his sojourn in the woods," Devlin said, his anger rising. "Both mares' breeding programs have been ruined, of course. Neither was to mate with that particular stallion."

"D'you think that breaks my heart?"

"No, but it might interest you, since I'm giving you the animals. The stallion is an unsure stud. His offspring tend to be either mediocre or outstanding, so there's no telling what those mares will produce. But he's a proven racer. He's won quite a few championships here in England. In that he's like my Caesar. I guarantee he'll beat anything your Highlands have to offer."

"So you think tae pay me off, d'you?"

"I prefer to think of it as a small amount of amends. Even if you don't want to breed the animals, that stallion will win you many a purse."

"*If* I take him," Lachlan replied. "But I dinna want your horses, mon. You're no' going tae clear your conscience that easily."

Devlin stiffened at that. "Then perhaps I'll give them to Lady Kimberly—as a wedding gift."

That pointed reminder of the new predicament that Lachlan had got himself in should have put him on the defensive. Instead he laughed, saying, "Dinna be thinking I'm regretting what was done, or feeling guilty for it. I *want* tae marry the lady, St. James. And now I've got her agreement, I'll no' be giving it up for any reason."

"Her father may have something to say about that," Devlin said.

"Dinna fash yourself. I'll deal wi' her da. 'Tis

no concern o' yours. And now I'll be having your apology, or were you thinking you could avoid it?"

Devlin's lips curled in a taut, humorless smile. "No, obviously not. You have it then. I apologize for the whole bloody mess, and for taking my fists to you without—current provocation. You weren't given a fair hearing, and believe me, I do regret that."

"Verra nicely done, but I canna accept."

Devlin came off the desk with a low growl. "The hell you can't."

Lachlan raised a brow. "You really mun do something about that temper o' yours. If it werena so hot, you'd no' have tae be apologizing. And I wasna finished. I canna accept your apology— yet."

In a flash, Lachlan drew back his fist and let it smash against Devlin's mouth. The duke fell back against the desk and half across it. When he lifted his head, it was to see Lachlan grinning at him.

"*Now* I can. And 'tis lucky for you, St. James, that I'm in such a good mood because o' the lassie, or we'd still be discussing your apology."

After that parting shot the door closed behind him. Devlin rolled slowly off his desk, back to his feet. He brought his fingers to his lips. They were numb, but he tasted blood. And suddenly he laughed. The gall of the man. If that damned Highlander didn't watch himself, Devlin was going to start to like him.

36

"Come along now, you're going to enjoy it," Megan said, practically pulling Kimberly across the lawn with her. "And correct me if I'm wrong, but I do recall that you thought it was a good idea."

"That was before—well, before my husband was decided for me in a moment of madness."

Megan blinked, but then she burst out laughing. "Madness? My, now that's a nice name for it, indeed it is. I'll have to remember that the next time Devlin makes me—mad. Oh, now, do stop blushing. It really is funny if you give yourself a moment to think about it."

Kimberly disagreed. "Except it *was* madness, and I still can't believe—"

Megan stopped abruptly to put her arms around Kimberly. "You have to stop castigating yourself over this. It wasn't madness, it was passion, and we all succumb to it at one time or another—and frequently if we're lucky. I remember something Devlin told me before we were married—now what were his exact words? Ah, yes, that desire isn't selective of place, time, or the individual."

"He spoke of that with you *before* you married?" Kimberly nearly whispered, because the subject wasn't exactly what one would call normal.

"Well, you see, we had a very—how shall I put this?—torrid courtship." Megan then chuckled. "Actually, it was more like war. And that day, he was complaining about my arousing him. He went on to say, 'When it happens to you, and it will eventually, you won't have any more control over it than I do. You either make love or suffer with it.' And I have to say, I've found that to be quite true. I imagine, that's what you've learned as well."

"But it's not something I should have learned before the vows are spoken. You didn't, and—"

"M'dear, I'm going to trust you with this little secret, because I hope it will relieve some of the agony you're putting yourself through, but I did in fact learn all about it before my elopement to Gretna Green."

"You did?" Kimberly asked, wide-eyed. "You and the *duke* did?"

"You don't have to sound that surprised. As it happens, my marriage began exactly as yours is going to, and I wasn't all that happy about it either—then. But now—I can only hope that your marriage is as wonderful as mine is, or at least, that you think so. And that is really all that matters, what *you* think, not what others think—well, I suppose you must take into account what your Highlander thinks also. Keeps peace in the family, don't you know."

Kimberly actually grinned at the duchess. And she was feeling better—a little anyway. But she still didn't want to go to the picnic that Megan had arranged in the conservatory. Especially since a great many of the houseguests would be there, and she had yet to face them en masse, having kept mostly to her room since it happened.

She said as much, "I still don't think I'm ready for this. They must all know—"

"So what? They also know you're going to marry him. Devlin saw to that announcement last night. You'll be amazed how forgiving people can be, as long as whatever wrong you do is righted in the end. And you are righting your wrong by marrying the Scot. Now, if you had *refused* to marry him, then you would indeed have to bury your head under your pillow for the rest of your natural days."

Kimberly smiled. "How do you manage to make everything sound so simple—and silly?"

Megan chuckled. "Because I *work* at it, m'dear. If I don't keep a fair amount of silliness in Devlin's life, then he'll revert to being that stuffy, condescending man he was before I met him, and that, believe me, would be cause for war again between us. Now come along, or all the baskets will be empty by the time we arrive."

"Is—is James going to be there?"

"No," Megan said gently. "He returned to his home yesterday afternoon."

Kimberly sighed. "I feel so awful about James. I believe he wanted to marry me himself."

"But there's no need to feel bad. It happens, and quite frequently during the Season. But he's a grown man, he'll recover, and likely continue to look for a wife, now the notion's occurred to him again. And besides, you have to follow your own heart, and accept your feelings for what they are.''

"But my heart isn't—"

"Shhh, you don't have to tell me," Megan said. "I know very well how much easier it is to deny and ignore what you're feeling. I was an expert at that myself. But I also know that any man who can bring you—to madness—has got a very strong pull on your heart. For what it's worth, I think you've made the right choice."

Right choice? Kimberly hadn't made any choice at all, her body had, but she wasn't going to argue that point with the duchess. Megan apparently had different views on love than she did. And Lachlan didn't have any claims on her heart, nor would he—as long as he continued to love someone else.

They finally reached the conservatory. It was pleasantly warm, almost humid, with so many people inside. A few tables had been brought in for the older folks who didn't want to sit on the ground, Lucinda and Margaret included, but most of the guests were on large blankets that had been spread out between the foliage.

Megan was warmly greeted as she passed by one group of guests after another—and Kimberly with her. No snubs, no disapproving looks or smirks. It was as if she weren't at the heart of another scandal, as if there *were* no new scandal.

There was, of course. And Kimberly had expected to be utterly embarrassed. That she wasn't was possibly because Megan was announcing her support, by walking in with her arms linked with Kimberly's. The Duchess of Wrothston did in fact carry a great deal of weight where people's opinions were concerned. Or it was possibly what Megan had suggested, that folks could be forgiving as long as the wrong you'd done was going to be righted. But whatever it was, Kimberly was immensely surprised—and relieved.

"Ah, there he is," Megan said, having located her husband. "And it doesn't look like he's dug too deep into that basket yet."

Kimberly grinned. "Possibly because he has that adorable cherub in his lap, keeping him busy."

"Yes, I suppose that would do it."

Kimberly had been privileged to be taken up to meet the Wrothston heir not long after she'd arrived at Sherring Cross. It hadn't taken her but moments to fall in love with the beautiful child, and she'd been back to visit him on many occasions.

She joined Megan on the large blanket now and held her arms out. "May I?"

"Good God, yes!" Devlin replied in relief and quickly handed his son over. "It's bad enough I'm at a picnic in the heart of winter." He paused to give his wife an exasperated look. "But I'm bloody well starving, yet couldn't eat a thing without Mr. Twenty-hands there snatching at it."

Megan chuckled. "Let me translate that for you, Kimberly. What he means is he's spent all his time thus far feeding Justin, and enjoyed doing it so much that he forgot to feed himself as well."

"Och now, mayhap there'll be enough food for the rest of us then."

Kimberly stiffened, but Lachlan still plopped down on the blanket beside her. No wonder she hadn't seen him when she entered the conservatory—and she'd looked. He'd been following behind her and Megan all along.

"Do join us, Lachlan," Megan said, somewhat dryly, since he already had.

He grinned, unabashed as usual. " 'Tis a fine afternoon for a picnic, lass," he told Megan, but then his warm green eyes moved immediately to Kimberly and stayed on her. "D'you no' agree, Kimber?"

"Yes, I suppose it is," she replied reluctantly.

She could no longer relax with him there, though. He simply had that effect on her. Neither could the duke apparently, though for other reasons. He did nod to Lachlan, however, albeit quite curtly. Kimberly was surprised. Evidently they were going to be on civil terms again, if somewhat on the let's-ignore-each-other side.

And the duke's puffy lip, well, Kimberly certainly wasn't going to ask about it. She had to wonder though.

"You look verra nice wi' a bairn in your arms, darlin'," Lachlan leaned toward her to whisper at the back of her ear. "But I'm thinking you'll look even nicer when 'tis my bairn you're holding."

Kimberly blushed furiously at that insinuation, though with Megan and Devlin both presently digging into the picnic basket and setting items out on the blanket for them all to share, neither of them had likely heard him. Which wasn't to say they wouldn't if he continued such inappropriate talk with others near to hand.

So she hissed at him, "The least you could do is confine yourself to suitable subjects when we're not alone. Or is that asking too much?"

"Aye, I fear it is," he said with a sigh, as if he

might actually regret that he couldn't—as if she might actually believe that. "There's just something about being near you that leads me tae be thinking o' procreation."

She gasped. She looked away from him. She wasn't going to address that remark at all. And behind her, she heard his soft chuckle.

"Careful wi' those blushes, darlin'. You ken how becoming I think they are on you. I may have tae kiss you tae be proving it."

Her head turned sharply so she could glare at him. "If you do I'll—"

"Aye, kiss me back, I know," he cut in with a nod. "And then you'll be blushing even more, I dinna doubt, and I'll be thinking about carting you off tae a place where I can be kissing you proper."

It was the oddest feeling, to be so outraged, and yet become excited about the very prospect of being carted off by him for some proper kissing. Proper, she assumed, as in *im*proper . . .

Gah, she *was* mad, to let him keep doing this to her, infuriating her with his audacity, inflaming her with his sensual banter, and in public, where she'd cause a scene if she tried to deal with him as he deserved. But he wouldn't persist if he didn't get a reaction. She really was going to have to work on denying him that reaction.

To that end, she said now to Megan, "If there's any fruit in that basket, I'll take a piece, please."

At her back, Lachlan whispered, "Coward." And his soft laughter had a devilish sound to it.

Kimberly didn't react. Well, at least she didn't say anything more to him. But she still blushed.

37

During the next few days, the mansion slowly emptied of all its guests. Some returned to their homes because the Christmas holidays were fast approaching. Others had to be nudged a bit, with Duchy having no qualms in announcing that the house party was officially over.

Kimberly and Lachlan weren't included in the exodus. They would in fact be married in the Sherring Cross chapel, a small service with just family and Their Graces attending. The duke had already obtained a special license for them, so they wouldn't have to wait the requisite three weeks for the posting of the banns. Actually, the only thing they were waiting on was Kimberly's father's arrival.

Devlin had already written to the Earl of Amburough, or so Kimberly had been informed. She didn't ask if he'd gone into detail about her shameful behavior. Likely not, as such things weren't suitable for letters. And besides, a simple "Your daughter will be married as soon as you arrive," would bring Cecil Richards posthaste. If the duke had been even more exact with something like, "Your daughter will be marrying the Lord of Clan MacGregor," there'd be even quicker results.

Actually, Lachlan's name probably had been mentioned, so it was pretty much guaranteed that her father wouldn't be showing up just to give the bride away. Exactly the opposite. All hell would be breaking loose instead, and if she knew her father the Earl of Amburough would not care who might be present to witness the unleashing of his temper.

As it happened, when he did arrive, it was late in the evening, so everyone was still gathered together. Having just finished dinner, they had all adjourned to the parlor for some quiet amusements, now that all the guests were gone and continuous entertainments were no longer necessary.

Lachlan and Margaret were in one corner of the room finishing a chess game. Megan was directing several servants placing unlit candles high on the Christmas tree that had been brought in that morning.

Kimberly was helping Duchy remove some carved wooden angels from their little velvet storage pouches, still more decorations for the tree. Devlin was merely watching the proceedings from his favorite spot by the mantel and volunteering a suggestion now and then about the candle placements while he sipped at his after-dinner brandy.

And then there was that ill-tempered voice that Kimberly knew so well, demanding from the doorway, "What in the bloody hell is a Scotsman doing at Sherring Cross, and fighting over m'daughter?"

"Good to see you again, too, Cecil," Devlin remarked dryly. "I assume you got my letter?"

"What letter? I came here because Kimberly's name has been linked with a Scotsman. I don't mind telling you how appalled I was. Who is this damned Scotsman, and what's he even doing here?"

"The 'damned' Scotsman is related to me," Devlin replied, his own tone indicating he didn't care for Cecil's one little bit.

"Good God, related?" Cecil exclaimed, as if he couldn't imagine anything more horrible. "How is it I never heard of this?"

"Possibly because my relations are no one's bloody business but my own," Devlin answered tightly. "And I would suggest we continue this discussion in my study, before my wife, who has a Scot or two in her own ancestry, has you evicted for your insulting rudeness."

At that point the earl did some blushing, never having had it pointed out so blatantly that he was making an ass of himself. Kimberly wasn't the least bit embarrassed for him, she was too used to his acerbity. She did regret that these nice people had to be subjected to his ill-humored ways.

Cecil looked for and assumed he'd found the duchess—he had—who was in fact frowning at him, "I beg your pardon, Your Grace. I sometimes forget myself when I'm upset, and this has upset me mightily."

"That's understandable," Megan allowed graciously. "Although it was a minor scandal that we have all forgot about—due to other things."

"Come along then, Cecil," Devlin said, quickly

crossing the room to lead him to his study before he could ask *what other things*.

Cecil nodded, but he caught sight of Kimberly before he turned, and with a scowl, he ordered her, "You will join us, gel, since you have some explaining to do."

He didn't wait for her compliance, didn't expect her to disobey. She thought about it though, she really did. His tirades could be emotionally exhausting, even when she did no more than just sit and listen. And this tirade was likely to be the worst she'd ever heard. But there really was no avoiding it. He was here. He didn't know yet that she was going to marry the Highlander, but he would very shortly, and—she might as well get it over with.

She stood up, but paused to glance over at Lachlan, whose expression was curiously inscrutable. "You might want to come along," she suggested. "I warned you that he wouldn't be happy about—" She hesitated, realizing this was not a subject to mention before others. So she hoped he would recall *what* she'd told him he wouldn't be happy about, and finished with, "You're about to find out why."

Kimberly didn't wait to see if he would follow. It wasn't necessary for him to be present during this "baring of the sinful circumstances," so it made no difference to her. It would merely save her having to relate the entire tale to him later. The earl was very predictable, after all.

Devlin was sitting behind his desk when she reached the study. There were a number of chairs about the room. She took one against the wall, out of the way, though she couldn't hope to remain unnoticed for very long. Her father was apparently going to remain standing. She knew he would prefer to, so used to that authoritative seat behind the desk himself, and this not being his study.

"You haven't seen your daughter for more than a month," Devlin was saying. "Would you like a few minutes alone with her to—"

"What for?"

Eloquently put, and very indicative of Cecil's feelings for his only daughter. Kimberly almost smiled at Devlin's surprise. She supposed some people might find the earl's sentiments unnatural. She found them perfectly normal—for him. At least they were what she was used to. If he'd ever been anything other than curt or surly with her, she didn't remember it. So anything on a warmer side, she would find unnatural—for him.

"Very well then," Devlin said. "Since you left before my letter reached you, I will tell you the gist of it now and we can discuss—"

"You needn't bother, Your Grace. I told you, I'd already heard the entire story. That's why I'm here, to find out how such a sorry affair could have come about."

"I presume you're speaking of that morning the Highlander attacked Viscount Canston because of your daughter?" the duke questioned.

"Yes."

"And that's the only tale you heard?"

"Yes." Cecil frowned now. "Why?"

"Because we're talking about two different things here. I made no mention of that incident in my letter to you. It was a minor occurrence that didn't hold anyone's interest for more than a day or two."

"Then what were you writing me about?"

"I wrote to let you know that Kimberly has accepted a proposal of marriage—"

"To Viscount Canston?" Cecil interrupted, and his whole demeanor improved with that thought. "Excellent! I knew his father quite well when he—"

"The viscount turned out to be a thief and a liar," Devlin cut back in coldly. "And we shall not mention that blackguard again, thank you."

"Now see here, St. James, that's a rather harsh accusation to be making about a member of the Canston family," Cecil said in his disappointment.

"But no less true, and proven, I might add."

"Then who is it wants the gel?"

Cecil's tone implied he hadn't thought anyone *would* want Kimberly, which was probably why Devlin gallantly mentioned, "She was very popular among our guests, and other offers would have been forthcoming, I've no doubt. But she has agreed to marry the MacGregor of Clan MacGregor, and in my letter, I informed you that I am in complete support of her decision."

"The hell you say!" Cecil shouted, too shocked to say more at the moment.

Devlin raised a black brow sardonically. "Was I not clear enough?"

"Clear enough? *Clear enough!*" Cecil was so livid with fury now, he could barely think. "The hell she will! Is this a joke?"

"Would I risk a reaction such as yours for a joke, Cecil? I don't think so."

Cecil came to his senses a bit, enough to say, "She knows better than to associate with Scotsmen, let alone even think of marrying one. This must be a joke, and I bloody well don't appreciate it."

Devlin sighed at that point and glanced at Kimberly. "I'm sorry, I had hoped to avoid the whys and wherefores, but your father isn't cooperating."

"That's quite all right, Your Grace," she said, even managing a weak smile. "Thank you for trying to spare us, but the sordid details will have to come to light for him to understand there is no choice involved here."

"Sordid details?" Cecil was glaring at her now. "What have you done, gel?"

"Nothing unusual, just highly scandalous," Kimberly told her father. "Lachlan MacGregor was discovered in my bed, you see. Unfortunately, I happened to be in it with him at the time."

Cecil got so red in the face, he was in danger of bursting a blood vessel. "Slut!" he roared.

He took the several steps that brought him in front of her. She cringed and closed her eyes, because his hand was already raised. He was about to smack her senseless, was angry enough for some serious damage.

But a new voice was heard from in a soft, though ominous tone. "Lay even one finger on her, and I promise you will regret it."

Kimberly glanced toward the doorway. So Lachlan had followed her after all—fortunately for her. Devlin had stood up, would have come to her aid, but she would have had a few bruises before he reached her.

Her father had turned toward the door as well. That Lachlan filled the area with his immense size might have been one reason the much shorter earl was momentarily disconcerted. But it was more likely because Lachlan's menacing tone was nothing compared to how truly enraged he looked.

Cecil had been startled, but he was too angry to remain silent for more than a few moments. However, his new tone wasn't nearly as belligerent, proving he'd definitely been intimidated and still was. Kimberly was utterly amazed.

"So you're the MacGregor?" Cecil sneered.

"I am that, but more tae the point, I'm the mon who will be marrying the lass here. That makes her mine tae protect, no matter what she is tae you."

"She is my daughter—"

"More's the pity, I'm thinking."

"—and she won't be marrying any Scot bastard, clan lord or not."

"Shall we refrain from insults, if you please," Devlin tried to interject, but neither man was paying him any mind at this point.

"Were you no' listening, mon?" Lachlan said to Cecil. " 'Tis no secret that I bedded her. All and sundry know of it by now. So there's no choice. She must marry me, or suffer the consequences—"

"Exactly," Cecil shot back. "She courted the consequences, she can bloody well live with them. And she can count herself lucky if I can find a penniless lord who will overlook her tattered reputation and take her off my hands for the dower that comes with her."

"You'd do that tae her, when my marrying her would end the scandal?" Lachlan asked incredulously.

Cecil snorted. "The gel did it to herself. She knew she'd never have my permission to marry a damned Scot. If she can never hold her head up again because of it, that's no one's fault but her own."

"What say you, Kimber?"

"I—" she began.

But her father cut her off. "She has no say. And she won't cross me on this," he added confidently. "She knows I'd disown her if she does, and that would be a scandal she couldn't live down."

"For yourself as well, I'm thinking," Lachlan said in disgust. "Are you that much of a fool, mon?"

Cecil went red in the face again. "The only fool here is you, Highlander. And you've no further business here, so I'll thank you to leave."

"Don't be kicking people out of my study, Richards," Devlin said coldly. "I reserve that right."

But Lachlan had already turned about with a muttered low curse and stalked off. And staring at that empty doorway, Kimberly felt the most devastating disappointment.

It wasn't quite what she'd expected. Actually, it wasn't what she'd expected at all. She'd warned Lachlan that he wouldn't be happy marrying her, true, but she *had* taken it for granted that he would do the right thing after all was said and done, and marry her anyway.

He'd put up a good showing, of course. And he obviously found her father and his harsh sentiments despicable. But it came down to the simple fact that Lachlan couldn't afford a penniless wife, when his own dire circumstances demanded a rich one. Disowned meant no dower, and in his mind, he needed that dower.

38

Kimberly was still exhausted when she came downstairs to breakfast the next morning. Funny, that she'd never had a problem with sleeping before she met Lachlan MacGregor, but now . . . actually, it wasn't funny at all. And last night, there hadn't been any noise to keep her awake. Instead, she'd gone to bed with a lump in her throat that just wouldn't go away, and it refused to let her have any peace.

She could put aside her common sense and tell Lachlan that her father's money didn't matter, that she was as rich, if not richer, with more money than he could ever need. He'd marry her then, and there'd be no doubt that it was because of the money, not because he wanted her. Of course, she'd already known that. But having it proved beyond a doubt would hurt. But would it be any more than she was already hurting?

The prospect of her father having to buy a husband for her, some man she'd never even met, was what was tearing her up inside, not that

Lachlan didn't really want to marry her. And seen that way, wherein was the difference? If she bought Lachlan instead, by telling him about her own money, at least she knew what she was getting. And there was the lovemaking. With him, it was very nice, too nice maybe. But with someone else . . . she shuddered to even think of it.

She could tell him the truth and leave it up to him. If he'd been just waiting for an excuse to get out of the marriage, however, then it would make no difference. He'd use the new scandal instead, of her father disowning her. Or he'd still marry her . . .

She decided to tell him. And her opportunity arrived sooner than anticipated. Lachlan was in the hall outside the breakfast room when she approached, and he came toward her to take her arm and steer her toward the parlor instead, which was empty that time of the morning.

She waited to find out what was on his mind first. He told her the moment he closed the doors behind them.

"It occurred to me, Kimber, that you're of an age tae no' be needing your da's permission tae marry."

"That's true enough," she replied carefully. "But he wasn't joking, Lachlan, in what he said last night. He really will disown me if I marry without his approval."

"I didna doubt that. 'Twas what I found incredible and utterly despicable, that a father could be that cruel tae his own blood."

She shrugged, very used to that reaction in people who had to deal with her father, but had never done so before. "Perhaps it might help if you understand why he hates all Scotsmen," she remarked and gave him a brief accounting. But when she finished, she conceded, "On second thought, it doesn't help to know, does it? His prejudice is and always has been of an unreasonable nature."

" 'Tis no' important why he is how he is," he replied. "Unless there is the chance of him changing. He didna seem like a man capable o' changing his ways tae me, but I dinna know him as you do."

She sighed. "I know it's possible to change bad habits, but with him, it's a bit more than that, I'm afraid. Even the fact that he's met someone new since my mother died, that he wants to marry, and he's very eager to marry her, hasn't changed his attitude. It's not just his prejudice, you see. That has only to do with Scots. It's the way he is normally, a harsh, autocratic man, and I don't think he's ever been any other way. So no, I wouldn't ever expect him to change."

"As I thought. Then I need tae ask if you'll defy him and marry me wi'out his blessing? I should've asked you last night, but I was tae angry and shocked, and only thinking o' wringing his blasted neck."

Kimberly had gone very still before he finished. "Do you realize what that would mean?"

"Aye, it'd mean you'd be cut off from your da for good, likely ne'er tae see him again. Can you live wi' that, darlin', or would you always be regretting—"

"Lachlan, I could not care less if I ever see the Earl of Amburough again. He's never been a father to me, as fathers should be. He's merely been the tyrant who lived in the same house as I did. But do you realize what my being disowned by him would mean to *you*? Aside from the scandal—"

"The MacGregors are no' strangers tae scandal." He grinned.

"—there would be no dower forthcoming."

"I didna think so."

She blinked. "You'd marry me without it?"

"Damned right I will."

He was being gallant. She could think of no other reason. What else could he say, after all, without appearing the complete cad?

"But as I understand it, you need the money," she reminded him. "Have you forgotten about that? Or has that situation changed suddenly?"

"Nay, we're cash poor, you ken, and debt ridden as well," he told her. "You've a right tae know that now. When my da died a few years ago, my stepmother disappeared with a trunk full o' money—he didna like banks, you see—as well as all the MacGregor jewels, neither of which she had any right tae take, and she's ne'er been found. So we've still land aplenty, but no assets tae speak of on any of it."

All the more reason he should be marrying for money, not making this sacrifice because *she* hadn't had the will to prevent him from making love to her. Certainly, he was at fault there too, but she could have stopped him, should have, and didn't. And he didn't even know that marrying her would solve his problems after all. She hadn't told him that yet, and at the moment, apparently didn't need to.

But she should still tell him. He was, as far as she could tell, being honest with her. However, her curiosity was aroused now.

"It sounds as if you still need the dower, so how will you manage without it?"

"Dinna fash yourself about that, darlin'. I'll find the money that's needed some other way. A rich wife was an easy solution. There are others."

He sounded so confident, she decided again not to mention her own wealth. Actually, she wanted to savor the feeling that he would be marrying her not for any monetary reason—not for the reason she would have preferred to be asked for either, but at least this did put her one worry to rest. She wasn't being married only for her money.

So she said, "Very well, then. If you truly want to do this, I'll still marry you."

He smiled then, quite brilliantly. She caught her breath, feeling her stomach flip over. And then it seemed to leap right into her throat as he bridged the gap between them and slipped his arms around her.

"I'll tell your da today."

With him so close that his body was touching her in all pertinent places, it was almost impossible to concentrate on what he'd just said, and it was several moments before she got out, "Perhaps you should let me tell him. You'll more than likely lose your temper in his presence again. He has that effect on people who don't know him well."

"But—aye, mayhap you're right. But I will be close by if you need me."

That warmed her. This tendency he was showing about protecting her, when they weren't married yet. And then his lips were warming her even more, and although she'd guessed he was going to kiss her, was ready and waiting for him to, her senses were still jolted as they'd been each time previously. It was just so thrilling having his mouth on her, so incredibly thrilling . . .

She didn't hear the door open, but she did recognize the soft cadence of the Widow Marston's voice. "Cecil, are you in here?" and then when she noticed the kissing couple, "Oh! I'm so sorry. I should've knocked . . ."

Kimberly felt Lachlan go stiff just before he stepped away from her to face the intruder, but she assumed it was because they'd been interrupted. She had no idea it was because he'd also recognized the widow's voice.

But she gathered that much when he said in nearly the same ominous tone he'd used with her father last night, "Hello, stepmother."

Winnifred Marston gasped, took a step back, her hand going to her throat. She looked horrified, frightened, and sounded it too. "Lachlan, m'boy, I can explain."

"Can you now?"

39

Kimberly stared incredulously as her soon-to-be stepmother's eyes rolled into the back of her head and she crumpled to the floor in a dead faint. That, on top of just hearing that Winnifred Marston was also Lachlan's stepmother . . . or had she misunderstood that? Yes, she must have. It would simply be too ironic if the same woman were to play the same role in both their lives.

Beside her, Lachlan made a sound of disgust as he also stared at the woman now sprawled on the floor. The sound, however, brought Kimberly out of her bemusement.

"Pick her up, Lachlan, and put her on the sofa, would you?" she suggested.

"Nay, if I touch her, 'twill be wi' my hands around her throat."

Kimberly was so startled by his response that she immediately made an exasperated sound herself. "Put her on the bloody sofa. You can save your neck-wringing until she's conscious and can appreciate it."

She didn't wait to see if he would follow her order. She stepped around Winnifred to get to the door to summon a footman for some smelling salts. When she turned back into the room, Lachlan was dumping the older woman off of his shoulder onto a rose and gold sofa, and none too gently.

"Do remind me never to faint when you're around," she said dryly.

Lachlan dusted off his hands as if they'd been made filthy by the chore, then glanced at her. "Nay, darlin', you'd be carried like a wee bairn. But she's no' deserving o' that care."

She came back to stand beside him. "Am I to understand that she's the woman you were only just telling me about? The one who stole your inheritance?"

"Aye. I dinna ken why she's here, but she'll no' be disappearing on me this time."

Kimberly frowned. She could guess why Winnifred Marston was suddenly at Sherring Cross. She'd obviously come here with Cecil, and had probably been shown to a room last night so that she could retire, as late as it was, while they were still in the duke's study. That would explain why they hadn't seen her sooner.

But this was still so—astonishing, she had to ask again, "*She's* your stepmother?"

"Aye."

"The Widow Marston is your stepmother?"

He glowered at her now. "Aye and aye, and dinna make me repeat it again. I dinna care what she calls herself now, but she's the same woman was married tae my da for twelve years, then snuck off in the dead o' night no' a week after he died, taking the MacGregor wealth wi' her."

He was growing annoyed at her persistence, but she still found this too ironic by half. "You couldn't be mistaken? Maybe she only closely resembles your stepmother?"

He snorted. "She fainted at the sight o' me. If there was ever any doubt o' her guilt, there's none now. But there wasna any tae begin wi'."

It was incredible. Kimberly had met and spoken with Winnifred Marston dozens of times socially, even before her mother died and her father became interested in the widow. She'd always seemed a nice enough sort, if a little self-centered.

The widow was in her late forties, had brown hair untouched yet by grey, light brown eyes, and a slightly plump, though very curvacious figure. And she wasn't very tall, certainly shorter than Cecil. She was a handsome woman for her age.

Kimberly had actually never given the woman much thought. She knew that Winnifred had refused to marry Cecil until Kimberly was herself married and was gone from his house. But that was understandable.

She knew many women who weren't related by blood that had trouble sharing the same household. There were even some troubles among those who were related. It was a matter of each wanting ultimate control of a household, when only one could fill that position. And she'd certainly had no problem with that, since she wanted out of her father's house as well.

She also knew that the widow was quite wealthy. She'd bought the old Henry house, a really large home, when she'd moved to Northumberland several years before. She employed dozens of servants. She entertained lavishly and frequently. With stolen money?

It was incredible. And her father, when he was told—good God, she couldn't begin to guess what his reaction was going to be. Actually, he'd never believe it, not with a Scotsman as the accuser.

She shook her head, still quite bemused. "I'm having a very hard time imagining Winnie as a thief, I really am."

"Winnie?" Lachlan said in surprise. "D'you know this woman, Kimber?"

Had that somehow not been mentioned yet? "Actually, you're going to find this—"

"Who fainted?" Megan asked as she sailed into the room, the footman apparently having fetched her along with the smelling salts. And then seeing Winnifred on the sofa, "Ah, our newcomer, Lady—Marston, is it? Was she taken ill? Should I send for a doctor?"

"I doubt a doctor will be needful," Kimberly replied, giving Megan a slight smile. "She was merely done in by the sight of Lachlan."

Megan lifted a brow in Lachlan's direction. "You have them swooning at your feet now, MacGregor? Maybe you should start carrying the salts around with you?"

He snorted. "She fainted in fear, and rightly so."

Megan's brow lifted much higher at that. "Did she now? Well, you've such a frightening face, no wonder. Yes, that I can surely imagine."

Lachlan's lips compressed in annoyance. Megan was sitting down on the edge of the sofa now, so that she could pass the smelling salts swiftly beneath Winnifred's nose. It did the trick, the widow's hand coming up to swipe at the offensive smell, then her eyes slowly blinked open.

She was confused at first, and seeing only Megan before her, asked haltingly, "What—happened to me? Why am I lying down?"

She stopped, her eyes suddenly widening in remembrance—and there was some definite alarm there too. She even gripped Megan's arm to ask her next question, which came out in a frantic whisper.

"Is he still here?"

"Who?"

"The MacGregor?"

"Well—yes, actual—"

The widow sat up immediately, in fact too quickly, causing her head to throb, and nearly knocking Megan onto the floor in the process. Winnifred groaned at the sharp pain she felt, but it was more important that she locate Lachlan. Doing so, she groaned again, even louder, and extended a beseeching hand toward him.

"Lachlan, you must let me explain first—before you do anything that we'll both regret."

"*Both* regret?" he replied coldly. "I assure you, lady, whatever I do, it will give me a great deal o' pleasure—and you none a'tall."

"Please, can we at least discuss this in private?" Winnifred pleaded, glancing with embarrassment at Kimberly and Megan. "There's no reason to disturb these ladies with a family matter."

"Family matter, is it?"

It was apparent, at least to Kimberly, that Lachlan was too angry to honor the widow's request. Nor did he care at the moment how embarrassed she might be. From his perspective, Kimberly certainly couldn't blame him, but she still took pity on the woman.

So she cleared her throat and gave a pointed

look at Megan. "I haven't had breakfast yet myself. Would you care to join me?"

Megan sighed, but nodded. Once beyond the door, however, she confessed, "I know you're right, m'dear, but I wouldn't have left there for the world myself. I'm simply too curious. Do *you* know what that is all about?"

"Yes, unfortunately," Kimberly replied. "And I don't believe Lachlan intends to keep it secret. Quite the contrary. When you have someone arrested, it's rather impossible to keep it under wraps . . ."

In the parlor, Winnifred was talking quickly. "I loved your father, Lachlan. You must know that. His dying was a shock, so unexpected. I was distraught and not thinking clearly—"

"We were all o' us distraught. If that's the only excuse you have tae offer—"

"I was also terrified."

"Of what?" he demanded.

"Of being alone."

"Are you daft?" he asked in amazement. "Alone wi' a whole castle full o' folk around you?"

"All MacGregor folk," she reminded him.

"Aye, and who else would be there but MacGregors? You were a MacGregor as well, or are you forgetting that?"

"It's not the same as being born a MacGregor," Winnifred insisted.

"How is it no' the same? Did you think we would kick you out? Nay, you know better. You would always have had a home at Kregora."

"Without your father?" she said, shaking her head. "I'd never made friends there—"

"Whose fault is that, lady?"

"Mine, I know, but it was still a fact. Your father was my life and my protection. Without him—I had nothing."

"If you're thinking that gave you the right tae steal my inheritance—" he growled.

"No, no, I know I did wrong. And I did it without thinking, because I was so frightened of being alone again. Believe me, I've regretted it so often."

"Did you now?" he scoffed, adding, "You've had a number of years tae correct what you did, but I've yet tae see the MacGregor jewels returned, or the money."

She winced. "I know, but I convinced myself that I needed it more'n you did. You were young, after all. And you were a man, able to earn money in ways that I couldn't."

"Aye, and mayhap that would've been no problem if there was only myself tae see about. But wi' my da's passing, it became my responsibility tae look after the clan, as well as the upkeep of Kregora. And how was I tae do that, when the college I attended was only a rounding off o' my education? I wasna there tae learn a trade. Nor could any trade have supported the many mouths I have tae feed, much less make the repairs on that old castle."

Hearing that, she began to panic. "Lachlan, you *have* to understand! I grew up very poor. My father had been a wastrel and a gambler. My mother died when I was but a baby. There were times when I didn't know if there would be food enough for another day. I couldn't go back to how it was before. Your father had been my salvation. With him gone, I was desperate again, don't you see?"

"Nay, Winnifred, no matter how you look at it, no matter your reasons, you stole from me and no' just from me, but from the clan. And I'll be having it all back, every pound, every ring and necklace—"

"The money's gone."

Lachlan went very still. His eyes had flared. Considering the amount of money that was taken, and the amount of time that had passed . . . no, he couldn't believe it. No one could spend that much money in only three years—unless they lived like a blasted king.

All he could think to say to such an outlandish statement was, "Gone?" Actually, he shouted it.

The widow was flinching. "I didn't mean to spend it all, truly. I even hid in a small cottage in Bath for nearly a year, going nowhere, doing nothing. But I got so bored, you see. I needed to be around people again. So I decided to play the bountiful widow for a while—under another name, of course, and moved to Northumberland where I bought a house so that I could entertain properly. And I gambled a bit, not much, but— I'm not very good at it, any more than my father was—"

"Enough!" he thundered. "Faith, but you're talking about more'n a hundred thousand pounds, woman! You canna have spent all o' that—"

"I still have the jewels," she quickly inserted. "At least most of them. I've only had to sell off a few of the pieces just recently. And there's the house I bought. I'll be glad to give it to you just as soon as I marry, and that will be very shortly now."

"Glad tae give me a house you bought wi' my money?" he asked incredulously.

He almost laughed. She didn't even see the absurdity of her offer, or realize that every blasted thing she owned belonged to him. The woman was a twit, a frivolous, self-centered nitwit, and he'd never been around her long enough when she lived at Kregora to actually realize that before now.

"I'm sure my fiancé won't mind the loss of my house," she went on to say. "He might even be persuaded to reimburse your funds for me. He's such a dear man, after all, and quite rich. I'm sure he wouldn't miss a few hundred pounds—"

"Hundred *thousand* pounds, lady!"

"Well, that too."

The door suddenly opened again, and Kimberly poked her head around it. "Do you realize you can be heard down the hall?"

"They can hear me in the next blasted county for all I care," Lachlan replied heatedly. "Do you ken the lady has squandered away more'n half my inheritance, Kimber? And she has the audacity to suggest her fiancé might replace a hundred thousand pounds of it!"

"Oh, I wouldn't count on that," Kimberly replied calmly. "She's engaged to marry my father, you see."

40

"I think it's rather funny, actually," Megan remarked as she dismounted and turned her mare, Sir Ambrose, over to the waiting groom.

That her horse was named after her husband, and before she'd ever met him, was—well, it was a long story. And Devlin certainly didn't mind the name anymore, though at one time he had.

They had just returned from a ride, where she had told him about the latest development in the MacGregor-Richards situation. Usually she rode in the early mornings, but if she wanted to ride with her husband, she had to make allowances for his busy schedule, and he'd been attending to business all morning—which was why he'd missed the newest scandal-in-the-making.

"And just what do you find funny?" he asked, taking her arm to lead her back to the house. "That I owe the Highlander another apology?"

"No, not that—" She stopped in surprise. "You do? What for?"

"Because I didn't believe that story of his,

about his inheritance being stolen," Devlin said sourly. "I thought it was just a good ruse on his part to gain him sympathy."

"Well, if *he* wasn't aware that you thought that, then there's no need to apologize to him."

"I feel there is. My assumption about him colored most of my thinking, you see. Had I accepted his story to begin with, I might have treated him differently, might not have jumped down his throat so quickly when the horses went missing, might not have—"

"Oh, dear, you really *are* feeling a tad guilty, aren't you?"

He nodded curtly. "A tad."

"Then by all means . . . but you know, it certainly won't change his mind about what he's going to do."

"Which is?"

"I haven't the faintest idea. I'm not so sure even MacGregor knows at this point. The Marston woman is such a silly scatterbrain, after all. It would be like punishing a child. But he's set his kin to guarding her. She won't be going anywhere until this is resolved."

"And what did the earl have to say about that?" Devlin asked as he resumed walking to the house.

"I don't believe he's been told yet—at least no one got around to it before we left. That could have changed by now. Let's hope so. It's going to be a rather—loud—undertaking, I imagine."

"Well, I did my duty last night, distasteful as it was. I'm staying the hell out of this one."

"Don't blame you a'tall," Megan replied. "Lord Richards is the most singularly unpleasant man I've met in a very long while. Amazing that

Kimberly turned out so decent, with a father like that. And I'm so *glad* she's going to marry the Highlander. As outrageous as he is, and charming, he'll bring laughter to her life, and long overdue if you ask me."

Devlin lifted a brow at her. "Ah, did I miss something, m'dear? I could have sworn I told you last night that the earl refused, unequivocally, to allow it."

Megan waved a dismissing hand. "Yes, yes, I know, but mark my words, those two will get married anyway."

"You think so, do you?"

"Absolutely."

Kimberly had expected to see Lachlan standing there when she opened the door to her room, and to hear what he had decided. He had been so exasperated by his talk with the widow earlier that he had simply escorted Winnifred to her room without saying another word to her, sent a footman for his kinsmen, and waited there until they arrived to set a watch on her. Then he'd gone off to "think about it" and Kimberly had returned to her room to do some thinking of her own, in preparation for her talk with her father.

She had intended to be very straightforward about her decision. There was nothing to discuss, after all, nothing to argue about, and no reason to broach the subject carefully. The earl might rant and rave a bit—she expected no less. But she was used to listening to his loud tirades with only half her attention. Otherwise, she never would have been able to survive them all these years.

But this thing with Lachlan's stepmother, Kimberly's *almost* stepmother, well, that was a different subject altogether. She had no desire to hurt her father. Cutting herself out of his life wouldn't hurt him at all, she had no doubt. But this . . .

Did he love the widow?

It was possible, but not very likely. In fact, Kimberly doubted he was even capable of that emotion. He might have claimed it was love, what he'd felt for that other woman all those years ago, but her guess was that it was more an obsession.

No, it was much more likely that he was re-marrying simply because he needed a hostess, and he couldn't depend on Kimberly, with her indifference to his needs, to fill that position for very long. That he had picked the Widow Marston could have been for no other reason than she was socially acceptable, and in their small community, quite popular.

So would he be upset if Winnifred was arrested and charged with her crime? Or would he see it only as a setback and a bother, while he looked for someone else to take her place? Kimberly really couldn't say.

However, there was also the fact that he'd invested a lot of time in courting the widow. He had, in fact, frequently gone to her home for dinner or one of her entertainments. She had been invited to their house as well.

And another thing, everyone knew they were engaged. If they didn't marry now, the earl would have to explain why, and knowing him, he'd find that quite an embarrassment. Instead, he'd probably come up with a good excuse that wouldn't come close to the truth—if the scandal could be contained and go no further.

If . . . if . . . and Kimberly was supposed to address this issue? Actually, as his daughter, it did fall to her to do so. Lachlan certainly wouldn't bother. And Winnifred, well, there was no telling what she would have to say about it.

And Kimberly had the opportunity to do it now, because it was the earl standing in her doorway scowling at her, not Lachlan. And apparently, he'd already worked himself into another rage.

"This is the fourth time I've come by here to see you," he complained right off. "Should have restricted you to your bloody room—"

"Did you want something, Father?"

"Yes, I came to tell you to pack your belongings. We're leaving here today."

"I don't think so."

"I beg your pardon?"

"You can leave, of course, but I'll be staying on, at least until I'm married."

"You found someone else to marry you this quickly? I don't believe it. Who?"

"No one else. I'm going to marry the Highlander as I had already agreed to do."

"I forbid it!"

"Yes, I know, but I'm going to marry him anyway," she replied calmly.

"That is complete defiance of my wishes! No daughter of mine—"

"I'm your only daughter—"

"Not anymore, by God! You are disowned. Disowned, d'you hear!"

"Yes, I know that too. And now that we have that out of the way—"

Kimberly paused because he'd turned away, red-faced in his fury. She was already dead to him, apparently. She no longer existed, so she didn't even warrant a farewell. He was going to simply leave . . .

She lost her calm completely. "Stop right there! I don't know why I should bother with this. It's nothing to me whether you marry Winnifred or—"

That snapped him back around to say, "You're damned right it's nothing to you—now."

"It never was, or haven't you realized that I have no interest in your life? But that's neither here nor there. What I was going to share with you was that the widow is in serious trouble, is likely to end up in—"

"What the bloody hell are you talking about?"

"If you'll stop interrupting me, I might manage to explain. You see, a few years ago she stole a lot of money from her stepson, more than a hundred thousand pounds, as well as a fortune in jewels. She had no right to either. This was his inheritance. Yet she walked off with both. Your bringing her here has allowed him to finally find her. He may wish to thank you for that, though I doubt it, since it's Lachlan MacGregor that I'm talking about."

His eyes showed that she had surprised him, but only for the briefest second, before he covered his surprise and demanded, "What kind of trick are you pulling here, gel? D'you really expect me to believe such nonsense?"

"Actually, I don't really care if you do or don't," she admitted. "I just felt that since you had intended to marry the widow, you had a right to know that she could be sent to prison for this crime."

"There is no crime! And I refuse to listen—"

"She fully admitted it, Father. She also admitted that the money is gone, squandered away. She has most of the jewels still, and those will be returned to Lachlan, along with her house, but I doubt he'll be satisfied with just that. We're talking about too much money here for him to just shrug off the loss. It was all the tangible wealth he had. But he's undecided at the moment, so you might want to talk to him about it. You'll want to talk to her as well, since I certainly don't expect you to take my word for any of this."

He stood there bemused now, staring at the floor. She understood the feeling perfectly.

After nearly a minute passed, he said, still in bewilderment, "How could she do such a stupid thing?"

It was one of the most singularly ordinary things she'd ever heard him say. It actually touched her, certainly made her feel sorry for him. So she wasn't about to answer, "Because you got yourself engaged to a bloody twit," which would have been her reply otherwise.

Instead she said diplomatically, "She had her reasons, though they don't excuse what she did. I'm sure she'll tell you all about it. Actually, she probably needs a good shoulder to cry on about now."

He snapped to himself then, his usual sour visage back in place. But he blushed, because Kimberly had still witnessed his moment of vulnerability.

And he cleared his throat before asking in a grumbling tone, "Just how determined is that Scotsman to have Winnie arrested?"

Kimberly blinked. She almost laughed. Never

would she have imagined herself in a bargaining position with her father, but damned if that wasn't what she was now in. So he *did* still want to marry the widow? Imagine that.

41

It took Kimberly over an hour to find Lachlan, but only because he wasn't staying in any one place long enough to be found, was just walking aimlessly about the estate. She finally found him coming up the path that led to the boating lake, where she'd been told he'd headed last.

He must not have stayed there long. The chill wind coming off the water, which was kept free of ice by the grounds keepers, had probably chased him away, because he hadn't dressed warmly enough for an extended outdoor jaunt. His hands were stuffed in his pockets now, his cheeks were wind-reddened, and his teeth were chattering. But he still had a warm smile for her when he noticed her heading toward him.

"Ah, darlin', would you be taking pity on me?" he asked without preamble.

"How's that?" she said as she reached him.

"I'm in need of a little warming."

Even as he said it, he slipped his hands inside her coat and around her to press her close to his chest. She shivered as those cold hands spread on her back. She heard him chuckle when he felt it.

"Bad as all that, is it?"

"No," she allowed, blushing slightly. "Just for a second it was. But this isn't going to warm you adequately. You need a fire and—"

"You'd be surprised," he murmured by her ear, "how quickly you can warm me."

She shivered again. They both knew it wasn't because of the cold this time. But then his icy nose touched her cheek and she was startled. She shrieked and jumped back from him. He laughed. She did too, because the sound he was making was contagious.

When he wound down, he sighed dramatically and said, "Verra well, I guess I mun settle for a fire tae do the warming—for now."

"You should have dressed warmer," she admonished as he took her arm to start them toward the mansion.

"Nay, this is mild weather they have here, compared tae the Highlands."

"I agree, it's much colder in Northumberland too, but how long have you been out in it?"

"Since I left you."

She shook her head at him. "You'll be lucky if you don't have the sniffles by this evening."

"Och, well, I'm owing you a cold as I recall."

His grin was too wicked by half, and had her blushing again. She, too, could remember that he'd caught her previous cold by kissing her. To get her mind off of that, she recalled the reason she'd sought him out.

"I've spoken with my father," she said abruptly.

He stopped to draw her back into his arms, surprising her with his sympathy. "I'm sorry, darlin'. Was it painful, his cutting you from his life?"

"No, but—"

He interrupted her, his tone gentle, "You dinna have tae pretend for my sake."

"Lachlan, really, we never had that kind of relationship." She leaned back to assure him. "If I never saw him again, it wouldn't bother me a'tall, and I'm sure he would say the same. But he didn't quite disown me. Well, he did, but then he sort of changed his mind."

"He realized the scandal of it would reflect worse on himself, did he? Aye, I was hoping he'd be figuring that out—for your sake."

She smiled wryly. "He might have, but most likely after the damage was already done and so too late to correct it. One thing I've noticed over the years is when he's angry, which is a great deal of the time, he tends to not think things through. So consequences are the least of his concern."

He let go of her, his confusion apparent. "Then you were able tae actually *talk* him out of it?"

"Bargain might better describe it."

"And what did you have tae bargain with?"

"You."

Lachlan blinked at that answer. She laughed at his startled expression and decided to tease him a bit. She hooked her arm through his again and made the effort to pull them up the path. That worked for only about three steps, before his feet dug in and she couldn't budge him another inch.

"You dinna think you can get away wi'out explaining that tae me, d'you, Kimber?"

"Actually . . . possibly . . . well, now that you mention it . . ."

He waited expectantly, but when she said no

more, just stared at him wide-eyed, he was surprised again. It was her grin, however, that gave her away, and after a moment, he slowly shook his head at her, and his own grin was entirely too—retaliatory. So when he reached for her, she knew she was in trouble, and with a shriek, she hiked up her skirt and took off up the path.

Of course, it was absurd to think she could outdistance him with those long legs of his, nor did she for more than a few moments. But she didn't expect to end up on the ground, sprawled on top of him in a most undignified manner, his chuckling bouncing her around on his chest.

"You're mad," she admonished, trying to get up, but he wasn't letting her. "We're not children, you know."

"When I'm too old tae play, darlin', I'll be using a cane and counting the hairs I have left on my head. Och, mayhap no' even then will I stop playing wi' you."

She gave him a stern look, but she couldn't hold it for more than a few seconds, not when he was looking so boyish, and mussed, and pleased with himself. And besides, what he'd said was rather thrilling if taken in a sensual context, which she was sure he'd meant, since things of a sexual nature seemed to *always* be on his mind.

So she ended up blushing instead, and when he saw it, he ended up kissing her. One thing led to another, and before she knew it, his hand was halfway up her skirt, his cold hand on her thigh contrasting with the heat of his lips, causing her to shiver in pleasure and with the chill.

And then he was gazing up at her with a thoroughly disgruntled look. "I have tae own, outdoors in the dead o' winter is no place tae be playing—this game."

"Not to mention, anyone could have come along," she pointed out.

"Och, well, that wouldna bother me—"

"It would me—"

"No' for long, darlin'. I promise you'll get used tae that real quick once I have you home wi' me."

Of course, she blushed again. Hopefully she'd also get used to his sexual innuendoes real quick, so she could stop looking like she was sunburned every time she was around him for more than a few minutes.

"Now, 'afore I'm letting you up," he said, quite serious of a sudden, "you'll be telling me what happened wi' your da, or did you forget what got you down here on the ground in the first place?"

She had forgotten. But then Lachlan had a way of making her forget anything and everything when he had his arms around her and . . .

"Well?"

"Well, I told him about Winnifred's little problem," she said.

"*Little* problem?"

She sighed. "Very well, *big* problem. And I suggested that if he still wanted to marry the woman, that he come up with a good portion of what she owes you. And then you might, *might*, mind you, be persuaded to drop the matter."

He rolled to sit up, setting her on the ground next to him, and with a snort, asked, "How hard did he laugh?"

"He didn't. My father is going to give you half of the money. I'll make up the difference."

"Oh, he is, is he? And that's supposed to make up for all the worry and deprivation she—what d'you mean, you will make up the difference? You've money o' your own?"

"Yes."

He was suddenly smiling. "You do?"

He was so delightfully surprised, she couldn't help it, she laughed. "Yes, I do."

"Faith, and when were you going tae be telling me that?"

"Oh, sometime after we were married, I imagine. But as I was saying, he'll give you half of the money. He still wants to marry her, you see. So as an added incentive, *if* you agree to drop the matter, he's also agreed not to disown me—officially at least, if I still marry you. But he wouldn't budge on the dowry. He still refuses to give that to a Scotsman." And then she laughed.

"What?"

"I wasn't going to mention this to him, but it works out about the same, you know. What he's going to give you and my dower, it's about equal. He'll have another fit, I don't doubt, once he realizes that. So what do you think? Does that sound acceptable to you?"

Lachlan rubbed his jaw, his look seriously thoughtful. "Och, I dinna know, darlin'. I'm thinking I'll have tae be giving it a lot of thought."

Her eyes narrowed. "There's nothing to— you're going to make him wait deliberately, aren't you?"

His eyes widened with feigned innocence. "Now would I be doing that, just because the man hates my guts and doesna want me marrying his only daughter? Just because he's mean-spirited and hot-tempered and deserves tae stew about it a wee bit?"

She'd heard Megan say it so often that the word came out automatically, "Absolutely."

Lachlan grinned. "Och, well, I like it that you think you know me so well. But in this case . . . well, in this case you do."

42

Kimberly didn't necessarily think making her father wait for an answer was a good idea, but she did agree that Winnifred should be made to wait. If Lachlan decided in their favor, took the money and the return of the jewels, and let it go at that, which Kimberly had no doubt he would do in the end, then the widow would have gotten away with the theft free and clear.

Making her wait, and doing so confined to her room, was the only punishment she'd receive for what she'd done. That was little enough for all the trouble and difficulties she'd caused the MacGregors, but at least it was better than nothing at all.

Her father, however, wasn't taking the wait very patiently. His mood was about as sour as it could get, making it *very* uncomfortable to be around him. But fortunately, he kept to his room mostly, or the widow's room, so the rest of them didn't have to suffer his unpleasantness very often.

Kimberly hadn't asked Lachlan, but she guessed he wasn't going to announce his decision until after they were married. That was rubbing her father's nose in it a bit more, and he'd be all for that. She was sure, positive, actually, that Cecil would have preferred to be gone before she committed this public defiance of his wishes.

He could, of course, not show up for the service. That might have embarrassed Kimberly if she had been expecting him to make an appearance. But she wasn't, so she really didn't care if he did or not. As long as Lachlan was there . . .

With Christmas so close, Megan had suggested they enjoy the holiday first—she wouldn't hear of them not staying for it—then have the wedding a few days afterward. And when the duchess made a suggestion, everyone pretty much agreed.

Kimberly saw nothing wrong with that arrangement. She had much to do anyway, shopping, difficult letters to write to her few closer friends in Northumberland, explaining why she wouldn't be back. And a long, detailed letter to the Richards' housekeeper, instructing her to pack all her belongings and send them on to the Highlands, as well as those things in the house that she considered hers.

Most important were the furnishings that had belonged to her mother, certain pieces that had become fixtures of the house after so many years. Like the mammoth painting that hung over the mantel in the parlor, the antique chinoiserie in the dining room, the Queen Anne walnut grandfather clock that had been handed down in her mother's family since the mid-seventeen hundreds.

These were things that held no meaning for her father, but were treasures to her, and she would fight tooth and nail to take them with her. Which wasn't necessary.

When she gave her father a list of the items she wanted, he merely nodded his agreement and turned back to what he'd been doing, dismissing her and the subject. And how familiar that was, exactly how he'd treated her most of her life.

Christmas arrived all too soon, and it turned out to be a really festive day, and one of the most enjoyable holidays Kimberly had ever experienced. She'd bought a little something for each of the St. Jameses, and gave her father a box of his favorite cigars. He'd never once, for any occasion, given her a gift from himself. Her mother used to tell her the presents she received were from the both of them, but once Kimberly was older and knew better she didn't pretend anymore.

But that she received nothing from him that day was no more than she expected, so it didn't bother her. Nothing, actually, could ruin that day for her, thanks to Lachlan, who teased her outrageously, and caught her beneath the mistletoe so often, everyone else was making jokes about it. And what was most delightful was that they'd both had the idea of giving each other gifts designed to be amusing.

Lachlan burst out laughing when she handed him a cane, remembering the day he'd mentioned one. And he warned her, "I'll be taking this tae your backside if you try counting the hairs I have left before I'm at least—thirty."

She studied his thick mane of auburn hair and replied seriously, "It's going to fall out that soon, eh? Well, there are wigs, of course, and I'll be sure to fix yours whenever it starts to fall off. Very messy, you know, when they fall in the soup—you do serve soup in the Highlands?"

"Nay, but we do serve sassy Sassenachs up for dinner quite frequently."

She couldn't hold a straight face any longer and chuckled. "I won't taste good, I promise you."

"Och, darlin', now that's a lie. I already know how good you taste."

And he proved it by dragging her back over to the mistletoe, smacking his lips loudly, then giving her a half dozen quick kisses that had her giggling before he was through. And Duchy had looked up from the new stationery set she'd been examining to remark, "Good God, there ought to be a law against noise like that. Dev, m'boy, why don't you show him how to do it right?"

And damned if the duke didn't, pulling a protesting, though grinning Megan over to join them beneath the mistletoe, and soon the rest of them were all laughing, because *they*, of course, didn't make a sound, and it didn't look like they had any intention of stopping either.

But not much later, Lachlan topped her silly gift by pulling a parasol out of his coat and offering it with a flourish.

Kimberly saw the humor in the gift, and with a slight smirk, said, "Brave of you."

"Aye, for you, darlin', I'll brave anything," he said, and she could have sworn he wasn't teasing in the least.

She smiled at him. He had a charming knack for saying all the right things, courting things. Then again, he said all the wrong things too, sensual, sexual things that shouldn't be for her ears—yet, and caused her all those blushes.

She'd also bought him a rather expensive pair of diamond cuff links that got her yet another kiss, this one without any mistletoe, and of the warm, lingering kind. But then he surprised her with another gift also at the end of the day, one she really hadn't been expecting.

It was in a small box, and while she opened it, he told her, "I bought that 'afore your da showed up."

After the box was opened, revealing what could be considered an engagement ring, she realized why he'd volunteered that information. It was his way of apologizing because it was on the plain side.

Even so, it was a small emerald of good quality, and she knew he'd had no money to speak of to buy it, and still didn't—yet. So she asked him, "How?"

He shrugged, trying to make light of it. "I sold my horse. I'm no' much of a horseman anyway, so the nag won't be missed. Mayhap I'll accept those three the duke tried tae give me, just tae get us home, mind you."

For some ridiculous reason, Kimberly was moved nearly to tears. He hadn't needed to do anything like that. He could have waited until he could have afforded it. She would have understood. She knew his circumstances. That he'd gone ahead and bought her the ring anyway, simply because he wanted her to have it before the wedding as was traditional, made it all the more sweet, and she would treasure it far more than any of her own jewelry.

But to keep from crying and making a fool of herself, she latched onto what he'd mentioned about possibly accepting the three Thoroughbred horses from Devlin and told him, "I already did."

"Did what?"

"Accepted them," she answered matter-of-factly. "They're a good investment. I happen to know about such things."

"D'you now?" he replied, his tone skeptical, until he noticed her smile was positively smug, then he allowed, "Aye mayhap you do, and faith, I'm glad tae hear it, darlin'. The MacGregors have-na had much luck in that area. I'm thinking we're due."

43

Kimberly was with Mrs. Canterby late the next afternoon, mere hours now before her wedding— she was counting the minutes too—when one of the servants came looking for her.

One of her new gowns had been ideally suited for a wedding—she was sure the seamstress had planned it that way when she'd made it—with just a few alterations and embellishments needed to make it perfect for the occasion, which the woman had been working on this last week. Kimberly was there for the final fitting and approval. But of course, she could find no fault with Mrs. Canterby's designs, with her subtle, yet elegant tastes.

The servant who showed up was a young girl, one of the upstairs maids, who requested a private word with her. Out in the hall, she proceeded to tell her in a whisper, "I cleans yer father's room, I do, and glad I am when 'e's not— well, 'e's there today, but 'e won't let me in, won't even answer me knocks. Yet I knows 'e's in there, 'cause I could 'ear 'im crying on t'other side of the door.''

"Crying?"

"Yes, mum."

"*Crying*?"

"Yes, mum," the girl repeated, bobbing her head now in a hopeful manner, as if that might help to get Kimberly to stop doubting her.

It didn't. Kimberly didn't believe it and wouldn't until she saw it for herself. What nonsense. It was probably no more than some cat that had found its way into the room and was now trapped and wanting out. Her father probably wasn't even in the room himself. And this girl couldn't tell the difference between a cat mewling and a human crying.

She sighed. "Very well, I'll go and see what's wrong as soon as I change clothes," she told the girl. "And thank you for bringing this matter to me."

Kimberly didn't hurry. It was too absurd, really. And by the time she left Mrs. Canterby's rooms, she had almost decided not to bother. Her father's room was in a different wing of the mansion than hers, after all, and no short walk between the two. It would be a waste of time . . . but there was still the cat. She couldn't just leave it there, when it was apparently desperate to get out.

So she headed for her father's room, and upon reaching his door, she heard not a sound from the other side. She knocked gently, but still no sound. Then she opened the door a bit, expecting a cat to come flying past her feet. None did. So she opened it a bit more. And there he was, sitting in a chair with one hand covering his eyes.

He was wearing a robe, as if he hadn't dressed at all since he'd gotten up that morning.

She was surprised. And then she actually felt a smidgen of concern. If he really had been crying—it was still impossible to believe—but . . .

"Are you all right?" she asked hesitantly.

Her voice startled him. His hand fell away to reveal some very bloodshot eyes, but no tears, and no trace that there had been any. There could have been, though. He could have wiped them away.

"All right?" he blustered. "Certainly. Why wouldn't I be all right?"

Kimberly blinked. Those words had definitely been slurred. And then she noticed the nearly empty bottle of spirits on the table next to him.

He was foxed. Incredible. Cecil Richards never drank to excess, just the opposite. One glass of wine at dinner and no more was all he'd allow himself. One glass of something at a party and no more.

She'd never seen him like this. She doubted anyone else had either. It was a unique experience, and so unexpected, but curious too.

Too curious not to ask, she said, "Why are you drinking in the afternoon?"

"Am I?"

She raised a brow. "I believe so."

"So I am." He snorted, then replied, "And why wouldn't I be, when that wretch you're planning to marry can't make up his bloody mind?"

So that was it? The waiting had really gotten to him, worse than she'd thought. But still, a more typical response from her father would be to have a good blowup about it, instead of this.

Unless he was worried about antagonizing Lachlan at this point.

"Reminds me of Ian," he went on to mumble.

"What does?" she asked, thinking he meant Lachlan's being indecisive.

"The drinking. He never could hold his liquor either, the sot."

"Who's Ian?"

He reached for the bottle, missed it, then promptly forgot about it as he answered, "My best friend, or he was, the bastard. You don't know him, gel. He's not worth knowing, so be thankful of that."

Best friend? She'd never known her father to have any close friends aside from Maurice's father, Thomas, and theirs had been more of a business relationship. His brusque attitude alienated people easily, keeping them at a distance. So this Ian he must have known a really long time ago. And perhaps he'd even had a more pleasant nature in those days, to allow for things like friendships. It was apparently the death of his true love that had turned him sour on the world, and that had happened before Kimberly was born.

But her curiosity had been satisfied as to why he was drinking. She wasn't curious about his past. Actually, she was wondering now how she might delicately suggest he go to bed and sleep off the liquor he'd consumed, because she didn't feel comfortable just leaving him like this.

So to get the same results, she asked, "What did Ian do when he drank too much? Sleep it off?"

He didn't take the hint. In fact, it was the worst thing she could have said. He went red in the face, giving every indication that one of his temper tantrums was about to begin. And in his present condition, she imagined that could get really ugly.

So Kimberly was already taking a step backward toward the door when he exploded, "What did he do? *What did he do*? He stole my Ellie, that's what, and killed her! May he rot in hell when he gets there!"

Good God, she'd never heard this before, only that the woman had been killed by a Scot, in Cecil's opinion, which was why he hated them all now. But in the opinion of everyone else, it had been an accident. Killed by a Scot . . . ?

"Ian was a Scotsman? You're saying you were best friends with a *Scotsman*?"

He glared at her. "That was a bloody long time ago, but yes, I was foolish enough to make that mistake in my youth. I've never regretted anything more, and will never make the mistake of trusting a Scotsman again, either."

"I don't understand. Why would he steal her, if he was your friend?"

"Because he loved her, too. And he kept it a bloody secret, didn't tell me until after she was dead. I wanted to kill him, I really did. I should have killed him. Always regretted that I didn't."

Kimberly had never heard exactly what had happened, just bits and pieces at different times, usually whenever her father was especially angry at her mother and throwing it up to her, that she'd been his second choice. She wondered if he'd tell her now?

"How did she die?" she asked carefully.

"Because Ian MacFearson was drunk, that's how! He never would have had the nerve to run off with her if he'd been sober. And he stole her in the small hours of the night and sped with her across the border. She fell off her horse; died instantly. To this day, I don't doubt that she jumped off deliberately, because she couldn't bear to be dishonored by that blackguard. He claimed it was an accident, that her horse stumbled into a chuckhole and broke its leg, throwing her." Cecil snorted. "Damned liar, just trying to place the blame other than where it belonged."

"If he—loved her too, how did he take her death? He must have been as devastated as you were."

"He blamed me, no doubt. Why else would he have wanted revenge?"

"Revenge?"

"Yes. I still needed a wife. Saw no reason to wait, since I didn't think I'd ever love again. So I picked your mother. And Ian bided his time, waiting until we were engaged, then he set out to seduce Melissa into falling in love with him. He wanted me to know what it felt like, to love a woman who loves someone else. That was his revenge, because Ellie loved me, she didn't love him. And it worked. I don't doubt Melissa loved him till the day she died."

Could that possibly be true? Kimberly had suspected there had been no love between her parents, knew there'd been no closeness, at least that she'd ever witnessed. They simply lived in the same house, went to the same functions together, but rarely spoke to each other. Through all those years, could her mother really have loved another man?

And then Cecil laughed, an ugly sound, and added somewhat smugly, "But the joke was on him, because I didn't love her. I only married her because I needed a wife, and I didn't care who. He moved back to Scotland, though, before I could tell him his efforts had been wasted. And I had the last laugh, because he didn't even know he'd left you behind, the fool."

Kimberly went very still, her breath suspended. "What do you mean, he left me behind?"

Cecil blinked, seemed surprised by her question. But then he shrugged, saying, "You're going your own way, foolish enough to marry that Highlander. So there's no reason for you not to know the truth now."

"*What* truth?"

"You ain't mine, gel. You're all over his, same eyes, same hair, same mouth—same smile. I despise that smile of yours, you know, the way it reminds me of him. And anyway, your mother admitted it, took pride in admitting it, by God. But I called you mine. There was nothing else to do, after all. And I didn't really care. Didn't expect to be having an heir off her anyway, since I wouldn't touch her, knowing she loved Ian. Couldn't divorce her, much as I'd have liked to later. The scandal, you know. So I was stuck with her—and you."

Kimberly slowly shook her head, so shocked she could barely get her next words out. "It's not true. Mother would have told me."

Cecil snorted. "When I made her swear she wouldn't? Don't be stupid, gel. Her promise was the only thing that kept me from kicking the both of you out and letting the world know about her shame."

He wasn't her father. He wasn't her father. He wasn't . . . The refrain kept running through her mind, trying to make sense, and then it really clicked, that this cold tyrant of a man wasn't related to her at all. And that little knot of guilt that she'd always carried, for not loving him, for actually hating him for most of her life, dissolved suddenly. She almost smiled. Actually, she felt like laughing.

He wasn't her father and she was—delighted.

And he'd never told anyone—until now. But knowing him as she did, Kimberly doubted that her mother's promise had kept him silent. It was more likely his desire to not have it publicly known that he'd been cuckolded, she thought cynically.

"Is he still alive?"

"Who?"

He'd dropped his head back on the chair, closed his eyes. The drink was catching up to him. But she wasn't about to let her question go unanswered.

"Ian MacFearson. Is he still alive?"

He struggled to get his eyes open again, then squinted them at her. "I sincerely hope not. I hope he's rotting in hell already."

"But you don't know for sure?"

"You think to find him?" He smirked. "He won't thank you for telling him he's got a grown bastard daughter. He didn't love your mother, you fool. He only seduced her because he thought it would hurt me. So why would he want anything to do with you?"

He was undoubtedly right. But if the man was still alive and out there somewhere, she could at least meet him, couldn't she? She wouldn't have to tell him that he was her father. She could keep that her secret. But at least she would know what he was like . . . and eat her heart out if he was nice and decent and everything Cecil Richards wasn't? To know what she'd missed all these years if she'd had a *real* father raise her with loving concern?

She sighed mentally. No, perhaps it was better not to know after all. It was enough, really, just knowing that Cecil wasn't her father.

Kimberly turned toward the door, but she stopped there, looking back at him, shaking her head. "You ought to get into bed and sleep the drink off. You'll likely have the decision you want tomorrow and—" She paused, remembering what had brought her there in the first place. "Why were you crying?"

"Crying?" He jerked upright, flushing with vivid color, and went on to grumble, "Crying? More like laughing, thinking of telling that blackguard after he marries you that he's married himself to a bastard."

He was lying, and obviously not going to admit that he'd done something so normal as crying. She supposed the drink had made him melancholy about his lost love, but she'd never know for sure—and didn't really care.

As for his threat, she merely smiled. "Why don't I save you the trouble, hmmm? Actually, Lachlan will probably be glad to know that I've got Scots blood in me."

44

"She's written another letter," Ranald said, dropping the envelope on Lachlan's bureau.

"Same as the others?" Lachlan asked.

"Aye."

Lachlan sighed. Nessa had really taken his getting married hard. She'd cried and screamed and pleaded with him not to go to England to find a bride. She'd refused to listen when he tried to explain once again that he wouldn't be marrying her either way, that it'd be like marrying his own sister, if he had one. She swore that she'd find the money they needed, somehow, and that would change his mind.

And then she'd written to him after he'd been at Sherring Cross for about two weeks, and a good half dozen times since, saying the same thing each time, begging him to come home, saying she'd gotten the money, all they'd need, but not saying how she'd managed to get it.

It was a lie, of course, a desperate measure, because she still thought she loved him, and didn't want to lose him to another woman. There was no way she *could* have come up with enough money to support the castle for any length of time. And even if it was true, it wouldn't have changed his plans. He'd found the woman he wanted. He'd even been willing to marry her when he thought no money would come with her, he wanted her that badly.

So he'd read only that first letter from Nessa, and was so distressed by it, because she simply wouldn't give up her obsession with him, that he'd told his cousins to read any other letters from her, if she wrote again. Which is what they'd been doing, embarrassing as they found the task.

"Yer no' going tae answer this one either?" Ranald asked curiously when Lachlan didn't even spare a glance at the latest letter.

"What's the point, when we'll be heading home tomorrow? Mayhap the sight o' my new wife will finally convince her that I mean what I say." And then he grumbled, "Faith, nothing else has been able tae."

"She'll no' like it," Ranald warned.

"I dinna expect she will, but she'll have tae get used tae it. I willna have dissension in my house."

"Ye'll hae nothing but, if I know Nessa," Ranald predicted with a grin.

"Nay, she'll accept my Kimber and wish me well—or she can go live wi' her uncle in the Hebrides."

That evening, Lachlan began to wonder if Kimberly hadn't somehow heard about Nessa and the trouble she might cause, she seemed so preoccupied. Her distraction could, of course, be no more than the fact that they were getting married in the morning. Nerves, jitters, or whatever you choose to call it. He was feeling none himself. But women looked at things differently, worried when they didn't need to, and—he finally asked her.

"What's wrong, darlin'? And if you tell me you've changed your mind, I'll drag you out o' here this second and off tae Kregora where we'll have tae live in sin till you come tae your senses."

She smiled at him. "That won't be necessary. I've just been thinking, is all."

"About what?"

Instead of answering him, she asked, "Do you know anyone by the name of Ian MacFearson?"

His eyes flared wide in surprise. "Faith, where'd you hear *that* name?"

"Do you know him then?"

"Nay—well, aye."

"Which is it?"

"I dinna know him, Kimber, but I've heard *of* him. I dinna think there is anyone in the Highlands who hasna heard of Ian MacFearson. Some even wonder if he's real, the tales of him are so unusual."

"What tales?"

"He's reputed tae be one o' the meanest, blackhearted rogues our side o' the border, that would as soon draw a dirk on you as look at you. Some say he hasna left his home since he returned tae it more'n twenty years ago, that he's no more'n an old recluse who's turned his back on the living. Others say he never married, but he's got so many bastards you need more'n two hands tae count them on, and they're every one of them as vicious and blackhearted as he is. They even say they entertain themselves by trying tae kill each other, and he sits back and encourages them."

"You're joking, right?" Kimberly asked, her expression incredulous.

"Nay, but these are only tales, mind you. I dinna think anyone really kens how much is truth tae them or how much embellishment. But mothers will use his name tae admonish their bairns, telling them that Ian MacFearson will be coming for them if they're no' good, tae feed them tae his bloodthirsty sons. And I remember when I was fifteen, my cousins and I set out tae find where he lives, tae see for ourselves if he was real or just legend."

"Did you?"

"We didna see him, nay. We found a house we thought might be his, an old brooding place set out on a promontory in the far north country, wi' barren trees about it, and black clouds hovering low o'er it, and we didna go any closer. A place like that, that actually looked evil, merely supported the tales, we were thinking."

"Or started the tales to begin with?" she suggested hopefully.

"Aye, mayhap, but I dinna care tae be finding out. Now where did you hear that name?"

"From my fa—from Cecil. Apparently, Ian MacFearson can add one more bastard to the count," she told him, then with a wry smile. "Myself."

He started to laugh, but she was suddenly looking too serious by half and he ended in a groan. "You're no' joking, are you?"

"No, and you're not happy about it, are you?"

she replied tightly. "It bothers you that I'm a bastard?"

He caught her hand and brought it to his lips. "Now why would that bother me? But Ian MacFearson's daughter—that is going tae take getting used tae."

That placated her enough that she admitted, "I'm not used to it myself yet."

"You mean he only just told you today? The day 'afore you get married? That lousy—"

"He was quite foxed. I don't think he had any intention of telling me, ever. But it slipped out, and—I was glad actually. He'd never behaved like a father to me, and this at least explained why. I thought you might even appreciate it, that I was half Scottish."

"What blood runs in your veins, darlin', isna important tae me—though Scots blood is nice," he added with a grin. "And 'tis glad I am myself that the earl is no' your da. I dinna mind admitting now that I had some powerful fears you'd turn out like him one day."

She grinned. "You did not."

"I did. However, are you *sure* you're the MacFearson's only daughter?"

"Only? You said he had bastards aplenty."

"Aye, so the tale goes, but every one of them sons, and few o' them wi' the same mothers."

She blushed at that bit of information. "Well, to answer your question, yes, I'm reasonably sure, and that's because I know Cecil didn't mean to tell me. He also said I take after the Scotsman, that even my smile is like his."

"A blackhearted rogue wi' the smile of an angel?" he said skeptically.

"I don't believe he was always a rogue. But I

guess only Ian MacFearson could verify it for certain, whether I'm his daughter or not. If he didn't know my mother or Cecil—they were apparently best of friends long ago—then it would all be a lie, wouldn't it?"

"Aye."

"Also, it's not something that Cecil would want known, not when he's claimed me as his all these years. It would be a blow to his pride, you know. And it wouldn't have slipped out if he wasn't quite foxed today. Then again"—she shrugged— "perhaps he planned the whole thing, wasn't really drunk, and thought the tale would get you to not marry me."

Lachlan snorted. "People with volatile tempers dinna usually have the patience for such deceit."

"Well, as I said, I believed him. I didn't at first, it was so unexpected. But it explained so much, about the way he treated both me and my mother over the years. And to be honest, I *want* it to be true. I don't even care that this Ian MacFearson isn't a nice man either. As long as the earl isn't my father, I don't really care who is."

"Aye, I could almost agree wi' that."

"Almost?"

"If your real da were anyone but a fearsome legend," he said, then, "You—ah—werena of a mind tae meet the MacFearson, were you?"

He looked so leery, she chuckled. "After what you've told me? No, I don't think so."

He sighed in relief, but quickly assured her, " 'Tis no' that I wouldna want tae take you tae meet the mon. If that is your wish, you'll have it. But I'm thinking 'twould be best if you dinna find out if the tales are true. Some things are better left tae the unknown."

"In this case, you're probably right," she agreed. "But speaking of the unknown, or at least what you likely don't know yet—I doubt my father will attend the service in the morning, but the duke has kindly agreed to give me away."

Lachlan raised a brow. "Did he now?" And then he laughed. "Och, well, I refused the last thing he offered me, but I'll have no trouble accepting you, darlin'."

45

Kimberly was floating in a cloud of happiness that she couldn't quite explain. She was getting married, yes, and that *should* be a joyful experience—except she was marrying a man who didn't love her. So she had no reason really to be so ridiculously happy.

She was standing at the altar now, her husband-to-be-in-a-few-minutes next to her, their shoulders touching. He'd looked so handsome when she'd joined him there, wearing his formal black, and his heart-stopping smile, that he'd taken her breath away.

It was almost easy to believe that he really wanted to marry her, that he wasn't just doing as honor demanded. But she supposed if she was going to find any peace in her marriage to him, she'd have to suspend her beliefs and do a little pretending, and just accept him as the charming, sensual man he was.

She felt beautiful herself. Her cream-colored gown with its new white lace bodice and train fit her to perfection. And her new maid, Jean, must have been trained by Megan's maid, because she had the same talent for creating soft, flattering coiffures.

Megan had picked the girl herself and sent her to Kimberly when she heard that Mary had been dismissed. She was young, had a sweet, eager-to-please disposition, and best of all, she was willing to move to the Highlands with Kimberly. "Going to a new place, with nothing familiar to you, you simply must have your own maid," Megan had told her. "And Jean will be loyal to you, m'dear, you won't have to worry about that."

Kimberly was forced to pay attention to the service as answers were demanded of her. To have and to hold . . . from this day forward . . . till death do us part. Such solemn vows, so serious, so at contrast with her bubbling happiness. She was hard pressed to keep a smile off her lips.

And then Lachlan was reaching for her hand, and she glanced down to see that he had not just a wedding band to slide onto her finger, but a magnificent diamond engagement ring to go with it, quite the largest gem she'd ever seen, surrounded by perfectly round pink pearls. It was one of the MacGregor jewels. They'd been fetched and returned to him just yesterday. She was so awed by it that she almost didn't stop him in time from removing her emerald so he could put the diamond in its place. But she did stop him.

He looked up at her, the question in his eyes, a frown about to form. She quickly whispered to him, "I like the first one you gave me, that is, I prefer to wear it—if you don't mind."

His smile came slowly, but soon it was blinding. And he wasn't supposed to kiss her yet, but he did anyway. The pastor had to clear his throat, more than a few times, before Lachlan stopped so the flustered gentleman could finish the service. Then he was kissing her again.

They were married, really and truly married. Kimberly was so entranced with that thought, she barely heard the congratulations that followed. And before long, they were riding away from Sherring Cross.

Devlin had offered them one of the ducal coaches for the journey—he had several. He even supplied a coachman and outriders. And he surprised them all, his wife included, by telling Lachlan he'd be welcome to visit again. He'd actually been sincere. Of course, he'd added, albeit with a grin, "Just not too bloody often, eh."

It had made the parting much more pleasant, when Kimberly had been near to tears, in saying good-bye to Megan. She'd made a friend in the duchess, the closest she'd ever had, actually. She was going to miss her dreadfully. But she'd promised to write. And Megan had promised to come visit them in the Highlands someday.

The plan had been to leave directly after the service. So Kimberly had gone to visit her—well, to visit the earl, one last time early that morning. He'd been sober, and barely awake, and his usual surly self. And she hadn't wasted any time hoping for a kind word in parting. In retrospect, it was amazing that that visit hadn't spoiled the rest of the day for her. Quite the opposite. Probably knowing that she'd never see the earl again had added to her happiness.

"I don't expect you to come to my wedding," she'd told him. "It would be hypocritical of you to do so, and you're not that."

He'd snorted. "No, I'm not, nor do I suffer fools lightly, and you're that if you still marry—"

"Let's not get into that, if you please. I will marry him, and it's nothing to you, so do keep your opin—I'm sorry. I didn't come here to argue with you."

"Ungrateful chit," he'd mumbled.

"No, I'm not ungrateful. Actually, I want to thank you for sharing your house with me all these years, for feeding me and putting clothes on my back. It would have been nice if you had also shared something of yourself with me, after agreeing to raise me, but despising me as you do, it's understandable why you couldn't."

She'd actually struck a nerve. He'd flushed and replied, "I never despised you, gel. I despised your father, and you reminded me too much of him."

"Well, you needn't worry about that anymore. I see no reason why we should ever see each other again after today. So this is good-bye. And I do hope you find some happiness with Winnifred."

"He's not going to charge her then? He's going to drop the matter?"

"He has the MacGregor jewels back, and the deed to Winnifred's house. If you arrange a bank draft and have it delivered to him before we leave this morning, yes, the matter will be forgotten."

"Thank you."

She'd blinked, shocked to hear those words from him. She'd only been able to nod, and turn away. But she had one last question that was burning to be asked, and only he could give her the answer.

So she'd paused at the door, stared at him a

moment, this man who for twenty-one years she'd thought was her father. But he'd never been a father to her, or a real husband to her mother, and what she wanted to know, needed to know, was why her mother accepted that.

So she asked him, "Why did she never leave you? She had the wherewithal to do so. Why did she stay, when she was so unhappy with you?"

He'd scowled at her, but he nonetheless answered, "Because she was raised to do what's right. Unlike you, she would never have disobeyed her parents, no matter what. She was told to marry me and she did. And she made the best of it, as was proper."

"Made the best of it?" she'd said incredulously. "She was miserable all those years, and you're saying it was because it was the proper thing to do?"

He'd flushed again. He wasn't going to say any more—and then he did. "She also stayed because of you. She didn't want you having the stigma of bastardy. She knew if she left that I'd no longer keep her secret."

Kimberly shook her head. "You really had her fooled, didn't you?"

"What the bloody hell are you talking about?"

"You were miserable, so she had to be miserable too, was that it?"

"I would have—"

"No, you wouldn't. Just as you won't tell anyone now that I'm not your daughter. Because who gets laughed at in the case of a cuckold, the erring wife, or the husband who was fool enough to let it happen? And you'll never willingly admit to being a fool. We both know that. I wish to hell my mother had known it as well. Actually, I wish you had kicked her out when you first found out. She would have been much, much happier if you had. I know I would have been."

"You're the fool if you think so, gel," he countered. "A woman alone, with a bastard child, she's shunned by one and all. Your mother had too much pride to be able to handle that. The scandal would have destroyed her. At least with me, she could hold her head up and keep her place in society, and she was grateful for that, believe me. And she wasn't completely miserable, by God. She had you. She bloody well doted on you. But ask me what I had? Nothing."

"You could have had me. You could have opened your heart and I would have loved you. But I forget. I reminded you of him."

"You think I don't have regrets, gel?" he'd said gruffly. "I do."

"Then I'm sorry. I'm sorry for all three of us, but mostly for Mother. She won't get a second chance to find happiness, but you and I will."

"Not if you marry that Scotsman, you won't," he'd predicted.

"I mean to prove you wrong in that."

46

I mean to prove you wrong in that.

Kimberly had been doing so all day. She'd been happy all day—after she'd left the earl for the last time and put that visit out of her mind. But for some reason, tonight, she was assailed with doubts again.

They had stopped for the night, not at a coaching inn, as she had assumed they would, but at one of the St. Jameses' properties that had been prepared especially for their wedding night, compliments of the duke and duchess. Lachlan was as surprised as she was. But their driver and the outriders had had their instructions. And the staff of the large cottage had been notified in advance.

Kimberly was led straight up to the master chamber, where a hot bath had been drawn for her in the separate bathing chamber. Two maids assisted Jean in getting her quickly into it. And when she came back into the main chamber, she discovered a dining table with soft candlelight had been set up there while she bathed, with some delicious aromas coming from a serving cart beside it.

And then yet another surprise. Draped on the large bed with its blue satin sheets already turned down was a new negligee and robe, compliments of Mrs. Canterby, no doubt, at Megan's behest. Of gossamer silk in a blue-green that had a jewel tone to it when it caught the light, it was not something that Kimberly would ever have chosen for herself. Thin straps that held up a deeply scooped neckline, a waistline that clung to her belly and hips, then flared only slightly on its way down her legs.

Having donned it, she was so shocked by the amount of skin the cleavage displayed, she reached immediately for the robe to cover it up—only to find the robe wasn't like any robe she knew. There were long sleeves, and an abundance of material at her back that would float behind her when she walked, but not a speck of material in the front to wrap around her. Well, that wasn't exactly true. There was a two-inch border of gathered black lace along the edges that ran behind her neck, just covered the straps of the gown, ran along the sides of her breasts and on down to her feet.

It was half a robe, was what it was, sort of like an over-the-shoulder cape with attached sleeves. It was designed as a complement to the gown, not as a means to hide it. And Kimberly was appalled that she was expected to dine with Lachlan tonight while wearing it.

She was shaking her head, completely balking at the idea, when one of the maids remarked, "I hope you like it, Lady Kimberly. Her Grace the duchess will be so disappointed if you don't."

Kimberly could have murdered the girl. Of course, now she *had* to wear the ensemble. She couldn't even claim she was too cold to wear it, the crackling fire in the room had it so toasty warm.

Jean, bless her, suggested she might like to wear her cameo with it. Yes, anything to cover a little more skin, even a very little more. But it still wasn't enough, her breasts were still bursting out of that low cleavage, and she felt more naked than if she wasn't wearing anything at all. And she had every intention of finding something else to wear, just as soon as Megan's servants left the room, and would have—if Lachlan didn't arrive first.

The cameo failed as an added cover. All it did was serve to draw Lachlan's eyes straight to her cleavage, and she went up in flames of embarrassment, because he seemed shocked too, or at least so surprised that his remark about the enticing smells of food as he walked into the room was cut off abruptly. Nor did he discreetly look away. He simply stared at her breasts, and stared, until one of the maids cleared her throat, and then he blushed as well.

But his charm surfaced, and he immediately set out to put them both at ease, remarking on the journey so far, discussing the route they would take the next day, mentioning the cottage and how he was no longer going to be surprised by the duke's generosity. He even confessed that Devlin had amazed him by apologizing because he hadn't believed Lachlan's story about his stolen inheritance.

Before Kimberly realized that she'd been so distracted she'd forgotten about her revealing cleavage, they were halfway through their dinner, and the maids had quietly departed. And that was when the doubts came to plague her.

Was it presumptuous of her to assume they would have a wedding night? Just because they were sharing a meal in the bedchamber didn't mean they'd be sharing the bed there as well. Lachlan had done his duty by marrying her. What if he had no intention of playing the husband thereafter? What if he expected a marriage just like her parents' dismal union? She'd have a hard time pretending she had a perfect marriage in that case, now wouldn't she?

She was startled out of her thoughts when Lachlan suddenly stood up, tossed his napkin aside, and came around the table to take her hand.

"What—" was all she got out before he was dragging her toward the bed, and stopping there, his hands coming to her cheeks, he gave her such a scorching kiss that her knees buckled and she sagged against him.

He groaned and said against her lips, "I dinna know how I restrained myself as long as I did. I wanted tae toss those blasted maids out the door. I wanted tae crawl across the table and eat you, no' the blasted food. If you ever wear a gown like this again, I willna be responsible for what I do. Do you ken, Kimber? I dinna need tae be provoked, when I'm already wanting you all the time."

He sounded angry, and yet his hands were extremely gentle as they caressed their way down her neck and catching on her robe, dragged it off her shoulders and down her arms. And there was such heat in his eyes as they fastened on her gown without its lacy frame.

"I had plans for tonight, darlin'. I was going tae love you so slowly, was going tae make you need me as much as I've needed you these many weeks. I was going tae make you beg me tae take you—but now I'm begging."

He dropped to his knees before her, his arms wrapping around her legs, his mouth pressing into her belly. She caught her breath. She could barely stand.

"Begging . . . for . . . what?" she managed to ask, she wasn't sure how.

"For your forgiveness, because I mun have you now—right now. I swear it feels like I'll be dying if I wait another minute."

Her hands came to the top of his head as she replied in a soft whisper, "I've no desire to be a widow so soon, Lachlan MacGregor."

He looked up at her, and then his smile came, so beautiful, so heart-moving. But he wasn't joking about his need for haste. He stood up, lifted her, and was on top of her on the bed almost all in one motion. And she barely had time to blink before his tongue plunged deeply into her mouth, and his manhood thrust even more deeply into her welcoming warmth.

He groaned again, that she was so ready for him, but why wouldn't she be? His mention of needing her had sent heat coursing through her. But then she'd known she'd be a sucker for those words if she ever heard them from him. And it only took seconds for her to feel the same tearing need as he drove into her again and again, so that she was there, meeting him on each thrust, and joining him when he soared over the edge on a pulsing wave of bliss.

It took a while for her heartbeat to return to normal, as well as her breathing. She held him close as she recovered, her hands gently caressing him, marveling at the uniqueness of lovemaking, and how powerful were its urges under the right provocation. Lachlan MacGregor was all the provocation she'd ever need.

His face was still buried in her neck, his breathing still hard, when she heard his whisper, "Did I mention something about doing this slowly?"

"I believe you did."

He leaned up to grin at her. "And something about begging?"

"No—you must have imagined that."

He chuckled. She rolled her eyes at him. It was a very long night.

47

Kimberly had heard Kregora Castle mentioned more than once, but somehow she had imagined something not quite so massive and definitely not so *old*. Well, most castles did have their old parts, the looming circular tower, the surviving great hall, the small but sturdy chapel, yet they also had their modern additions that blended in so nicely that the original castle sections were hardly discernible among all the chimney tops and fancy gables and moldings of more recent architecture.

Kregora, however, was just the opposite. If there was anything modern behind its high stone walls, you couldn't tell it as you approached. Turrets and crenellations were visible on two huge rectangular towers and—good God, even a drawbridge and portcullis. Could the thing possibly still work after hundreds of years?

After her initial surprise, though, Kimberly had to admit it was a very impressive edifice, sitting as it was on a high bluff of a large lake that wandered and curved through the countryside like a river. And just across the water, hills and mountains rose up to form a varied background for the castle, with the occasional small stone cottage here and there, and even another castle in the far distance, though one not nearly so large as Kregora.

This time of year there was no green to speak of, but those ice-topped mountains and hills were a grand sight on their own, truly magnificent. The entire scene took Kimberly's breath away, it was so beautiful.

Lachlan had been watching for her reaction, and it was a bit apparent in her expression. He grinned, pleased, and said, "Welcome home, darlin'."

"For all the stark barrenness of these Highlands of yours, it is rather lovely country, isn't it?"

"You've noticed that, have you?" he replied with a good deal of pride.

"And your Kregora, too."

"Aye, that she is."

"But are there fireplaces in there? Warm bedding? Hot bricks?"

The last leg of the journey had been extremely cold, the farther north they traveled, so it was understandable that such things should be on her mind—even if she was teasing him.

And Lachlan laughed. "Dinna fash yourself, Kimber, I'll be keeping you warm and comfy and the rats away."

"That's good to—*rats*?!"

"Och, well, mayhap only a few wee mice."

Her eyes narrowed on him, afraid he wasn't just teasing her back this time. Castles were known to harbor such creatures, after all. But then so did any place that wasn't kept properly cleaned.

"Well, if you do have any mice running about, I promise you they'll soon be looking for a new home," she said with a determined glint in her eyes.

Lachlan smiled at the thought. Winnifred, to give her her due, had been an excellent housekeeper. She'd kept Kregora running smoothly without ever seeming to be active at it. Nessa, who had taken over the same responsibilities, would rather be out in the kennels playing with her favorite hounds, or out hunting grouse. The castle had deteriorated under her supervision, though she had too much pride to ever acknowledge that.

Thinking of his tomboyish cousin, Lachlan asked, "Did I tell you about Nessa?"

"Your cousin who fancies herself in love with you and thought you ought to have married her instead?" she replied. "That Nessa?"

Lachlan flushed with ire. "Which of those frog-kicking devils told you?"

She smiled at him. "Actually, they both did, and not together but separately, unaware they'd both had the same idea. I thought it was rather amusing when Gilleonan was telling me the exact same thing Ranald already did."

"I would have been telling you myself," he said in a low grumble.

"Yes, I can see that. But they both felt they were doing you a service, so you have no reason to be annoyed with them. They wanted me to be assured that you only have brotherly affections for the girl. They seemed to be worried that I might get jealous or some silly thing like that, if I didn't

understand the way of it." And then she all but
snorted. "As if I have a jealous nature."

Lachlan grinned, remembering that day at an
ice-skating pond when her nonexistent jealous
nature had come galloping to the fore—just as his
had. "Well, I'm hoping Nessa can set aside her
stubbornness and come tae her senses about this
after meeting you," he said earnestly. "There's no
reason the tae o' you canna be friends."

Two women loving the same man, not very
likely . . .

Kimberly went very still. Her eyes closed. No,
she didn't just have that thought. She was to have
remained detached, to enjoy him, yes, to have fun
with him, yes, to make him a good wife, yes, but
to keep her heart her own. If she loved him, she'd
be wanting his love in return, and forever, but
she wasn't going to be getting that.

It was a shame her mood had to be spoiled,
just as they arrived at Castle Kregora, driving
over the drawbridge. But she would work on re-
gaining a proper perspective on the matter, so
that she could exist here with some modicum of
peaceful accord with her husband—and get back
to pretending that all was just as she would want
it to be.

The lord's return had been anticipated for days,
and word had been sent ahead again this morning as to their approximate time of arrival. So the
large inner courtyard beyond the high outer walls
was filled to capacity with MacGregors who had
come from miles around to welcome Lachlan
home—and to have a look at his English bride.
They were a boisterous lot, some of the men in
tartans despite the frigid weather, the blue, green,

and black of the MacGregor in ample display on men, women, and children.

What with all the warm greetings and good wishes, it took them quite a while to finally make it through the doors to the great hall, or what Kimberly had assumed would be a great hall. But coming through those mammoth double doors, she was pleased to find that although Castle Kregora hadn't been changed on the outside, it had definitely undergone complete remodeling on the inside.

What had once been a great hall had been divided into the rooms one would expect to find in most homes, a parlor, a normal-sized dining room, a billiards room, and a few other rooms she would get around to examining later, all with thick wooden walls. In fact, she was to find that every bit of stone inside the castle had been covered with wood for insulation, and some with wainscotting and wallpaper on top of that.

She had already discovered the perfect spot to put her mother's grandfather clock, there in the wide entry hall. And a quick glance into the dining room they passed showed no china cabinet at all, so the chinoiserie, which should have been delivered already with the rest of her belongings, was actually needed.

"So this is her, then?"

Kimberly hadn't seen the young woman come up behind them, but she had a feeling that sneering tone would belong to Nessa MacGregor, and as Lachlan made the introductions, she found she was right.

She was petite. Kimberly actually looked down on her by at least six inches. And she was strikingly beautiful, with long black hair in an unadorned single braid, and large, stormy grey eyes. She was also reed thin, and struck a regal pose, despite her diminutive height and size.

After the introduction, which she hadn't acknowledged, and after no more than a brief, derisive glance in Kimberly's direction, the girl said to Lachlan, "Well, she mun be rich as a queen, because she sure isna pretty. And she's a blasted giant! What could you be thinking o', Lach, tae be marrying such a homely looking lass as this?"

It was said loudly, for the benefit of one and all, and dozens of people had followed them into the hall and fell silent now. Kimberly had gasped, her cheeks glowing, never having experienced such direct malice from a woman before. Nessa smiled smugly.

At least she was smug until Lachlan growled, "You little witch. She has a unique beauty of her own, and you're blind if you dinna see it. And she's no giant. For me, her size canna be more perfect. If you dinna think so, 'tis because you're no bigger than a child yourself."

That struck a nerve apparently, and had Nessa shouting, "A *child* who came up wi' the money you needed! You didna have tae go marrying no damned Sassenach just for her money!"

"As it happens, Nessa, I asked the lady tae marry me when I thought she was poor as a kirk mouse. Did it no' occur tae you in your one-sided thinking that I might love her? And dinna be calling her a Sassenach again, when she's got a father as Scottish as you and me."

"Who?"

"Never mind who—"

"Aye, as I thought," the girl interrupted with

a smirk. " 'Tis a lie tae try and make her acceptable here, which she'll ne'er be."

Lachlan's scowl turned positively black at that accusation and he gritted out, "So now I'm a liar, am I? 'Tis Ian MacFearson if you mun know—" The collective gasp that followed had him glancing about the hall to add, "And I dinna want that spreading beyond Kregora. I'd as soon the legend doesna pay us a visit."

There were many nods of agreement, and that last had apparently worked to silence Nessa as well. Lachlan was still furious that she'd managed to spoil his homecoming with her jealousy, and embarrass Kimberly, who was still tight-lipped and pink cheeked.

Kimberly was more than embarrassed, she was shocked. Jealousy was no excuse for that type of mean-spirited behavior, words meant to cut to the quick. The girl deserved a good slap. Had no one ever taught her better?

Apparently not, and Kimberly had little doubt that this wouldn't be the end of her spite. Was she expected to put up with such verbal attacks every time she and Nessa came upon each other? Not bloody likely.

Lachlan had come to her defense. It wasn't the first time, and it was apparently his nature to do so. But in this case, she was his wife. He could do no less in front of his kin. And he'd even lied, in reference to loving her. Well, actually, he hadn't needed to. The way he'd put the question, it implied much, but didn't admit a thing.

However, Nessa lived here. There would be times when Lachlan wouldn't be available to intervene. And Kimberly had no idea how much abuse she could put up with before she fought back. She supposed she was going to find out.

48

Kimberly would have preferred to remain tucked away in her room until she fully recovered from that disastrous first meeting with Nessa. But the *laird* was home and a gala banquet was planned for that first night at Kregora, with all clan members invited, as well as close neighbors.

Lachlan had apologized profusely for Nessa's behavior when he took Kimberly upstairs to show her their suite of private rooms. He'd tried to tease her out of her upset by pointing out that out of the four connecting rooms—one was a very large bathing chamber that was thoroughly modernized with hot and cold running water— she could have one of the extra rooms for dressing or whatever she chose to use it for, as long as she didn't try sleeping in it. There'd be only one bed, he'd told her, and they'd be sharing it.

He hadn't gotten a blush out of her, hadn't gotten much of a response at all. And he'd finally left her alone there to rest and settle in.

Rest wasn't needed, but activity was. Yes, that

was definitely one cure for rotten moods. So Kimberly had helped Jean put her belongings away, while the maid had chattered nearly nonstop, between mumbles about barbarian wenches, to try and keep her distracted.

Kimberly had then sent her to find where her things from Northumberland had been stored. She wasn't going to feel like Castle Kregora was truly her home until her treasures were dispersed to their appropriate locations, leaving her mark, as it were.

Lachlan's rooms were very nice, she found, when she got around to really noticing them. There was a lot of light from large windows in each room that offered that splendid view of the lake and the mountains beyond. The bedchamber, the largest of the rooms, even had a small balcony with French doors that looked down on a boating dock far below. She imagined it would be nice having breakfast out there come summer.

Dark emerald drapes in soft velvet framed each window, drawn back with tasseled ropes. The wallpaper was in several shades of pastel blues, with numerous paintings of ladies and gentlemen of the French court from the era when white powdered wigs was the fashion for both men and women. Thick rugs were so large, they nearly covered every inch of the wood floors, and had likely been specially made, since they were in leafy swirls of blue and black on a green background, the colors of the MacGregor tartan.

One of the rooms Lachlan had definitely been using for dressing—the wardrobe was full of his clothes—as well as for private relaxing. There was a chaise lounge there, a large desk, several reading chairs and tables. It was quite big enough to serve both purposes. As was the other chamber, which Kimberly would use as a dressing-sitting room, at least until it was time to plan a nursery. That was if there wasn't already a nursery somewhere nearby.

Thoughts of her own children running through those rooms someday did much to lighten Kimberly's mood. She was even looking forward again to exploring the rest of the castle. And when Jean came back to tell her that her belongings that had been delivered from Northumberland had been stored in the cellar—well, she didn't question why they had been put there, her clothing included. She simply took the maid with her to find out if the cellar wasn't something other than what one might expect, just as the great hall had been.

It wasn't. It was dark and dank, and the one place inside the castle where the original stone walls were still in use, and the home of countless spiders. It was also filthy, being the storage area for coal, the main fuel source since Scotland didn't have an abundance of trees.

They'd had to backtrack to find a lantern, as well as a couple of stout servants to carry the trunks and furniture upstairs once they found it. Locating it was another matter. There were a lot of rooms down there, small cubbyholes that might have been cells at one time, larger rooms, and a lot of narrow halls that went off in all directions. Centuries of stuff seemed to be stored down there, mostly old furniture all covered in cobwebs.

But the room was finally found where Kimberly's belongings had been brought, and her smile of relief lasted all of one second as she held the lantern high and surveyed the total destruction of her family heirlooms.

The grandfather clock lay on its side, the hour hands missing, the body cracked, dented, raw chips of wood sliced open as if an ax had been taken to it. The legs were gone from the chinoiserie, the doors broken off their hinges, more raw slices in the intricate wood carvings, again, as if an ax had chopped and hacked at it.

The mammoth painting looked like someone had stood on one end of it and pulled the other end down until the frame and canvas cracked in the middle. The small tables, the three-hundred-year-old hall bench, the antique vases, the deeply carved Chinese bedding trunk, everything was broken, sliced open, shattered. Even her clothes trunks had been ripped open, the clothing dumped about the dirt floor.

Kimberly stared, and stared, so horrified she couldn't breathe. She took a step forward, another, then dropped to her knees, her hand stretching out, but not reaching anything, and the tears started. This was all she had left of her mother, and it was gone now, broken junk, good only for firewood. The willful destruction, and even in her shock, she had no doubt it was deliberate, was unbelievable. And there was only one person here who she could think would do such a thing.

Kimberly got slowly to her feet, the name on her tongue: "Nessa . . ."

"My lady, these broken things—they aren't what we were looking for, are they?" Jean asked beside her, the same horror in her voice.

Kimberly didn't answer, she looked at one of the confused castle servants and demanded softly, icily, "Where would Nessa be now?"

One shrugged, the other said, "Where the laird be, most like. The lassie's always been his shadow."

"And where would he be?"

Now they both shrugged. Kimberly asked no more questions. She'd find him—and her, if she had to search every inch of the entire castle, inside and out. And there was going to be worse than hell to pay when she did. She was choking with hurt, and so beyond furious that she didn't know what she was going to do, but murder wasn't to be excluded.

She found Lachlan first, easily, in an office of sorts. The greetings over, dozens of his kin still required some of his time, for reports, complaints, good news and the like. And there was little formality at Kregora, as she was to find, nor much privacy. Instead of all those people waiting out in the hall to see him individually, they were all of them crowded into that room, which was fortunately a large room.

He smiled when he saw her enter—until he noticed her tears, which she didn't even realize were still coursing down her cheeks. She barely spared him a glance, though, searching the room for his young cousin, but she didn't see Nessa and almost turned about to leave. But then she did spot her, and only because Nessa had lifted her head to see what had gained Lachlan's attention.

The girl had been sitting on a footstool against the wall, unobtrusive, just listening to the proceedings. It was doubtful Lachlan even knew she was there.

"Kimber, what happened?" Lachlan asked with concern on his way to her.

She didn't hear him. She had Nessa in her sights and all she could think about was getting to her. But Nessa saw her coming and didn't stay put. She leaped to her feet and ran around the desk there, putting it and about a half dozen people between them.

"You keep that giant away from me, Lach!" Nessa shouted. "She's crazy!"

"Crazy, am I?" Kimberly said, still working her way around the crowd. "Do you even know what you did? Those were priceless heirlooms you destroyed! All that I had left from my mother, who's dead!"

"I didna destroy anything! 'Twas all delivered just as you saw it!"

That gave Kimberly pause, until she remembered the ax marks. "I don't believe—"

" 'Tis true," Nessa insisted, adding quickly, "The wagon driver said he'd lost a wheel, and everything spilled out because it hadna been tied down properly."

"Falling a few feet wouldn't account for every single item being broken!"

" 'Twas more'n that. It happened at the side of a gully, and everything hit the rocks below."

It was possible. Completely unlikely, but possible. And just because Nessa had already shown her true colors didn't mean she was responsible for this too.

Kimberly stopped the chase, deflated that she couldn't have immediate satisfaction. "I'll hear it from the driver himself then."

"He's no' here. Why would he still be here? He's gone back tae wherever he came from."

Kimberly stiffened. There was simply too much smugness in Nessa's expression now. She knew she was lying. And then she had it confirmed.

"There's nae need tae be askin' the driver," one of the men said, giving the dark-haired girl a disapproving look. "Yer a liar, Nessa MacGregor, and I'm ashamed tae call ye my kin right now. I helped tae unload that wagon. There wasna a thing wrong wi' any o' those goods, and I even asked ye why ye wanted such fine things put down in the cellar."

Nessa went red in the face. So did Kimberly as her fury returned tenfold. And while Nessa was still glaring at her accuser, she closed the distance between them and brought her hand down sharply against Nessa's cheek.

It staggered the much smaller girl, whose eyes rounded incredulously as her hand went to the burning area on her face. "How dare—!"

"You're lucky I don't take an ax to you, as you did to my treasures. What you did, Nessa, in your vicious spite, is irreparable. And I refuse to live in the same house with anyone as malicious as you are."

She realized her mistake immediately, in making an ultimatum like that, because pride wouldn't let her back down from it. But it was too late, she'd said it. However, to her immense relief, her husband was in agreement.

"You'll no' have tae, Kimber," Lachlan said behind her as his arms wrapped around her. "She'll be packing her bags tonight and leaving in the morn, because I'll no' have anyone that spiteful living in my house either. And I swear tae you, I'll find the finest artisans tae repair your mother's things, and Nessa will be paying for it herself wi' the money she claims tae have found."

Nessa had gone pale, listening to him, then

paler still when he finished. "This is my home,"
she said with a catch in her voice.

"No' anymore. Your behavior has lost you the
right tae call it so."

"That isna fair! She should be the one leaving,
no' me! She doesna belong here, I do!"

"Nessa lass, do you no' even see the wrong
you've done?" Lachlan said sadly.

It was probably the disapproval in his tone that
brought her anger back. "This is the thanks I get,
after all I did for you? And you didna even ask
me how I got the money for you. I sold myself
tae Gavin Kern, that's how!"

She threw it at him as if she expected it to hurt.
It did surprise him. And it did anger him, but not
for the reason she'd hoped.

"Then we'll be having us another wedding,"
Lachlan said with cold finality.

"I won't marry him!" Nessa screamed.

"You slept wi' him, you'll marry him, and
that's the MacGregor telling you that, Nessa."

She paled again. Kimberly realized that his putting it that way apparently made it an indisput-
able fact. And then Nessa ran from the room.

Into the uncomfortable silence that followed,
someone said, "She'll be going into hiding, I warrant, hating Gavin Kern as she does."

"He's asked her tae marry him a dozen times,"
another pointed out. "At least he'll be glad she's
boxed herself into this corner and can no longer
refuse him."

"If he can find her."

"Go, detain her," Lachlan ordered abruptly,
nodding to the two men nearest the door. "And
someone else fetch Gavin here for his wedding.

We'll be having it tonight, or I'll be knowing why."

Kimberly, incredibly, actually felt sorry for Nessa after hearing that. She didn't approve of forcing a woman to marry a man she despised. But she kept her opinion to herself. After all, she didn't feel *that* sorry for the girl.

49

Most everyone enjoyed themselves that night at the banquet, with a few notable exceptions, too few to dampen the high spirits of a homecoming though. And once Lachlan made his announcement concerning Winnifred, that she'd been found at last and his inheritance returned to him, well, that merely doubled the mood of celebration.

Modernization did have its drawbacks, however. With the great hall converted, there wasn't a room in the castle that was big enough to accommodate so many people for a normal-type banquet, let alone a really large one as was thrown that night. So the food was set up in the dining room, but it was the hallway and parlor that became the eating areas, with chairs and benches aplenty brought in to line the walls and fill in most of the empty spaces.

Nessa was one of those exceptions, of course. She sat in a slump on one of the sofas, her arms crossed, her expression mutinous and occasionally baleful, if anyone tried to speak to her. Not many did.

Kimberly tried to put a good face on it, because that was the proper thing to do. A lady didn't share her sorrow with the general public. But she was hurting too deeply to manage too many smiles. Lachlan's assurance, after he'd gone to examine the damage, that it could all be fixed and looking brand-new again, hadn't helped. For one thing, she doubted it was possible, the damage from the ax too extensive. For another, she didn't want her things looking new. They were antiques. They were supposed to look old, but well preserved.

But she would wait and see. Her husband was determined to correct this wrong. If it was at all possible, he'd see it done and done right. And that alone lightened the pain a bit—and warmed her heart toward him a little more, not that her heart needed any encouragement whatsoever in that regard.

Gavin Kern, now, was a very happy man tonight. He'd apparently been asking Nessa to marry him for quite a few years now. Kimberly was still bothered that the girl was being forced to marry him, until she found the opportunity to talk with Gavin alone for a few minutes.

Lachlan, who had been staying close to her side all evening, was called away to deal with a disturbance between two quick-tempered brothers before it escalated into physical blows. He'd been speaking with Gavin at the time, so his abrupt departure left Kimberly alone with him, and allowed her to appease her curiosity.

Gavin, she had discovered, belonged to that castle across the lake, or rather, it belonged to him. He'd been born there, so had always been a neighbor, though in his early thirties, he was far enough older than Lachlan and Nessa, that they hadn't been younger companions together. But he'd been one of the first to notice when Nessa had begun to mature into a little beauty. She'd still been a tomboy, still had no interest in men, but that hadn't stopped him from courting her from that time on, all to no avail.

Kimberly had learned all of this when she'd asked him, "It doesn't bother you to marry a woman who—ah—?"

"Despises me?" he helpfully finished for her. "But she doesna. She always says she does, and I used tae believe it, but I know better now. She always comes tae me when she needs help. She always cries on my shoulder when she's the need tae be doing that. She tells me her dreams. She tells me her desires. And I was sick tae my soul o' hearing how she loves the MacGregor, until I realized 'twas nae more'n a habit she had since she was a wee bairn."

He seemed like a really nice man, too nice for the vindictive Nessa. He had blond hair a bit darker than her own, and amiable brown eyes. He was no taller than Kimberly, and he had pleasant features, nothing extraordinary like Lachlan's, but strong, friendly.

"She went to great lengths for a habit," Kimberly remarked. "She even came to you—" Again she couldn't finish, embarrassed by the subject.

But again he understood, replying, "As I said, she always came tae me for help when she was needing it. In this case, she could've just asked for the money, and I'd have given it. She knew that. But she's prideful, you ken, and she knew

she'd have nae way tae repay it, sae she offered
herself. I should've refused, but"—he blushed
here—"I've wanted her tae long, and I was hoping, praying, that this is what would happen
when the MacGregor found out."

"That he'd force her to marry you?"

"Aye," he said, then he smiled. "And I dinna
doubt she knew this would be his reaction as
well. She'd turned me down tae many times, you
see. Her pride was in the way o' her accepting
me now."

Kimberly was amazed. "You're suggesting
she'd changed her mind and wanted to marry
you, but couldn't bring herself to say so?"

He nodded. "I've—spent the night wi' her, you
ken. Much was revealed tae me that night o' her
feelings, that even she wasna aware of. She's protesting now, but 'tis all for show, I'm thinking,
for her pride's sake. She's a complicated lass, is
my Nessa."

And malicious and destructive and—well,
Kimberly wouldn't have to figure the girl out after tonight. Nessa could be as complicated as she
liked, as long as she was doing it across the lake
and not at Castle Kregora.

They'd spoken a bit more before Lachlan returned. And not long after, the wedding cere-
mony took place, right there in the parlor.

Nessa continued to look mutinous. She hadn't
changed her clothes into something more appropriate for the occasion, or fixed her hair. She
hadn't eaten any of the food offered to her. And
she refused to answer the questions put to her
during the wedding.

But it was a MacGregor performing the cere-
mony for them, and whenever he got no response

from Nessa when she was supposed to respond, he would simply look up at the crowd and say something to the effect of, "And the MacGregor says she agrees, which is good enough for me."

A bit medieval in Kimberly's opinion, but Nessa certainly didn't seem surprised that she was getting married without her permission, and neither did anyone else. And when it was over, the soft-spoken, unpretentious Gavin Kern let out a whoop of joy, tossed Nessa over his shoulder, and walked out with her like a conquering hero.

The MacGregors cheered at this bold display. And Nessa finally found her voice to shout, "I've got feet, you lummox. Put me down!"

Gavin replied with a hearty laugh, "No' until I've got you safely stowed away on my side o' the loch, Nessa m'darlin'."

"If you're thinking marriage gives you the upper hand—" Nessa paused to rethink that, because marriage did in fact do that. But stubbornly she maintained, "Well, we'll be seeing about that."

Beside Kimberly, Lachlan said, "Aye, I've put her in capable hands, I'm thinking."

Kimberly gave him a sideways glance. "It sounds as if she disagrees with that."

Lachlan grinned at her. "Nay, she'd be swearing tae cut out his heart if she bore any malice toward him. I give it a month and she'll be thanking me."

"Or swearing to cut out *your* heart."

He laughed, and in front of the whole assemblage, kissed her soundly. The cheers went up again. And even though she was embarrassed by the display, she was warmed by those cheers. At least the rest of the MacGregors accepted her.

And Nessa—well, Nessa was a Kern now.

As eventful as the day was, and emotional for Kimberly, she retired early that night. Lachlan made his excuses to the guests so he could join her, but he didn't try to make love to her as she thought he would. He just held her in his arms and whispered soothing bits of nonsense when she started crying again. And most of those tears weren't for her mother's things. They were because she didn't think she could get back to being blasé about Lachlan's not loving her, now that she knew for certain that her heart wasn't her own anymore, that it now belonged completely to him.

50

It was about a week later that the riders showed up, some thirty or forty of them—they were hard to count, all wearing the same red and green tartan baldrics across their heavy coats. They rode across the drawbridge as if they owned the castle, and lined up in the inner court before the greater tower shouting for the MacGregor to come out.

Lachlan witnessed their arrival from the parlor with a good deal of dread mixed with annoyance, and figured he had Nessa to thank for their appearance. She'd probably sent off a message to them in a fit of pique and even if she'd regretted it after, it would have been too late. And now they were here. There was nothing for it but to go out and deal with them, and harshly if necessary.

But when he threw open the front doors, it was to see Kimberly just reaching them. She'd been leaving the stable when they arrived, and warily worked her way around the riders to get back to the hall, not knowing who they were. Lachlan would as soon keep it that way for now.

So he grabbed her about the waist and ushered her into the hall, closing the doors on her with the admonishment to "Stay inside."

Phrased like that, as an order and without explanation, it was little wonder she didn't obey, curious lass that she was. The doors opened again just as he shouted, "I'm Lachlan MacGregor. What is it you're wanting?"

A dark-haired young man in the center of the line had apparently been elected their spokesman. "We've been tald ye've got our sister here. We've come tae have a look at her."

"You're *all* o' you her brothers?" Lachlan asked incredulously

"Nay," the spokesman said and raised an arm.

At that signal, one horse moved forward out of the line, then another, then another. By the time they finished, it was damned near half of them and just as bad.

And then Kimberly whispered at Lachlan's back, "Who are they talking about?"

"You, darlin'," Lachlan said with a sigh. "They're MacFearsons, the lot o' them." Then to the speaker, "You can see her, but dinna be thinking you can take her wi' you. She belongs to Kregora now and tae me."

The young man nodded curtly and dismounted. Kimberly had stepped out from behind Lachlan by then, her eyes wide, staring out at that long line of horsemen. Those that had moved forward and were also dismounting were all young men, at least half near her in age, the rest of them younger still, the youngest around seven years.

Her brothers? She counted them, too awed for words. There were *sixteen* of them, sixteen replicas—well, they did all bear a marked resemblance. Most also had the same dark gold hair as her own, the same dark green eyes.

And Kimberly saw now where she'd gotten her height from, not her mother's family as she'd always supposed. The one who'd spoken appeared to be the oldest among them, and he was almost as tall as Lachlan. Four others were as tall as him, five more almost as tall, and the younger ones, well, they weren't done growing.

This was too incredible. She'd grown up with no siblings at all, and now she had—too many to count on two hands. That was one of the tales, and if that one was true, how many of the other things about the legend known as Ian Mac-Fearson were also true?

"We're no' known for our patience, Mac-Gregor," one of the younger boys said as they all gathered there at the entrance. "Will you be fetching her?"

Another boy elbowed that one in the ribs and jerked his head toward Kimberly, giving her an impish smile as he did. There were a few chuckles. And then they were *all* smiling at her, and talking near all at once.

"Faith, she's older'n you, Ian One. You'll no' be lording *that* o'er us anymore, I'm thinking."

"Ye'll still be licking my boots, Johnny, if I've a mind tae have them cleaned," Ian One replied, giving the younger Johnny a look that promised his boots would soon require some cleaning.

Johnny glared back at him, but before he could retaliate, another brother was saying, "You dinna think she's tae small tae be a MacFearson?"

"She's a lass, you twerp," still another brother replied. "She's supposed tae be a wee size."

"I always wanted a sister," a red-haired brother said bashfully.

"Donald has a sister," one of the younger boys pointed out with some confusion.

"But Donald's sister isna a MacFearson, Charles, and no' yer sister or mine. This one's a MacFearson and belonging tae all o' us, ye ken."

"She looks like Ian Six. D'you see it?"

Ian Six was apparently the youngest lad, because he blushed and mumbled, "Does not."

Kimberly smiled at Ian Six. The numbers added to the names was amusing, making her recall that these brothers of hers all had different mothers, or most did. She imagined those mothers had proudly wanted to name their sons after the father and had done so, despite the confusion it would cause. The numbers were to lessen the confusion, she supposed.

She wondered how she would ever remember all their names, once she learned them. Would they be here long enough for her to make the effort to figure out who was who? Right now she wanted to hug this youngest lad among them. Actually, she wanted to hug them all. But they were a fearsome lot, with their shaggy manes and dirks strapped to their legs, their great size for all that they were each younger than her, and their sheer numbers. There were just so *many* of them, and brothers or not, they were still strangers to her.

"Och, she's all o'er hisself wi' that smile," a black-haired lad said in surprise. "He'll no' be doubting she's his now."

"Aye, and mayhap we'll be seeing the end o' his black mood now."

"After he has Ian One's head for keeping him waiting," Johnny smirked.

Ian One flushed with color to have forgotten his orders, and abruptly turned to nod at one of the men still mounted. Kimberly felt a frisson of trepidation, having forgotten that there were other MacFearsons there, cousins, second cousins, even third she was to learn later. But quickly scanning the line of men who were still mounted, she didn't see a one that was old enough to be her father.

She started to relax, until one of those men turned his horse about and rode back through the portcullis. If Ian MacFearson was out there beyond the walls . . . but what did she really have to fear? That he wouldn't like her? That she wouldn't like him? According to Cecil, this man had seduced her mother—for revenge. How *could* she like him, knowing that? And yet, her mother had loved him. Cecil had admitted that, too. There must have been something decent about him for the gentle Melissa to love him.

And then the man who had left returned, and behind him came a very large man, made even bigger by the bulky sheepskin coat he wore. It gave him a wild look, added to by his dark gold hair worn very long, and lightly streaked with grey. His features were craggy, harshly chiseled, yet there was a handsomeness underneath that might at one time have turned a young woman's heart.

His eyes had gone directly to Kimberly as soon as he came through the portcullis, and they remained on her as he slowly approached, sharply piercing, disturbing, as dark green as her own, but with a coldness to them, a deadness, as if the man had no joy of living.

A path was quickly cleared for him when he was close enough to dismount. Kimberly had unconsciously moved closer to Lachlan, whose arm came around her shoulders protectively. She wasn't ready for this, she really wasn't.

And then he was standing there in front of her, Ian MacFearson, the legend, the nightmare of little children—her father—and she released her suspended breath when she finally noticed the guarded wariness in his own expression. He was as nervous as she was, as uncertain, and that knowledge won her over.

She smiled. "Hello, Father."

51

Kimberly handed Ian a glass of warmed, spiced wine before she joined him on the sofa in her sitting room. She was probably going to have bruises along her sides from the bearlike hug he'd given her outside, before she'd managed to get them all in out of the cold.

Ian had cried. She was still amazed about that, wouldn't even have known it, smothered in his arms as she had been, if one of her brothers hadn't remarked on it.

Lachlan had taken on the duty of seeing to the sleeping arrangements for so many guests, so that she could have some time alone with her father. She wasn't sure that was such a good idea, this soon, when they weren't comfortable with each other yet. But she had so many questions for him, her curiosity wasn't going to let her wait.

"How did you know I was here?" she began carefully.

"I had a letter from Cecil Richards this week. I thought it was a bad joke at first. He told me his wife had died." His eyes closed, still stricken with that thought, but he continued, "He said he saw no reason to claim Melissa's bastard as his own any longer."

"That isn't exactly true, at least, it was not a decision that he actually made voluntarily, I don't think. My mother died more'n a year ago, but he only told me a few weeks ago that you were my father, not him. And he didn't mean to tell me, it slipped out. But since it did, I suppose he thought I might try to find you, and he wanted to be the one to tell you first."

"I still can't bear the thought that she's gone," he said quietly. "I gave up all hope of having her for my own years ago, or of ever seeing her again, but I never stopped loving her. That was forever. And I never imagined her dying—" He choked up and it was a moment before he added, "I'm sorry, lass. 'Tis as if she only just died for me, and I havena fully accepted it yet."

"I understand, but I'm confused too. Cecil said it was Ellie you loved, that you only seduced my mother as a means to have revenge on him."

He flushed with anger, hearing that. "The bastard. He's become a liar, has he, tae hide his own faults? If anyone was wanting revenge, 'twas him."

"What really happened then?"

"He loved Eleanor, loved her dearly. He couldna see what a greedy opportunist she was. She could do no wrong as far as he was concerned. And she agreed tae marry him. She wanted his wealth and the position of being an earl's wife—or she thought she did. The truth was, she couldna stand him, and just 'afore the wedding, she decided the money wasna worth it, that she couldna bear to live wi' him."

"She told him, called off the wedding?"

"Nay, he'd given her tae many fancy, expensive presents that she wanted tae keep, you see. She knew he'd be wanting them back and rightly so, if she didna marry him. But I only realized that afterward. At the time, she cried and begged me tae take her away and hide her in Scotland. She claimed they'd had a terrible fight, and he was going tae beat her if he found her. I knew Cecil had an unpredictable temper. 'Twas possible she was telling the truth, or so I thought. But I was a damned fool for believing her."

"There'd been no fight?"

"Nay, 'twas just her excuse tae get me tae help her. She even admitted it after we'd crossed the border, and laughed because I was so gullible. I should have just let her go and told Cecil the truth, letting him search for her if he was fool enough tae still want her. But I was angry enough tae take her back tae face him. And that was my second mistake."

"Why?"

"Because she refused tae go back, and when I insisted, she laughed and raced off into the night. I hadna even enough time tae decide whether tae chase her down, when I heard her scream. She was dead when I reached her, her horse crippled. And I'm ashamed tae say I felt more grief for having tae put her horse out o' its misery than I did for her death, conniving manipulator that she was."

"But Cecil thought you loved her too, and had been trying to steal her away from him? At least, that's what he told me. Why would he think that?"

"Because I didna have the heart tae tell him she was running away from him. It would have crushed him totally, and I wanted tae spare him that. So I told him I loved her too, and was drunk enough tae think I could make off with her and she'd actually stay wi' me. I thought 'twould be better for him tae hate me, if he couldna forgive me, than for him tae know how she really felt about him."

"I think that was your third mistake. He's hated all Scotsmen since then, and he's been a bitter, cold man all the years I've known him."

" 'Tis glad I am tae hear it."

That surprised her. "You've hated him as much as he does you? Then why did you try to protect him from Eleanor's perfidy?"

"Because that was 'afore he had his revenge on me, when I was still his friend and feeling sae guilty for the whole damn mess."

Kimberly frowned. "This is where I am confused. Cecil claims it was you who took revenge on him. *Did* you seduce my mother?"

"Nay, hinny, I loved your mother. I'd always loved Mellie, but I didna think I'd ever be having a chance wi' her. She was rich, you ken, and I knew her parents wanted her tae marry a title. My family wasna poor, but we werena in their social class by any means. But then I found out she felt the same way about me, and I was the happiest man alive."

"This was before she married Cecil?"

"Aye, and 'afore he'd asked for her. We were going tae elope. We kept our feelings secret, because her parents wouldna have approved. But Cecil figured out that I was interested in her. I was tae happy for him no' tae notice."

"So he tried to steal her from you?"

"He didna just try, he succeeded. And I was tae blind tae see what he was up tae," Ian answered bitterly.

"But how?"

"He came tae me one day, told me he understood what I'd done wi' Eleanor, that no mon could help but love her, and he forgave me for it."

Kimberly's eyes widened in disbelief. "Cecil said he *forgave* you?"

"It was a lie, hinny, but I didna know it then. He said my presence was reminding him tae much o' what happened, and he asked me if I'd go away for a while, tae give him a chance tae get over it wi'out the constant reminder. I could hardly refuse, as guilty as I felt for lying tae him about loving her, just tae spare him that pain. I should've confessed the truth that day, yet another mistake on my part, though I doubt he would have believed it by then. Yet it might have changed his mind about what he was planning tae do."

"So you left?"

"Aye, I agreed tae go for a short time."

"Why didn't you just take my mother with you then? You were already planning to elope with her."

"She was in London at the time. Her mother was having a grand birthday party there. But 'twas tae London that I went tae find her. Yet every time I called on her there, she was out, or indisposed, and even then, I didna suspect anything was wrong. I just kept coming by their town house each day, and kept getting turned away."

"You're saying she didn't want to see you?"

"Nay, she didna know I was there. She wasna told. What she *was* told was that her da had found out about us, and he'd paid me off. Wi' her da doing the telling, she believed it, thought I'd forsaken her for money, and she was devastated. I dinna know what Cecil told the mon, but he got him tae lie about me, and tae agree that Cecil should marry Mellie immediately. And she was tae brokenhearted tae care."

"My God, her own father—"

"Dinna blame him, hinny. The mon probably thought he was protecting her from me. God knows what Cecil told the mon, but he instigated and manipulated us all wi' his lies, so he could have the woman he knew I loved. He didna even want her for himself. He just wanted tae make sure that I'd be denied having her."

Kimberly shook her head sadly. "So they were married in London, before you could even speak to her to tell her the truth?"

"Nay, they were married as soon as she returned tae the country, but it was more'n a week more 'afore I realized she wasna even in London anymore. And by then I was tae desperate tae see her tae stay away any longer for Cecil's sake, so I returned tae Northumberland as well. And was told by a neighbor that she'd been married just days 'afore I got there."

"Why didn't you take her away anyway?" Kimberly asked him almost angrily. "Why did you leave her there to be miserable with him?"

"You think I didna try? It nearly killed her tae tell me nay, she couldna go wi' me, she was married."

"Even knowing you'd both been tricked?"

"Aye, her morals were too strongly ingrained. The deed was done. The vows were for better or worse. Though she loved me still, she'd no' break those vows."

Kimberly slumped back against the sofa. She vaguely remembered a few things from her childhood now, that she had long since forgotten, her mother never staying in the room with her when her grandparents came to visit, or even speaking to them, and she hadn't gone to their funeral when they'd died together in a carriage accident.

"If it helps any, I don't think she ever forgave her parents. I was too young at the time to even wonder why she never spoke to them when they visited."

He reached for her hand and squeezed it. "Nothing can help the tragedy of three misspent lives, hinny."

"No, I suppose not." She sighed. "And she didn't even tell you about me?"

" 'Twas so soon after—I dinna think she knew about you when we last spoke."

She blushed slightly. It was difficult to think of her mother making love with this man out of wedlock. Yet they had planned to marry, to live their lives together. That was more than she could say for herself and Lachlan. Yet she and Lachlan had ended up married, but the two who should have, would have, if not for the perfidy of others, didn't.

"I know you came home to the Highlands, but did you never go back?"

"Nay, not once. I knew that if I ever saw her again, I'd be stealing her away against her wishes, and she'd be hating me for it. And if I ever saw Cecil again—well, murder was on my mind for many a year. So I drowned myself in whisky and women and—'' He shrugged here. "You've met the results o' my overindulgence.''

He said that so casually, without a bit of embarrassment. Sixteen bastards he had, well, seventeen, counting her. And he was apparently doing right by them, raising the lot, because they all lived with him. Now, if she could discount the tale about them trying to kill each other for entertainment . . .

She smiled. "Yes, you have some fine sons there.''

"And no' a single grandchild out o' them as yet,'' he mumbled.

She almost choked. "Well, none of them are married yet, are they?''

He raised a bushy brow at her, as if to say, "What has that to do with it?'' and in his case, it certainly hadn't been a necessity. She wondered if all his sons' mothers were living with him as well, but she wasn't about to ask.

"I take it you would like some grandchildren?'' she asked instead.

"Aye, bairns are a pleasure tae have around at my age, but the lass I favor now, she's barren. You wouldna be breeding yourself, would you?''

Kimberly's cheeks filled with heat. "No, I've only just married,'' she said, which apparently had not much to do with it in her unusual family, of course, but thankfully, he didn't point that out.

"You're happy wi' the MacGregor, are you?''

"He doesn't love me, but we do very well together.''

Now why had she admitted that? And he was frowning at her because of it, and wanting to know, "Then why did you marry him, lass?''

A logical question, and her blush must have answered it for him, because he snorted. But fortunately, Lachlan entered the room at that moment . . .

"So you dinna love my daughter, Lachlan MacGregor?" Ian demanded abruptly.

Kimberly's face went up in flames. She couldn't believe Ian would actually say that, even if they had just been discussing it. And Lachlan had been smiling when he came in, but he certainly wasn't now.

"O' course I do. Who says I dinna love her?"

"She does."

Those light green eyes came to her and there was surprise in them, then disappointment. He sighed. And then he was bending to her and lifting her over his shoulder.

Between her gasp and her father's chuckle, Lachlan said, "You'll be excusing us, Ian, but I've a few things tae be explaining tae your daughter, like the difference 'atween bedding a lass and making love tae her. Apparently, she doesna know there is a difference."

"You didn't just say that to my father!" Kimberly wailed. "You *didn't*."

Lachlan had carried her just one room away, into their bedroom, and dumped her on the bed there. He was now leaning over her and looking too serious by half, but Kimberly was still too embarrassed to care.

"Och now, I heard the words myself. He did as well. Mayhap you're the only one who didna hear me say it?"

"But how could you?"

"Your da is a lusty mon, Kimber. Proof is the

time I've just spent scrounging sleeping space for his brood. Only you were embarrassed by what I said, and well you should be, because if you tell *me* you've never heard me say I love you, I'll be blistering your—"

"You haven't. Not one single time, so I defy you to point out even once that you did."

"The day we arrived here I told Nessa, and I know you heard me say it. But that is beside the point. How could you no' realize I love you, darlin', when every time I look at you or touch you, and especially when I make love tae you, I'm telling you how much I love you?"

Her mouth opened for another denial, but closed slowly as it sank in, exactly what he'd just said. At that moment, it didn't matter a bit to her when or how he'd told her before, because he'd just told her now.

"You love me?"

He gave her an exasperated look for sounding so surprised. "You still want that blistering, do you?"

She smiled and wrapped her arms around his neck. "No, but I'll take some of that loving you were talking about, the kind that tells me things I'm apparently too dense to pay attention to."

He chuckled. " 'Tis that English blood in you, no doubt. But lucky for me that I'm no' as dense. I knew long ago that you'll be loving me forever."

"Forever is an awfully long time, Lachlan. Could you settle for fifty years or so?"

"Nay, darlin', wi' you, 'tis forever I'm wanting."

52

"God God, this is positively medieval. Will you look at that, Megan."

Megan peered out the coach window, then leaned back against her husband. "Looks like a castle to me, and what were you expecting, with a name like Castle Kregora?"

"Just because a bloody name has castle in it, doesn't necessarily mean—"

"But usually does."

He glared down at her. "If I have to bathe in a wooden tub, I'm leaving."

She chuckled. "Will you stop complaining, please. I've been looking forward to this visit with Kimberly. You aren't going to spoil it for me by looking disgruntled the whole time we're here, are you?"

"I might."

She lifted a brow at him. "Very well, be stubborn if you must. And I might just tell Lachlan that the matched breeding pair we've brought along for Melissa's christening gift was *your* idea."

"Brat."

She gave him a really sweet smile. After a moment he laughed and leaned down to give her a brief kiss—well, that had been his intention. But as it happened, they were still kissing when the coach rolled to a stop before the castle doors. And just Devlin's luck, it was Lachlan who got to the coach first to open it.

"We've a nice drive along the loch if you're no' ready tae end your journey," he offered with a chuckle.

The Duke and Duchess of Wrothston broke apart, Megan blushing prettily, Devlin scowling. "Perhaps another time, MacGregor. Right now, we've a mind to see this relic you call home."

"Och now, I'll be pleased tae give you a tour once you're settled in. She's been under extensive repairs this year and is eager tae be shown off."

At Megan's curious frown, Devlin said helpfully, "I believe he's talking about the castle, m'dear."

"Well of course, I knew that. And you can tour all you like, it's Kimberly and her daughter that I'm eager to see. Just point me in their direction, if you would, Lachlan."

"My ladies are holding court in the parlor just now, entertaining Kimber's family. They've come tae visit again for the christening too."

"Cecil's here?" Devlin exclaimed. "Good God, now I *know* I'm not staying long."

Megan jammed her elbow into his side, saying in exasperation, "I think he means the Mac-Fearsons. I could have sworn I told you about them."

"Ah, quite right. Must have slipped my mind."

To which Lachlan laughed. "After you meet them, *that* will never happen again."

He wasn't exaggerating, they were to find. The MacFearsons were a fascinating lot. And all contained in one room, not five minutes could pass that a few of them weren't arguing about something and coming near to blows. But Kimberly had an amazing effect on her brothers. She merely had to catch their attention, and with a simple look, they would be blushing and quieting down.

And they all doted on Kimberly's baby, named after her mother. Kimberly had written to Megan, telling her something of that tragic story, and that this Melissa was going to have the happiness her grandmother had been denied. Megan had no doubt of that. The little darling had sixteen uncles. She was going to be positively spoiled.

"I hate to say I told you so, but I did," Megan whispered to Devlin, nodding toward Kimberly who was smiling at Lachlan. "Have you ever seen a more happy woman?"

"Hmmm, possibly you?"

Megan appeared thoughtful before she answered, "Yes, I do suppose I make an exception."

"Suppose?"

"Well, I can't have you thinking you can stop working at it. It requires a lot to keep me happy, you know."

"Does it indeed?" he growled by her ear.

She grinned. "But you do manage, indeed you do."

"I told you it wouldn't be so bad," Kimberly said as she joined Lachlan in bed that night. "Admit it. You and Devlin actually enjoyed each other's company today."

He pulled her to his side as he did every night, waiting for her head to settle on his shoulder. They usually spent time talking before going to sleep—or doing other things. It had become a nightly ritual they each savored.

"I suppose he's no' such a bad sort, when he unbends a wee bit," Lachlan allowed grudgingly.

"Well, there must be something there to like, for Megan to love him so much."

Kimberly stiffened, wishing she hadn't brought Megan up—but then again, she'd been meaning to broach the subject for a long time, she'd just never gotten around to it.

"What?" Lachlan asked.

She smiled. He was so sensitive to her moods. She rather liked that.

"I was just wondering—I know you love me—"

He drew her onto his chest for a hug. "Wi' all my heart, darlin'."

"—but do you have any feelings left for the duchess?"

He was quiet so long, she finally leaned up to look at him—and found him silently laughing. "You're a silly lass sometimes, Kimber. You havena been worrying yourself wi' that notion, have you?"

"Well, no, actually, but I used to."

He shook his head. "Darlin', even when I was telling the bonny Megan that I loved her, 'twas you I was thinking about, you that had already stolen my heart. She put it best herself. 'Twas no' real, what I felt for her, when I didna even know her. And she was right. It wasna real, just an infatuation wi' her beauty. But you, on the other hand, drive me tae distraction, I love you so much. Will you be admitting it now?"

"What?"

"That you'll love me forever? I want more'n one lifetime wi' you, darlin'. Forever may no' even be long enough."

She smiled at his whimsy. "On one condition—"

"Nay, unconditionally."

She stared at him for a long moment before she allowed, "Oh, very well, but—"

"No buts, darlin'."

"*But*—you have to promise I'll be able to find you in this forever of yours. If I had to live even one lifetime without you—"

"Nay, never, Kimber," he said emphatically. "You'll always be by my side, and I by yours. And that's the MacGregor telling you that."

She laughed. That, of course, meant she could believe it would be so.

We are pleased to announce
the publication of Johanna Lindsey's
SAY YOU LOVE ME
from Avon Books.

It wasn't such a bad place, this place that was going to witness her sale to the highest bidder. It was clean. Its decor was quite elegant. The parlor she had first been shown to could have belonged in the home of any one of her family's friends. It was an expensive house in one of the better sections of London. It was politely referred to as a House of Eros. It was a place of sin.

Kelsey Langton still couldn't believe that she was there. Ever since she had walked in the door she had been sick to her stomach with fear and dread. Yet she had come here willingly. No one had carried her inside kicking and screaming.

What was so incredible was she hadn't been forced to come here, she had agreed to—at least she had agreed that it was the only option available. Her family needed money—and a lot of it— to keep them from being thrown into the streets.

If only there had been more time to make plans. Even marriage to someone she didn't know would have been preferable. But her Uncle

Elliott was likely right. He had pointed out that no gentleman with the wherewithal to help would consider marriage in a matter of days, even if a special license could be obtained. Marriage was simply too permanent to be jumped into without careful consideration.

But this . . . well, gentleman *did* frequently acquire new mistresses on the spur of the moment, knowing full well that those mistresses would be every bit as costly as a wife, if not more so. The great difference was that a mistress, though easy to acquire, could also be easily disposed of, without the lengthy legalities and subsequent scandal.

She was to be someone's mistress. Not a wife. Not that Kelsey knew any gentlemen personally she could have married, at least none who could afford to settle Uncle Elliott's debts. She had had several young beaux courting her in Kettering, where she had grown up, before The Tragedy, but the only one with a large income had married some distant cousin.

Everything had happened so swiftly. Last night she came down to the kitchen as she did each night before retiring, to heat a bit of milk to help her sleep. Sleep was something she'd had difficulty with ever since she and her sister Jean had come to live with their Aunt Elizabeth.

Her insomnia had nothing to do with living in a new house and town, nor with Aunt Elizabeth. Her aunt was a dear woman, their mother's only sister, and she loved both her nieces as if they were her own daughters, had welcomed them with open arms and all the sympathy they had desperately needed after The Tragedy. No, it was the nightmares that disturbed Kelsey's sleep, and the vivid recollections, and the ever-recurring thought that she could have prevented The Tragedy.

Aunt Elizabeth had suggested the warm milk all those months ago when she had finally noticed the dark smudges beneath Kelsey's gray eyes and had gently prodded her for the reason. And the milk did help—most nights. It had become a nightly ritual, and she usually disturbed no one, the kitchen being empty that time of night. Except last night . . .

Last night, Uncle Elliott had been there, sitting at one of the worktables, not with a late repast before him, but a single, rather large bottle of strong spirits. Kelsey had never seen him drink more than the one glass of wine Aunt Elizabeth allowed with dinner.

Elizabeth frowned on drinking, and so naturally didn't keep strong spirits in her house. But wherever Elliott had obtained that bottle, he was more than halfway finished. And the effect it had had on him was quite appalling. He was crying. Quiet, silent sobs, with his head in his raised hands, tears dripping down onto the table, and his shoulders shaking pitifully. Kelsey had thought it was no wonder Elizabeth didn't want strong drink in her house . . .

But it wasn't the drink that was causing Elliott such distress, as she was to discover. No, he'd been sitting there, with his back to the door, assuming he wouldn't be disturbed while he contemplated killing himself.

Kelsey had wondered several times since if he would have had the courage to actually go through with it if she had quietly left. He'd never struck her as being an overly brave man, just a gregarious, usually jovial one. And it was her presence, after all, that had presented him with a solution to his troubles, one that he might not have considered otherwise, one that *she* certainly would never have thought of.

And all she'd done was ask him, "Uncle Elliott, what's wrong?"

He'd swung around to see her standing behind him in her high-necked nightgown and robe, carrying the lamp she always brought downstairs with her. For a moment he'd appeared shocked. But then his head dropped back into his hands and he'd mumbled something she couldn't quite make out, so she'd had to ask him to repeat himself.

He'd raised his head enough to say, "Go away, Kelsey, you shouldn't see me like this."

"It's all right, really," she'd told him gently. "But perhaps I should fetch Aunt Elizabeth?"

"No!" had come out with enough force to make her start, then more calmly, if still quite agitated, he added, "She doesn't approve of my drinking . . . and . . . and she doesn't know."

"Doesn't know that you drink?"

He didn't answer immediately, but she had already assumed that was what he meant. The family had always known that he would go to extremes to keep Elizabeth from unpleasantness, apparently even that of his own making.

Elliott was a large man with blunt features and hair that had gone mostly gray now that he was approaching fifty. He'd never been very handsome, even when he was younger, but Elizabeth, the prettier of the two sisters, and still beautiful today at forty-two, had married him anyway. As far as Kelsey knew she loved him still.

They'd never had any children of their own in

the twenty-four years of their marriage, and that was possibly why Elizabeth loved her nieces so dearly. Mama had mentioned once to Father that it was through no fault of their not trying, that it simply was not meant to be.

Of course, Kelsey shouldn't have heard that. Mama hadn't realized that she had been within earshot at the time. And Kelsey had overheard other things over the years, of how confounded Mama was as to *why* Elizabeth had married Elliott, who was frankly homely and had had no money to speak of, when she'd had so many other handsome, wealthy suitors to choose from instead. And besides, Elliott was in trade.

But that was Elizabeth's business, and the fact that she'd always been a champion of the less fortunate might have had a great deal to do with her choice—or not. Mama had also been known to say that there was no accounting for love and its strange workings, that it wasn't, nor ever would be, governed by logic or even one's own will.

"Doesn't know that we're ruined."

Kelsey blinked, so much time had passed since she had asked her question. And that wasn't the answer she'd anticipated. In fact, she could barely give it credit. His drinking could hardly be cause for social ruin, when so many gentlemen—and ladies, for that matter—drank to excess at the many gatherings they frequented. So she'd decided to humor him.

"So you've created a bit of a scandal, have you?" Kelsey had chided.

"A scandal?" He'd seemed confused then. "Oh, yes, it will be, indeed it will. And Elizabeth will never forgive me when they take this house away."

Kelsey had gasped, but once again, she'd drawn the wrong conclusion. "You've gambled it away?"

"Now, why would I do a fool thing like that? Think I want to end up like your father? Or perhaps I should have. At least then there would have been a slim chance for salvation, when now there is none."

She'd been utterly confused herself by that point, not to mention thoroughly embarrassed. Her father's past sins, with the accompanying reminder of what those sins had wrought, shamed her.

So with high color in her cheeks that he probably didn't notice, she'd said, "I don't understand, Uncle Elliott. Who, then, is going to take this house away? And why?"

He'd dropped his head back onto his hands again, unable to face her in his shame, and mumbled out the story. She'd had to lean close to catch most of what he was saying, suffering the fumes of sour whiskey to do so. And by the time he'd finished she'd been shocked into silence.

It was much, much worse than she'd thought, and it really was so reminiscent of her own parents' tragedy, though they'd handled the situation quite differently. But in Elliott's case, he hadn't had the strength of character to accept a failure, buckle up, and go on from there.

When Kelsey and Jean had come to live with Aunt Elizabeth eight months before, Kelsey had been too much in mourning over the deaths of her parents to notice anything amiss. She hadn't even thought to wonder why Uncle Elliott was home more often than not.

She supposed it wasn't something they thought

it necessary to tell their nieces, that Elliott had lost his job of twenty-two years and was so distraught that he hadn't been able to hold another position for very long since. And yet they had continued to live as if nothing had changed. They'd even taken in two more mouths to feed when they could hardly afford to feed themselves.

Kelsey wondered if Aunt Elizabeth even knew the extent of their debt. Elliott had been living on credit, which was a standard practice for the gentry, but it was also standard to pay those creditors before they took matters to the courts. But with no money coming in, Elliott had already borrowed all he could from his friends to keep the creditors at bay. He had no one left to turn to. And the situation was out of control.

He was going to lose Aunt Elizabeth's house, the house that had been in Kelsey's family for generations. Aunt Elizabeth had inherited it, being the older sister. And the creditors were threatening to take it away. In three days' time.

And that was why Elliott was drinking himself sick, hoping to find some courage in that bottle to end his own life, because he didn't have the courage to face what was going to happen in the next few days. It was his duty to provide for them—for his wife, anyway—and he'd failed miserably.

Of course, killing himself wasn't an option. She'd pointed out how much worse it would be for Elizabeth if she had to face eviction and a funeral as well. For Kelsey and Jean, well, they'd already faced one eviction. Yet they'd had somewhere to go that time. This time . . . Kelsey simply couldn't let it happen. Her sister was *her* responsibility now. It was up to her to see to it that Jean was raised properly, with a proper roof over her head. And if that meant that she had to . . .

She wasn't quite sure how it had come up, the selling of her. Elliott had first mentioned that he'd already thought of marrying her to the best offer, but he'd put off broaching the subject with her for so long that now it was too late for that, and he'd explained why it was too late, the need for serious deliberation for something that important that couldn't be done in just a few days.

Perhaps it was the drink that had loosened his tongue, but he'd gone on to relate how the same thing had happened to a friend of his many years ago, how he'd lost everything, but his daughter had saved the family by selling herself to an old reprobate who prized virginity and had been willing to pay extremely well for it.

Then, in almost the same breath, he told of approaching one gentleman he knew fairly well to find out if he'd be interested in a young wife. The reply had been, "Won't marry the gel, but I'm in need of a new mistress. Pay you a few pounds if she'd be willing . . ."

Which was how the talk of mistresses in relation to wives had arisen, how some rich lords would pay very handsomely for a fresh young mistress they could show off to their friends, especially a girl who hadn't already made the rounds of those friends, and pay even more if she happened to be an innocent in the bargain.

He'd planted the seeds well, showing her the solution without actually asking her to sacrifice herself. She'd already been shocked by the talk of mistresses and heartsick over the situation and how it would affect them all, but mostly she'd been desperately worried about Jean, and how this could ruin her chances for a decent marriage one day.

Kelsey could find a job, possibly, but hardly one that would keep them much above the level of poverty, especially if she took on the responsibility of supporting them all. She couldn't imagine Aunt Elizabeth working, and Elliott, well, he'd already proven pathetically that he couldn't be depended on to hold a job anymore, not for very long.

It was visions of her young sister resorting to begging on the streets to help out that had prompted Kelsey to ask, albeit in a mortified whisper, "Do you know of some man who would be willing to—to pay enough if I—if I agreed to become his mistress?"

Elliott had looked so hopeful, and so damn relieved, even as he'd replied, "No, I don't know a single one. But I know of a place in London that the rich lords frequent, a place where you can be presented to receive an excellent offer."

She'd stood there, silent for a long while, still so hesitant about such a monumental decision and so sick to her stomach that this did, in fact, seem to be their only option. Elliott actually broke out in a sweat before she finally nodded her consent.

And then he'd tried to console her, as if anything could just then. "It won't be so bad, Kelsey, really it won't. A woman can make a great deal of money for herself this way if she's smart, enough to become independent—even marry later, if she chooses."

That wasn't a bit true, and they both knew it. Her own chances for a good marriage would be gone forever. The stigma that would be hers when she went through with this would follow her for the rest of her days. She'd never be welcomed in polite society again. But that was her cross to bear. At least her sister would still have the future she deserved.

Still in a state of shock over what she'd agreed to, she'd suggested, "I will leave it to you to tell Aunt Elizabeth of this."

"No! No, she mustn't know. She'd never permit it. But I'm sure you will think of something reasonable to tell her to excuse your absence."

She had to do this, too? When it was doubtful that she'd be able to think of anything other than the appalling truth of what she'd agreed to?

She'd been ready to finish off that bottle of spirits herself by the time she left him. But she had come up with a weak excuse to tell the others. She'd told Aunt Elizabeth that Anne, one of her friends from Kettering, had written that she was seriously ill, the doctors not offering much hope. Kelsey had to visit, of course, and give what comfort she could. And Uncle Elliott had offered to escort her.

Elizabeth hadn't noticed anything amiss. Kelsey's pallor could be credited to worry over her friend. And Jean, bless her, didn't badger her with her usual hundreds of questions simply because she didn't recognize the name of this particular friend. But, then, Jean had matured a great deal during the past year. A tragedy in the family had a way of interrupting childhood, sometimes permanently. Kelsey would almost have preferred the hundreds of questions from her twelve-year-old sister that used to test her patience. But Jean was still mourning.

And when Kelsey didn't return home from the

visit to Kettering? Well, she would have to worry about that later. Would she ever even see her sister or Aunt Elizabeth again? Did she dare, when they might discover the truth? She didn't know. Right then, she only knew that nothing would ever be the same for her again.